MALORIE BLACKMAN has written over sixty books and is acknowledged as one of today's most imaginative and convincing writers for young readers.

She has been awarded numerous prizes for her work, including the Red House Children's Book Award and the Fantastic Fiction Award. Malorie has also been shortlisted for the Carnegie Medal.

In 2005 she was honoured with the Eleanor Farjeon Award in recognition of her contribution to children's books, and in 2008 she received an OBE for her services to children's literature. She has been described by *The Times* as 'a national treasure'.

Malorie Blackman is the Children's Laureate 2013–15.

Chosen and introduced by

MALORIE BLACKMAN

CORGI BOOKS

LOVE HURTS
A CORGI BOOK 978 0 552 57397 9

First published in Great Britain by Corgi,
an imprint of Random House Children's Publishers UK
A Penguin Random House Company

Penguin
Random House
UK

This edition published 2015

1 3 5 7 9 10 8 6 4 2

Introduction and HUMMING THROUGH MY FINGERS
copyright © Malorie Blackman, 2015
Illustrations © Lisa Horton, 2015
Short stories and extracts © individual authors; see Permissions.

The right of Malorie Blackman to be identified as the editor of this
work has been asserted in accordance with the Copyright, Designs and Patents Act 1988.

Every effort has been made by the publishers to contact the copyright holders of the
material published in this book; any omissions will be rectified at the earliest opportunity.

The Random House Group Limited supports the Forest Stewardship Council® (FSC®),
the leading international forest-certification organisation. Our books carrying the FSC
label are printed on FSC®-certified paper. FSC is the only forest-certification scheme
supported by the leading environmental organisations, including Greenpeace. Our paper
procurement policy can be found at www.randomhouse.co.uk/environment.

MIX
Paper from
responsible sources
FSC
www.fsc.org   FSC® C016897

Set in Bembo Reg 12.5pt

Corgi Books are published by Random House Children's Publishers UK,
61–63 Uxbridge Road, London W5 5SA

www.randomhousechildrens.co.uk
www.totallyrandombooks.co.uk
www.randomhouse.co.uk

Addresses for companies within The Random House Group Limited
can be found at: www.randomhouse.co.uk/offices.htm

THE RANDOM HOUSE GROUP Limited Reg. No. 954009

A CIP catalogue record for this book is available from the British Library.

Printed and bound in Great Britain by CPI Group (UK) Ltd, Croydon CR0 4YY

CONTENTS

INTRODUCTION

Love Hurts. Sometimes. If it didn't, a significant proportion of the stories throughout the world would disappear.

So what is love? Chemical reactions in our brains? Electrical impulses? A universal energy? The manifestation of our souls? An intertwining of our ephemeral existences? Yes, I know that last one is vomit-inducing! But seriously, what is it? Is love the one true unifying force that links all of us? Is it any, all or none of the above?

Maybe reading about love is our way of trying to figure it out. It's one of those intangibles that you can't hold in your hand and which words cannot, perhaps ever, adequately convey, but is shown in how we act towards and speak to and treat others. And while we may never find the words to effectively express just what love is, that certainly shouldn't stop us from trying.

Star-crossed lovers have always been at the heart of

our stories, from Orpheus and Eurydice, Kintu and Nambi, Paris and Helen, Tristan and Isolde, Romeo and Juliet, the butterfly lovers Liang Shanbo and Zhu Yingtai, Lancelot and Guinevere, Layla and Qays (Majnun), Heathcliff and Cathy, right up to Buffy and Angel, Spider-Man and Gwen Stacy, Katniss and Peeta.

I have never described my own book *Noughts & Crosses* as a love story, but the relationship between Callum and Sephy lies at the very core of it. It is the beating heart of my story. Without that, the rest of the plot just wouldn't work. Our relationships with others are an integral part of our lives. Surely love provides a point and purpose to life? Those who cannot find it or do not have it perhaps seek lesser and maybe more destructive alternatives, or are resigned to a life which doesn't reach its full potential.

Stories serve many purposes – to illuminate, educate, entertain. Love stories let us know that sometimes, in spite of many and varied obstacles thrown in our way, love can triumph. But sometimes it doesn't. That's love – and life. In love stories, it's the journey, not the destination, that is all important. The stories in this anthology aren't all hearts and flowers. God forbid! I like my love stories to have a bit of spice and bite! These stories contain love lost, love found, the start of love, the end of love, love bitter and love sweet.

The stories and extracts of stories contained within this anthology are old and new favourites of mine, as well as some wonderful new stories. They show that

✖

'the course of true love never did run smooth' (thank you, Lysander from *A Midsummer Night's Dream*). I hope the extracts and short stories will whet your appetite and encourage you to seek out more books by these authors.

I know these stories will amuse, entertain, surprise, and maybe provoke thought and discussion. I really do believe there's something in this anthology for everyone.

Enjoy!

Malorie Blackman

HUMMING THROUGH MY FINGERS

BY
MALORIE BLACKMAN

My hands slowed down, then stilled on my book as I listened. I turned my head and sniffed at the wind. Mum always said I had ears like a bat, but if it wasn't for the wind blowing in my direction, I doubt if even I would have heard this particular conversation.

I listened for a few moments until I'd heard enough, then returned to my book – which was far more interesting. Nine pages on and I was interrupted. He stood directly in front of me, blocking the sunlight, making my arms and face feel instantly cooler. I'd thought I'd get at least twelve pages on before he plucked up the nerve to come over.

'Hi, Amber. It's me. Ethan. Ethan Bennett.'

I sniffed the air in the direction of his voice. He didn't have to tell me his name. I recognized his voice. Ethan Bennett – the new boy in my brother Joshua's class. Well, when I say new, I mean he'd joined Josh's class last September and been to our house four or five times when I was there, but this was the first time he'd said anything other than 'Hi' to me.

The last time he left our house, I had tried less than subtly to ask Joshua about him. 'Josh, what's Ethan like?'

'Why?' asked my brother, suspicion lacing his tone.

'I like his voice,' I replied.

'He looks like Quasimodo and he's constantly farting,' Josh replied. 'He's lactose intolerant so God help you if you're around him without a gas mask after he's had a pizza or a glass of milk.'

So much for trying to get a straight answer out of my brother.

'Hello, Ethan.'

'Can I sit down?'

'I don't know.' I shrugged. 'Can you?'

'Huh?'

I smiled. A teeny-tiny smile for a teeny-tiny joke.

'No, I . . . er . . . meant, d'you mind if I sit down?' Ethan's voice was anxious, eager for me to understand.

'Help yourself.' Why ask me if he could sit down? Did I own the field or the grass in it? I carried on reading my book while he parked.

'What're you reading? Is it any good?'

'It's *Misery* by Stephen King. I've read it before, and yes, it is good.'

'If you've read it before, why're you reading it again?' asked Ethan.

'It's one of my favourite books.' As I spoke I

carried on reading, my fingers skimming over the page. But then my fingers unexpectedly touched Ethan's and an electric shock like summer lightning stung through my fingers and up my arm.

'Ouch!' Ethan exclaimed.

With his touch still humming through my fingers, I drew my hand away. 'What happened?'

'I just got a shock.' Ethan dismissed it easily. I could hear that he was still shaking his sore fingers. He mused, 'I don't see how we could've been shocked sitting on grass.'

I said nothing. There'd been something un-expected in his touch, something more interesting than the obvious, but harder to read. It was this that stopped me from telling him to get lost.

'Sorry about that,' said Ethan. 'I just wanted to see what Braille was like.'

'Why?'

I could smell his surprise at my question. 'I've never seen a Braille book before. How does it work?'

Here we go again. I sighed inwardly. Another explanation. Another embarrassed pause followed by a murmur of sympathy and, if the usual pattern was followed, a sudden mumbled excuse to leave.

'Each of the series of raised dots represents a letter or a number. I use my fingers to read the dots rather than my eyes to read the words on a page, that's all.'

'Can I have a try?'

'Go ahead.'

I picked up the book and held it in Ethan's direction. He took it from me, careful not to touch my fingers this time.

'It must take ages to learn all this lot. It would take me years.' Ethan whistled appreciatively. 'How long did it take you?'

'Quite a few months, actually, and I'm still learning.' OK, I admit it, I was surprised. No pity, no sympathy, just two people talking.

'Were you born blind?'

Another surprise. No one over the age of ten ever asked me about my eyesight – not directly, at any rate. It was a taboo subject, conspicuous by its absence. How come Ethan had never got round to asking my brother or one of his other friends? Too afraid they'd mistake his questions for interest? I wondered who else was present, who else was listening. I sniffed the air. I couldn't smell anyone else nearby. Just Ethan – and his lie. Not lies plural. Just one lie.

'No.' I was going to say more, but the words didn't seem to want to come out of my mouth.

'Here's your book back.'

I reached out my hand. Ethan placed it in my upturned palm.

'So how did you become blind, then?' he asked.

Wow! Direct much? Truth to tell, I kind of liked it. It was refreshing.

'I'm a diabetic and I'm one of the unlucky few

6

who developed diabetic retinopathy.' I faked a nonchalant shrug. 'I played fast and loose with taking my insulin and watching my diet. My vision started going fuzzy and I didn't put two and two together until it was too late. So here I am.'

'What d'you miss most?'

'People's faces — and colours.' Silence stretched between us as I listened to Ethan search for something else to say. 'What would *you* miss most?'

'Pardon?'

I repeated the question and smiled inwardly as I felt Ethan frown. 'I don't know,' he answered at last. My question had disturbed him. 'Josh told me that you see things with your other senses, though.'

I didn't reply. Slowly, I closed my book and waited.

'He said that you can hear colours and sense certain things that most people can't.'

Hearing colours — was that why I'd been singled out by Ethan? Was that all there was to it? Check out the weird girl and have a laugh while doing it?

'Is that true?' Ethan persisted.

I shrugged. I'd have to have a serious word with Josh when I caught up with him. He wasn't meant to tell anyone about that. It wasn't even his secret to tell, it was my secret. Who else had my brother blabbed to?

'I hope you don't mind me mentioning it. Josh swore me to secrecy and he hasn't told anyone else — at least, that's what he said.'

'Why did he tell you?'

'I don't know. Maybe he thought he could trust me.' Pause. 'He could see I wanted to know more about you.'

Hhmm! I shrugged noncommittally, careful to keep my expression neutral.

'I've never heard of anything like that before,' Ethan stated.

'It's called synaesthesia. I've always had it but it became heightened when I lost my sight. About ten people in every million have it, so don't go thinking I'm a fruit loop or something.' An edge crept into my voice.

'I didn't think anything of the kind,' Ethan laughed. 'What's it like?'

'What's it like to see using your eyes?'

'It's . . . well, it's . . . it's a bit difficult to explain. Ah! OK!'

And I knew then that he'd got the point. 'Exactly.'

Wanting to change the subject, I asked, 'So what d'you think of Belling Oak, then?'

'It's not bad, actually. It's a lot better than my old school. How come you don't come here with your brother?'

Whoosh! Instantly my face flamed, in spite of myself. I turned away, listening to the distant cheers and the shouting as the 100 metres sprint race started.

'I was here for four years, but . . . there were problems,' I said, still half listening to the race.

'What sort of problems?'

I sighed inwardly. I'd say one thing for Ethan: he was persistent. 'The teachers spouted on and on about how it would be too dangerous for me, too hazardous, too nerve-racking, how I'd be teased and bullied – stuff like that. The Head insisted Belling just wasn't set up for students who were visually challenged. He couldn't even say the word – blind.'

'Sounds like excuses to me.' Ethan sniffed.

I turned to face him again. 'It was. I already had friends here, I'd already been here for four years since junior school and after the first year I could've found my way around blindfolded. Mum, Dad and I kept telling him that I was willing to put up with the rest, but he wouldn't have it. Then he started quoting health and safety regulations at us and they said it would cost too much to have the school converted so that I could find my way around without help. So it didn't happen.'

'You must've been disappointed.'

'Of course. I'd set my heart on staying at Belling.' I looked around, seeing it with my memory. All around me were the acres of grounds, divided by a trickling stream known as 'The Giggler' because of the sound it made. I remembered the intensity of the green of the grass in spring, how in spring and early summer it was always covered in daisies and buttercups. From the upper classroom windows the daisies made the ground look like it was covered in summer snow, they were that thick on the ground. And then there were the tall, sprawling oaks fringing the stream on both sides. The oaks had always been my favourite. They whispered amongst themselves, using the wind for cover. At one end of the upper field was the red-brick school building and way across on the other side, past the lower fields, were the tennis and netball courts which doubled as basketball courts. And the whole thing had been so beautiful. I only started appreciating its beauty when I started to lose my sight. Precious little time left to drink in the sights and sounds of the place before I got bounced out.

'So where d'you go now?' asked Ethan.

'Arenden Hall. We've already broken up for the summer, though.'

'Never heard of it.'

'It's a college for the blind, about ten kilometres from here.'

'D'you like it?'

I shrugged. 'Yes, I do. They treat me like I'm more than my eyesight there. They know that my blindness isn't the one and only thing to define me.'

I turned back towards the sports field. I was seated near the stream, under the arms of one of the huge oak trees that gave Belling its name. Every sports day, I always sat in the same spot. Far enough away from everyone else so that I wouldn't have to worry about being knocked over or swept aside by the enthusiastic crowds, but close enough to hear what was going on. Some of my Belling friends thought it strange that I would want to sit by myself for most of the afternoon, but they were used to me by now. To be honest, I liked my own company. That and the fact that my friends made me remember . . . different times. I forced my mind away from the past to concentrate on the here and now.

Joshua, my twin brother, was due to run in the Upper Sixth 200 metres later on. He'd come last, or close to it. He always did, but he didn't mind, and neither did anyone else. It would've been good to see him run, although my friends said he didn't so much run as saunter. Josh always said that he was built for endurance, not speed. In cross-country runs, he invariably crossed the finish line first and fresh as a daisy while his friends collapsed all around him several minutes later.

'I'm sorry if I asked too many questions,' said Ethan. 'I didn't mean to upset you.'

'It's OK.' But I didn't deny that he'd upset me. 'May I ask you something?'

I heard him nod, then catch himself and say, 'Yeah! Sure!'

'Why are you over here? I mean, why aren't you with everyone else watching the races?'

Please tell me the truth. Please.

'I saw you over here and I just wanted to say hello. We've never really had the chance to have a proper conversation before.'

'I see.' The heat from his lie swept over me like volcanic ash, tasting bitter and acrid against my tongue.

Ethan cleared his throat. 'Actually, I wanted to ask you something. Would you . . . er . . . I'm going for a pizza after all the events are over. I don't suppose you'd like to come with me?'

Silence stretched between us like a rubber band.

'You're inviting me to go for a meal with you, my brother and your friends?'

'Well, I thought if you agreed to have a pizza with me, we could go by ourselves?' Ethan cleared his throat again at the end of his rushed sentence. He obviously did that when he was nervous. Useful to know.

'OK,' I said, at last.

'Really? Great!'

The obvious relief in his voice made me stifle a smile. It meant that much to him?

'Aren't you lactose intolerant, though?' I said. 'Is a pizza wise?'

'What did Josh say about me?' Ethan sounded mortified.

'Is it true?'

'I have a mild case and it's cumulative. I'm OK with just one pizza.'

'You will keep away from the ice cream with your dessert though, right?' I teased.

Ethan didn't reply but I could've been on Mars and still felt his embarrassment.

'Are you in any of the races?' I took pity on him and changed the subject.

'No, athletics isn't really my thing.'

'What is?'

'Rugby. And tennis sometimes.'

'Oh, I see. Are you heading back to your friends to watch the rest of the races now?' I asked.

'No, I thought I'd stay here with you, if that's all right?'

Whoa! So he was going for it, was he? Two could play that game.

'Sure. Tell you what, let's go for a walk,' I said.

'A walk?'

'Around the grounds. Away from everyone else.'

'Can you . . . ? I mean, do you want . . . ?'

I laughed. 'It's my eyes that don't work, my legs are fine.'

'Yeah, of course. Sorry.' I heard Ethan get to his feet. I stood up, ignoring the hand he put out to help me.

'Let's walk downstream towards the car park, then cross the stream and walk round behind the tennis courts,' I suggested.

'Fine with me.'

We started walking. Ethan stuffed his hands in his pockets until I placed my hand on his bare forearm. He must've been wearing a short-sleeved shirt. And there it was again, that strange humming through my fingers. Ethan's arm started to flap about like a fish out of water. He didn't know what to do with it, where to put it so I could rest my hand on it. I stopped, withdrawing my hand as I waited for him to figure it out. After a moment or two, he took my hand and placed it on his forearm, which was now steady. We carried on walking in a strangely amiable silence.

'So tell me what you can see,' I said.

'Huh?'

'Describe what you can see.' I smiled at Ethan. 'Unless, of course, you'd rather not.'

'No, I don't mind. I just . . . OK . . . well, we're walking beside the stream now and there are oak trees on either side of the stream and over there is the car park and over there is the school and—'

My hand gently squeezed his arm. 'That's not what I meant. Tell me what you can *see*.'

'But I just did.'

I gave him a hard look. 'Ethan, are you wearing your school tie?'

'Yes. Why?'

'Could you take it off and put it around your eyes?'

'Come again?'

I smiled. 'You heard me right the first time.'

'Why d'you want me to do that?' Ethan asked.

'I'm going to take you around the school grounds.'

'With my eyes blindfolded?' Ethan asked, aghast.

I laughed at the panic in his voice. 'That's right. You're going to have to trust me.'

'But you . . . you can't see.'

'Oh my God! Thanks for telling me. I hadn't noticed!' I teased. 'So are you going to do it, or are you too much of a chicken?'

Slowly, Ethan removed the tie from around his neck and tied it around his eyes.

'You've got to do it so you can't see anything,' I told him.

'I have.'

'No, you haven't.'

'How d'you know?' The amazement in his voice was very gratifying. 'OK! OK! My eyes are totally covered now.'

'Let me touch your face.'

I felt him lean forward. I raised my hands to run my fingers lightly over his face. My fingers began to hum again as I touched his skin. He had a large forehead (lots of brains!), a strong nose and a firm chin, and his lips were full and soft. I couldn't tell about his eyes because they were covered with his tie. His tie smelled of sweet green and sharp, tangy gold. Belling Oak colours. I would've been able to tell the colours even if I didn't already know what they were. Satisfied that his eyes were indeed completely covered, I linked his arm with my own. He instinctively stiffened at that.

'Don't worry, your friends won't be able to see us over here.'

'It's not that,' he denied. 'But suppose we end up in the stream or something?'

'Then we'll get wet!'

There was a pause, then Ethan laughed. His body relaxing, he said, 'All right then. D'you know where you're going?'

'I know this school like the back of my hand. Don't worry. Now . . . which way are we facing again?'

A sharp intake of breath from Ethan had me cracking up.

'You're not funny,' he grumbled.

We walked for a minute, listening to the distant cheers and the occasional birdsong.

'What d'you think of this tree?' I asked.

'What tree?'

'The one right in front of us. It's my favourite of all of them here,' I said, adding, 'No, don't,' when I felt his other hand move upwards to remove the tie from around his eyes.

'But I can't see it. I can't see anything.'

'See it without using your eyes.'

'How do I do that?' Frustration began to creep into Ethan's voice.

I took Ethan's hand and stretched it out in front of him until it touched the tree trunk. 'What does it feel like?' I asked, my hand resting lightly over his so I could feel what he was doing.

'Rough.'

'What else?'

His fingers began to move slowly across the tree bark. 'Cool. Sharp in places. Here's a smooth bit.'

'And what does it smell like?'

Ethan looked over towards me.

'Go on!' I encouraged. 'It's international hug-a-tree

day! Tell me what it smells like and feels like. Don't be shy.'

Reluctantly, Ethan moved closer to the tree. He stretched out his arms to hold it. Waves of 'what-the-hell-am-I-doing?' rippled out from his entire body.

'It feels . . . strong. Like it could be here for ever if it was left alone.' Ethan's voice grew more quiet, but more confident. 'And it's got secrets. It's seen a lot of things and knows a lot of things, but it's not telling. And it smells like . . . like rain and soil and a mixture of things.'

'Come on,' I said, taking his arm again.

'Where're we going?'

'To our next stop.'

I led Ethan further down the stream before I turned us to our left and walked a few steps.

'Now you have to do exactly what I say,' I told him, leading him down a gentle slope.

'Are we going to cross the stream here?' he asked, a frown in his voice.

'That's right.' I smiled. 'We're going to jump across.'

'But . . . but I can't see where I'm going,' said Ethan, horrified.

'Then use your other senses. I'll help you.'

'Why can't we use one of the bridges?'

'Because everyone does that. We're going to be more adventurous. I want you to jump from here. It's less than half a metre to the other side at this point. Just jump, then let your weight fall forward and grab hold of one of the tree roots sticking out of the ground. OK?'

No answer.

'OK, Ethan?'

'D'you really think this is a good idea?'

'Trust me. And once you've grabbed the tree root, haul yourself up out of the way 'cause I'll be right behind you.'

'All right,' Ethan said dubiously.

I placed my hands on his shoulders and turned him slightly to straighten him up so he wouldn't be jumping at an angle. 'Don't worry, Ethan. My nan can jump half a metre and she's got bad knees – always assuming I've led us to the right bit of the stream, of course.'

'You mean, you're not sure?' Ethan was appalled.

'I'm only winding you up,' I told him gleefully.

'You're enjoying this, aren't you?'

'You'd better believe it! Now then. After three. One . . . two . . .'

'Three!' Ethan shouted. And he jumped.

To be honest, I was impressed. I thought he'd need a lot more coaxing. I heard an 'Ooof!' followed by the mad scramble of his hands as he sought and found a tree root. The ground here was covered in exposed tree roots so I knew he'd have no problem. He hauled himself up the bank to the level ground beyond.

'Here I come!' And I jumped. In a way, I'm sorry

Ethan didn't see me. A sighted person couldn't have done it better. I landed cleanly, then stepped up the bank, pushing against the roots beneath my feet. No need to get my hands dirty.

'Are you OK?' I asked.

'I think so.'

'How did it feel to jump?'

'I don't know,' said Ethan.

'Yes, you do.'

His sharp intake of breath told me that I was right. 'I was a bit nervous. I know the water is only a few centimetres deep but it suddenly felt like it was kilometres deep and kilometres down.'

'And how did you feel when you landed on the other side?'

'Relieved!'

'Anything else?'

'Yeah. Kind of proud of myself.'

'Being blind is like jumping off a cliff – except you jump never knowing what's on the other side. Everything is an adventure for me. Walking along the street, going into a shop, meeting new people, even reading a book. I see things I never saw before. D'you know how much I hate reading the phrase, "How could I have been so blind?" when the author is using it to mean stupid? That really pisses me off, but I never even noticed it before losing my sight. I travel through life never knowing what I'll come across or what I'll find, whether I'll be delighted or disappointed, hurt or happy.

Everyone else travels that way but most take it for granted. I don't. Not any more. Does that make sense?'

'I think so.' Ethan didn't sound sure at all. But it was enough.

I reached out to link arms with him again. 'Have you still got the tie around your eyes?'

'Yes.'

'Then it's time for our next stop.' I led the way along the fence and past the car park.

'I have no idea where we are,' Ethan said, perplexed.

'That's OK. I do.'

We walked on for another few minutes before I stopped.

'Where are we now?' asked Ethan.

'By the tennis courts. What can you hear?'

Ethan was still for a moment. 'Birds and a faint droning sound.'

'That drone is the traffic on the other side of the school building.'

Ethan turned his head slightly. 'I can hear some cheering now from the sports field but it's very faint.'

'Anything else?'

'I don't think so.'

'OK. Kneel down.'

'Why?'

'Trust me!'

Ethan shook his head but he still knelt down. I smelled what I was looking for. The scent was overwhelming. I took Ethan's hand and put it out to touch the thing I could smell.

'Just use your index finger and thumb to touch this,' I said. 'Rub it gently between your fingers but don't touch anything else except this bit.'

When Ethan's fingers were on the object, I let go of his hand.

'What is it?' he asked.

'What d'you think it is?'

'I don't know . . .' Ethan said slowly. 'It feels like a bit of velvet but there wouldn't be velvet around the tennis courts.'

I reached out and touched the object, my fingers next to Ethan's. 'A deep yellow velvet.'

'How can you tell what colour it is?'

'Yellow has got quite a high voice. This yellow's voice is slightly lower, which means the shade is deeper, but it's definitely yellow.'

'Do you know what it is I'm touching?'

'Yes, I do.' And all at once I didn't want to do this any more. I felt wistful and sad. 'Take off your tie now. Have a look at what you're touching.'

Ethan removed his tie at once and gasped. 'It's . . . it's a flower . . .' he said, shocked.

'Beautiful, isn't it?'

'A deep yellow flower,' Ethan whispered.

'There's more to seeing than just looking, Ethan,' I told him. 'Your eyes work. Never forget what a gift that is. I can feel colours and I'm grateful. But to see . . .'

'A flower.' Ethan's voice was awestruck. I didn't have his full attention. I wondered if he'd even heard me.

'Ethan, touching that flower and seeing it with your fingers – that's what seeing with my other senses is a tiny bit like. I see things in ways that you can't or won't because you don't have to. I'm grateful for that as well, because I can still appreciate the things around me. Maybe even more than a lot of sighted people do.'

I sensed Ethan looking at me then. Really looking – for the first time. I wondered how he saw me now. I smiled at him.

'I . . . look, I have to tell you something,' Ethan began uneasily.

'Forget it.'

'No, it's important. I—'

'Harry and Jacob bet you that you couldn't get me to go out for a pizza with you and get a kiss out of me. But for your information, they've both asked me out and I've always turned them down flat, so they reckoned you had no chance.'

Silence.

'Stop it. You're staring!' I laughed.

'How did you know that?'

'What? About the bet or that you were staring?'

'Both.'

'I could tell you, but then I'd have to kill you,' I teased. 'And by the way, I wouldn't tell my brother about the bet if I were you. He's massively

over-protective where I'm concerned and he'd probably want to punch your face into next week.'

'I'm sorry, Amber. I . . . I suppose you don't want
anything more to do with me.'

'I knew about the bet before you'd even said one
word to me – remember?'

'I still don't understand how.'

'I heard you.'

'You couldn't have. We were practically across the
field,' Ethan protested.

'Exaggerate much? You were only a few metres
away and the wind was blowing in my direction.' When
Ethan didn't answer, I said, 'I have ears like a bat. Always
have done. And I've always had a sixth sense when it
comes to spotting when people are lying to me.'

A profound silence followed my words. How I
wished I could see Ethan's face at that moment.

'We'd better get back,' Ethan said at last, his tone
strange.

Now it was my turn to be bemused. 'What's the
matter?'

Ethan took my hand and rested it on his arm. His
touch lingered a little longer than was necessary on the
back of my hand. We started back towards the sports
field, my hand lightly resting on his arm. I knew the
way back without any problem but I wanted to sense
what he was feeling. From the way his muscles were
bunched and tense beneath my fingers I could guess
what was going on in his head. He wasn't happy.

'Ethan?'

'I'm really sorry, Amber. You must think I'm a real dickwit. And I don't blame you.' His words came out in a rush of genuine embarrassment. And there was something else, something more behind them.

'Why would I think your wits are dickish?' I smiled.

Ethan looked at me then. And his gaze hadn't changed back – I could tell. He was still looking at me with the eyes of someone who could see *me*. Not a blind girl and nothing else. Not someone to be pitied or patronized or mocked. Not someone who was less than him. But a girl who could see without using her eyes.

'Can I . . . can I touch your face?' said Ethan.

Surprised, I nodded. He moved to stand in front of me. A moment later his fingers were exploring my face, starting from my forehead and working their way down, skimming over my eyebrows, my closed eyes, my nose, my cheeks, my lips, my jaw, my chin. He leaned in closer. I could feel his warm breath on my face. He smelled of mints and chocolate. Was he going to kiss me? Ethan's hands dropped to his side as he straightened up.

'Why did you do that?' I asked, wondering why I felt so disappointed.

'I . . . I don't know.' He took my arm in his and we carried on walking.

'What about Jacob and Harry? Didn't you have to kiss me to win your bet?' I asked.

'Those two can go . . .' Ethan swallowed the next word. '. . . themselves. If I kiss you it won't be to win some stupid bet.'

I smiled. 'So where are we going for this pizza, then?'

Stunned, Ethan stopped walking and turned to look at me. 'You still want to go out with me?'

'Course I do. I'm starving.'

The sigh of relief that came from Ethan made me giggle.

'D'you know something?' Ethan looked around. 'I never noticed it before, but everything around me is so . . . so . . .'

He shut up then. I raised my hand to touch his radiating cheek.

'I could fry an egg on your face.' I grinned. 'A couple of rashers of bacon too.'

'Shut up!' said Ethan.

I burst out laughing. 'Come on,' I said. 'Let's go and watch my brother come last in the four-by-one-hundred relay.'

And we walked over the bridge together to join the others.

FROM

MORE THAN THIS

BY
PATRICK NESS

'Don't you think I hate it, too?' Gudmund whispered fiercely. 'Don't you think it's the last thing I want?'

'But you can't,' Seth said. 'You can't just . . .'

He couldn't say it. Couldn't even say the word.

Leave.

Gudmund looked back nervously at his house from the driver's seat of his car. Lights were on downstairs, and Seth knew Gudmund's parents were up. They could discover he was gone at any moment.

Seth crossed his arms tightly against the cold. 'Gudmund—'

'I finish out the year at Bethel Private or they don't pay for college, Sethy,' Gudmund practically pleaded. 'They're that freaked out about it.' He frowned, angry. 'We can't all have crazy liberal European parents—'

'They're not that crazy liberal. They'll barely look at me now.'

'They barely looked at you before,' Gudmund said. Then he turned to Seth. 'Sorry, you know what I mean.'

Seth said nothing.

'It doesn't have to be forever,' Gudmund said. 'We'll meet up in college. We'll find a way so that no one—'

But Seth was shaking his head.

'What?' Gudmund asked.

'I'm going to have to go to my dad's university,' Seth said, still not looking up.

Gudmund made a surprised move in the driver's seat. 'What? But you said—'

'Owen's therapy is costing them a fortune. If I want college at all, it has to be on the faculty family rate where my dad teaches.'

Gudmund's mouth opened in shock. This hadn't been their plan. Not at all. They were both going to go to the same university, both going to share a dorm room.

Both going to be hundreds of miles away from home.

'Oh, Seth—'

'You can't go,' Seth said, shaking his head. 'You can't go now.'

'Seth, I have to—'

'You can't.' Seth's voice was breaking now, and he fought to control it. 'Please.'

Gudmund put a hand on his shoulder. Seth jerked away from it, even though the feel of it was what he

30

wanted more than the world. 'Seth,' Gudmund said. 'It'll be okay.'

'How?'

'This isn't our whole lives. It isn't even close. It's *high school*, Sethy. It's not meant to last forever. For a goddamn good reason.'

'It's been—' Seth said to the windshield. 'Since New Year, since you weren't there, it's been—'

He stopped. He couldn't tell Gudmund how bad it had been. The worst time of his life. School had been nearly unbearable, and sometimes he'd gone whole days without actually speaking to anyone. There were a few people, girls mostly, who tried to tell him they thought what was happening to him was unfair, but all that did was serve to remind him that he'd gone from having three good friends to having none. Gudmund had been pulled out of school by his parents. H was hanging out with a different crowd and not speaking to him.

And Monica.

He couldn't even think about Monica.

'It's a few more months,' Gudmund said. 'Hang in there. You'll make it through.'

'Not without you.'

'Seth, please don't say stuff like that. I can't take it when you say stuff like that.'

'You're everything I've got, Gudmund,' Seth said quietly. 'You're it. I don't have anything else.'

'Don't say that!' Gudmund said. 'I can't be anyone's everything. Not even yours. I'm going out of my mind with all this. I can't stand the fact that I have to go away. I want to *kill* someone! But I can take it if I know you're out there, surviving, getting through it. This won't be forever. There's a future. There really is. We'll find a way, Seth. Seth?'

Seth looked at him, and he could now see what he hadn't seen before. Gudmund was already gone, had already put his mind into Bethel Private, sixty-five miles away, that he was already living in a future at UW or WSU, which were even further, and maybe that future included Seth somehow, maybe that future really did have a place for the two of them—

But Seth was only here. He wasn't in that future. He was only in this unimaginable present.

And he didn't see how he'd ever get from here to there.

'There's more than this, Sethy,' Gudmund said. 'This sucks beyond belief, but there's more. We just have to get there.'

'We just have to get there,' Seth said, his voice barely above a whisper.

'That's right.' Gudmund touched Seth's shoulder again. 'Hang in there, please. We'll make it. I promise you.'

They both jumped at the sound of the door slamming. 'Gudmund!' Gudmund's father shouted from the porch, loud enough to wake the neighbours. 'You'd better answer me, boy!'

Gudmund rolled down his window. 'I'm here!'

he shouted back. 'I needed some fresh air.'

'Do you think I'm an idiot?' His father squinted into the darkness where Seth and Gudmund were parked. 'You get back in here. Now!'

Gudmund turned back to Seth. 'We'll email. We'll talk on the phone. We won't lose contact, I promise.'

He lunged forward and kissed Seth hard, one last time, the smell of him filling Seth's nose, the bulk of his body rocking Seth back in the seat, the squeeze of his hands around Seth's torso—

And then he was gone, sliding out of the door, hurrying back into the glow of the porchlight, arguing with his father on the way.

Seth watched him go.

And as Gudmund disappeared behind another slamming door, Seth felt his own doors closing.

The doors of the present, shutting all around him, locking him inside.

Forever.

FROM

THE INFINITE MOMENT OF US

BY

LAUREN MYRACLE

The park, when they arrived, was inhabited by drunk college kids – Wren assumed they were college kids because of their Georgia Tech T-shirts, and because they looked old in a way that even Tessa and P.G. couldn't yet pull off – and they were as loud as the bat killers back at the graduation party had been, if not louder.

There could be no talking here. No nice boy to unsadden her. Her heart felt heavy, and after a Frisbee flew at her out of the darkness, making her duck, she exhaled and said, 'We should go.'

'Already?' Charlie said. 'We just got here.'

'Yeah, but . . .' She gestured at the partiers by the swing set.

One of them cupped his hands over his mouth and called, 'Yo! Frisbee! Sorry 'bout that!'

Charlie knelt, grabbed the Frisbee, and threw it deftly back at the group. To Wren, he said, 'One second.' He started for his car, then stopped. Came back for Wren and took her hand. 'Actually, come with me.'

Wren's tummy turned over. Charlie was . . . why was Charlie holding her hand? She'd held his arm earlier, but that was to get him away from Tessa, and she hadn't thought about it first. She'd just done it. But unless she was mistaken, he was holding her hand on purpose.

She looked at their linked hands as if the answer lay there. She noticed the stitches on his thumb from his visit to Grady Hospital two days ago. She took in, again, how strong and capable his fingers were. With his hand curled protectively around hers, she felt safe – only, as soon as she recognized the feeling, she tugged her hand free. Or tried to. He tightened his grip, striding across the grass.

'What about Starrla?' she said.

Charlie stopped. She bumped into him.

'Ow,' she said, rubbing her nose with her free hand.

'Why are you asking about Starrla?' he said. He held her hand tightly.

'Uh, because you two are going out?' Wren said. A guy wasn't supposed to hold another girl's hand when he had a girlfriend. Even if he was handsome. Even if he smelled like pine needles. Even if he looked dismayed at the very thought of . . . well, whatever he was thinking of.

'I'm not going out with Starrla,' he said. 'I thought
. . . well, no, I guess he couldn't have.'

'Huh?'

Charlie's shoulders relaxed. 'Nothing.'

'Well, good,' Wren said. 'I mean—'

Hush, she told herself. She was glad, very, that
Charlie wasn't claiming Starrla, even if she was fairly
certain Starrla still claimed Charlie. This morning,
before the graduation ceremony, Starrla had caught
Wren looking at Charlie and narrowed her eyes. *Back
off*, Starrla's expression had said. Her lips, curving into a
smile, had added, *Don't even. You are weak, and I am
strong.*

But Charlie was with her, holding her hand, and
Wren had her own brand of strength, brought to the
surface by the dim glow of the streetlight and the
whisper of night air on her skin. It was new to her. Her
heart beat with a low, thumping exhilaration.

'Starrla and I did . . . date,' Charlie said. 'Once. A
long time ago. But now we're just friends.'

'Oh,' Wren said. 'Um, thanks. For explaining.'

The moon was full, lighting up Charlie's face. He
looked as if he wanted to say something more, perhaps
to make sure she truly knew they weren't together
anymore. Then he furrowed his brow adorably – he *was*
adorable – and squashed the thought, whatever it
might have been. He fished in his pocket for his car
keys and popped the trunk, all the while not letting go
of Wren's hand.

What am I doing? she wondered. *What is happening?*

Go with it, she told herself. *For heaven's sake, stop thinking for once.*

With a coarse army blanket tucked under his arm, Charlie shut and locked the trunk. 'This way,' he said, and Wren allowed herself to be led across the far corner of the park and into the bordering grove of trees. Cautions from her mother burbled through her – never, ever go to an isolated spot with a stranger, you don't do that, Wren – but Charlie wasn't a stranger. Also, Wren wasn't her mother.

'You carry a blanket with you everywhere?' she asked. She was trying to tease him, as in, *Just how many girls do you take into the woods when the sun sets?*

He looked puzzled, and Wren felt dumb. She wasn't her mother, but she wasn't Tessa or some other flirty girl, either. She needed to just be Wren.

'One of my . . . um, at one of the houses I was in, the dad was a scoutmaster,' he explained. '"Always be prepared." That was his motto.'

'Oh. That's cool.' To try and normalize things, she added, 'Was he a nice guy? That dad?'

'No,' Charlie said.

'Why not?'

He was quiet, and she wished she hadn't asked.

They were thick in the woods behind the park now, and she had to watch her footing. Then the ground sloped down, and the trees thinned out. They reached a small ditch – maybe a ravine that had been eroded by running water? Behind them were trees, and on the other side of them were trees, but the ditch itself was clear and dry. There were leaves and a few sticks and a mat of prickly grass, but once Charlie let go of Wren's hand and spread out the blanket, none of that was a problem.

He had climbed to the bottom of the hollow on his own, and now he held out his hand. Wren accepted it, grasping him as she slid-hopped down. Following Charlie's lead, she sat on the blanket. Gingerly, she leaned all the way back, her body at an incline on the ditch's banked slope.

'Oh,' she said, enthralled. Through the gap in the trees she could see the sky. The moon, luminous and huge, peeked through the leafy branches. 'Beautiful.'

They lay next to each other, not speaking. Wren could feel the heat radiating from Charlie's body. Tiny hairs on her neck and on her forearms seemed to prickle awake and stand alert. Wren felt very strongly that, since he had brought her here, to this secret place, it was her job to keep the conversation going. Just not by talking about foster families. At first she thought, Guatemala, but she realized she didn't want to talk about Guatemala, either.

Guatemala would work itself out. She'd bought her plane ticket the very day she got her Project Unity acceptance letter – and yes, she probably should have used her savings to pay back the money her parents had spent on her college fees, but she didn't – and either her parents would get used to the idea of her leaving or they wouldn't. She hoped they would.

But she didn't want to think about Guatemala, or leaving for Guatemala, right now. Right now, amazingly, she was exactly where she wanted to be.

'Your thumb seems better,' she said.

Charlie held out his hand, examining it in the pale moonlight. His fingers, splayed against the stars, seemed . . . more than. More than fingers. More than a part, or parts, of a whole. Just as one plus one is more than two, she thought, not knowing where the idea sprang from, or why.

'Good as ever,' he said. He turned his head towards hers just enough so that she could make out his grin. 'Better.'

She smiled back. She felt her pulse in the hollow of her throat, and she felt the night air on her throat as well. She didn't think she'd ever noticed that sensation in that specific location.

'Bodies are funny, aren't they?' she said.

'How so?' Charlie asked.

She stared at the sky. She was nervous. She didn't want him to laugh. 'Just . . . are they us? Are we them?'

Charlie was silent long enough for Wren to regret her words. Then he said, 'Do we have souls, you mean?'

Relief pressed her deeper into the scratchy wool blanket. 'Yeah. I guess. Or are we just, you know, chemicals? Brain cells talking to brain cells, talking to lung cells and spine cells and thumb cells?'

'Like when Ms Atkinson compared us to computers with organic hard drives?' Charlie said. 'A blow to the head can create a system failure? A disease, like Alzheimer's, is a computer virus?'

Wren nodded. She didn't like that concept, because if it were true – if a human was a highly specialized computer, but a computer nonetheless – where did that leave the 'human' part?

'My dad's an atheist,' she said. He wanted Wren to share his beliefs, but she didn't.

'My foster mom teaches Sunday school,' Charlie replied. 'And during the church service, when it's time for "A Moment with the Kids," she plays "Jesus Loves Me".'

'"A Moment with the Kids"?'

'When the youth minister calls up all the kids and tells them a story that has to do with the day's Scripture.'

'Didn't know,' Wren said. She rolled onto her side to face him. 'So, you go to church?'

She bent her knees slightly to get more comfortable, and her thigh touched Charlie's. She inhaled sharply. Charlie didn't move his leg. Neither did she.

What passed between them, even through the fabric of their jeans – it felt like way more than computer circuitry.

'Sometimes,' Charlie said. 'Pamela likes it when we

do, me and my brother. But Chris usually stays home and works. When I can, I like to stay and help out.'

'In the wood shop?'

'The cabinet shop, yeah.' He raised his arms and clasped his hands beneath his head, and she saw the hard slope of his biceps. The expanse of skin stretching from his bicep to his shoulder, paler than his forearm and more vulnerable, disappearing into the shadow of his sleeve. Not an entirely private place, but not a part of this boy – *Charlie* – that everyone had seen, either.

And, again, not just a part. More than.

'I think souls are real,' Wren said in a burst. 'Maybe they're not things you can measure or hold or feel—'

'You can feel them,' Charlie said in a low voice. He turned his head, and she saw his cheek meet his upper arm.

I would like to feel that arm, Wren thought. I would like to touch that cheek.

She swallowed. 'What about trees?'

His lips quirked. 'Trees?'

'Do they have souls?' she asked, because at that moment they seemed to. Leaves rustled, saying *shushhhh, shushhh*. Branches formed a canopy high over their heads. Add in the matted grass below them, and Wren and Charlie were nestled in . . . a set of parentheses. They were in a moment outside of time. Just the two of them. Their eyes locked. Their bodies, as Charlie rolled onto his side, forming parentheses

44

within the parentheses, and within the parentheses, their souls reached out. Like roots. Like fingers. Like wisps of clouds and slivers of radiant moonlight.

Wren shivered.

'They probably don't,' she said. 'That's just in fairy tales, right? Druids and dryads and alternate worlds?' She was babbling, but her heart was fluttering, and she was helpless to stop her string of words from issuing forth. 'Anyway, I'm a scientist. Or will be, probably, since doctors are scientists. I know that's silly – trees with souls – but I just . . . I guess I just . . .'

She waited for Charlie to jump in and rescue her from her stupidity. He didn't, and when Wren checked his expression, when she let herself truly see his expression instead of hiding from it, she realized he was waiting for her to finish. Not because he was enjoying watching her make a fool out of herself, but because he cared about her thoughts and was interested in hearing them.

His auburn eyes weren't auburn in the dark ditch. They were dark and liquid. A well to fall into. The ocean.

'I guess I think the world is more connected than people realize,' she said, choosing her words carefully. You're allowed to have thoughts, she reminded herself. Just because others might scoff, that doesn't mean Charlie will.

She tried to steady her breath. 'I think . . . some-times . . . that scientists . . . *some* scientists . . . want to package things up into neat little boxes. Explain, explain, explain, until there aren't any mysteries left.'

'I think you're probably right,' Charlie said.

'Well . . . I like the mysteries,' she said. Her skin tingled. Those little hairs stood up again, all over her. It wasn't as if she were undressing in front of him, and yet that's how it felt. And she wanted to keep on going, even so. What had this boy done to her?

'I want to understand them, or try to,' she said, 'but I don't want to put them away in boxes. And if there doesn't seem to be any explanation for something, I don't want that to scare me away. I don't want to force an explanation to fit or throw my hands in the air and give up. You know?'

He nodded. A faint shadow of stubble ran from his hair-line down and along his strong jaw.

She swallowed. 'Does that make any sense?'

He pulled his eyebrows together endearingly, like a little boy trying to act grown up. 'You're saying the mysteries are worth examining, even if they're too big to be understood. That maybe they're bound to be too big to understand, but that doesn't take anything away from them, and in fact just adds to their beauty. Is that close?'

'That's it exactly,' she said. He put it into words so beautifully: Marvel and wonder all you want. There will always be more. She laughed, and the surprised smile she got from Charlie was a pure gift.

Then he grew serious. He pulled his eyebrows

together again, but this time he didn't look like a little boy at all.

'Hey,' he said. He propped himself up on one elbow. With his other hand, he reached out and lightly, lightly stroked her cheek.

Wren's chest rose and fell. She almost felt as if she were out of her body, except she was very much in her body, and her body knew what it wanted.

Charlie leaned in, and she leaned to meet him. His mouth found hers, and her thoughts flew through her, as loud and raucous as magpies. *My first kiss. I am eighteen, and this is my first kiss, unless I count Jake What's-His-Name in eighth grade, which I don't. Because this is . . . different. So different.*

And then her thoughts dissolved into lips. Breath. A soft sigh, a shifting thigh. She gave herself over to Charlie and the night and the world, full of mysteries. She allowed herself to just be.

More than.

Charlie wanted to see Wren again. She was all he could think about – kissing her, touching her, being with her – and he wanted to do it again. Right away.

He called her the morning after P.G.'s party.

'Charlie?' she said when she answered, and his heart jumped.

'Hey,' he said.

'Hey.'

'How are you?'

'I'm good. How are you?'

'I'm good,' he said. His conversation skills sucked. He couldn't talk worth a damn, but last night he kissed her, and she kissed him back. So, yeah. He was very, very good.

'I was wondering whether you'd like to do something,' he said abruptly. 'I'd like to see you.'

'Today?'

'I could grab some sandwiches if you want. I could come pick you up. I was thinking we could go on a picnic, if that sounded like something you might like. Is that . . . something you might like?'

'Um, sure,' she said.

'Great. Awesome. *Great.*'

She giggled. 'What time?'

'Now,' he pronounced, and she giggled again. He was too thrilled to be embarrassed. 'I'll be at your house in fifteen minutes. Hey – are you afraid of heights?'

'Of heights? Why?'

'No reason. See you soon.'

He took her to a spot along the Chattahoochee River where the sky was wide and blue. Trees lined the bank, and birds sang as they flitted from branch to branch. The water was brown, but it glinted and turned to gold when it splashed over the moss-covered rocks.

Charlie drove here when he needed to think. Until today, he'd always come alone.

'It's beautiful,' Wren said after climbing out of the car. She was wearing a sundress, or some sort of dress, and it swished against her thighs. She had on cowboy boots, and her hair was pulled into a ponytail. *She* was beautiful.

'Come on,' he said, almost reaching for her hand. He didn't, and he cursed himself.

He headed up the trail. She followed.

'Do you go hiking a lot?' she asked.

'Um, what do you mean by hiking? You mean like what we're doing now?'

'I guess,' she said. 'Being outside – is that something you like?'

'Oh,' he said. 'Yeah. When I was a kid, I was inside a lot, so yeah, I'd rather be outside if I can.' He glanced back at her. Her skin was smooth and creamy. When she stepped over a log, he caught a glimpse of the paler skin of her inner thigh. There, and then gone.

Take her hand, he told himself, and this time he did.

'And you?' he said. They started back up the trail. 'Do you like being outside?'

'Mmm-hmm,' she said. 'Especially the ocean. Oh my gosh, I *love* the ocean. I love catching waves and getting all salty, and hungry – I get so hungry after swimming in the ocean – and then flopping down all wet on my towel and letting the sun soak in.'

She made a small sound that was almost a moan, and Charlie's cock stirred. Wet and warm and salty?

Damn. Everything she said, she said so innocently, and yet she drove him so crazy. She drove him more crazy because she was so innocent.

Discreetly, he tugged at his jeans. 'I've never been.'

'To the ocean? You've never been to the ocean?'

He shook his head. 'One day.'

'Oh, Charlie, you have to,' she told him. 'If you like being outside – wow. You will love the ocean. It makes you feel so . . . I don't know. Small, but not in a bad way. Small because you realize you're part of something bigger. It gets you out of your head, if that makes sense.'

She almost tripped on a root. Charlie caught her.

'You all right?' he said.

'Yeah, thanks,' she said, looking embarrassed. She let go of his hand. He wished she hadn't. Then, after a moment's hesitation, she looped her arm through his, and he was elated. Her breast brushed against him. She brought her other hand across her body and rested it on his biceps, above their linked elbows.

She smiled shyly up at him. 'Is that okay? I'm not making it hard for you to walk or anything?'

She was, but not in the way she meant. Yes, it was okay.

'Do you think that life has patterns in it?' she asked.

'Patterns? Like what?'

She exhaled in a sweet way. 'Like, in a non-random way. Like, do things happen for a reason?'

'Hmm,' Charlie said. Science and math were subjects he did well at, and in general, he was more comfortable with ideas that could be expressed in formulas than ideas that couldn't fully be explained. Then again, scientific theories started with the seed of an unexplained idea. Mathematical formulas often described phenomena that couldn't be physically verified.

'I'm not sure,' he said. 'I'm certainly not willing to discount it.'

'Me either,' she said. 'And, okay, this is going to sound silly, but when you called me this morning . . .'

'Yeah?'

'Well, when I heard your voice I felt . . .'

He waited.

She blushed and squeezed his arm, and he realized that she wasn't going to answer. But he thought that if the world was layered with meaning, then she was the evidence, right here. She was the mystery and the explanation, both.

They reached the place in the trail Charlie had been waiting for, and he gestured with his chin at what lay ahead.

'Hey,' he said. 'Take a look.'

She caught her lower lip between her teeth. 'Whoa.'

'Yeah,' Charlie said.

'How did I not know this was here?' Wren said. 'How have I never been here before?'

'Let's go up,' Charlie said, leading her toward the embankment. Above them stood a decaying railroad bridge that was built probably a hundred years ago. The wooden support beams stretched like a row of giant As into the clouds. The steel rails that trains once rode on were long gone, but the underlying tracks remained.

At first, Wren kept her arm linked in his as they climbed. Then the dirt grew loose, and she had to use her hands for balance and to clutch at branches. Charlie, behind her, glimpsed the curve of her ass and a flash of panties.

He took several big steps to pass her. From the top of the rise, he extended his hand.

'Oh wow,' she said, breathing hard. 'We're as high as the treetops.'

'Let's go out,' he said. He squeezed her hand. 'You want to go out?'

'To the middle of the bridge?'

'Yeah, come on.'

Two rotting wooden tracks, each approximately three feet wide, stretched across the gulley below. They were sturdy enough to walk on – Charlie would never put Wren in danger – but the ground dipped steeply away several yards past the top of the embankment. Walking along them was like walking along a wide balance beam, only much higher off the ground. Charlie went first and kept Wren's hand in his.

FROM
IF I STAY

BY
GAYLE FORMAN

'Have you ever heard of this Yo-Yo Ma dude?' Adam asked me. It was the spring of my sophomore year, which was his junior year. By then, Adam had been watching me practice in the music wing for several months. Our school was one of those progressive ones that always got written up in national magazines because of its emphasis on the arts. We did get a lot of free periods to paint in the studio or practice music. I spent mine in the soundproof booths of the music wing. Adam was there a lot, too, playing guitar. Not the electric guitar he played in his band. Just acoustic melodies.

I rolled my eyes. 'Everyone's heard of Yo-Yo Ma.'

Adam grinned. I noticed for the first time that his smile was lopsided, his mouth sloping up on one side. He hooked his ringed thumb out toward the quad. 'I don't think you'll find five people out there who've heard of Yo-Yo Ma. And by the way, what kind of name is that? Is it ghetto or something? Yo Mama?'

'It's Chinese.'

Adam shook his head and laughed. 'I know plenty of Chinese people. They have names like Wei Chin. Or Lee something. Not Yo-Yo Ma.'

'You cannot be blaspheming the master,' I said. But then I laughed in spite of myself. It had taken me a few months to believe that Adam wasn't taking the piss out of me, and after that we'd started having these little conversations in the corridor.

Still, his attention baffled me. It wasn't that Adam was such a popular guy. He wasn't a jock or a most-likely-to-succeed sort. But he was cool. Cool in that he played in a band with people who went to the college in town. Cool in that he had his own rocker-ish style, procured from thrift stores and garage sales, not from Urban Outfitters knockoffs. Cool in that he seemed totally happy to sit in the lunchroom absorbed in a book, not just pretending to read because he didn't have anywhere to sit or anyone to sit with. That wasn't the case at all. He had a small group of friends and a large group of admirers.

And it wasn't like I was a dork, either. I had friends and a best friend to sit with at lunch. I had other good friends at the music conservatory camp I went to in the summer. People liked me well enough, but they also didn't really know me. I was quiet in class. I didn't raise my hand a lot or sass the teachers. And I was busy, much of my time spent practicing or playing in a string quartet or taking theory classes at the community college. Kids were nice enough to me, but they tended to treat me as if I were a grown-up. Another teacher. And you don't flirt with your teachers.

'What would you say if I said I had tickets to the master?' Adam asked me, a glint in his eyes.

'Shut up. You do not,' I said, shoving him a little harder than I'd meant to.

Adam pretended to fall against the glass wall. Then he dusted himself off. 'I do. At the Schnitzle place in Portland.'

'It's the Arlene Schnitzer Hall. It's part of the Symphony.'

'That's the place. I got tickets. A pair. You interested?'

'Are you serious? Yes! I was dying to go but they're like eighty dollars each. Wait, how did you get tickets?'

'A friend of the family gave them to my parents, but they can't go. It's no big thing,' Adam said quickly. 'Anyhow, it's Friday night. If you want, I'll pick you up at five-thirty and we'll drive to Portland together.'

'OK,' I said, like it was the most natural thing.

By Friday afternoon, though, I was more jittery than when I'd inadvertently drunk a whole pot of Dad's tar-strong coffee while studying for final exams last winter.

It wasn't Adam making me nervous. I'd grown comfortable enough around him by now. It was the uncertainty. What was this, exactly? A date? A friendly favor? An act of charity? I didn't like being on soft ground any more than I liked fumbling my way through a new movement. That's why I practiced so much, so I could rush myself on solid ground and then work out the details from there.

I changed my clothes about six times. Teddy, a kindergartner back then, sat in my bedroom, pulling the Calvin and Hobbes books down from shelves and pretending to read them. He cracked himself up, though I wasn't sure whether it was Calvin's high jinks or my own making him so goofy.

Mom popped her head in to check on my progress. 'He's just a guy, Mia,' she said when she saw me getting worked up.

'Yeah, but he's just the first guy I've ever gone on a maybe-date with,' I said. 'So I don't know whether to wear date clothes or symphony clothes – do people here even dress up for that kind of thing? Or should I just keep it casual, in case it's *not* a date?'

'Just wear something you feel good in,' she suggested. 'That way you're covered.' I'm sure Mom would've pulled out all the stops had she been me. In the pictures of her and Dad from the early days, she looked like a cross between a 1930s siren and a biker chick, with her pixie haircut, her big blue eyes coated in kohl eyeliner, and her rail-thin body always ensconced in some sexy get-up, like a lacy vintage camisole paired with skintight leather pants.

I sighed. I wished I could be so ballsy. In the end, I chose a long black skirt and a maroon short-sleeved sweater. Plain and simple. My trademark, I guess.

When Adam showed up in a sharkskin suit and Creepers (an ensemble that wholly impressed Dad), I realized that this really was a date. Of course, Adam would choose to dress up for the symphony and a 1960s sharkskin suit could've just been his cool take on formal, but I knew there was more to it than that. He seemed nervous as he shook hands with my dad and told him that he had his band's old CDs. 'To use as coasters, I hope,' Dad said. Adam looked surprised, unused to the parent being more sarcastic than the child, I imagine.

'Don't you kids get too crazy. Bad injuries at the last Yo-Yo Ma mosh pit,' Mom called as we walked down the lawn.

'Your parents are so cool,' Adam said, opening the car door for me.

'I know,' I replied.

We drove to Portland, making small talk. Adam played me snippets of bands he liked, a Swedish pop trio that sounded monotonous but then some Icelandic art band that was quite beautiful. We got a little lost downtown and made it to the concert hall with only a few minutes to spare.

Our seats were in the balcony. Nosebleeds. But you don't go to Yo-Yo Ma for the view, and the sound was incredible. That man has a way of making the cello sound like a crying woman one minute, a laughing child the next. Listening to him, I'm always reminded of why I started playing cello in the first place – that there is something so human and expressive about it.

When the concert started, I peered at Adam out of the corner of my eye. He seemed good-natured enough about the whole thing, but he kept looking at his program, probably counting off the movements until intermission. I worried that he was bored, but after a while I got too caught up in the music to care.

Then, when Yo-Yo Ma played 'Le Grand Tango', Adam reached over and grasped my hand. In any other context, this would have been cheesy, the old yawn-and-cop-a-feel move. But Adam wasn't looking at me. His eyes were closed and he was swaying slightly in his seat. He was lost in the music, too. I squeezed his hand back and we sat there like that for the rest of the concert.

Afterward, we bought coffees and doughnuts and walked along the river. It was misting and he took off his suit jacket and draped it over my shoulders.

'You didn't really get those tickets from a family friend, did you?' I asked.

I thought he would laugh or throw up his arms in mock surrender like he did when I beat him in an argument. But he looked straight at me, so I could see the green and browns and grays swimming around in his irises. He shook his head. 'That was two weeks of pizza-delivery tips,' he admitted.

I stopped walking. I could hear the water lapping below. 'Why?' I asked. 'Why me?'

'I've never seen anyone get as into music as you do. It's why I like to watch you practice. You get the cutest crease in your forehead, right there,' Adam said, touching me above the bridge of my nose. 'I'm obsessed with music and even I don't get transported like you do.'

'So, what? I'm like a social experiment to you?' I meant it to be jokey, but it came out sounding bitter.

'No, you're not an experiment,' Adam said. His voice was husky and choked.

I felt the heat flood my neck and I could sense myself blushing. I stared at my shoes. I knew that Adam was looking at me now with as much certainty as I knew that if I looked up he was going to kiss me. And it took me by surprise how much I wanted to be kissed by him, to realize that I'd thought about it so often that I'd memorized the exact shape of his lips, that I'd imagined running my finger down the cleft of his chin.

My eyes flickered upward. Adam was there waiting for me.

That was how it started.

12:19 p.m.
There are a lot of things wrong with me.

Apparently, I have a collapsed lung. A ruptured spleen. Internal bleeding of unknown origin. And most serious, the contusions on my brain. I've also got broken ribs. Abrasions on my legs, which will require skin grafts; and on my face, which will require cosmetic surgery – but, as the doctors note, that is only if I am lucky.

Right now, in surgery, the doctors have to remove my spleen, insert a new tube to drain my collapsed lung, and stanch whatever else might be causing the internal bleeding. There isn't a lot they can do for my brain.

'We'll just wait and see,' one of the surgeons says, looking at the CAT scan of my head. 'In the meantime, call down to the blood bank. I need two units of O neg and keep two units ahead.'

O negative. My blood type. I had no idea. It's not like it's something I've ever had to think about before. I've never been in the hospital unless you count the time I went to the emergency room after I cut my ankle on some broken glass. I didn't even need stitches then, just a tetanus shot.

In the operating room, the doctors are debating what music to play, just like we were in the car this morning. One guy wants jazz. Another wants rock. The anesthesiologist, who stands near my head, requests classical. I root for her, and I feel like that must help because someone pops on a Wagner CD, although I don't know that the rousing 'Ride of the Valkyries' is what I had in mind. I'd hoped for something a little lighter. *Four Seasons*, perhaps.

The operating room is small and crowded, full of blindingly bright lights, which highlight how grubby this place is. It's nothing like on TV, where operating rooms are like pristine theaters that could accommodate an opera singer, *and* an audience. The floor, though buffed shiny, is dingy with scuff marks and rust streaks, which I take to be old bloodstains.

Blood. It is everywhere. It does not faze the doctors one bit. They slice and sew and suction through a river of it, like they are washing dishes in soapy water. Meanwhile, they pump an ever-replenishing stock into my veins.

The surgeon who wanted to listen to rock sweats a lot. One of the nurses has to periodically dab the perspiration from his face with gauze that she holds in tongs. At one point, he sweats through his mask and has to replace it.

The anesthesiologist has gentle fingers. She sits at my head, keeping an eye on all my vitals, adjusting the amounts of the fluids and gases and drugs they're giving me. She must be doing a good job because I don't appear to feel anything, even though they are yanking at my body. It's rough and messy work, nothing like that game Operation we used to play as kids where you had to be careful not to touch the sides as you removed a bone, or the buzzer would go off.

The anesthesiologist absentmindedly strokes my temples through her latex gloves. This is what Mom used to do when I came down with the flu or got one of those headaches that hurt so bad I used to imagine cutting open a vein in my temple just to relieve the pressure.

The Wagner CD has repeated twice now. The doctors decide it's time for a new genre. Jazz wins. People always assume that because I am into classical music, I'm a jazz aficionado. I'm not. Dad is. He loves it, especially the wild, latter-day Coltrane stuff. He says that jazz is punk for old people. I guess that explains it, because I don't like punk, either.

The operation goes on and on. I'm exhausted by it. I don't know how the doctors have the stamina to keep up. They're standing still, but it seems harder than running a marathon.

I start to zone out. And then I start to wonder about this state I'm in. If I'm not dead – and the heart monitor is bleeping along, so I assume I'm not – but I'm not in my body, either, can I go anywhere? Am I a ghost? Could I transport myself to a beach in Hawaii? Can I pop over to Carnegie Hall in New York City? Can I go to Teddy?

Just for the sake of experiment, I wiggle my nose like Samantha on *Bewitched*. Nothing happens. I snap my fingers. Click my heels. I'm still here.

I decide to try a simpler maneuver. I walk into the wall, imagining that I'll float through it and come out the other side. Except that what happens when I walk into the wall is that I hit a wall.

A nurse bustles in with a bag of blood, and before the door shuts behind her, I slip through it. Now I'm in the hospital corridor. There are lots of doctors and nurses in blue and green scrubs hustling around. A woman on a gurney, her hair in a gauzy blue shower cap, an IV in her arm, calls out to 'William, William.' I walk a little farther. There are rows of operating rooms, all full of sleeping people. If the patients inside these rooms are like me, why then can't I see the people outside the people? Is everyone else loitering about like I seem to be? I'd really like to meet someone in my condition. I have some questions, like, what is this state I'm in exactly and how do I get out of it? How do I get back to my body? Do I have to wait for the doctors to wake me up? But there's no one else like me around. Maybe the rest of them figured out how to get to Hawaii.

I follow a nurse through a set of automatic double doors. I'm in a small waiting room now. My grandparents are here.

Gran is chattering away to Gramps, or maybe just to the air. It's her way of not letting emotion get the best of her. I've seen her do it before, when Gramps had a heart attack. She is wearing her wellies and her gardening smock, which is smudged with mud. She must have been working in her greenhouse when she heard about us. Gran's hair is short and curly and gray; she's been wearing it in a permanent wave, Dad says, since the 1970s. 'It's easy,' Gran says. 'No muss, no fuss.' This is so typical of her. No nonsense. She's so quintessentially practical that most people would never guess she has a thing for angels. She keeps a collection of ceramic angels, yarn-doll angels, blown-glass angels, you-name-it angels, in a special china hutch in her sewing room. And she doesn't just collect angels; she believes in them. She thinks that they're everywhere. Once, a pair of loons nested in the pond in the woods behind their house. Gran was convinced that it was her long-dead parents, come to watch over her.

Another time, we were sitting outside on her porch and I saw a red bird. 'Is that a red crossbill?' I'd asked Gran.

She'd shaken her head. 'My sister Gloria is a cross-bill,' Gran had said, referring to my recently deceased great-aunt Glo, with whom Gran had never gotten along. 'She wouldn't be coming around here.'

Gramps is staring into the dregs of his Styrofoam cup, peeling away the top of it so that little white balls collect in his lap. I can tell it's the worst kind of swill, the kind that looks like it was brewed in 1997 and has been sitting on a burner ever since. Even so, I wouldn't mind a cup.

You can draw a straight line from Gramps to Dad to Teddy, although Gramps's wavy hair has gone from blond to gray and he is stockier than Teddy, who is a stick, and Dad, who is wiry and muscular from afternoon weight-lifting sessions at the local YMCA gym. But they all have the same watery gray-blue eyes, the color of the ocean on a cloudy day.

Maybe this is why I now find it hard to look at Gramps.

Juilliard was Gran's idea. She's from Massachusetts originally, but she moved to Oregon in 1955, on her own. Now that would be no big deal, but I guess fifty-two years ago it was kind of scandalous for a twenty-two-year-old unmarried woman to do that kind of thing. Gran claimed she was drawn to wild open wilderness and it didn't get more wild than the endless forests and craggy beaches of Oregon. She got a job as a secretary working for the Forest Service. Gramps was working there as a biologist.

We go back to Massachusetts sometimes in the summers, to a lodge in the western part of the state that for one week is taken over by Gran's extended family. That's when I see the second cousins and great-aunts and uncles whose names I barely recognize. I have lots of family in Oregon, but they're all from Gramps's side.

Last summer at the Massachusetts retreat, I brought my cello so I could keep up my practicing for an upcoming chamber music concert. The flight wasn't full, so the stewardesses let it travel in a seat next to me, just like the pros do it. Teddy thought this was hilarious and kept trying to feed it pretzels.

At the lodge, I gave a little concert one night, in the main room, with my relatives and the dead game animals mounted on the wall as my audience. It was after that that someone mentioned Juilliard, and Gran became taken with the idea.

At first, it seemed far-fetched. There was a perfectly good music program at the university near us. And, if I wanted to stretch, there was a conservatory in Seattle, which was only a few hours' drive. Juilliard was across the country. And expensive. Mom and Dad were intrigued with the idea of it, but I could tell neither one of them really wanted to relinquish me to New York City or go into hock so that I could maybe become a cellist for some second-rate small-town orchestra. They had no idea whether I was good enough. In fact, neither did I. Professor Christie told me that I was one of the most promising students she'd ever taught, but she'd never mentioned Juilliard to me. Juilliard was for virtuoso musicians, and it seemed arrogant to even think that they'd give me a second glance.

But after the retreat, when someone else, someone impartial and from the East Coast, deemed me Juilliard-worthy, the idea burrowed into Gran's brain. She took it upon herself to speak to Professor Christie about it, and my teacher took hold of the idea like a terrier to a bone.

So, I filled out my application, collected my letters of recommendation, and sent in a recording of my playing. I didn't tell Adam about any of this. I had told myself that it was because there was no point advertising it when even getting an audition was such a long shot. But even then I'd recognized that for the lie that it was. A small part of me felt like even applying was some kind of betrayal. Juilliard was in New York. Adam was here.

But not at high school anymore. He was a year ahead of me, and this past year, my senior year, he'd started at the university in town. He only went to school part-time now because Shooting Star was starting to get popular. There was a record deal with a Seattle-based label, and a lot of traveling to gigs. So only after I got the creamy envelope embossed with THE JUILLIARD SCHOOL and a letter inviting me to audition did I tell Adam that I'd applied and been granted an audition. I explained how many people didn't get that far. At first he looked a little awestruck, like he couldn't quite believe it. Then he gave a sad little smile. 'Yo Mama better watch his back,' he said.

The auditions were held in San Francisco. Dad had some big conference at the school that week and couldn't get away, and Mom had just started a new job at the travel agency, so Gran volunteered to accompany me. 'We'll make a girls' weekend of it. Take high tea at the Fairmont. Go window-shopping in Union Square. Ride the ferry to Alcatraz. We'll be tourists.'

But a week before we were due to leave, Gran tripped over a tree root and sprained her ankle. She had to wear one of those clunky boots and wasn't supposed to walk. Minor panic ensued. I said I could just go by myself – drive, or take the train, and come right back.

It was Gramps who insisted on taking me. We drove down together in his pickup truck. We didn't talk much, which was fine by me because I was so nervous. I kept fingering the Popsicle-stick good-luck talisman Teddy had presented me with before we left. 'Break an arm,' he'd told me.

Gramps and I listened to classical music and farm reports on the radio when we could pick up a station. Otherwise, we sat in silence. But it was such a calming silence; it made me relax and feel closer to him than any heart-to-heart would have.

Gran had booked us in a really frilly inn, and it was funny to see Gramps in his work boots and plaid flannel amid all the lacy doilies and potpourri. But he took it all in stride.

The audition was grueling. I had to play five pieces: a Shostakovich concerto, two Bach suites, all Tchaikovsky's *Pezzo capriccioso*, which was next to impossible, and a movement from Ennio Morricone's *The Mission*, a fun but risky choice because Yo-Yo Ma had covered this and everyone would compare. I walked out with my legs wobbly and my underarms wet with sweat. But my endorphins were surging and that, combined with the huge sense of relief, left me totally giddy.

'Shall we see the town?' Gramps asked, his lips twitching into a smile.

'Definitely!'

We did all the things Gran had promised we would do. Gramps took me to high tea and shopping, although for dinner, we skipped out on the reservations Gran had made at some fancy place on Fisherman's Wharf and instead wandered into Chinatown, looking for the restaurant with the longest line of people waiting outside, and ate there.

When we got back home, Gramps dropped me off and enveloped me in a hug. Normally, he was a handshaker, maybe a back patter on really special occasions. His hug was strong and tight, and I knew it was his way of telling me that he'd had a wonderful time.

'Me, too, Gramps,' I whispered.

3:47 p.m.

They just moved me out of the recovery room into the trauma intensive-care unit, or ICU. It's a horseshoe-shaped room with about a dozen beds and a cadre of nurses, who constantly bustle around, reading the computer print-outs that churn out from the feet of our beds recording our vital signs. In the middle of the room are more computers and a big desk, where another nurse sits.

I have two nurses who check in on me, along with the endless round of doctors. One is a taciturn doughy man with blond hair and a mustache, who I don't much like. And the other is a woman with skin so black it's blue and a lilt in her voice. She calls me 'sweetheart' and perpetually straightens the blankets around me, even though it's not like I'm kicking them off.

There are so many tubes attached to me that I cannot count them all: one down my throat breathing for me; one down my nose, keeping my stomach empty; one in my vein, hydrating me; one in my bladder, peeing for me; several on my chest, recording my heartbeat; another on my finger, recording my pulse. The ventilator that's doing my breathing has a soothing rhythm like a metronome, in, out, in, out.

No one, aside from the doctors and nurses and a social worker, has been in to see me. It's the social worker who speaks to Gran and Gramps in hushed sympathetic tones. She tells them that I am in 'grave' condition. I'm not entirely sure what that means – grave. On TV, patients are always critical, or stable. Grave sounds bad. Grave is where you go when things don't work out here.

'I wish there was something we could do,' Gran says. 'I feel so useless just waiting.'

'I'll see if I can get you in to see her in a little while,' the social worker says. She has frizzy gray hair and a coffee stain on her blouse; her face is kind. 'She's still sedated from the surgery and she's on a ventilator to help her breathe while her body heals from the trauma. But it can be helpful even for patients in a comatose state to hear from their loved ones.'

Gramps grunts in reply.

'Do you have any people you can call?' the social worker asks. 'Relatives who might like to be here with you. I understand this must be quite a trial for you, but the stronger you can be, the more it will help Mia.'

I startle when I hear the social worker say my name. It's a jarring reminder that it's me they're talking about. Gran tells her about the various people who are en route right now, aunts, uncles. I don't hear any mention of Adam.

Adam is the one I really want to see. I wish I knew where he was so I could try to go there. I have no idea how he's going to find out about me. Gran and Gramps don't have his phone number. They don't carry cell phones, so he can't call them. And I don't know how he'd even know to call them. The people who would normally pass along pertinent information that something has happened to me are in no position to do that.

I stand over the bleeping tubed lifeless form that is me. My skin is gray. My eyes are taped shut. I wish someone would take the tape off. It looks like it itches. The nice nurse bustles over. Her scrubs have lollipops on them, even though this isn't a pediatric unit. 'How's it going, sweetheart?' she asks me, as if we just bumped into each other in the grocery store.

It didn't start out so smoothly with Adam and me. I think I had this notion that love conquers all. And by the time he dropped me off from the Yo-Yo Ma concert, I think we were both aware that we were falling in love. I thought that getting to this part was the challenge. In books and movies, the stories always end when the two people finally have their romantic kiss. The happily-ever-after part is just assumed.

It didn't quite work that way for us. It turned out that coming from such far corners of the social universe had its downsides. We continued to see each other in the music wing, but these interactions remained platonic, as if neither one of us wanted to mess with a good thing. But whenever we met at other places in the school – when we sat together in the cafeteria or studied side by side on the quad on a sunny day – something was off. We were uncomfortable. Conversation was stilted. One of us would say something and the other would start to say something else at the same time.

'You go,' I'd say.

'No, you go,' Adam would say.

The politeness was painful. I wanted to push through it, to return to the glow of the night of the concert, but I was unsure of how to get back there.

Adam invited me to see his band play. This was even worse than school. If I felt like a fish out of water in my family, I felt like a fish on Mars in Adam's circle. He was always surrounded by funky, lively people, by cute girls with dyed hair and piercings, by aloof guys who perked up when Adam rock-talked with them. I couldn't do the groupie thing. And I didn't know how to rock talk at all. It was a language I should've understood, being both a musician and Dad's daughter, but I didn't. It was like how Mandarin speakers can sort of understand Cantonese but not really, even though non-Chinese people assume all Chinese can communicate with one another, even though Mandarin and Cantonese are actually different.

I dreaded going to shows with Adam. It wasn't that I was jealous. Or that I wasn't into his kind of music. I loved to watch him play. When he was onstage, it was like the guitar was a fifth limb, a natural extension of his body. And when he came offstage afterward, he would be sweaty but it was such a clean sweat that part of me was tempted to lick the side of his face, like it was a lollipop. I didn't, though.

Once the fans would descend, I'd skitter off to the sidelines. Adam would try to draw me back, to wrap an arm around my waist, but I'd disentangle myself and head back to the shadows.

'Don't you like me anymore?' Adam chided me after one show. He was kidding, but I could hear the hurt behind the offhand question.

'I don't know if I should keep coming to your shows,' I said.

'Why not?' he asked. This time he didn't try to disguise the hurt.

'I feel like I keep you from basking in it all. I don't want you to have to worry about me.'

Adam said that he didn't mind worrying about me, but I could tell that part of him did.

We probably would've broken up in those early weeks were it not for my house. At my house, with my family, we found a common ground. After we'd been together for a month, I took Adam home with me for his first family dinner with us. He sat in the kitchen with Dad, rock-talking. I observed, and I still didn't understand half of it, but unlike at the shows didn't feel left out.

'Do you play basketball?' Dad asked. When it came to observing sports, Dad was a baseball fanatic, but when it came to playing, he loved to shoot hoops.

'Sure,' Adam said. 'I mean, I'm not very good.'

'You don't need to be good; you just need to be committed. Want to play a quick game? You already have your basketball shoes on,' Dad said, looking at Adam's Converse high-tops. Then he turned to me. 'You mind?'

'Not at all,' I said, smiling. 'I can practice while you play.'

They went out to the courts behind the nearby elementary school. They returned forty-five minutes later. Adam was covered with a sheen of sweat and looking a little dazed.

'What happened?' I asked. 'Did the old man whoop you?'

Adam shook his head and nodded at the same time. 'Well, yes. But it's not that. I got stung by a bee on my palm while we were playing. Your dad grabbed my hand and sucked the venom out.'

I nodded. This was a trick he'd learned from Gran, and unlike with rattlesnakes, it actually worked on bee stings. You got the stinger and the venom out, so you were left with only a little itch.

Adam broke into an embarrassed smile. He leaned in and whispered into my ear: 'I think I'm a little wigged out that I've been more intimate with your dad than I have with you.'

I laughed at that. But it was sort of true. In the few weeks we'd been together, we hadn't done much more than kiss. It wasn't that I was a prude. I *was* a virgin, but I certainly wasn't devoted to staying that way. And Adam certainly wasn't a virgin. It was more that our kissing had suffered from the same painful politeness as our conversations.

'Maybe we should remedy that,' I murmured.

Adam raised his eyebrows as if asking me a question. I blushed in response. All through dinner, we grinned at each other as we listened to Teddy, who was chattering about the dinosaur bones he'd apparently dug up in the back garden that afternoon. Dad had made his famous salt roast, which was my favorite dish, but I had no appetite. I pushed the food around my plate, hoping no one would notice. All the while, this little buzz was building inside me. I thought of the tuning fork I used to adjust my cello. Hitting it sets off vibrations in the note of A – vibrations that keep growing, and growing, until the harmonic pitch fills up the room. That's what Adam's grin was doing to me during dinner.

After the meal, Adam took a quick peek at Teddy's fossil finds, and then we went upstairs to my room and closed the door. Kim is not allowed to be alone in her house with boys – not that the opportunity ever came up. My parents had never mentioned any rules on this issue, but I had a feeling that they knew what was happening with Adam and me, and even though Dad liked to play it all *Father Knows Best*, in reality, he and Mom were suckers when it came to love.

Adam lay down on my bed, stretching his arms above his head. His whole face was grinning – eyes, nose, mouth. 'Play me,' he said.

'What?'

'I want you to play me like a cello.'

I started to protest that this made no sense, but then I realized it made perfect sense. I went to my closet and grabbed one of my spare bows. 'Take off your shirt,' I said, my voice quavering.

Adam did. As thin as he was, he was surprisingly

built. I could've spent twenty minutes staring at the contours and valleys of his chest. But he wanted me closer. I wanted me closer.

I sat down next to him on the bed, perpendicular to his hips, so his long body was stretched out in front of me. The bow trembled as I placed it on the bed. I reached with my left hand and caressed Adam's head as if it were the scroll of my cello. He smiled again and closed his eyes. I relaxed a little. I fiddled with his ears as though they were the string pegs and then I playfully tickled him as he laughed softly. I placed two fingers on his Adam's apple. Then, taking a deep breath for courage, I plunged into his chest. I ran my hands up and down the length of his torso, focusing on the sinews in his muscles, assigning each one a string – A, G, C, D. I traced them down, one at a time, with the tip of my fingers. Adam got quiet then, as if he were concentrating on something.

I reached for the bow and brushed it across his hips, where I imagined the bridge of the cello would be. I played lightly at first and then with more force and speed as the song now playing in my head increased in intensity. Adam lay perfectly still, little groans escaping from his lips. I looked at the bow, looked at my hands, looked at Adam's face, and felt this surge of love, lust, and an unfamiliar feeling of power. I had never known that I could make someone feel this way.

When I finished, he stood up and kissed me long

and deep. 'My turn,' he said. He pulled me to my feet and started by slipping the sweater over my head and edging down my jeans. Then he sat down on the bed and laid me across his lap. At first Adam did nothing except hold me. I closed my eyes and tried to feel his eyes on my body, seeing me as no one else ever had.

Then he began to play.

He strummed chords across the top of my chest, which tickled and made me laugh. He gently brushed his hands, moving farther down. I stopped giggling. The tuning fork intensified – its vibrations growing every time Adam touched me somewhere new.

After a while he switched to more of a Spanish-style, finger-picking type of playing. He used the top of my body as the fret board, caressing my hair, my face, my neck. He plucked at my chest and my belly, but I could feel him in places his hands were nowhere near. As he played on, the energy magnified; the tuning fork going crazy now, firing off vibrations all over, until my entire body was humming, until I was left breathless. And when I felt like I could not take it one more minute, the swirl of sensations hit a dizzying crescendo, sending every nerve ending in my body on high alert.

I opened my eyes, savoring the warm calm that was sweeping over me. I started to laugh. Adam did, too. We kissed for a while longer until it was time for him to go home.

As I walked him out to his car, I wanted to tell him that I loved him. But it seemed like such a cliché after what we'd just done. So I waited and told him the next day. 'That's a relief. I thought you might just be using me for sex,' he joked, smiling.

After that, we still had our problems, but being overly polite with each other wasn't one of them.

TUMBLING

BY
SUSIE DAY

I am a late person. Notoriously late. Lategirl, with the effortless power of lateness.

I get to Speedy's at 10.33 a.m.: twenty-seven minutes early.

She's not even here to appreciate the gesture. Obviously.

Speedy's is the café on Baker Street, the café with the glossy black front door to 221b beside it, the flat's two windows directly above, where Sherlock Holmes lives with his hair and his cameraphone and that cushion with the flag on, solving hard clues in a sexy brainy way.

Not really.

Actual Benedict Cumberbatch has the good sense to live somewhere less fangirlable, probably.

The cushion and the cameraphone are in a studio in Wales.

Speedy's is on North Gower Street, and sells

omelette and chips under walls coated with fanart and Setlock photos. Sherlock would find that a bit rum. (There's a fic in that; someone will have already written the fic of that; never mind. My mind on a loop.)

I hold the camera for a series of tourists, posing in front of the red canopy. A Japanese girl clutches a deerstalker, guiltily. We have the Season Three Talk (short version). We hug before she leaves. It hurts. My hands shake holding her camera. I need to sit down.

Twenty-three minutes.

Twenty-three minutes and **vaticancameltoes** will be here.

My girl. My friend. My Sherlock.

'I'm not allowing it,' my mum says at breakfast this morning. 'My babygirl, meeting a stranger.'

'She's not a stranger.'

'She could be a pervert. A rapist. She could be anyone.'

'She's not anyone.'

She is **vaticancameltoes**.

She's Tumblr-famous.

17, consulting fanartist, Inverness says her bio in 8pt Helvetica, beside the endlessly mobile face of Sherlock Holmes whipping his blue scarf from his neck in a ridiculously flouncy yet charming way.

(I'm **eye_brows**. I keep my bio blank to retain the alluring mysteriousness that variations on 'homeschooled 16-year-old made entirely of hair and ailments' do not.)

'She's coming all the way from Scotland. We're meeting in a public place. *Mum*.'

Mum sighs. 'I don't even know what you'd do with a girlfriend.'

Yasmin's face goes taut, appalled. 'Please don't be asking what I think you're asking.'

(Yasmin is my sister: nineteen, college girl, quite heterosexual enough for the both of us, thank you very much.)

I squirm. 'Erm. They probably do a pamphlet at the GP's?'

Mum makes a face, then tries unsuccessfully to take it back in case I'm going to be all psychologically damaged by rejection.

'No! Only . . . you can't go out much, babygirl. And you *like* your quiet time, your quiet things. Being on the computer, your books, your television. You tell us off if we talk when your programme is on.'

(I do. There is no talking during *Sherlock*. Especially when Mum is all 'Which one is he?' and 'I do like a man in a coat, your father had a coat like that,' and 'Is this *Doctor Who*?' It's like living with Mrs Hudson.)

'Girlfriends watch television. Girlfriends have computers,' I tell her, drawing on my wealth of experience of girlfriends and their ways.

Mum pats my hand sadly. 'What you want is a cat.'

'Or you could just be alone for ever with a wide

selection of imaginary friends,' says Yasmin. 'No one'll mind.'

Yasmin leaves for college.

Mum leaves for work.

'I don't have imaginary friends,' I announce to the empty flat, logging into Tumblr.

I've just got one, my brain echoes back.

Like a normal human person who is utterly capable of having a girlfriend.

Right?

eye_brows – i don't think i ship them
i just want them to go shopping for curtains
eat eggs for breakfast
and play cluedo forever
vaticancameltoes – that is the legal definition
of shipping

On 15 January 2012, around 10.24 p.m., Sherlock Holmes fell from the roof of St Bart's Hospital and died.

It's OK. He's done it before. Repeatedly, since 1893. It never sticks.

He falls.

He falls again.

He is a professional tumbler, cheekbones gracefully slicing the air. Angel pose on the edge of the roof, coat billowing. Dignified back view. Then the fall. He dies very prettily: artistic bloodstains and bright blue eyes.

(I've watched it a lot. For science.)

It's OK. He always comes back.

For his Watson, says VC.

(There is a school of viewers – and readers, dating back beyond even 1893 – who interpret the relation-'ship' between Sherlock Holmes and Dr John Watson as more than crime-solving professionalism: courtship, romance, erotica. Friends with bennies. Repressed Victorians with unresolved sexual tension. A homoromantic asexual and his bisexual flatmate. A couple. Whatever.

VC is a dedicated Johnlock shipper.)

For his Watson, says VC, whenever it comes up, which is often, which is all the time because 15 January 2012 is exactly 365 days ago and we still don't know how he did it, or what happens now, and there is nothing new to talk about.

Only the agony of waiting.

But we know he isn't dead.

And John Watson doesn't. John Watson only *believes* it. Which seems harsh, or would if he was real. Which he isn't. But I seem to have cried a lot about him anyway. I'd like to write him a letter (there's a fic in that; someone will have already written the fic of that; never mind) to let him know that knowing doesn't help. *Dear John, I've written to the BBC Scheduling Department but there's no airdate for Season Three yet. Sorry you don't get to find out what happens to fictional you for probably like ages.*

So now we're stuck, waiting. Fangirls in aspic. We're all John Watson now.

Except for her.

Never her.

She's the one worth waiting for.

In Speedy's café, just like the real thing.

I go inside, buy a bottle of water, fumble the change, fingers stiff and face red. I sit by the window, facing out. Twenty-one minutes.

> **vaticancameltoes** – I think I ship us.
> **eye_brows** – Is that allowed?
> **vaticancameltoes** – Do we care?

She's not a stranger.

I don't know what she looks like but she's who makes me feel better at 3 a.m. when I can't sleep.

She lives 444 miles away (Inverness to London: 444 miles as the crow flies; 596 by road; 444 is prettier, though) but she is the person who laughs at my jokes, the person I tell them for.

She lives in my laptop, like I do.

She lives in my Tumblr, and Tumblr is the happy place.

> **vaticancameltoes** – Your turn: worst date or first date?
> **eye_brows** – ahahahaaha

I've been on a date precisely once. His name was Eddie, and I was fifteen and never been kissed, and at the end I was still fifteen and never been kissed because Eddie wanted to take me to Pizza Express (so fancy) to tell me all about how very agonizingly gay he was and how school was bringing him down and his family were bringing him down and how he didn't know how to deal and could I help while eating dough balls. My brain went

– well this didn't escalate at all

– why did i think this was a date

– why is he telling me does he think i am a dude there are breasticles under this shirt bro behold my brastrap

– this is flattering though, i have ally face, i am officially team nice

– also thank god i don't have to kiss him

– oh wait

– OH WAIT

And that is the one date that I have been on.

vaticancameltoes – Oh man, I'm so sorry
Please tell me he paid
eye_brows – He did pay!
Free chicken and a life revelation.
At some point maybe my love life could be less about the gay menfolk tho.

Seventeen minutes.

I *think* this is a date.

444 miles, plane tickets and a night in a hostel, a fabricated university open day to bunk off school. That's some Mycroft shit right there.

Though I am totally going to apply to a buttload of London unis anyway, she said.

For their impressive nightlife and high academic status?

For her Watson?

I have been on one date, and it wasn't a date. I don't know how you tell.

VC made an art once, where they're both cats in a box. It's called

John and Sherlock: Schrödinger's boyfriends.
dead/not dead
falling/not falling
kissing/not kissing
together/together
How does anyone know?

Sixteen minutes.

I rattle out today's med #3 and swallow, ignoring the pass-agg mumble from a coughing old man in one of those Russian-looking fur hats, on the next table. Then I lay my head flat on the plastic table, because I'm exhausted and I hurt and it's not a good look.

Fifteen.

My phone hums.

        Hello London! now pls pls tell me
        what you look like cos I really don't
        wanna say smoochie helloes to some
        random

We don't do selfies. We are not those girls. But the
smoochie helloes, I like.

        i have ketchup on my lapel and my
        fingernails suggest i am a typist

        what am i some kind of detective?

        Ok, i don't look like my icon

        You are not a painting of an angry
        lady with hibiscus growing out of her
        head? I AM CANCELLING THE APOCALYPSE

The angry hibiscus lady is Frida Kahlo: Mexican
painter. Also famous for her eyebrows, which stride
across her forehead in an unapologetic straight line and
meet in the middle to fuck. I am a hairy lady. (It's a
Persian thing – thanks, Dad! – although hello, ladies
have hair growing out of their faces, art dudes, why is
the world's most famous painting the one where she
doesn't even HAVE eyebrows?) Also also, Frida mostly
painted self-portraits because she got in a terrible
hideous accident that left her effectively paralysed with

chronic pain, but she was a badass so she propped a mirror up by her bed and just painted the thing she could see. Also also also she had a pet monkey, which I think we can all agree is not the very most amazing thing about her but.

Frida Kahlo is my sparkly unicorn Beyoncé.

Magical. Unique. Mine.

And VC doesn't know who she is.

Is this what having your first fight is like?

Are we not even going to get to have our first fight, because we are plainly incompatible?

I mean, if we met across a crowded Starbucks (autumnal Sunday afternoon, I'm writing on my laptop wearing adorable knitwear, she carries her signature hot chocolate to the next table and we catch eyes as she does the can-I-use-the-plug-point-under-your-leg mime and I nod and shimmy my violet betighted calf aside, we type side by side, my fingers slow as instead of wording my brain retraces her face, her smile, her teeth, and I steal glances of her elbow and her macbook until I hear a gasp and we both simultaneously realize we are on tumblr, reblogging the same gifset: welcome to my imagination, I can only apologize) it wouldn't matter. Romantic prospects are allowed to not love all the same things if they meet adorably in Starbucks, with knitwear and miming. These are the things they will discover together, adorably. 'There is an amazing Kahlo exhibition at the National,' I would say and she would say, 'Would you take me?' and boom, first date. Adorable.

But us: we haven't got to elbows and teeth. All we have is shared Liking Of Things. That's our glue.

I've just sort of assumed our Venn diagram would be busy in the overlap. Then we'd hold hands, and gradually as we talked the two circles would slide closer and closer to fit exactly on top of one another, like a lid on a tin. Perfect match. Love.

But our interconnections are basically *Sherlock* and *a declared fondness for girlkissing*.

I know she likes *Galaxy Quest* because she quoted *Galaxy Quest* one time, but then, who hasn't? What if deep down she likes ponies and death metal and people with non-broken endocrine systems? What if she only dates girls who can eat dairy products while mountaineering?

And even if 444 miles and my exciting medical history are not a dealbreaker –

Can anyone have a relationship based on six episodes of one TV show?

eye_brows – i have a theory
we love stories because they let us try on being helpless/frightened/beloved
we love fandom because it tells us we are not alone
fandom = training wheels for our personal lifebicycle

vaticancameltoes – So glad I'm prepped for all the gigantic hounds and 'Oriental' acrobat killers my lifebicycle is going to run over.

eye_brows – are you mocking my lifebicycle my profound lifebicycle

vaticancameltoes – little bit

eye_brows – YOU WERE THE BEST AND MOST HUMAN HUMAN BEING I HAVE EVER KNOWN

vaticancameltoes – Oh jesus

eye_brows – YOU WANT SINCERITY I GIVE YOU JOHN HAMISH WATSON

vaticancameltoes – shut up john

eye_brows – STOP BEING DEAD

vaticancameltoes – I will. Read a book, you idiot. Did I teach you nothing about research?!

eye_brows – MYCROFT STOLE MY LIBRARY CARD

vaticancameltoes – that little bitch

I scroll back back back through old favourites and messages, our fannish family album, until the fear rolls back and I remember: this is us.

Yasmin is currently dating a guy because she likes the shape of his skull. (She sits behind him in lectures. He has 'a hot neck', apparently. She spent a whole term posting sexy notes down his collar and blowing on his ears.)

Six episodes of a TV show is entirely reasonable. It's plenty.

I mean, they're long episodes.

You can rewatch them. A lot.

It's practically the same as being in the same room ever.

She's not a stranger.

I'm just wondering what the back of VC's head looks like when my phone hums with a new message, and suddenly I'm looking at the front of it.

```
I know we said we wouldn't but
Selfie
```

This is VC.

Not 8pt Helvetica font and a ridiculously flouncy Cumberbatch scarf-removal gif.

White girl, face shaped like a strawberry, pretty, straight blonde hair with a fringe. Eyeliner wings, pierced eyebrow. A green T-shirt with some anime giant cat thing on it I am not cool enough to know. Skinny. Huge close-lipped smile.

I freeze.

She's not my type.

My type is:

– Kristen Stewart: in *The Runaways* NOT *Twilight*

– Alexis Bledel: *Gilmore Girls* Season Four the haircut years

– Michelle Rodriguez: in a vest

– no one because I have only ever been on one

date and that was two years ago and not even a date.

She looks like Taylor Swift-Malfoy. She's going to expelliarmus me then write a song about how much I suck.

Which I do.

This is never going to work.

I should've told her. I should've warned her. She's turned up all human-like and pristine, expecting someone human-like and pristine, and I'm . . . not. My body is all sand dunes, dimples and hills, and it is fundamentally broken. We are not going to hold hands and run across London. I will not be magically cured by the presence of adventure and the thrill of the chase.

Oh god oh god why isn't she still a gif of a manface pulling off a scarf? Why can't I have a date with one of those? Why did I think I could go on a date at all?

I grab my phone to text VC and cancel – and it rings.

(Season Two soundtrack, track 1: *Irene's Theme*. Shut up.)

Not her, demanding a return selfie of my stupid giant hairy head.

Aish: my official I Am Meeting A Friend From The Internet guardian, checking I'm not being murdered.

'Are you being murdered?' she says.

'Yes. Right this second. Ow, the murdering.'

The Russian-looking hat man gives me another stare. If this was *Sherlock*, that would be him, in disguise.

I'm warming to reality.

'You promised!'

'OK. Sincere mode: locked. I'm fine. Apart from, you know, the terror. Is terror a necessary part of dating?'

'You're asking me?'

Aish isn't meant to even speak to a boy till he's met her parents and they've met his. In her universe, I am worldly and maybe a bit of a slut. I'm not quite noble enough not to like that. Except now she's meant to be my wingwoman and I need honest advice, from someone more experienced than me, i.e. beyond hand-holding/one date that was not actually a date.

(Handholding: Samira, age 12, Brixton ice rink. Technically she was helping me not fall over but I came home and wrote a poem about her hair and then burned it. Formative, no?)

'Sorry.' I explain about Venn diagrams and how love is two circles becoming one, but less mathsy than that sounds.

Aish isn't convinced. 'The only thing my parents have in common is they're my parents. Opposites attract though, yes? So perhaps it's better if you hate all the things she likes, and yell about that before sitting in separate rooms, angrily.'

'That sounds very advanced for a first date.'

'Hm. True. So maybe all you need is chemistry? Do you have chemistry?'

'How the hell do I know? How do you tell?'

'Kissing, I think. Kamila snogged Shahan on Friday

night even though he's going out with Priya, because she found him irresistible.'

I have no idea who any of these people are.

'Your advice is that I should snog VC to see if we have chemistry?'

There's a pause down the line. 'Given the challenging time and distance constraints you face, I think it may be the most practical move. If you have nerves, I suggest writing her a note asking permission. No one dislikes politeness.'

Sexy politeness. Well-known aphrodisiac. It's what the ladies love.

vaticancameltoes – Season 3 wishlist:
– hugs
– someone gets punched in the face
– homoerotic crying
– sex

Truthfully, I like Unresolved Sexual Tension as much as the next human – but I like Resolved Sexual Tension more. Because reasons.

eye_brows – BUT BUT BUT
I mean, yes. Obviously.
BUT
The Chase Is Always Better Than The Kill.
vaticancameltoes – bzuh?
eye_brows – what if this is it

what if this is as good as it gets
what if everything up until What Happens When
He Comes Back is the very pinnacle of our
fannish existence and engagement and love
and from the moment the theme plays at the
start of the next episode begins the slow
crushing of our souls with disappointment
hammers
what if we have reached Peak Sherlock
what if
what if
halp
vaticancameltoes – ATTENTION WORLD
eye_brows just broke Sherlock

I've thought about this a lot. (365 days.)

Sherlock comes back to solve the case of the Empty House, wearing a false moustache, and since this is TV everyone pretends it was, like, no big thing.

Sherlock comes back for his Watson, who is traumatized by the deceit and their friendship is eternally now odd and cold and unrescuable. John gets married. Sherlock grows a beard (not a disguise beard, a Season Three Stop-Objectifying-Me-Fangirls beard). Viewing figures drop. The fandom moves on. My dash fills with gifsets of some other curly-haired white boy with an Eton accent.

He comes back for his Watson, and they kiss with tongues.

These are all on the table.

No, but really.

Maybe not really?

But maybe?

'Why do you care so much?' Yasmin asks, all the time, eating biscuits over my shoulder as I replay and cry; read fic and cry; stare at pictures of two old dudes running through London holding hands and smile.

Yasmin does not have the fannish gene. You do or you don't.

'Why don't you obsess over the girl ones? Like – the doctor with the ponytail, and . . . oh.'

(Sherlock's ladies are splendid but they are few.)

'Is it – you like them being gay? Because I see they're a little gay. That bony one is, anyway. Public schoolboy thing, yeah? But – are you queer ladies that hard up that you compulsively string together every conceivable man plus man just to feel like you're, you know, kind of represented?'

Yes.

No.

'You can be bi, babygirl,' she says too, because Mum hasn't, and she doesn't want me to feel all psychologically damaged by rejection either. 'You can come out all over again, we won't mind.'

'Um. Thanks? But – I'm not bi.'

VC is. She has two first-date stories, and they both have kissing (but no free chicken, she was kind enough to point out). She has two worst-date stories too. I thought that was handy – like, someone else is driving this thing thank god.

Maybe?

'So – babygirl, how come you like staring at pretty white boys so much?'

'It's complicated.'

I think I understand it. Kind of. Like, number one: it's kind of hard to like popular culture if you *don't* like staring at pretty white boys. All the girls I get to stare at look straight back at me, so done with this shit. And yeah, for whatever reason I get butterfly flappings in my heart at the way that one particular dark brown curl sits when he sips tea, and the way that blue silk dressing gown fits just so, and his skin, his Buckingham Palace skin. But it's not legrub-sexytimes–may I climb you like a tree-type liking. Urgh. I am equally invested in his Secret Childhood Manpain, his taste in wallpaper and his mind palace (although if I was John we'd have words about that, because palaces are terrible).

I like the idea of him. I like the idea of them.

Sherlock and John. John and Sherlock.

Them.

They are fun and joy and glee and agony and I want to be them and watch them both at once. They *fight crime!* and face peril and giggle inappropriately at crime scenes – but above all this they like each other. They really very much like each other. Chalk and chalk. Cheese and crackers.

I'm not his date.

Who even says that?

Who even runs across London holding hands?

Only – now I like the idea of them. What happens if I like the idea of them more than I like *them*?

I slide my phone onto the table – nine minutes, *nine*, is that too near or too far away? – and bring up her profile. **vaticancameltoes**, carried in my pocket. 8pt Helvetica and a flouncy scarf.

I spin back to her selfie.

In nine minutes that strawberry-faced girl'll be a breathing alive human sitting in that crap plastic chair, there, here, in a café that smells of old fried egg.

The Chase Is Always Better Than The Kill.

444 miles. Plane tickets, hostel, fabricated open day. Some Mycroft shit right there.

Only it isn't, because Mycroft is made up and this is not a set and

breathing

alive

(blonde, pretty, gosh she is pretty)

human

in nine minutes.

Eight.

The flouncy scarf-removal repeats on a loop: cheek-bones, errant curl.

What if I like the idea of her more than I like her?

It's OK for me. I know I'm a disappointment.

And suddenly, it hits: I only have to be John. I'm the short friend. The other one. A custard cream in human form, politely apologizing for the human whirlwind.

I'm asking her to be him.

I've made a terrible mistake.

It's a bit not good.

Only there's a black cab outside and a girl is climbing out, shivering on the pavement, staring up at the oh-so-familiar red Speedy's canopy with that glowing look, clutching a backpack and her phone and mine buzzes on the table and it's too late.

I'm early. Meet you outside?

i'm early too. inside, right window, person waving at you like a dork

Oh! Hey you

hey yourself

I like your hair

thank you. i like your hat

Thank you.

and your capacity to stand outside typing

Perfect: I can do *this* all day. Onscreen, where I resemble sense and can delete my stupid. It's cute. It's our adorable knitwear. *Hey kids, when we met we spent the first six months of our relationship without actually using human speech, because we are like so twenty-first century.*

Then she strides in, slipping off a glove, and reaches out a hand, bold, easy, to shake, like shaking hands is a mature adult sensible thing she does all the time, and she says, 'I'm Candy and I so can't believe I'm actually here, oh my god,' in a thick Scottish accent and I see the braces on her teeth and hear the hitch in her voice and, OK.

I've seen films. People with braces are statistically unlikely to be evil.

'I'm Shirin,' I tell her, and my face smiles without me. 'I can't believe you're actually here either.'

When she sits down we're still holding hands.

We do small talk like grown-ups: travel, weather, hostel bed linen and strangers who snore.

When she talks, her forehead moves constantly, the silver bar in her right eyebrow – her left, my right – lifting with amusement. Three creases line up above it and I want to smooth them out with a thumb. I want to touch her. She lets go of my hand to slide off her thick padded winter coat, the kind that looks like a human-shaped sleeping bag, and I leave my empty one on the table for her to grasp again but then she's up, reading menus, taking photos of the photos on the walls.

'God, I need coffee. And I'm starving. Share a bowl of chips?'

I can't drink coffee. Chips do unspeakable things to my intestines.

But I nod anyway. I want to say yes to all the things.

She stands at the counter to order and I watch the cling of her green T-shirt travelling her spine, rising in folds at the waistband of her jeans.

Apparently I stare at pretty white girls too. Yasmin will be thrilled.

She laughs with the guy behind the counter, pays, slides into the chair and gazes at me.

What are we going to talk about now? Sherlock and John talk about crime. Should I have laid on some crime, some minor not-that-illegal crime, for ice-breaking purposes?

'I found a map,' she says, excitedly spinning it up on her phone. 'Locations. The full tour. Plus the real Baker Street, and there's a museum, and this well cheesy pub if they'll let us in . . .'

I take a breath; hold it; breathe out slow, riding it out. 'Sorry. We can – I can do—'

The three creases reappear on her forehead, worried now.

Here goes.

I guess this is me, then, on the roof of St Bart's, arms out. This is me, giving up everything.

There is not really a short version of my medical history but I do my best: juvenile secondary fibromyalgia, which means both chronic and acute musculoskeletal pain, which means I don't sleep, which means fatigue, which means more pain, and brainfog, round and round. (I don't mention antidepressants, arthritis, the day in Year 11 I got so tired in school that Mr Grayson had to carry me down the stairs to French like a swooning damsel and how I never went back, or the word *bowel*, because one disease at a time. We have chemistry. Biology is extra.)

Air keeps getting stuck between my top lip and my teeth as I speak, like a robot with faulty pneumatics.

She squinches her lips into an unhappy rose.

'Wow. You never said.'

'Sorry.'

'No! You didn't have to – I mean – I just, I don't know. If I was always hurting I'd be screaming about it all the time.'

I shake my head slowly. 'You wouldn't. You'd want to forget about it and post cat pictures and porn like everyone else.'

Tumblr is the happy place. Tumblr is where I am not tramadol and fluoxetine, CBT statements that don't work, my hips on cushions at 3 a.m. Autumn isn't the arrival of cold that makes every muscle burn brighter; it's gifsets of treelined Parisian avenues, new episodes, a million odes to pumpkin spice. I am **eye_brows**: the best me, ordinary, pain-free. And no one looks at me like she is looking at me now.

Sadface.

Poor you.

I wish I'd known not to bother.

That's what I'm giving up.

My safety net.

The training wheels for my pretentious lifebicycle.

A girl who's a gif and thinks I'm funny and an angry hairy painting and just like her.

Then my Sherlock – VC – Candy – her – she smiles like a Saturday morning and slides her palms across the table, bumping fingertips.

'This is amazing.'

'It's not.'

Please no. I'm not a project, you can't fix me, I am not your inspirational poster, I am not—

'No – Shirin' – she lifts her fingertips and presses the pads of each finger on top of each of my fingernails: gossamer touch, barely there, so intimate I lose my breath – 'I thought – it could be awkward? I thought we might run out of things to say. But' – she looks into my eyes – 'I know **eye_brows**. I like **eye_brows**. Now I get to like Shirin things.'

I'm glad her fingers are there, holding me, so I don't float up to the ceiling.

'Tell me *everything*,' she says.

I tilt my head, then pull my hands away and place

them over the backs of hers, flat on the table, feeling her skin, her warmth, her.

I smile like my face is broken, good–broken, and it doesn't know how to stop.

'You first.'

She still lives 444 miles away. I still need a sit down and three prescription meds before elevenses.

But we hold hands. We learn. We laugh.

Chalk and chalk. Cheese and crackers.

That's it.

That's our first date.

And then?

BBC *Sherlock* Season Three, episode one, *The Empty Hearse*, airs on New Year's Day, 1 January, 2014.

Inside Schrödinger's box –

We are all, still, always John Watson, waiting to find out.

We are all, still, always Sherlock Holmes, tumbling off rooftops.

falling/not falling

kissing/not kissing

together/together

FROM
TROUBLE

BY
NON PRATT

FRIDAY 8TH JANUARY

Hannah
My day starts with a text:

> Hey Hannah, u might want 2 check FB.
> Hope ur OK, Anj

A text from Anj that does not contain a question about French homework is big news.

It takes me about ten seconds to log in to Facebook.

Fifteen minutes later I'm still there. I don't think I can move, let alone put my clothes on. It's like my body's in shock or something. Even my brain seems to be broken – I actually can't believe what I'm seeing. I keep hoping that I'm having one of those dreams where you think you've got up but you haven't.

It took me a while to work out that a lot of the comments on my newsfeed were about me. Then I clocked the posts on my wall – some nice, some not so. I've got a few messages too. I don't read them.

There's another text on my phone. It's Gideon.

```
Not sure if congrats is what ur
after, but JIC — yay! Gx
```

My throat catches as I read it, but I grind my teeth together and tell myself to focus. I need to know how this happened. I only told . . . and she . . . she couldn't? She *wouldn't* . . .

I open Katie's profile. She's changed her picture – it's now a close-up of her cleavage with faces drawn on each boob winking at each other. It used to be a photo of me and her dressed up for Jay's party. I check out her status, but it's the same as when I last checked.

No longer an airplane blonde ☺

Comments are split between people who get the joke and people who don't. I notice that Marcy has liked Rex's comment – about having *first-hand experience [pun intended]* – and I go through to her page. Marcy hasn't bothered sorting out her privacy settings so it doesn't matter that we aren't friends.

And it means that the whole world can read her status:

OMG. Hannah Sheppard is 4 months pregnant. Hands up who saw that one coming!

Aaron

There's something in the air. I missed registration because the car wouldn't start, and the people I share a bench with in Chemistry wouldn't know what was on the grapevine unless someone plucked the information off and turned it into a smokable substance. I hurry to Geography, hoping to catch Anj before the lesson starts.

As I turn the corner I see that she's standing with Gideon, who should be the other side of the school in my dad's class.

'I always thought she was exaggerating . . .' Gideon is saying when he sees me coming and shoots me a grin.

'She was. You only have to sleep with one guy to get pregnant.' Anj has her back to me, but I heard her loud and clear.

'Who's pregnant?' I say, breathing a little too heavily after my semi-sprint from the Science block.

It's Anj who tells me.

'Hannah's pregnant.'

'Hannah who?' says my mouth because it's not actually connected to my brain.

'Sheppard.' But I knew that.

'How?' I say. Which isn't what I mean. I wish my

mouth and brain could communicate. Gideon gives me a cheeky smirk and says something about a 'special cuddle', but Anj elbows him.

'It's all over Facebook,' Anj says.

'He's not on Facebook,' Gideon tells her before I can. It's the first time I've heard someone's looked for me and I feel awkward. Best to focus on Hannah.

'Is that how she told everyone?' I can't believe this is true.

'Not exactly . . .' Anj looks uncomfortable.

Gideon fills me in. 'Apparently Katie told Marcy whilst they were out last night. I'm pretty sure it wasn't meant to be a global announcement, but then Marcy put it as her status and now everyone's talking about who the father is.' He slides a glance through the open door at Fletch, who's at his desk, head in hands, but it's me that Anj is looking at.

'Anyone tried asking her?' I say.

'No one's seen her,' Anj says, getting out her phone. 'I texted this morning . . .'

'I think she might be lying low. There's loads of people posting on her wall and saying some pretty harsh stuff,' Gideon says.

I wish I found this hard to believe.

Anj taps on her phone, breaking school protocol, before emitting a shocked, 'Oh my God!' We look at her and she turns the phone towards us so we can see the screen.

It's a Facebook page called 'Whos the Daddy? Yous

the Daddy?' Normally I'd be appalled by the terrible English, but for now I'm more horrified by the content.

There's a picture of Hannah in her school uniform and someone's drawn a cartoon bump over the top with a question mark inside. There's loads of members – presumably all from our school – and people have already started posting suggestions as to who might be the father. One of the posts near the top catches my eye.

Whoever suggested Mr Tyler is way off – his son's deffo the daddy!

I don't know the kid who wrote it, but he looks about ten in his profile pic. Nice.

Anj clicks on the pictures page and I glimpse a few familiar faces badly Photoshopped onto some less familiar bodies doing . . . well, doing the nasty. Why would anyone do that?

Hannah

I'm all cried out for the moment and I feel sick. Mum offered to miss her hair appointment and stay home with me, but what's the point? It's not like her being here will change anything. I'll still be pregnant. I'll still have a giant knife wound where my best friend stabbed me in the back. No need for Mum to have crap hair as well. This is the first time Mum's ever let me stay off school without taking my temperature. She's beside herself with rage about Katie telling Marcy – I'm guessing that's what happened, anyway; I can't imagine it was anyone in my family.

The doorbell rings.

'Go away,' I whisper.

It rings again after a while. I risk peering out of my bedroom window and see Aaron at the front door, fiddling with his phone. If he's ringing me, he'll be disappointed. I turned my phone off an hour ago. I head down and open the door though.

'Hi.'

'Hi.'

I open the door wider and he steps inside. He smells nice, safe.

Then he does something unexpected – he hugs me. As I lean into him and rest my head on a shoulder broader than Mum's, I think how strange this is. We've not hugged before today, we've not really even talked *that* much, but Aaron's the only person who's hugged me during all this without being pushed.

'Shouldn't you be at school?' I say into his blazer.

'Shouldn't you?'

'Point taken.' I let go and walk towards the kitchen. 'How'd you know where I live?'

'Anj. And Fletch asked me to send his love. Well, something like that. I think he's convinced himself that he's about to become a dad.'

'Oh God,' I mutter and shake my head as I offer Aaron a drink from the fridge.

'How are you?' Aaron asks, as he cracks open his can of choice (Diet Coke – huh).

'Pregnant,' I say. This is so weird. I feel like I'm having tea with the queen or something.

'So I hear. How's that working out for you?'

I look at him. He's a funny one. I can't figure him out. He's so direct about stuff but at the same time it's as if he's far away from it all, not a part of things.

'Pregnancy's fine – it's just my friend that's a bitch.' I sip a glass of milk. MILK. I used to hate milk, but these last few days I can't get enough of it.

'You know most people are just curious, they're not actually hating you or anything.' He looks away, embarrassed almost. 'I guess you've seen the Facebook page?'

'What Facebook page?'

Aaron

I show her on her laptop upstairs, hating myself for it, figuring it's worse *not* to know something like this . . . but I've seen more expression on my dad's face when he's checking the BBC weather page.

She clicks off the page and shrugs.

'You OK?' I'm the epitome of lame.

'Not really.'

'As I said, most people . . .'

'. . . are just curious,' she finishes. 'Well, it's none of their fucking business, is it?'

Hannah gets up and kicks the chair out of the way before storming downstairs and, since I don't know what else to do, I follow her. She's opening the back door and rushing outside, then she's standing in the middle of the lawn and screaming so loud I think her voice will break.

'*I'm pregnant. All right?*' She spins round to look at the neighbours' twitching curtains. 'ALL RIGHT? And I'm fifteen! Fuck off!'

'Hannah . . .' I say, edging closer, not sure if now's the right time to point out that she's still in her pyjamas and slippers.

'FUCK OFF!' She screams right in my face before collapsing forward so fast I nearly drop her, and she's kneeling in the cold, wet grass, sobbing and screaming and growling – actually growling. We stay like that a while, me crouching awkwardly, treading the corner of my blazer into the grass, Hannah contorted into my arms, crying herself into silence. I wonder what the neighbours are making of this and I look up to see an old lady and her husband staring out of one of the windows. I give them the finger and enjoy their outraged reaction. They shouldn't be looking. This is private.

'I'm wet,' Hannah mumbles and staggers to her feet. 'Got to shower.'

I follow her indoors and stand in the hallway where she turns, halfway up the stairs, and asks me if I'll stay, apologizes for being mental. I tell her not to worry and that I'll wait in the kitchen. There's a book in my blazer pocket, one I've read before, but since

I don't have anything better to do I start at the beginning once more. Maybe it was a mistake to come here – it's not as if I was invited. But Hannah needs someone and that someone may as well be me . . .

'Hi.'

I jump.

'I didn't hear you,' I say, putting my book down.

Hannah smiles, picks up the book to look at the cover and wrinkles her nose. 'Never heard of it,' she says before pouring herself another glass of milk and digging out a pack of ginger nuts. I decline the offer as she sits down next to me – she smells of coconut and her hair's still wet. When I look at her, I see someone I recognize: myself, I think. Not in a literal sense. I don't wash my hair with coconut shampoo and I have certainly never worn a Little Miss Naughty T-shirt. But she looks soul-weary and I know about that.

'Thanks,' she says and meets my eyes. 'I mean it. It takes guts to tell a person what they don't want to hear. Most people would be too scared to face up to it.'

'You're not,' I say.

'Wrong. Facing up would have been telling Mum sooner, or my best friend.'

'You didn't tell anyone?' I say, surprised.

Hannah smiles. 'I told Gran.'

I smile too, but hers has turned into a sigh and she slumps forwards, her forehead resting on the tabletop.

'Fletch isn't the dad,' she tells the table.

'Thank God for the baby. Anybody would make a

better dad than him.' It's meant to be a joke, but something tells me she's a long way from finding it funny.

'You think I don't know who it is, don't you?'

'I never—'

'That's what my mum thinks.' Hannah lifts her head to look at me, the imprint of the tablecloth on her forehead.

'I don't think anything.' I should leave it there. 'Except—'

'Except what?'

'Whoever it is has a right to know.'

Hannah winces at this. 'He will not want to know. Trust me.'

So she *does* know who it is. 'I would,' I say.

'Well, he's not you.' She looks at me with such intense sorrow that any suspicion we were talking about Tyrone dissipates. 'Can we just leave it?'

'OK.' Hannah obviously has her reasons. 'Consider it left.'

She looks at me for a moment longer, her face softening before she puts her head back on the table. 'Thank you.'

'Don't mention it.' I finish my can and look for a change of topic. 'Can I have a ginger nut?'

She pushes the packet towards me and then waggles her fingers for one, still face down on the tablecloth.

'Anything else?' I ask, wondering if she needs a top-up of milk.

'A dad for my baby?' she says with a laugh.

Hannah

My joke wasn't exactly funny, so I don't think his silence is rude as I sit up and down the dregs of my milk. It's only when I start to stand, turning to offer him another drink, that I realize he's watching me.

'Me,' he says.

'You what?' I say, caught somewhere between sitting and standing.

'I could do it, if you wanted.'

I sit down with a thump.

'You could say I was the father.'

FROM
RANI AND SUKH

BY
BALI RAI

Rani

There were tears falling down my cheeks as Parvy finished telling us the story. I had hold of Sukh's hand and, looking down at it, I realized that I had squeezed it so hard, his fingers had gone almost white. I let go and wiped away the tears but they were soon replaced by more. Parvy looked at her brother then got up and came over, crouching in front of me. I didn't know what to think or do. It was such a shock. How come I'd never heard the story from my own family? I didn't even know that I had another aunt. And then I realized that my father would never have told me about it − it undermined all his lectures about filthy white girls . . . But surely someone in my family . . . my brothers . . . ?

'It's OK,' Parvy told me, putting her hands on my knees.

'Why didn't I know about all of this already?' I

asked her, trying really hard not to cry. And failing.

'I don't know,' Parvy told me. 'I really don't know.'

Sukh stood up and started pacing the room. No one spoke for a few minutes before he broke the silence.

'This is so messed up, man. I didn't know any of this – none of it,' he told me.

'Our families have had this thing going on for years,' said Parvy. 'Dad thought that it was all over – and he didn't want you to know. He wanted you to grow up without having to deal with the same stuff he had to – all the shame and the sadness and stuff. I only found out because I walked in on an argument, back when you were about six. He sometimes talks about Rani's dad, Mohinder – they were good friends once.'

'I kinda *thought* Rani's name rang a bell when we met but I put it out of my mind. I thought that I was just being stupid . . . And now I find out there's a feud . . .' said Sukh, talking to his sister but looking at me.

'Yeah – although it's been years since anything major happened between our families. Some of the younger idiots kick off now and then – but they just use it as an excuse for fighting and acting like animals.'

I looked at Sukh and then at Parvy. I was confused. How could I not have known? How could my family not have told me? 'So your uncle, Billah, was killed?' I asked.

'Yeah.'

'What happened to my aunt? Something must have happened because until just now I didn't even know about her.'

Parvy looked away. 'She killed herself – jumped in a well, I think. No one really knows because they never found her body. Just her shawl – lying next to the well.'

'But she was . . .' I began.

Parvy put her hand on mine and squeezed. 'I know, I know . . .' she said.

'Oh, this is horrible!' I shouted suddenly, and then wished that I hadn't. But what was I supposed to do? I didn't know what to think. My family hated Sukh's family, and there we both were, seeing each other.

Parvy stood up and walked over to the window. She started to speak but stopped and thought for a while. Then she went on, 'Our family had to leave the village after Billah died and Kulwant vanished. The elders thought it would be the best way to stop any more blood being spilt. But the feud continued. Both our fathers moved to Leicester in the nineteen sixties and there've been incidents between them, off and on, over the years . . .'

I shuddered. My mind was going in about a million directions at the same time and I felt numb. Sukh tried to take hold of my hand but I pushed him away. I didn't want to – it just happened that way. I couldn't control it.

Parvy turned and looked at me. 'There've been fights between our uncles, our cousins – we even go to separate *gurudwara*. It's been calm for a few years now though.'

'But it just doesn't make any sense,' I told her. 'How could me and Sukh not have known about it?'

'I dunno how someone didn't let it slip.' Parvy shrugged. 'But I'm sure Dad told everyone not to tell you about it, Sukh. When I found out he told me never to mention it again. He said that it was like cutting open an old wound . . .'

Sukh just sat where he was, looking from me to Parvy and feeling a little hurt at my rejection, I think. I just didn't want to be there. Didn't want to be around them. I needed to think . . . I needed to call Nat. I needed to cry again too.

Something in my head snapped and I shot up from my seat. 'Gotta go,' I mumbled, not looking at Sukh or Parvy. I headed for the door.

'Rani . . . wait,' said Sukh, coming after me, but I didn't wait.

I ran to the door, threw it open and went out into the corridor. I rushed down the stairs and out into the street, the glass door to the foyer slamming shut behind me. I looked up, tears blurring my sight, made out a taxi and ran to it, got in and told the driver to go. As he pulled away I saw Sukh standing across the street from me, shouting. I think he was still telling me to wait. I don't know. I didn't want to talk to him, didn't want to touch him. Just wanted to go home. Just wanted to . . .

Sukh

Three days after Parvy had told him and Rani about the feud, Sukh sat on his bed with some R & B thing playing on his CD. He wasn't listening to it. He was sitting thinking, watching the signal light on his mobile flash on. And off. And on. And off. Rani hadn't answered her phone since she'd run out of Parvy's flat. Sukh had only heard from her once. She'd sent a text telling him that she didn't want to talk to him. Her phone had gone straight to answer every time he'd tried calling. Each of the thirty or forty times. And she wasn't replying to his text messages either. He'd just sent the latest one and was sitting staring at his phone, willing the message tone to bleep at him and put him out of his misery; imagining her face in his mind, thinking about her touch and her smell and the way she tasted when he kissed her.

His family wasn't really talking to him. He'd returned from Parvy's flat angry and sullen and had told his dad to fuck off. His dad had reacted with measured calm, not slapping him or swearing back – just walking away, shaking his head. That had been three days ago and since then only his mum had tried speaking to him, in vain. Sukh wasn't in the mood to talk to anyone. Not his parents, nor Parvy and definitely not his mates. Jaspal had sent him loads of messages and rung three times each day but Sukh had ignored him. He couldn't think of anything but Rani. He wasn't hungry, he couldn't sleep. He didn't care what time it was. He just wanted Rani to call or send him a text to say that he should meet up with her. Hold her hand. Make her laugh. Like it was before he'd taken her to meet Parvy and ruined it all. Like it was before . . .

The mobile bleeped three times in quick succession and Sukh's heart jumped into his mouth. He grabbed the thing and pressed the READ NEW MESSAGE button. His heart went back to where it had come from. Jaspal. Sukh deleted the message without reading it and threw the phone back down on the bed. The CD finished and he leaned over to where the player sat and started it again, the thump of the bass not getting him going like it usually did. He got up off his bed and paced his room, usually so tidy but looking now like someone had played a bhangra gig in it. He paced for about five minutes, all the while looking at his mobile and turning it round in his hand as the signal light flashed on. And off. And on. And then he sat back down.

Ten minutes passed as Sukh sat and stared at the wall, then he picked up his phone again and scrolled through the menu to WRITE MESSAGE. He looked at the small screen for a moment and then began to type in another message.

```
PLS LET ME NO THAT U R OK. CALL ME
PLS. LOV U.
```

For the next twenty minutes Sukh went through the same routine, sitting on his bed, pacing his room and thinking about Rani. The signal light flashed on and off but there were no bleeps from his phone. He tried again.

PLS CAL ME.I LOV U. JUST WANNA TALK. CANT SLEEP. PLS RANI.

When he realized that Rani wasn't going to reply, no matter how many times he sent her messages, Sukh got angry and threw his phone on the floor, grabbed his jacket and stormed out of his bedroom, downstairs and into the street, not knowing where he was going . . .

Rani

'Just call him.'

Nearly a week after I'd run out of Parvy's flat I was watching the rain fall outside my bedroom window, holding my mobile to my ear and trying to listen to Natalie.

I hadn't spoken to or seen Sukh for all that time and it was killing me. But I didn't know how to sort out the mess that I had created when I ran away. When I had sent him that text, telling him that I didn't want to talk to him, I had been angry, upset. I hadn't meant never again . . .

And now I didn't know if *he* would want to talk to

me. I hadn't had any messages in the last couple of days. What if he was angry? What if he wanted to drop me? And what was I supposed to say? Hey Sukh, sorry for being so rubbish but I'm back now and I'm OK about it all . . . ?

'Are you listening to me?' asked Nat.

'Yeah I'm listening,' I told her.

'You've got to *hear* me too, babe,' she replied, sounding a bit exasperated.

'I'm sorry, Nat.'

'That's what you need to tell Sukh too,' she said.

'He'll just tell me to get lost.'

'No he won't.'

'How do *you* know?'

'Let me think . . .' she began.

'I didn't reply to any of his messages, Nat, and now he's stopped sending them. He'll probably drop me like a stone . . .'

She sighed for about the tenth time since I'd called her. 'Look – do you love him?' she asked.

'More than anything . . .'

'And you're OK with this whole feud thing?'

I grinned despite myself. 'It is a bit Bollywood—' I began, but Nat cut me off.

'Answer the question, minx.'

'Yes – I'm fine now. I just wanted to think about things – that's all . . .'

'And he's sent you what – thirty-odd messages?'

134

'Yeah.'

'So call him, apologize for being crap and meet him somewhere, for God's sake.'

'But what if—?'

'That's it – I'm going. You're doing my head in now . . .'

'I'm sorry, Nat . . .' Just what I needed. My best friend getting pissed off with me too.

'Look – you haven't got time for this shit. We've all got GCSEs coming up. The last thing—'

'I don't know what to say,' I admitted, tears suddenly appearing.

'Don't cry, honey . . .'

'But, Nat – he's going to hate me now.'

'Right, sod this. Get your little ass over here,' she demanded.

I thought about having to make up a reason to go out for my parents. 'I dunno if—'

'Rani – we're going to *revise* together, not have a sex-and-drugs-and-naughty-things party . . .'

'Let me ask – I'll call you back.'

Nat didn't reply straight away.

'*Nat?* You still there . . . ?'

'Tell you what,' she replied. 'Leave it for a couple of hours. Come round about five.'

'But you said to—'

'I've got a plan, Stan,' she said.

'Nat?'

But the line was dead.

★ ★ ★

I went downstairs about an hour later, after trying to concentrate on maths homework without success. My dad was in the living room, snoozing, and my mum was out in the jungle-like conservatory, watering her zillion and one plants. She heard me approach and turned to me.

'What do you want?' she asked in Punjabi.

'What makes you think that I want anything?' I said, pretending to be offended.

'Rani – you have on that face. Every time you want something you look like that.'

'I'm sorry for being alive,' I replied flippantly.

'Shut up! You never talk like that . . .' she told me.

'I just wanted to go over to my friend's to revise for my exams,' I said, waiting for her to say no.

'*Rebise?*' said my dad from behind us. He'd obviously woken up. And still not learned how to pronounce 'v's correctly, something lots of older Punjabis couldn't do.

'I want to go and revise at my friend's house,' I repeated.

'When?' he asked me, totally ignoring my mum's part in the conversation.

'Five o'clock,' I said. 'I'll be back by nine—'

'*Nine?*' he replied, going off the idea.

'Dad – it's only four hours . . . and Gurdip can pick me up later.'

The mention of my brother sealed the deal and my

dad told me I could go, as long as I didn't turn off my mobile and only if I was really going to 'rebise' and not mess about.

'Dad, I've got my GCSEs in under five months. I want to do well . . .' So I can get out of here, I thought to myself.

'OK – *beteh* – you going,' he replied, in English this time. 'Ju calling Gurdip at the half-eight, telling him where to picking you up.'

'Thanks, Dad,' I said, before going back upstairs to ring Natalie.

Natalie & Sukh

Natalie stood outside Sukh's parents' house, wondering how much money it would take to buy such a big place. It was a mock-Tudor mansion with a double garage and long driveway. The iron gates at the front had a Sikh symbol as part of the overall design and the word BAINS. Very tasteful. She rang the bell again and then turned to admire the pebble driveway, sectioned off in three colours, white, brick-red and green. The borders were immaculate, with purple and green shrubs. Not a weed in sight. No one answered the door but from somewhere she could hear the beat of an R & B tune. She rang once again, wondering where everybody was and whether Sukh would get into trouble because a white girl was calling for him. It had been known to happen. In fact she had never even been round to her boyfriend Dev's house. Didn't know what it looked like or what his parents were like. She smiled as she remembered Dev telling her that it was an 'Indian' thing. She rang one more time.

Finally, deciding that no one was going to come to the door, Natalie walked round the side of the garages to a smaller gateway, through which she could see a landscaped garden. She debated whether or not she should try the gate, walk down the side of the house and try to get someone's attention. Someone was definitely in because they were playing a crappy tune by some generic R & B artist. By the time she had finished debating with herself, all of thirty seconds later, she was already standing underneath a veranda-style balcony at the back of the house, framed at the sides by ivy-covered trellises, the leaves a deep shade of green. Above her, the window furthest to her left was open, the source of the music. She called out to Sukh but got no reply.

Turning to face the garden, she saw a patio area made up of white pebbles and walked over to pick up a handful. From beneath the window she gently threw a pebble up. It hit the wall to the side, not really having the desired effect. She tried again, this time hitting the window with a slight tap. The third pebble flew in through the opening and announced her presence. *Someone* was in. *Someone* shouted a few very naughty words . . .

★ ★ ★

Sukh stuck his head out of the window, after turning his CD off, ready to shout at the idiot throwing pebbles, or to call the police if it was a burglar. As if he didn't have enough to deal with, he thought to himself. Down below him he saw Natalie and once the initial shock was gone, his stomach turned over. Rani. It had to be about Rani . . .

'*Natalie!* What the fuck . . . ?'

'But, soft!' she began, a big smile cracking across her face, 'what light through yonder window breaks? It is the east and Sukhy boy, my son!'

'NAT! What—?'

'Sukhio! O Sukhio! Wherefore art thou Sukhio? Deny thy father and . . .'

Sukh groaned and considered finding the pebble that Nat had chucked through the window so that he could fling it at her stupid head. He couldn't see where it had landed. Instead he turned to Natalie again. 'What do you want, Natalie?'

Nat grinned up at him. 'So much for bloody romance!' she said. 'I'm here to see *you*. You lettin' me in or what?'

'What do you wanna see me about?'

'Doh! Whaddya think, sexy boy?'

Sukh groaned again and told her to go round to the front of the house. 'I'll be down in a minute.'

Natalie waited, as patiently as someone with her itchy feet could manage, for Sukh to open the door to her.

When he eventually did she let him have another sick-eningly sweet smile and asked him what had taken him so long.

'Nothing,' replied Sukh sullenly.

'Putting your trousers back on?' asked Nat, annoyingly.

'Look . . . what is it that you want, man?'

'Our mutual love is coming round to mine at five and I want you to be there,' said Natalie seriously.

'Why?' asked Sukh, trying to sound cool but spitting out his reply just a bit too quickly.

'Why do you think . . .?'

Sukh looked away as he spoke, still trying to seem cool. 'She wants to see me she should reply to my messages an' that . . .'

'She feels stupid,' replied Natalie, unmoved by Sukh's attempted nonchalance, 'and, to be fair, she should.'

'What if I don't wanna see her?' asked Sukh.

'What if I just bang both your heads together?' said Natalie, meaning it.

'What if you just mind your own—?'

'Look – I don't have to be here,' Natalie reminded him. 'You want to carry on sitting around in your boxer shorts, listening to shite music and sending fifty messages an hour, that's your prerogative. Me, I'm just trying to help – so if you're gonna be all *wankyboy* about it . . .'

Sukh looked at her and then smiled for the first

time in a week. 'I'm sorry,' he told her. 'I really *do* want to see her.'

'Thought as much,' said Natalie, taking his hand. 'Are you OK?'

Sukh took his hand away, regretting it instantly, and then looked to the floor. 'Yeah . . . No – I'm just . . .' He didn't really know what he was, apart from being just a little excited at the thought of seeing Rani. Excited and nervous too.

Natalie smiled warmly at him.

'Come in for a bit,' he said. 'I need to have a shower.'

'Are you sure? Wouldn't wanna get into trouble with Mummy and Daddy Bains.'

'Stop being such a dickhead, Nat, and wait in the lounge,' he replied.

'Only thinking of your needs, Sukhy, my boy . . .'

'Shut up, Nat.'

Sukh showed Natalie into the living room, told her not to break anything and to get herself a drink if she wanted one, before heading up for a shower. Nat thanked him, sat down on a deep, aubergine-coloured leather sofa and waited.

FROM
YOU AGAINST ME

BY
JENNY DOWNHAM

Ellie

Ellie opened the door of the Queen's Head slowly and was immediately hit by the warm stink of food and beer. She felt primitive coming in from the mist, as if she was a wild girl and warmth and shelter meant little to her. She was a girl who invited boys to graveyards and dared them to jump in rivers. She was a girl who boldly entered the information office and demanded to know where every pub in the vicinity of the harbour was. The man had even let her borrow his pen so that she could mark them on the map with red ink.

If he was in here, she would shimmy up behind him, her hand on her hip like the world owed her something, and she'd fix her eyes on him until he felt an irresistible pull at his heart. She'd make him turn round simply by looking at his back.

The woman behind the bar frowned as Ellie

approached. She was wearing a name badge that said SUE, MANAGER.

'I can't serve you without ID,' she said.

'It's OK, I don't want a drink. I'm looking for someone who might work here. A boy.'

The woman laughed. 'Are you now? Well, only two lads work for me – Mikey or Jacko. Which one are you after?'

She knew it wasn't Jacko, because he was the boy in the car the other day. Ellie found herself grinning.

'It's Mikey I want.'

'I thought you might say that.' The woman pointed beyond the bar to a carpeted dining area. 'There he is, right at the back.'

He was standing at a table with a group of elderly women smiling up at him. He looked solid and confident, entirely unlike any boy at school. Adrenalin flooded her body as she watched him.

'He the one?'

'Yes, that's him.'

The woman tutted. 'Bringing his love life to work again, is he? I'll be having words with Mister McKenzie.'

'McKenzie?'

'Yes, love, and if you're his new girlfriend you can wait till he's on his lunch break, which will be in precisely five minutes. And since you're very evidently not eighteen, could you please step away from the bar.'

Mikey *McKenzie*? But that meant . . .

The name affected her physically. She felt light-headed and nauseous.

'Take a seat in the family lounge, please, and I'll tell him you're here.'

She lurched to the seats the woman pointed to and sat down. She wanted to get to the door, to get away, but if she moved that far, something might break. Nobody took any notice of her – the customers in the other seats were chatting to each other, or staring blankly at the TV screen. Her world had shifted and nobody knew it but her.

The manager came back. 'He's on his way, and you can tell him from me that if he spends one minute longer than his regulation half-hour with you, he can consider himself sacked.'

She smiled to show she didn't really mean it, but Ellie didn't smile back. She couldn't. She could barely breathe.

He came over slowly, with a strange reluctant walk. He said, 'What are you doing here?'

She squinted at him, as if the mist was in the bar, as if she'd brought it in with her. She could see the resemblance now – the same dark hair and eyes. Why hadn't she seen it before? It was all so obvious and terrible – he was Karyn McKenzie's brother.

He sat down, frowning. 'How did you know where I worked?'

'You said a pub by the harbour.'

'I didn't say which one.'

'Well, I was just passing this one and thought I'd check it out.'

'Just passing?'

She felt such an idiot. She'd been out in the mist and got hold of some stupid fantasy that he'd be pleased to see her, that she meant something to him. Her face was burning with shame as she stood up. 'You know what? I'm going to go.'

'What's the matter?'

'Nothing.'

He shook his head. 'Something is.'

How could he read her better than anyone she knew? Better than her own brother?

'I'm fine. I had an argument with someone, that's all.'

'You want to talk about it?'

'Not really.'

'I'm a good listener.'

Her heart lurched. That was sweet. Maybe he didn't know who she was after all. Maybe it was all some amazing coincidence that meant they were destined to be together for ever.

But then she noticed his name badge. 'So, you're called Tyler?'

He looked down at himself and frowned. 'It's not my real name.'

Tom said Karyn McKenzie was a liar. Obviously the whole family was, since everything about this boy was fake. He'd targeted the party, rather than stumbled across it, he'd deliberately chatted her up because he knew who she was. Even now, as he looked her up and down, his eyes warm and flirtatious, it was only an act.

'You look nice,' he said. 'Windswept, but pretty.'

She didn't even blush, didn't say something dumb, like, *Oh no, I don't*, because she knew he didn't mean it, he was trying to manipulate her.

'I'm going now,' she said. 'I'll see you around.'

'You'll see me around? You came all this way and now you're going?'

'I'm sorry. It was a stupid idea.'

'It wasn't. Don't go, I've got a break now. Let me get my jacket and we can sit outside.'

'It's cold out there.'

'Then we'll have to sit very close together.'

He smiled, and she couldn't help it, she smiled back. She was pathetic. Even when she knew he was trying to trick her, she still liked him. She was like some brainless girl in a horror movie, the kind of girl you scream at from the sofa because she can't see that she should leave *right now* or she'll be turned into mince.

'I'll just be a minute,' he said. 'Don't go away.'

She stood outside the main door, running the choices through her head. She could get the bus back into town and never see him again. Or she could stay and find out what he was up to.

The McKenzies were liars, which meant Tom was

telling the truth. And if Tom was telling the truth, then she needed to put aside her stupid doubts about what happened that night and help him, as any sister should.

If she asked Mikey the right questions, if she flirted and got him to let his guard down, she might find out stuff which could get the case thrown out of court. She'd end up a hero and Dad and Tom would be grateful for ever.

She took a breath and switched on a smile. It was too good an opportunity to miss.

Mikey

Something had changed in her by the time he came back with his jacket, because she took his hand, actually took his hand, and led him across the car park to the sea wall.

'There's a bench over there,' she said. 'Come on.'

The tide was out and a stretch of sand had opened up. Mikey looked in both directions, up and down the beach, but apart from a bloke with a dog, and another bloke fishing, there were no people about.

'I think we should go down,' he said. 'It'll be less windy.'

'No, let's stay here. It's a better view.'

She sat on the bench and patted the space next to her. She really was very pretty. It was like it was dawning on him, like she got prettier and prettier the longer he looked. Her skin was so smooth and she had the most amazing eyes – blue with splashes of grey in them.

He cast a quick look around. Did it matter if they sat up here? It was more exposed, but apart from Jacko, no one round here would know who she was. He yanked his hood up just to be safe and sat down.

She shuffled close and leaned in to him.

'Look at that,' she said. 'So much water just for us.'

Mikey had seen people do this plenty of times, just sitting watching the sea doing its thing – in and out. It wasn't that he didn't like the wind, or the smell of the beach or the way the waves never gave up, it was that he'd never seen the point of it. But today was different. Today he was with Ellie.

He had to do things right, treat her right. What was it his mum always said? *If you want a girl to like you, you have to listen like a woman and love like a man.* She reckoned that men hardly ever ask questions and when they do, they never listen to the answers.

He'd start with something simple, to get into the swing of things.

'So, why aren't you at school?' he said.

'I bunked it.'

'Second time in five days, eh?'

'Oh, I've got no shame.'

That sent a thrill of something through him. He wanted to touch her, especially her hair. It was loose and snapping in the wind. Seaside hair with strands of blonde among the gold. He coughed, shuffled about on the bench and adjusted his jacket, tried to concentrate.

'How did you get here?' he said. 'Did you walk or get the bus?'

'My brother gave me a lift.' A pause, then, 'You met my brother, didn't you?'

He nodded, fumbled in his pocket for his tobacco. 'Yeah, at the party. Just for a minute, near the end.'

'Ah, yes,' she said, 'the party. The one you gate-crashed.'

He pinched tobacco into a paper and rolled it, aware she was looking at him. 'You sound like a cop.'

'Which makes you the criminal.' She was so quick at answers. She glittered with cleverness.

He offered her the finished rollie. 'You want this?'

'I don't smoke.'

'Sensible.'

Still she was watching him. He lit up and took a drag, pulled it down hard. 'So,' he said, 'tell me about this argument, who was it with?'

'It's too long to tell.'

'I've got time.'

'I'd rather talk about you.'

That wasn't what was meant to happen next. What was the point of asking girls questions if they refused to answer? And what were you supposed to do when they turned it round and asked you stuff?

'Tell me a secret,' she said. 'Tell me something about you that I don't know.'

What was she expecting? A confession that he was married or gay or something? He took a drag of his

152

cigarette, then another, before he thought of the perfect thing.

'OK,' he said. 'I don't really go to college.'

She looked surprised. 'Why did you say you did?'

'I thought you wouldn't like me if I wasn't clever. I work here full-time, but I'm learning stuff I'd never discover at college. There's a great chef and he's teaching me.'

He wasn't sure she understood how important this was and he wanted her to know. 'I've always liked those cooking programmes on the telly – you know the ones? I want to be like Jamie Oliver and run a whole kitchen. It's very complicated, takes years to learn.'

Ellie nodded as if she was really listening. She asked him how long he'd worked in the pub and what his hours were. She asked about Jacko and how long they'd known each other. He told her everything, including his dream of working in a top London restaurant. He hadn't meant to let that one out, but she was so easy to talk to, taking every word somewhere deep inside. He could have sat there all day talking. But then he remembered his mum's advice.

'You tell me a secret now,' he said.

'OK.' She leaned in close. 'Here's my secret. I'm hopeless at cooking, I can't even make cakes from packets, or follow recipes or anything, but' – and here she moved closer, her breath hot in his ear – 'I think boys who cook are very sexy, and, one day, I'd like you to show me how you do it.'

He laughed out loud. 'That's a promise.'

It was weird. At the pub she'd seemed frightened, as if she was worried he hadn't wanted to see her. But out here, it was like she was running the show. She was totally flirting with him, it was great. It was obvious she wanted something to happen between them. It gave him confidence.

'So what else do you find sexy, then?'

'Easy.' She held out a hand to count on her fingers. 'Boys who play guitar, boys who make me laugh, boys who have a nice smile and boys who never lie.'

Shit! That was a lot to live up to, especially the no-lying bit.

'Can you play guitar?' she said.

'No, but I had a drumming lesson once.'

She rolled her eyes as if that was a total let-down. Well, maybe he should try and be funny then.

'I'll tell you my little sister's favourite joke,' he said.

'Go on then.'

'OK, what do you call a sheep with no legs?'

She wrinkled her nose to think about it. He liked that. She had a smattering of freckles across the bridge of her nose that he'd never noticed before.

'I give up.'

'A cloud.'

She groaned, rather than laughed. But she leaned in to him to do it, and her hair brushed his face. He kissed the top of her head, suddenly, out of the blue. He hadn't meant to, it just happened – right there on a bench outside the pub. And although a faraway part of him knew it was a bad idea, there was a much closer, bigger part of him that wasn't going to stop. Not while she didn't move away, not while his kisses climbed down her hair to her neck and one of his hands crept inside her coat to pull her closer.

'You're beautiful,' he whispered.

She went very still, then slowly pulled away. She looked startled. He felt a bit surprised too – as if he'd said he loved her, which he never had to any girl. It was one of his rules.

Her eyes flickered. 'Beautiful?'

'Totally.'

'What about my scar?'

'I like it.'

She looked down at herself. 'What about my legs? I've got horrible legs.'

'No, you've got beautiful legs.' To prove it he got off the bench and inspected both ankles, cupping each foot in turn.

'My shoes might be dirty.'

She was wearing her school skirt and tights, like before. It filled him with longing and fear to be down there, close to her feet, close to her ankles, her knees, her thighs.

She took a handful of his jacket and pulled it gently, so he had to look up.

'Maybe you should come and sit back down?'

But he couldn't move. He was an animal, wild

and hungry. He let his tongue hang out, did that panting thing dogs did, hoping for a smile. He rubbed his head against her thigh like he wanted stroking.

But she didn't stroke him. In fact, she went a bit quiet and moved along the bench and looked at her mobile.

'Don't you need to go soon?' she said. 'Won't you get sacked or something?'

It was very complicated, the way she went from flirting to cool, but he knew she liked him, however much she was avoiding it now.

'I want to see you again,' he said. 'Will you meet me after my shift? I finish at ten.'

'I'm busy tonight.'

Of course, she was only sixteen and it was a weekday evening – what was he thinking?

'I get a half-day on Saturday,' he said. 'I'll meet you in the afternoon, we'll do something.'

She stood up, made a big show of adjusting her bag on her shoulder, then folded her arms at him. 'What will we do?'

He should've thought before he opened his big mouth. It had to be quality with a girl like her. Not a pub or a club, but somewhere amazing – hot-air ballooning, or a trip in a space ship. It also had to be somewhere far away from everywhere.

'I know. I'll borrow my mate's car and we'll do that wild swim thing. You remember telling me about some place where the waves are really massive?'

She frowned at him, like that was the worst idea in the world. But he was burning with it. It was what he wanted to do more than anything else. Just for a bit. For a day. A half-day. An hour. To be alone with her.

Seconds went past. Ellie chewed her lip and stared down at the beach. The bloke with the dog was still there and the dog was yapping because the bloke was holding a ball a fraction out of its reach. Ellie watched them. Out of the corner of his eye, Mikey watched her.

This was deep for her. She was only in Year Eleven and he was two years older and knew stuff about the world. It was his job to make her feel OK.

'Nothing can happen unless you want it to,' he said.

Which wasn't strictly true – just look at Karyn. But it would be true for Ellie. Eventually she'd give stuff away about her brother, and he wasn't going to hurt her while he looked for it. They'd hang out, kiss some more. No harm done.

'Ellie, come out with me, come on. What are you scared of?'

'Not of you.' She whipped round, her eyes shining. 'All right, let's do it then.'

It was like she was accepting a dare.

Ellie

All sensible websites suggest that you meet a potentially dangerous stranger in a crowded place, and that you tell a family member or a friend what you are doing. And here Ellie was, Saturday lunchtime, about to break the rules. In less than two hours, Mikey McKenzie would arrive at her house, and no one knew he was coming and no one but her would be in.

RSN, he texted.

He was right, it was going to be *real soon now*.

Ellie threw the phone onto her bed as if it was hot, then opened her bedroom window and looked out at the storm, at the dark clouds and fat splashing rain. She leaned on her elbows and watched. A cat dived for cover, cracks in the lawn sucked water into their grooves and all the trees sighed.

She gave revising a try, lay on her bed with Geography books and tried to care about the movement of people from rural to urban areas following the industrial revolution. But thinking of big stuff made her feel small, and when she felt small, she stopped caring about revising and GCSEs and what happened next. It was easy to break any taboo when nothing mattered, so she picked up her phone and texted, *TAU*. It was true, she was thinking about him. He was pretty much all she'd been thinking about since Monday at the harbour.

His text came whizzing back: *XOXOXO*.

A series of hugs and kisses.

She needed food. Diets didn't count in a crisis.

Her parents were sitting holding hands at the kitchen table. Cups of coffee and empty plates in front of them. They looked up and smiled as she walked in. It was lovely, like a normal family again.

'Hungry?' Mum said, pushing her chair back. 'I've just made your dad a bacon butty. Want me to make you something?'

'No thanks.'

Ellie knew what she wanted — one of Tom's double chocolate muffins, kept in the bread bin and not to be eaten by anyone but him.

She ignored her mum's frown as she helped herself and sat down to unwrap it. 'You guys still going out?'

Her father nodded absently. 'As soon as this rain eases up.'

They all looked out of the window, at the garden sinking under the weight of water. And that was it. Extent of conversation. Ellie's journey down the stairs and into the kitchen had lightened the mood for a nanosecond. It was weird how there was nothing left to say or do that didn't relate to Tom. They fell back into grief so easily.

Eventually, Mum took a sip of her coffee, grimaced and put the cup back down. 'I can't believe it's the weekend again,' she said. 'I keep thinking any minute this will stop and we'll go back to normal.'

Dad wiped a hand across his brow. He looked tired. 'We shouldn't expect normal any more. Not if that little bitch insists on going through with this.'

That was new, that word, and the way he spat it out.

'Should you be calling her that, Dad?'

He looked at Ellie open-mouthed. 'She's in the process of ruining your brother's life!'

'It's a horrible word, that's all.'

He shook his head as if she was clearly mad and let his eyes slide back to the window.

When she was a kid, Ellie had spent every Saturday morning with Dad in the park – they'd go to the playground, feed the ducks on the lake, see if they could find decent trees for her to climb. Mum did a yoga class, Tom had football, it was only the two of them. 'Wild child,' Dad called her, and he'd pick leaves and sticks from her hair and let her choose whatever she wanted from the café for lunch. But something changed when she got to eleven, like he shrank away. She was *too big* for cuddles, *too old* for games and messing around. It was a slow retreat. But sometimes, if Ellie really thought about it, she realized he hadn't taken proper notice of her for years.

'Twenty-five miles in this weather,' Dad said, 'and when we get there, she won't even recognize us.'

'Simon,' Mum said, 'that's my mother you're talking about.'

He held up his hands. 'So shoot me!'

Ellie sighed, checked her mobile. Just over an hour to go. No new messages. 'So,' she said, 'are you coming back at the usual time?'

Her mum nodded. 'Should be.'

'Definitely,' Dad said.

'You're only going to see Gran, right? Nothing else? You're not going to the cottage to do more clearing out?'

'Why all the questions?' Dad said.

'No reason.' She pushed her plate away. She suddenly felt sick.

'You shouldn't've taken that muffin if you didn't want it,' Mum said. 'In fact, you shouldn't've taken it anyway.' She slipped the muffin into the bin, licked her fingers then slotted her chair back under the table and began to rinse the plate in the sink.

Ellie checked her phone again. 'And Tom's out all day, is he?'

Her mum gave her a sad smile. 'Might as well let him have fun while he can.'

'Golf club,' Dad said. 'He'll be indoors on the swing simulator if he's got any sense. Exactly where I'd like to be right now, in fact.'

Ellie see-sawed her fork, tilting it backwards and forwards. It left indents in the tablecloth.

Dad frowned at her. 'Are you up to something, Eleanor?'

Yes, don't leave me alone. I've done this foolish thing . . .

He said, 'You're supposed to be revising today, that's what we agreed.'

History notes were scattered on her bedroom floor, her Art project lay half finished on her desk, she hadn't even begun revising Spanish. If her father knew the extent to which she was falling behind, he'd freak. She'd probably be grounded until she was eighteen.

'So,' he said, 'what subject is it today?'

She told him Geography – the only subject she'd done any work on since Monday.

'Ah,' he said, 'ox-bow lakes.' And he patted her briefly on the hand. 'I envy you, Ellie. I wish I had something to take my mind off all this.'

Maybe she should tell him. *I've invited Mikey McKenzie to the house. You know him, sure you do, he's Karyn McKenzie's brother. I've got a plan. Trouble is, it terrifies me . . .*

'This rain isn't stopping,' Mum said from the sink. 'What shall we do?'

Dad stood up. 'Let's go. Get it over with.' He looked down at Ellie. 'Any messages for Gran?'

'Um no, not really. Tell her I'll come and see her soon. Tell her I miss her.'

He nodded, bent down and brushed the top of her head with a kiss. 'Work well then.'

Warmth flooded through her. He hadn't done that for years and years.

And now the ritual of finding things. Mum fumbled in her handbag for the car keys, which she eventually found in her coat pocket. Dad watched her in a distracted way before checking his own pockets for the keys she'd already found. He scooped up his wallet, turned on his mobile and then realized he had no idea where his glasses were. Mum, meanwhile, was convinced she'd lost her purse and had to root through her entire handbag again.

How vulnerable they seemed. How old and grey they'd be one day. *I could come with you*, Ellie wanted to say. *I'll look after you. Let me sit in the back of the car and we'll sing songs. When we get to the nursing home, Gran will give us Murray Mints and we'll take her out for a spin in her wheelchair.*

But, really, she knew how that kind of day would work out, and it didn't solve anything. At least if she stayed at home, everything would be different by the time her parents got back.

Mikey

When Mikey walked into the lounge, his mum switched off the vacuum cleaner to admire him. Holly and Karyn looked up from their game of Snakes and Ladders and wolf-whistled simultaneously.

He laughed. He had on his new T-shirt and favourite jeans. He'd shaved, showered and even used mouthwash. He knew he looked good and gave a male-model strut across the carpet to prove it.

'Look at my son,' Mum said. 'Look at my gorgeous boy.'

'Who's it today, then?' Karyn asked as she shook the dice and threw them on the table. ''Cos that's more effort than most of them get.'

She gave him that cheeky half-smile he'd forgotten about and he felt a bit bad then. But there was no way he could tell her about Ellie, not until he'd got all the information he needed. She wouldn't understand.

Holly reached for his hand, tucked her own into it. 'Where will you take her?'

'Don't know yet. Out and about.'

He sat at the table and watched them play. Karyn was going down ladders as well as snakes to let Holly win. She winked at him when she clocked he'd noticed.

Mum switched the vacuum back on and they pulled their knees up so she could get to the spaces under their feet. It made Mikey feel like a kid.

'I'm going to buy some new cushions,' Mum yelled over the noise. 'They've got some nice ones in the market with embroidery on. New cushions would look lovely in here, don't you think? And maybe a rug.'

Mikey nodded in agreement, then checked the clock. Twenty minutes to go. He tapped his pocket for the car keys. He felt crap lying to Jacko, but there was no way he'd have lent him the car and agreed to postponing the golf-club recce a second time if he hadn't.

'There are things they look for,' Mum said as she switched off the vacuum and coiled the lead up. 'They look for dirt, but they also look for smells. I've had the windows open all morning and I got one of those plug-in air fresheners.'

She stood, hands on hips, pleased with herself.

'It's been like zero degrees with those windows open and she wouldn't let me shut them,' Karyn said, her eyes amused.

Mum smiled across at her. 'You're cold because you don't eat enough, and that's what's happening next – toast.'

Karyn packed the game away and got Holly some paper and pens instead. Mum made four cups of tea and buttered some toast, even spread it with jam and cut it into squares. She placed Karyn's plate gently on the table in front of her.

'It's ages since I saw you eat anything,' she said.

Karyn sighed with pleasure and picked up a square of toast. Easy as that.

She looked happier than Mikey had seen her for days. He knew why. She thought every day was going to be as cheery as this from now on. She thought Mum would save her.

It was easy to believe as they sat there together, sipping their tea and eating toast. Things had been better since Gillian's visit on Monday. Mum had sobered up and collected Holly, then phoned the social worker to apologize. Monday night, she'd sat down with the three of them and promised never to disappear like that again. 'Everything's going to be different from now on,' she said.

Over the last four days she'd spring-cleaned the hallway, the lounge and the kitchen. The whole flat was beginning to look bigger and brighter. Over the week-end she planned to work her way upstairs. Mikey knew what would happen then. She'd fill dustbin bags with old toys and clothes. She'd get ridiculous with it, start throwing things away that people still wanted. Mikey remembered his denim jacket going that way last year, and Holly weeping for hours over her football card collection. Next week, if Mum still hadn't run out of energy, she might get the local paper and look for jobs. She'd circle them, maybe cut them out and put them in a pile somewhere. And then she'd start saying stuff about how they all took her for granted, how nothing good ever happened to her. And then she'd give herself a little reward – maybe a cheap bottle of red from Ajay's over the road. 'Just the one,' she'd say.

And round and round they'd go again. It was so predictable.

'OK, Mum,' he said, 'a little test before I go. Monday morning. *Ding-dong*, there's the social worker again, all smiles, wanting to help. You've been cleaning for days and in she comes, very impressed. First question: *Why has Holly been off school?*'

'She won't ask me that.'

'She might. What will you say?'

'I'll say she was sick.'

'What was wrong with her?'

'She had a headache.'

'Kids don't get headaches.'

Mum moved the ashtray a centimetre to the left, matched the lighter with the edge of the table, making patterns. 'It's all right, I can handle it. I told you, it's going to be different now.'

'Tell them a fever and a cough, or that she kept

throwing up. Not a headache. And don't smoke in front of her.'

He knew how important his mum's fags were, how they kept her calm. He knew he was being unkind.

'Stop worrying,' she said. 'It's only a support visit, nothing else. I'll sit by the window. I'll tell her I never do it with Holly around.'

'Show her the smoke alarm,' Holly said, pointing up at the ceiling with the end of her felt-tip pen.

Mikey followed her gaze. Sober for days, and a tidy flat was one thing, but a fully-installed and working smoke alarm was definitely something new.

Mum grinned at him. 'You're impressed.'

He couldn't help smiling back.

She glanced at the clock. 'Go and have fun, Mikey. Go on, you've done enough.'

He checked his mobile. No new messages, but that was OK. It was all agreed. Two-thirty at Ellie's house. He'd leave in a few minutes.

'Like my drawing?' Holly said.

She held it up for them all to see. It was Karyn, outside with her hair streaming behind her in the wind. She was holding a piece of string with a dragon on the end and a flaming sword.

'Nice picture,' Karyn said.

Holly smiled, carefully tore the page from her book and laid it on the table. 'I'm going to draw you at school next.'

'Let me keep the dragon,' Karyn laughed. 'I'll need it if you're sending me back there.'

Mikey took the plates to the kitchen, had a quick look in the fridge while he was there. It was stuffed – juice and yoghurts, cheese and milk, all sorts. Mum had even bought a pack of bacon and some sausages.

By the time he'd washed up the plates, all three of them were huddled together on the sofa watching a re-run of *TopGear* – some mountain climber was talking about how he got frostbite and later, after surgery, he had a very hot bath and his toe came off and he left it on the side of the sink for his wife to find. They cackled like witches at it. Mikey smiled, wanted to leave them with something. He went over and put ten quid on the table.

'Here,' he said, 'get yourselves a DVD and some sweets.'

You'd think he'd given them a fortune, the way they passed it between them.

He almost didn't want to leave. It wasn't that long ago when this would have been his idea of a perfect Saturday afternoon and he'd happily have squeezed in with them on the sofa.

'I'll be off then.'

Mum raised her cup of tea. 'Have a lovely time.'

Ellie blushed, actually blushed, when she opened the door. Mikey wanted to sweep her up and kiss her, but he had to save that until they were safely away from the house.

'Ready?' he said.

She smiled apologetically. 'Not yet. I haven't made the picnic.'

'We'll get fish and chips.'

She wagged a finger at him. 'Every adventure has a picnic. Come inside, it'll only take a few minutes.'

'Why don't I wait in the car?'

She shook her head. 'There's nobody home, don't worry.'

What choice did he have?

When Ellie closed the door behind them, a dim blue light shone through the coloured glass and splashed the floor. There were paintings on the wall and a statue on a stand – a man and a woman wrapped together. Mikey touched it with a finger, surprised at how smooth it felt.

'It's not real,' Ellie said.

He pulled his hand away, embarrassed.

'It's a copy. Well, of course it's a copy. No one has a real Rodin.'

He nodded, as if that was obvious, mentally cursing himself for knowing nothing about anything.

She led him through a sitting room – sofa, chairs, display cabinet full of family photos (Ellie looking sexy with a swimming trophy) – through to the kitchen, right at the back of the house and smaller than he remembered. On the table was a chopping board, bread, various things for the picnic all spread out. The back door was open and beyond was the garden, that cool expanse of green that amazed him again with its endless lawn and trees.

A dog lay on a blanket and flapped its tail sleepily at them. It was an old dog, with grey hair round its nose. Here was something he recognized at least. He knew what to do with dogs.

'What's his name?'

'Stan, but she's a girl.'

'Does she bite?'

'Only if you're a biscuit. Stroke her if you like. No one else gives her any attention.'

Girls liked blokes who liked animals and he didn't even have to pretend. He took great care, was gentle and slow. The dog turned belly up and let him fuss her. Mikey smiled, forgetting where he was for a minute. 'She's a lovely dog.'

'She's my gran's. We've got her goldfish as well.'

He glanced up quickly. 'Is your gran here?'

'No, no, she's in a nursing home. Cup of tea while you wait, or do you want something else?'

His heart thumped. 'What have you got?'

'Wait there.'

She wasn't gone long. He heard her run down the hallway, heard a door open and shut. She came back with a bottle of wine and passed it over. She was trying to impress him.

He unscrewed the top, took a couple of gulps and

passed it back. She tipped the bottle to her mouth and took the smallest of sips. She wiped her mouth with the back of her hand.

'What about this picnic then?' he said.

'It's only sandwiches.'

'Well, let's make them.'

They really had to hurry up. He wouldn't relax until they were out of here.

He started sorting through the stuff on the table – a bag of expensive lettuce, some cheese in a wooden box, tomatoes, olives. She'd been planning on some complicated sandwiches, though the fresh ingredients were going to be interesting to work with. She yanked more stuff out of the fridge – a red pepper, a handful of rocket.

'You want butter?' she said.

'Not if it's been in the fridge. You got mayonnaise?'

She passed it, along with a knife from a wooden holder on the cabinet. He sliced the bread and spread it with mayo, shredded the lettuce and cut up tomatoes. He liked her watching, knew it looked cool. He unpacked the cheese from its box and laid thin slices on the bread with the salad.

'Got any black pepper, any salt?'

She came over with the grinders and did it for him. When she twisted, her hips swung and her skirt shifted. It was pretty the way her skirt did that, like it was part of her.

He cut the sandwiches in half diagonally, wrapped

them in foil and stepped back from the table with a bow.

'There you go.'

'You could be a chef,' Ellie said, 'the care you took.'

They smiled at each other.

'Shall we be off then?' he said.

She glanced at her mobile, then sat down at the table, pulled a packet of tobacco from a drawer, papers, a lighter and a small hunk of dope.

'What's that for?' he asked.

'What do you think it's for?'

She hadn't a clue how to make a joint, it was obvious. She forgot to heat the dope, then when she figured it out, put way too much in and could barely handle the rolling at all. He wanted to tell her she didn't need to do this to keep him interested, but wasn't sure how to say it.

'I didn't know you smoked,' was all he managed, as she licked the paper and stuck it down.

'I don't.'

'What do you call that then?'

She looked at the joint in her hand as if it had nothing to do with her, gave a little shrug. 'I call it exceptional circumstances.'

She made a roach for it then, tearing a strip from the Rizla packet and rolling it small.

'That'll be too tight,' he said.

She unrolled it and started again. Every now and then she threw him a glance, but he pretended not to notice. He wasn't going to let her freak him out. Or the situation. He kept hearing noises even though he was sitting really still. The afternoon seemed full of them and he couldn't work out if they meant anything or not. Maybe they were regular noises that houses made – boilers and radiators and all the special objects sparkling. But maybe they meant something. Maybe they were noises that mattered, even in the distance. The noise of a car pulling up the drive or footsteps on gravel, or a key in the lock.

'So, where is everyone?' he said. He couldn't help himself, needed to check.

'At work.'

He shot her a look. That was a lie. Rich people didn't work weekends.

'And my brother's playing golf.'

Heat rose from Mikey's chest to his neck, to his face.

'Done it,' she said, wiggling the finished joint at him with a smile.

'Well, do you want to smoke it in the car?'

'No, let's have it here.' She shoved it at him. 'You do the honours.'

He sparked up, took a couple of tokes and passed it to her. She took one puff, didn't even inhale, then handed it back.

He shook his head. 'I'm not really into it, to be honest.'

She looked surprised, stubbed the whole thing out on a saucer and picked up the wine. 'You want some more of this?'

Why weren't they leaving? Jacko's car was outside, the picnic was ready. He took the bottle, had a couple of glugs to calm himself down.

'Shall we go now?' he said.

She checked her mobile. 'How about a tour?'

'What do you mean? A tour of the house?'

'Yeah, why not?'

And she stood up, grabbed the wine bottle and simply walked out of the kitchen.

Like an estate agent with no hope of a sale, Ellie named rooms that lay behind closed doors. Cloakroom, study, bathroom, spare room. Outside her brother's room, Mikey slowed down. It was padlocked, still a crime scene. He laid his hand flat against the door. Ellie kept on walking.

They ended up in her bedroom, sitting together on her bed. There were books and revision papers spread on the desk and all over the floor, but when he tried to crack a joke about it, she ignored him. There was something cold about her, not warm like at the river, not flirty like at the harbour. It was messing with his head.

He got his tobacco out and rolled a thin one. She knelt up on the bed, opened the window and leaned out. He imagined her climbing up on the window ledge like a bird might, her arms open wide. Maybe she could fly. She seemed capable of anything today.

She said, 'Come over here if you're going to smoke.'

He knelt next to her and together they looked down at the garden, all green and leafy with its electric gate keeping it safe. You could have heard anything fall – feathers, dust. How did a place get to be so quiet?

'Don't you want to go swimming any more?' he said.

'Sure I do. We'll leave in a minute. Here.'

She handed him the wine and he took another swig. She had her finger in her mouth as she watched him. *Suck, suck, suck*, she went. He couldn't stop looking.

'What are you thinking?' she said.

'I'm not thinking anything.'

'Yeah you are, people are always thinking.'

He frowned at her. 'OK, I'm thinking you're being really strange.'

'Am I?'

'It's like you've gone away inside yourself. Why have you done that?'

'I don't know what you're talking about.'

A car spluttered in the distance, making them both jump. And that's when she yanked her T-shirt over her head and let it fall to the floor. She was wearing a bra, white lace.

'What are you doing?'

'Getting changed.'

She sauntered to the wardrobe and began to lazily flick through the hangers. He was getting turned on watching her. He could see every bone of her spine. Her shoulder blades looked like wings.

She held up some see-through thing and waved it at him. 'What about this one?' But she didn't put it on. He kept telling himself that this was ordinary. This was what rich girls did when they invited blokes to their bedrooms. But at the same time he knew it wasn't ordinary at all.

He said, 'Ellie, what's going on?'

She turned and stood before him. She looked so gorgeous standing there, smiling like there was light shining from inside her.

She said, 'You tell me.'

And he knew then why she was stalling, and he felt so dumb for not realizing it earlier. She'd got him to come to the house when everyone was out, tried to create a vibe with wine and dope, invited him upstairs. She wanted him to make a move on her.

He smiled, took a step towards her. 'No one's here, right?'

She turned to the door and locked it, put the key in her skirt pocket, turned back to him. 'They're all out.'

'When are they back?'

'Not yet.'

He held out his arms. 'Come here then.'

But she shook her head. And in the space between them something shifted, like the room got colder.

She said, 'I know who you are.'

'What?'

'You're Karyn's brother.'

'What are you talking about?'

She slapped the closed door with the flat of her hand. 'Don't even bother denying it.'

His heart was pounding. Standing there in her bedroom with a massive hard-on, he knew he was totally shafted.

She said, 'I'll read you your rights, shall I? You don't have to say anything. But it might harm your defence if you don't mention something that happens to be true. Like the fascinating fact that you're related to Karyn.'

'Fuck off.'

'*You* fuck off. My parents will be back soon and we've got CCTV at the gate, so it will have recorded you arriving. You've got fifteen minutes to tell me what's going on, or I'll tell them you tricked your way in, helped yourself to drink, smoked drugs in their house, then forced me upstairs and made me take my clothes off. See how easy it is for people to get themselves into compromising situations? See how bad this will look for your sister?'

'You set me up?'

Her eyes hardened. 'You did it to me first.'

She could do anything, say anything. She could say he touched her, that he made her do stuff.

'Did you think I wouldn't find out?' she said. 'Do you think I'm stupid?'

He sat down on the edge of the bed and wiped a hand across his eyes. 'How long have you known?'

'Since the pub. Your boss let it slip. But I knew all along you were only pretending to like me – all that chat at the party and then at the river. I didn't believe any of it.'

He shook his head. 'I wasn't pretending.'

Her eyes were stone. 'OK, let's get this straight. You crash my brother's party, you hit on me, then ask for my number. Why?'

'I liked you.'

'Bollocks.'

'OK, I liked you *and* I thought you might know stuff.'

'What kind of stuff?'

He shrugged. 'Something that might help my sister.'

'Why would I?'

'You were in the house when it happened. Karyn remembers you.'

She gave him a look. It was the strangest look, like a veil lifted, like what he was saying made some kind of sense. 'You didn't ask me anything at the river. You didn't mention my brother once.'

'I forgot.'

She looked puzzled. 'You forgot?'

'I was having a good time.' He was aware of how gravelly his voice was and gave a quick cough. 'Courts are crap, you know that. Your brother'll get off for sure and I wanted Karyn to know someone cared. I thought I'd get information out of you – where your brother

178

hangs out, that kind of stuff. I wasn't ever going to hurt you.'

'You were going to hurt my brother?'

He shrugged. 'He raped my sister.'

Ellie's face closed down again. 'Karyn *wanted* him. It's not Tom's fault she changed her mind in the morning. She flirted with him all night – laughing and joking, knocking back the booze.'

'She fancied him. Haven't you ever done that?'

'I've never offered myself on a plate to a boy, then woken up and cried rape.'

'That's not what happened. I know her and she's not making this up.'

'I know my brother and neither is he.' She took a step forward. 'Why would he rape her when she was clearly going to give it to him anyway?'

Mikey's stomach gripped. He held on tight to the edge of the bed. 'I don't know, but he did.'

'Maybe your sister got so drunk she forgot she said yes – you ever thought of that?'

'He should have looked after her if she was drunk, not taken advantage.'

Ellie glared at him. 'Why did it take her twenty-four hours to go to the police?'

'I don't know! I don't know all the answers.' He ran a hand through his hair. 'She was scared, I know that. She still is.'

'Yeah, well it's not easy for any of us.'

And that's when they heard the car, a door

slamming shut down there. 'That'll be my parents.' She looked at him with a strange fake smile and calmly turned round and unlocked the door. 'I'm going to introduce you. Come on.'

'What? Are you crazy?'

'Let's go and say hello. I'm sure they'd love to hear all about your plan to trick their daughter and hurt their son.'

He couldn't believe she was opening the door, was walking out onto the landing, expecting him to follow. She was only half dressed. Her parents would kill him.

'Ellie, come back!'

She swung round, her eyes furious. 'Why should I?'

And that was when someone yelled, 'Ellie, you up there?' which sounded like a threat and made her flinch, and footsteps came pounding up the stairs.

FROM
13 LITTLE BLUE ENVELOPES

BY
MAUREEN JOHNSON

Only three people showed. Since two people had already purchased tickets before Ginny got there and she had used one herself, this meant that absolutely *no one* she had given tickets to had come. Her Japanese girls had let her down.

The result of this was that the cast of *Starbucks: The Musical* outnumbered the audience, and Jittery seemed very aware of the fact. That might have been the reason he decided to skip intermission and keep right on going, eliminating any chance of letting his audience escape. For his part, Keith didn't seem to mind at all that hardly anyone was there. He took the opportunity to dive into the seats and even to climb one of the fake palm trees that sat on the side of the room.

At the end, as Ginny leapt up to make her escape, Jittery suddenly jumped down off the stage as she was reaching down to get her bag. He dropped into the empty seat next to her.

'Special promotion, eh?' he said. 'What was that about?'

Ginny had heard tales of people being tongue-tied, of opening their mouths to find themselves incapable of any speech. She never thought that was literal. She always thought that was just another way of saying they couldn't think of anything else to say.

Well, she was wrong. You could lose the ability to speak. She felt it right at the top of her throat – a little tug, like the closing of a drawstring bag.

'So tell me,' he said, 'why did you buy three hundred quid's worth of tickets and then try to give them away on the street?'

She opened her mouth. Again, nothing. He folded his arms over his chest, looking like he was prepared to wait forever for an explanation.

Speak! she screamed to herself. *Speak, dammit!*

He shook his head and ran his hand over his hair until it stuck up in high, staticky strands.

'I'm Keith,' he said, 'and you're . . . clearly mad, but what's your name?'

Okay. Her name. She could handle that.

'Ginny,' she said. 'Virginia.'

Only one name was really necessary. Why had she given two?

'American, yeah?' he asked.

A nod.

'Named after a state?'

Another nod, even though it wasn't true. She was

named after her grandmother. But now that she thought of it, it was technically true. She was named after a state. She had the most ridiculously American name ever.

'Well, Mad Ginny Virginia from America, I guess I owe you a drink since you've made me the first person in all of recorded history to sell this place out.'

'I am?'

Keith got up and went over to one of the fake palm trees. He pulled a tattered canvas bag from behind it.

'So you want to go, then?' he asked, tearing off the Starbucks shirt and replacing it with a graying white T-shirt.

'Where?'

'To the pub.'

'I've never been to a pub.'

'Never been to a pub? Well, then. You'd better come along. This is England. That's what we do here. We go to pubs.'

He reached behind once again and retrieved an old denim jacket. The kilt he left on.

'Come on,' he said, gesturing to her as if he was trying to coax a shy animal out from under a sofa. 'Let's go. You want to go, yes?'

Ginny felt herself getting up and numbly following Keith out of the room.

The night had become misty. The glowing yellow orbs of the crossing lights and the car headlights cut strange patterns through the fog. Keith walked briskly, his hands buried in his pockets. He occasionally glanced over his shoulder to make sure Ginny was still with him. She was just a pace or two behind.

'You don't have to follow me,' he said. 'We're a very advanced country. Girls can walk beside men, go to school, everything.'

Ginny tentatively stepped beside him and hurried to keep up with his long stride. There were so many pubs. They were everywhere. Pubs with nice English names like The Court in Session and The Old Ship. Pretty pubs painted in bright colors with carefully made wooden signs. Keith walked past all these to a shabbier-looking place where people stood out on the sidewalk with big pints of beer.

'Here we are,' he said. 'The Friend in Need. Discounts for students.'

'Wait,' she said, grabbing his arm. 'I'm . . . in high school.'

'What does that mean?'

'I'm only seventeen,' she whispered. 'I don't think I'm legal.'

'You're American. You'll be fine. Just act like you belong and no one will say a word.'

'Are you sure?'

'I started getting into pubs when I was thirteen,' he said. 'I'm sure.'

'But you're legal now?'

'I'm nineteen.'

'And that's legal here, right?'

'It's not just legal,' he said. 'It's mandatory. Come on.'

Ginny couldn't even see the bar from where they were. There was a solid wall of people guarding it and a haze of smoke hanging over it, as if it had its very own weather.

'What are you having?' Keith asked. 'I'll go and get it. You try and find somewhere to stand.'

She ordered the only thing she knew – something that was conveniently written on a huge mirror on the wall.

'Guinness?'

'Right.'

Keith threw himself into the crowd and was absorbed. Ginny squeezed in between a clump of guys in brightly coloured soccer shirts who were standing along a little ledge. They kept punching one another. Ginny backed as far into the wall as she could go, but she was sure they would still manage to hit her. There was nowhere else to stand, though. She pressed herself in close and examined the sticky rings on the wood shelf and the ashy remnants in the ashtrays. An old Spice Girls song started playing, and the hitting guys began to do a hit dance that brought them even closer to Ginny.

Keith found her there a few moments later. He carried a pint glass full of a very dark liquid that was coughing up tiny brass-colored bubbles. There was a thin layer of cloudy foam on top. He passed her the glass. It was heavy. She had a brief flash of the thick, warm Ribena and shuddered. For himself, Keith had gotten a Coke. He glanced behind him and placed himself between the dancing guys and Ginny.

'Don't drink,' he explained, seeing her staring at the soda. 'I fulfilled my quota when I was sixteen. The government issue me a special card.' He fixed her again with his unwavering stare. His eyes were very green, with a kind of gold starburst at the center that was just a little off-putting and intense.

'So, are you going to tell me why you did this strange thing or not?' he asked.

'I . . . just wanted to.'

'You just *wanted* to buy out the show for the week? Because you couldn't get tickets for the London Eye or something?'

'What's the London Eye?'

'The bloody great Ferris wheel across from Parliament that all the normal tourists go to,' he said, leaning back and eyeing her curiously. 'How long have you been here?'

'Three days.'

'Have you seen Parliament? The Tower?'

'No . . .'

'But you managed to find my show in the basement of Goldsmiths.'

She sipped her Guinness to buy herself a second

before answering, then tried not to wince or spit. Ginny had never tasted tree bark, but this was what she imagined it would be like if you ran it through a juicer.

'I got a little inheritance,' she finally said. 'And I wanted to spend some of it on something I thought was really worth it.'

Not totally a lie.

'So, you're rich?' he said. 'Good to know. Me, well, I'm not rich. I'm a hooligan.'

Before he began setting the names of coffee drinks to music, Keith had led a very interesting life. In fact, Ginny soon found out, he spent the ages of thirteen to seventeen being a parent's worst nightmare. His career began with crawling over the fence to the garden of the local pub and begging for drinks or telling jokes for them. Then he figured out how to lock himself into his local at night (by hiding in an under-used cupboard) and get enough alcohol for himself and his friends. The owners got so sick of being robbed that they gave up and hired him under the table.

There followed a few years of breaking things for no reason and setting the occasional small fire. He fondly recalled razor blading the word *wanker* into the side of his schoolmaster's car so that the message would show up in a few weeks, after it rained and rusted. He decided to try stealing. At first, he stole little things – candy bars, newspapers. He moved up to small appliances and electronics. It finally ended for him after he broke into a takeout shop and was arrested for grand theft chicken kebab.

After that, he decided to turn his life around. He created a short documentary film called *How I Used to Steal and Do Other Bad Things*. He sent this away to Goldsmiths, and they thought enough of it to accept him and even give him a grant for 'special artistic merit'. And now he was here, creating plays about coffee.

He stopped talking long enough to notice that she wasn't drinking her Guinness at all.

'Here,' he said, grabbing the glass and finishing off the remainder in one long gulp.

'I thought you said you don't drink.'

'That's not drinking,' he said dismissively. 'I meant *drink*.'

'Oh.'

'Listen,' he said, moving closer, 'as you've effectively paid for the entire show – and cheers for that – I might as well tell you this. I'm taking it to the Fringe Festival, in Edinburgh. You know the Fringe?'

'Not really,' Ginny said.

'It's pretty much *the* biggest alternative theater festival in the world,' he said. 'Lots of celebrities and famous shows have come out of it. Took me forever to get the school to pay to send us up there, but I did it.'

She nodded.

'So,' he said, 'I take it you'll be coming to the show again?'

She nodded again.

'I've got to pack everything up after the show tomorrow and move it out for the night,' he said. 'Maybe you'd like to join in.'

'I'm not sure what to do with the rest of the tickets . . .'

Keith smiled confidently.

'Now that you've paid for them, they'll be easy to unload. There aren't a lot of people around since it's June, but the international office will take anything free. And the foreign students are usually still here, wandering around.'

He looked down at her hands. She was clutching at her empty glass.

'Come on,' he said. 'I'll walk you to the tube.'

They left the smoke of the bar and stepped back into the fog. Keith walked her along a different route, one that she would never have been able to find on her own, to the glowing red circle with the bar cutting through it that read UNDERGROUND.

'So, you'll be back tomorrow?' he asked.

'Yeah,' she said. 'Tomorrow.'

She fed the ticket eater and passed through the clacking gate, descending down into the white-tiled tube station. When she got to the platform, she saw that there was a pineapple sitting on the rails of the tracks. A whole pineapple in perfect condition. Ginny stood on the very edge of the platform and looked down at it.

It was hard to figure out how a pineapple could end up in a situation like that.

She felt the whoosh of wind that she now knew accompanied the approach of the train. Any second now it would come blasting through the tunnel and cross right over this spot.

'If the pineapple makes it,' she said to herself, 'he likes me.'

The white nose of the train appeared. She stepped away from the edge, let the train go, and waited for it to pass away.

She looked down. The pineapple wasn't broken or whole. It was simply gone.

FROM
JUNK

BY
MELVIN BURGESS

We got to the squat in the end. I was impressed, actually. I mean, he'd found a place to stay, got himself a bunch of people who weren't just prepared to put him up, they were even willing to *feed* him. He'd only been away two weeks and he had the whole of that side of it worked out. The only thing he didn't have was a scene . . . you know, people to hang around with. Friends. You couldn't put Richard, Jerry and Vonny in that class. They were too old and too nice. To tell the truth I found it a bit put on. The girl, Vonny, came over and gave me a kiss and a hug, and I hugged her back and grinned, but she hardly knew me. And I didn't get the impression she approved of me all that much.

Richard was a bit weird, grinning all over the place, but he was fun. I think he was shy or something. Jerry was okay, he was fairly normal but even he was putting it on a bit. I felt like they could have been vampires in disguise for all I saw of the real them. You had the feeling they were nice because they'd decided it was the fashion to be nice. For all I knew they were probably no nicer than I am.

Now, if it'd been me, I'd have been sleeping in doorways and eating toenail clippings. But I'd have found a crowd to do it with, I expect. I guess I'm not all that interested in niceness. Sometimes people call me nice but that's just because I can make them feel happy. Inside, I just want to have a good time, enjoy myself.

I expect I'll get found out one day.

The first bad sign was that the meal Richard had made for us was drying out in the oven. Richard didn't care. When I said we'd been sightseeing he beamed at the ceiling as if it was the most exciting thing in the world and said, 'Oh, that's all right.' Vonny was a bit put out, though, even though she hadn't cooked it. Well, except she'd made an apple pie for pudding.

Over the apple pie Vonny said, 'How long are you staying with us, Gemma?' And there was this pause. I could feel them all looking at me.

I thought . . . oho. Because it wasn't, do you think you'll like living here, but, how long . . .

I just smiled and I said, 'I don't know. I just don't know . . .' And I smiled and they smiled and Tar smiled.

Like I say . . . they were all very nice.

Later on we went to the pub. It was good, sitting in there drinking half pints of lager. They had to sneak me and Tar in slightly, in case the barman refused to serve us.

They wanted to know if I'd heard anything about Tar's mum. So we talked about that for about an hour which made him utterly miserable. Mind you, they seemed to have a good time.

After a bit it turned out they were all anarchists. That took me back a bit. I mean, I don't know much about it, but aren't anarchists supposed to go around blowing people up, not hugging one another? It turned out they had this big plan for Sunday night. They were going to go out and superglue all the locks in the banks.

Richard got really beside himself about this. He kept putting his beer down and grinning wildly at the ceiling with the sheer delight of ruining the banks' trade for a day. I said, 'Don't banks have back doors, then?'

'Oh, we'll glue those up, too. And the night safes.' And he beamed all round the pub like a man who had been given a million pounds.

It was all arranged. Me and Tar were going along with them. I got quite excited about it. I thought, This is different. I always looked down on the vandals at home – you know, having a good time by smashing up the kiddies' playground. Great fun, eh? But this had a purpose and anyway, I'd have given anything to see the bank manager's face when his lock wouldn't open. We all had a good laugh about that.

I told them about my mum and dad and they seemed very sympathetic. Richard was quite distressed about it. 'My parents used to let me misbehave all I wanted,' he said, and he grinned in that mad way he had at the ceiling. 'I made plenty of use of the opportunity,' he added happily.

I was getting to like Richard.

We started swapping stories about mums and dads and how terrible they were. Tar was a bit quiet. Well, he would be, wouldn't he? But I was beginning to get the giggles. I'd had a vodka and orange on top of the lager and was thinking how just at that very time my parents would be beginning to get utterly furious. It was ten thirty and I was just one hour late. They'd be sitting there grinding their teeth and planning new restrictions, which frankly would be taxing even their imaginations because there wasn't much left to restrict. They'd be wondering who I was sleeping with, what I was taking, etc. etc. It really cracked me up, thinking about them raging around at home and ringing round all my friends and promising themselves they'd be tougher tomorrow. And all the time I was a hundred miles away . . .

They'd find out on Monday morning when my letter came through.

And then, Vonny turned to me cool as a cucumber and she said, 'Don't you think you ought to ring your folks up and tell them you're all right?'

I just gaped at her. The hypocrisy of it! There we'd

been swapping stories about parental horror and now she wanted me to start being nice to them!

'What for?'

'But they must be feeling awful. At least you could let them know you're all right.'

'And tell them when to expect me back?' I asked. 'And to send on the woolly vests.'

'No, like I said – just let them know you're okay.'

'I think that would be a good idea,' said Richard to the ceiling.

Well, I was cornered, wasn't I? I went on about the letter coming on the Monday morning but it wasn't good enough. Mum and Dad were worried *now*. I tried to point out that at this stage in the proceedings, incandescent fury would be a more typical reaction, but no. Even Tar rounded on me. Then of course he wanted to ring up *his* mum and we had to argue him out of that. I hoped that'd put them off the scent but as soon as he backed down they started on me again.

They even had a whip round so I wouldn't get cut off in the middle of something important. And before I knew it I was standing there in front of the pay phone stuffing in pound coins and thinking, Pig, pig, pig. How did this happen?

'Gemma . . . where have you been? Where are you now?'

'I'm all right, I'm just—'

'We've been worried sick—'

'It's only half past ten—'

'It's eleven o'clock and you should have been in an hour and a half ago. I thought we were past this, I thought things were getting better. Your mother . . .'

'Look, I'm ringing up to let you know I won't be back tonight . . .'

'You . . . you'd better be back. Picked up with some of those seafront friends again, have you? . . . It isn't good enough, Gemma . . . blah blah rant . . .'

And he was off. That's all it took. I held the phone away from my ear and I whispered, 'Please, please don't do this to me . . .' I was in the corner of the pub but I was aware of all of them looking over at me. I couldn't talk to him, he was shouting so much. I couldn't even look upset because they were all watching. I just had to pretend I was having a normal conversation with a normal person.

'Oh, we're having a great time, thanks. Yes, okay, I'll be careful. Yeah, thanks, Dad. I'll see you tomorrow . . . Yeah, give Mum a big kiss . . .'

And he was going, 'Why are you speaking to me like that, are you being sarcastic? Gemma, what's going on? Look, let's overlook this slip. You get back here WITHIN THE HOUR and we can discuss—'

'No, I've already eaten, we had baked potatoes. I'll give you a ring again, tomorrow probably. Okay, see you, Dad, thanks, bye . . .'

And I put the phone down.

I don't know why it upset me so much. I just wasn't ready for it. I was leaving home, I was running away, I just wasn't ready to start talking to them. I guess it took me by surprise.

I stood there for a bit staring at the wall trying not to cry. It wouldn't do for them to see me cry after talking to my folks. Vonny came up to me after a minute and tried to peer into my face but I turned away.

'Are you okay? Gemma?' She came up close and touched my arm. 'Is everything okay at home?'

The stupid cow! What did she think things were like at home? I closed my eyes and nodded my head. It felt like she was drilling a hole in my skull. She just made everything so hard. I managed to whisper, 'Look, I've done it, is that enough?' She thought about it and nodded. I went out to the toilet to fix my face.

Afterwards they were going to a party, but I didn't fancy it by this time. I'd really been having a good time but now I felt shattered, totally shattered, as if I'd flown to the moon and back instead of catching the coach to Bristol.

Me and Tar went back and sat in his room. I was furious with him for siding with them. We almost had an argument and then I started to cry and . . .

I couldn't really be angry with him for long. Once he saw me cry he got really upset about it. He started hugging me and saying, 'Sorry, sorry . . .' and getting all wet-eyed. And I thought, I'm not coming all this way just to fall out with Tar about that pair of sergeant majors.

We got ourselves cosy. I wanted to light a fire but we weren't allowed to in case the neighbours thought the house was on fire and called the fire brigade. They weren't supposed to know the house was squatted. We weren't allowed to have the lights on either, for the same reason. I was beginning to get a bit irritated with the list of things we weren't allowed to do. But Tar stuck loads of candles in bottles and made coffee and we sat on the floor in a pile of cushions and had a bit of a cuddle, and we talked for ages about . . . I dunno, everything.

Then bedtime came along. I had my bedroll with me that I used for camping. Tar had his mattress and he kept going on and on about me sleeping on that. I could feel myself losing my temper about it so I just said, 'Okay, okay.' I had his present to give him and I didn't want to spoil this.

I was feeling shy by this time. I put the bedroll down next to the mattress and got undressed and into my bag while he was out of the room.

And I thought, right. I've done my bit. He can do the rest.

Tar came in. He blew out the candles, got undressed in a corner and into his pyjamas. Then he slid into his bag and just lay there.

I was furious. Livid. I had the bag up around my nose so my hair and my eyes were peering out at him, three feet away with his eyes closed, all set to go to sleep. The worst of it was, I was getting cold and if this kept on I'd have to sneak out and get my pyjamas on.

I lay there for about ten minutes getting really chilly. And then he said, 'Can we have a cuddle?'

'All right, then.'

He pushed his mattress across so he lay next to me and hugged me. He didn't try to kiss me. Then he put his hand on my neck and I could feel his fingers slide down to my shoulder . . .

I was watching him. I saw his eyes open and catch me looking at him and he closed them again, quickly. Then in a moment the fingers slid down a little further, down my waist, to my hips.

That was my present, see. Me. I wasn't wearing a stitch.

Tar opened his eyes and smiled at me and I smiled back and said, 'It's a double. The sleeping bag.'

'Oh . . .'

The big oaf.

'I've taken two bags and zipped them together.'

He got out of bed and was just about to slide in next to me when I said, 'Have you got anything?'

'Oh . . . no . . .'

It was such a pain. I was so cross. I sat up in bed and seized a cup of cold coffee I had by me. 'Do I have to do everything?' I snapped, and started slurping the coffee.

'I'm sorry, I'm so stupid . . .'

Well . . . I suppose I should have supplied them. How was he to know? Still, Tar was never a Boy Scout, that much was clear.

Then he said, 'Hang on . . .' And he ups and outs the room with his jeans on and I thought . . .

'Oh, no!' I knew what he was doing. He was going to borrow some off Vonny and Jerry . . . I was half amused, half furious . . . because, I mean, this was my first time. I didn't want to use boring old borrowed anarchist condoms!

And then he was away for *ages*. He must have been half an hour and then he came back quietly in case I was asleep, all sheepish.

'Sorry . . .'

'What happened?'

'They were a bit reluctant to lend them.'

'Why?'

'Well, you're only fourteen, see, and . . .'

I got the picture. There'd been a big discussion about whether Gemma was old enough. I was livid. I sat there and steamed. He was dithering around the room. He came and sat next to me and asked me if I didn't want to any more. It was dreadful. This was exactly the sort of thing I'd wanted to avoid. I thought he'd discover me wearing nothing at all under my sleeping bag and it would just happen. Now he was sitting there in his blue jeans and I had my jumper back on, I'd got so cold waiting.

I said, 'Oh, never mind,' and I turned away and wrapped myself back up in my sleeping bag as if I wanted to go to sleep. I could feel him standing there for a moment, then he got into his. He lay close and cuddled up to me.

Well. Sometimes you've got to work harder than you want to. I turned round and he kissed me and he slid out and into my bag and he lay there very still for a bit, although I could tell he was really excited. He can be very tactful sometimes. We cuddled and it got very warm and then a bit steamy and pretty soon my jumper found its way up around my neck . . .

Later on, Tar said in a little voice, 'I love you.'

And I said . . .

Oh . . . I felt so sorry for him, but I hadn't anything else to give him, you know? It was just a moment we had together. I mean, he was a really special person to me, but . . . I just felt that someone could come along and blow hard and I'd fly away from him, go in the wind and end up . . . next door or on another planet with someone else, anywhere. Just because the wind blew.

I didn't want to hurt him.

I put my finger on his lips and I said, 'Ssssh . . .'

I could see him looking at me. He was hurt and I felt cross because I'd done my best. And what right had he got to love me?

I said, 'Don't say that.'

There was a long silence and then he said this funny thing . . . 'Dandelion.'

I just looked at him, it was so out of context. I said, 'What's that supposed to mean?'

He sort of smiled and shrugged and I smiled back because I realised . . .

He'd given me a picture he'd done of a dandelion. It was a lovely picture. I didn't know what the dandelion meant to him but I knew what he was saying. He was saying that he still loved me, even though . . .

I wanted to say something to him . . . to tell him that I felt so much for him, even though I didn't love him. I couldn't say dandelion so I said, 'Ladybird.' It just came into my head.

He laughed and said, 'Why ladybird?'

I said, 'Because they're nice, and everyone likes them, and they're pretty and red . . .' He began to kiss my mouth.

'. . . and they like dandelions. A lot,' I said. I touched his nose with the tip of my finger, as if I was telling him off.

Tar smiled and nodded.

'Dandelion,' he said.

'Ladybird.'

'Dandelion.'

'Ladybird.'

And I really did love him in that moment, more than anyone, more than myself, even though tomorrow it might all be over.

He kissed my mouth and we snuggled up as close as we could get.

FROM

NOUGHTS & CROSSES

BY

MALORIE BLACKMAN

Sephy

It took a while before I heard the strange tip-tapping at my window. And once I was conscious of it, I instinctively knew that it'd been going on for a while. Not bothering to wipe my face, I headed for my window and opened it. Tiny stones lay at my feet.

Callum . . .

Callum in our back garden. I leaned over my balcony and saw him at once.

'What . . . ?' I lowered my voice. 'What're you doing here?'

'I need to see you.'

'I'll come down.'

'No. I'll come up.'

I looked around anxiously. 'OK. But be quick.'

'How do I get up there?'

'Just a sec. Er . . . can you climb up the drainpipe and use the ivy for footholds?'

'I'll break my neck.'

'Hang on, I'll tie some sheets together then.'

'No, don't bother.'

Without another word, Callum clambered up the drainpipes and the ivy, reaching my balcony in about ten seconds flat. My heart leapt up into my throat as I watched him. If he fell now . . . The moment he reached my balcony, I hauled him over, terrified he'd plummet to his death.

'Did you phone me? I didn't hear your signal,' I told Callum, confused.

'I didn't phone. I came straight here,' Callum replied. 'I hid in the rose garden until the coast was clear.'

We stood in the middle of my room. He looked at me and I looked at him and all the events of our lifetimes finally caught up with us. I wanted to say sorry for everything that'd happened to his dad, sorry for everything that was still happening, but even in my head the words sounded trite and totally inadequate. Better to say nothing. Safer. And I couldn't forget the way he'd looked at me as the prison clock struck. I was the first to look away. I'd known Callum all my life and yet I felt as if we'd only just met.

'Is there anything I can do?'

Or maybe I'd done enough. Me and my kind . . . I risked a glance at Callum. He didn't answer. He just watched me.

'How's your mum . . . ?' Stupid question. 'Is she still staying with relatives or friends? Is she . . . ?'

'She's at my aunt's house,' Callum replied.

I looked around my room. Should I sit or stand? What should I say? What should I do? Inside, I was beginning to panic.

I ran to lock the door. The last thing either of us needed was to have my mother or sister enter the room. Sighing with relief at the click of the key in the lock, I turned, only to bump straight into Callum. Dazed, I looked up at him.

'I . . . I thought you were going to get help,' Callum told me.

I shook my head, shocked. Why would he think such a thing? 'Listen, if I wanted to get help, you wouldn't have made it to my bedroom window,' I told him.

But he was hardly listening. He just kept staring at me, his expression freezing by degrees.

'Callum . . . ?'

'Your father must be so proud of himself.' Callum's eyes narrowed. 'An innocent man is going to rot in prison and just like that his political reputation is restored.'

'No . . .' I whispered. 'It wasn't like that . . .'

But it was – and we both knew it.

'Is this the way it's going to be from now on? Whenever a politician is in trouble in the polls, if they can't start a war, they'll just search out the nearest nought to imprison or hang – or both?'

I didn't take my eyes off Callum's face. Out of the

corner of my eye I saw him slowly clenching and unclenching his fists. I didn't move. I didn't blink. I hardly dared to breathe. Callum was hurting so much, it was tearing him up inside. And he wanted to hurt someone.

'And what about you, Sephy?' he asked.

'W-what about me?' I whispered.

'No more you and me, I take it,' Callum said with contempt. 'After all, you wouldn't want to ruin your future career prospects by being spotted with the son of the Dundale bomber.'

'I know your dad didn't do it.'

'Oh yes? Well, so did the jury – for all the difference it made. D'you know how long they deliberated? One hour. One lousy, stinking hour.' His head slumped in despair.

'Callum, I'm so sorry . . .' I touched his cheek.

His head shot up. He glared at me with white-hot, burning hatred. My hand fell quickly to my side.

'I don't want your ruddy pity,' he shouted.

'Shush . . .' I pleaded, glancing at my bedroom door.

'Why should I?' Callum challenged. 'Don't you want anyone to know you've got a blanker in your room?'

'Callum, don't . . .' I didn't even realize I was crying until a salt tear ran into the corner of my mouth.

'I want to smash you and every other dagger who crosses my path. I hate you so much it scares me,' he told me.

'I . . . I know you do,' I whispered. 'You've hated me ever since you joined Heathcroft and I called you a blanker.' I realized it as I said it. And in that moment I realized a lot of things, including why I'd started knocking back wine.

'And you've hated me for turning my back on you at school and not being there when you needed me,' said Callum.

I didn't deny it.

'So why're we still together?' Callum spoke softly to himself, almost forgetting that I was right in front of him. 'Why do I still think of you as . . . ?'

'As your best friend?' I supplied. 'Because you know that's how I think of you. Because . . . because I love you. And you love me, I think . . .'

My words snapped Callum out of his reverie with a vengeance. A hard, mocking look flashed over his face. I waited for him to do something; laugh, lash out, deny it, leave − anything. But he didn't.

'Did you hear what I said?' I tried again. 'I love you.'

'Love doesn't exist. Friendship doesn't exist − not between a nought and a Cross. There's no such thing,' Callum replied.

And he meant every word.

'Then what're you doing in my room?' I asked, choking inside. 'Why did you come?'

Callum shrugged. 'I'm damned if I know.'

With a sigh I moved over to the bed and sat down.

After a moment's hesitation, Callum came and sat down beside me. I can't remember either of us ever feeling more awkward. I struggled desperately to find something to say. Risking a glance in Callum's direction, I saw at once from the look on his face that he was having exactly the same problem.

I had so many things I wanted to tell him. The words tumbled and jumbled around in my head, making me dizzy. But nothing would come out. I turned to Callum and slowly held my arms out towards him. He looked puzzled, then his expression cleared. He watched me intently. My gaze dropped. Another of my stupid ideas. I started to lower my arms. Taking hold of my hands, he shuffled along the bed towards me.

Wrapping his arms around me, he lay down on the duvet cover, taking me with him. We faced each other, our eyes locked. I licked my lips nervously. Now what? Callum kissed me. And I kissed him back. We were comfort kissing, that's all. We wrapped our arms around each other for solace. Bear hugging. Squeezing the life out of each other as if we were trying to merge together. When at last we loosened our grip, in a strange way we were both more . . . calm. Physically, at least. Not mentally.

'Turn around,' Callum whispered.

I was about to argue but then I thought better of it. I did as I was asked. He wrapped his arms around me. We were cuddled up like a couple of spoons in a cutlery drawer. I toyed with the idea of suggesting that we get under the covers but I decided not to push it. I didn't want to give Callum a reason to panic and leave. Maybe there was some way to suggest it . . . gently? I raised an eyebrow. Gently? Yeah, right! But it would've been wonderful. Just Callum and me locked together, locking out the whole world. Bliss. But one step at a time. And besides, what we were doing now wasn't too shabby! Better to settle for this than his hatred. Better this than nothing at all.

Callum sighed. I shuffled back to get closer to him. I felt him relax, his body warm against mine. My sigh echoed his.

'Are you OK?' His breath was warm and soft in my ear.

'Uh-hm!' I mumbled.

'I'm not squashing you?'

'Uh-uh!'

'You're sure?'

'Callum, shut up.'

I felt rather than saw him smile. His first smile in a long while, I think.

'Don't leave without giving me your new address and phone number,' I murmured. 'I don't want to lose you again.'

I don't even know if he heard me and I was too comfy to find out. Then I thought of something else. Something which struggled through my lethargic haze. Something that'd been troubling me for a while now.

'Callum,' I whispered. 'I'm sorry I sat at your table.'

'What're you talking about?'

'Your table. At school,' I said, sleepily. 'And I'm sorry for what happened at Lynette's funeral.'

And sorry for all the million and one other well-meant but badly thought out things I'd done in my life. Acts to make me feel better. Actions that had hurt Callum rather than helped him. Sorry, Callum. Sorry. Sorry.

'Forget it. I have,' Callum's warm breath whispered across my cheek, before he kissed it.

I closed my eyes and allowed my mind to drift away. I was cuddled up with Callum and for once this time was ours and no one else's. With that thought in my mind, I drifted off to sleep, with Callum still holding me.

Callum

Sephy was out like a light. Lucky her. I lay on her bed with my arms wrapped around her, wondering how on earth we'd managed to end up like this. I'm not sure what'd been on my mind when I came to see her, but this wasn't it! Strange the way things turn out. When I'd come into her room, I'd been burning up with the desire to smash her and everything else around her. Sephy was a Cross I could actually hurt. And yet here she was, asleep and still holding on to my arms like I was a life-raft or something. There's not a single millimetre of space between her body and mine. I could move my

hands and . . . And. Anything I liked. Caress or strangle.
Kill or cure. Her or me. Me or her.

I lifted my head, to make sure she was really asleep.
Eyes closed, regularly breathing, in-out, in-out. Dead to
the world. Lucky her.

She turned in her sleep to face me, her arms
instinctively reaching out to hug and hold me close to
her. I lowered my head back down to the pillow. Each
time Sephy exhaled, her breath tickled my cheek. I
moved my head down slightly so that our noses were
almost touching. So that when she breathed, she'd have
to breathe my breath and I'd have to breathe hers. And
then I kissed her. Her eyes opened almost immediately,
sleepy but smiling. Her hands crept up to frame my
face and, closing her eyes again, she returned my kiss,
her mouth open, her tongue dancing against mine.
Fireworks were shooting through my body. I was finding it hard to breathe. So was she. I pulled away
abruptly.

'Why are you kissing me?' I asked, frustrated anger
creeping into my voice. 'Passion or guilt?'

Sephy looked so sad, so hurt, that I instantly regret-
ted my words. She went to roll away from me, but I
held her arm and wouldn't let her.

'Sorry,' I murmured.

'Maybe you should go . . .' Sephy whispered, still
not looking at me.

'Not yet. Please. I'm sorry.' I placed my hand under
Sephy's chin and raised her head so that she could look

at me and know I meant it. She tried to smile. I tried to smile back.

I opened my arms for her. 'Let's just get some sleep – OK?'

Sephy nodded. I lay on my back and Sephy settled down to lie with her head on my shoulder. She was asleep again in less than a minute. Lucky, lucky, lucky. Ten minutes must've passed. Then fifteen. I couldn't stand it any longer.

'Sephy, d'you want to know a secret,' I mouthed against her ear.

She moved her ear slightly away from my mouth. My breath must've tickled her. But she was still fast asleep.

'Here is my confession,' I whispered. And I told her what I'd never told anyone else. What I hadn't even admitted to myself. The biggest secret of all.

God, if you are up there – somewhere – you've got a very peculiar sense of humour.

Sephy

'Miss Sephy? Are you all right in there?'

'Persephone, open this door. At once.'

The dream I was having was so warm and comfortable, apart from that incessant calling somewhere in the background. I opened my eyes slowly, only to have them fly right open when I saw whose shoulder I was perched upon. Callum's. His arm was around my shoulders and he was fast asleep.

'Persephone, open this door right this second or I'll get someone to break it down,' Mother yelled.

'Miss Sephy, are you OK? Please.' Sarah pulled at the door handle.

I sat bolt upright. 'Just . . . just a minute,' I yelled, shaking Callum awake.

'What . . . what's the . . . ?' Callum began sleepily.

Putting one hand over his mouth, I pointed to the bedroom door. He got it at once. I pointed to my bathroom door. Callum jumped off the bed and ran towards it.

'Look, why don't I just let them in,' I whispered. 'I want Mother to know about us. Besides, we haven't done anything wrong.' The look Callum gave me instantly changed my mind. 'Bad idea?'

'Duh!!' Callum replied.

I looked down at my clothes. I still had my Jackson Spacey dress on – although by now it had so many creases in it that it looked like the skin on a day-old macaroni cheese. If Mother saw it, she'd kill me.

'Just a minute, Sarah. I'm just putting on my dressing gown,' I called out.

After pulling the belt tight and making sure none of my dress could be seen, I ran to the door, waiting until Callum had scooted into my bathroom before I turned the key in the lock.

'What's the matter? Is the house on fire?' I asked as Sarah and Mother bustled past me.

'D'you know what time it is?' Mother asked.

'So I overslept a few minutes. Big deal,' I said, annoyed.

'A few minutes? It's almost noon and your door is locked. You never lock your door,' Sarah said suspiciously.

'Maybe I decided to bring a little excitement into your lives,' I yawned.

And then I saw them. Callum's trainers, right by my bed in plain, full, multi-colour view. My heart dropped to my ankles then bounced right up to my mouth.

'I'll be down as soon as I've had my shower.' I smiled brightly. 'I promise.'

'There's nothing wrong?'

''Course not. What could be wrong?' I said, a little too emphatically judging by the deepening look of suspicion on Sarah's face. She looked around slowly, stopping abruptly when she caught sight of the men's trainers on the floor. She gave me a profoundly shocked look and I knew at once what was going on in her head. Pursing my lips, I fought hard to stop myself from looking guilty. I hadn't done anything wrong. And if Callum and I had been at it all night like bunny rabbits instead of fast asleep, it still wouldn't have been any of her business.

'There's something strange going on around here,' Mother said slowly.

'Just 'cause I overslept?' I asked, more to focus her attention on me than for any other reason.

Sarah walked towards Callum's shoes as Mother

scrutinized my face. Although my eyes were on Mother, I was aware of Sarah's every movement. She was going to hold up Callum's trainers with a flourish for Mother to feast on.

'Sarah, what . . . ?'

As Mother turned around, Sarah kicked the trainers under my bed. All Mother saw was Sarah tidying up my bedclothes as if she was making my bed.

'Don't do that, Sarah,' Mother admonished. 'My daughter is quite capable of making up her own bed. That's not your job.'

Sarah dropped my duvet with a prim 'Yes, Mrs Hadley.'

Mother marched out in high dudgeon, followed by Sarah trotting behind her.

'Get Callum dressed and out of here!' Sarah whispered urgently as she passed me.

'How did you . . . ?' My mouth snapped shut. I shut the door behind them, carefully locking it so neither of them would be alerted by the noise.

'OK, Callum. You can come out now.'

Callum popped his head around my bathroom door and had a look around before he came back into my bedroom. We looked at each other and burst out laughing. And it felt so good.

'How am I going to get out of here?' Callum asked.

I had a long, hard think. 'We'll have to sneak

out of the house and across the grounds to the beach. If we see anyone, I'll distract them whilst you sneak past.'

'Just your ordinary average Sunday–morning activity!' Callum said dryly.

'Never a dull moment,' I agreed.

'Fancy another cuddle in the bed first?' asked Callum.

I smiled. 'You betcha!'

Callum

'*Ryan Callum McGregor, the convicted bomber of the Dundale Shopping Centre, was killed this morning whilst trying to escape from Hewmett Prison. He was electrocuted whilst trying to scale the electrified fence surrounding the prison. Ryan McGregor, who was due to hang four days ago, received a dramatic last-minute reprieve from the Home Office. His family are said to be devastated at the news and were unavailable for comment. Officials have launched an immediate enquiry.*'

Sephy

Dear God,

Please leave Callum's family alone. But it's not you, is it? My mistake. This has nothing to do with you. This is more like the devil's work. Another mistake? Maybe hatred has nothing to do with the devil either. Maybe it's something we've invented. And then we just blame it on you, God, or on the devil, because it's easier than blaming ourselves. I'm not

thinking straight. I can't think. Dear God, look after Callum
and his family. Help them. Help us all.

Callum

I entered the burger bar and waited my turn in the
long queue. This Friday was just like the Friday before
and would probably be exactly like the Friday to
follow. My days stretched out before me like some kind
of galactic desert. Funny how the days could go so
slowly and time could pass so fast. They'd killed . . .
they'd murdered my dad in July and when he died,
I think something inside me had died as well. And
although since then the weeks had come and gone, it
still cut like a knife every time I thought of my dad –
which was all the time. Officially, the authorities might
call it suicide, but I and every other nought knew
differently.

And I hadn't seen Sephy since the Saturday night-
Sunday morning I'd spent with her. Sarah hadn't given
us away but she'd made sure it was practically impossible for me to slip back into the house again. A
guard was now on permanent patrol.

I'd visited the beach a few times but to be honest
I never stayed very long. Going to the beach felt like
trying to recapture the past – an impossible task. Too
much had happened over the last year. I never saw
Sephy anyway, which was probably just as well. At
least the memory of that night in her bed was beginning to fade a little. Not much. But a very little. If I

tried very hard to think about something else — and rubbed my stomach and patted my head at the same time! I forced myself to think of Dad. What were the thoughts running through his head as he stood before the fence? What was the last thing he thought of before he died? I'd never know. Something else to hate the Crosses for.

I gave my order to the cashier, ignoring the plastic smile on her face as she served me, and waited for my food. When I'd received my burger, french fries and milk, I sought out the darkest corner of the burger bar. I finally sat down with my back to the throng and slowly chewed on a chip. I wasn't even hungry. It was just something to do to pass the time until the afternoon had passed. Now that I wasn't at school, I never knew what to do with myself. Totally aimless, I had nothing to do and nowhere to go. Since Dad's death, Mum was lost somewhere deep inside herself where I couldn't reach her. No one could. I had tried, but it was hopeless. Maybe if I'd been Lynette, her favourite child, or Jude, her first-born son, but . . . I chewed on another chip. I was sixteen and a half, and already it felt as if my life was over. The good times, the *best* times, were over.

'Hi, little brother.'

I looked up and my eyes began to hurt I was staring so hard. Jude . . . *Jude!* I leapt up and, leaning across the table, I hugged him — hard!

'I've missed you,' I told him.

'Get off. Are you mad, or what?' Jude glanced around before sitting opposite me. I sat back down, beaming at him.

'Stop grinning like an idiot!' Jude told me sourly.

'It's great to see you too!' I replied. 'Where've you been? I really have missed you.'

Jude took another look around. 'I've been keeping my head down for a while.'

My smile disappeared. 'You . . . you know what happened to Dad?'

'Oh yes, I know,' Jude said grimly. 'I know all about it. And it's payback time.'

'What d'you mean?'

Jude sat back in his chair. His eyes darted here, there and everywhere and although he sat perfectly still, he reminded me of a nervous cat, ready to leap off at a nanosecond's notice.

'I hear they booted you out of Heathcroft,' Jude said at last.

'I wasn't booted. I walked,' I told him huffily.

'Good for you. That wasn't the place for you, little brother.'

'I know that now.'

'It's a shame you didn't listen to me when I told you months ago. It would've saved you a lot of grief.'

I shrugged. What else was there to say?

'So what're you up to now?' Jude asked.

'I eat chips.' I pointed at my polystyrene tray.

'Would you like to do something more worthwhile?'

'Like what?'

Jude stood up. 'I have to go now. Someone will be in touch.'

'Jude, don't do your "Man of Mystery" routine on me.' I frowned. 'What am I meant to tell Mum?'

'Don't tell her anything,' Jude said vehemently. 'Where we're going, she can't follow.'

'And where are we going?'

'I think you know, little brother.'

'Stop calling me that,' I protested. 'What're you up to, Jude?'

'Just tell me one thing,' Jude said. 'Are you in or out?'

He was deliberately being enigmatic, answering each of my questions with a question of his own. And it was really cheesing me off. But I knew what he was asking. This was my chance to link up with the Liberation Militia. And I knew in my gut that if I turned Jude down now, I'd never be asked again.

'Well?' Jude prompted.

I licked my lips, trying to delay the moment of decision.

'This is your chance to make a difference,' Jude told me.

And just like that, I felt a calmness, a *purpose* I hadn't felt in a long, long time. I looked at Jude and said, 'I'm in.'

Jude nodded, satisfied. 'Then go home, pack your bags and make your peace with Mum. You'll be contacted tomorrow some time. After that you won't be seeing Mum or anyone else we know for that matter for a while. Are you still in?'

I nodded.

'Welcome to the lifeboat party, little brother,' Jude said, adding, 'I hope I can trust you.'

And a moment later, he was gone.

Sephy

Dear Callum,

I was going to phone you but I knew I'd bottle out and never say what I wanted to say. So I've decided to write it all down. I've thought and thought about it and I think I've found a way for both of us to get away from all this madness. You're sixteen, nearly seventeen and I'm almost fifteen so don't say I'm too young or anything stupid like that. Just read this letter with an open mind, that's all I ask.

I think you and I should go away together. Somewhere. Anywhere. Just the two of us. For good. Before you throw this letter in the bin, my brain hasn't dropped out of my ear. I know what I'm saying is right. I want to be with you and I think you want to be with me. I'm not going to swear undying love or any of that other stuff you despise so much, but if we don't leave now and together, then something tells me we never will. I'm not talking about the two of us becoming lovers or anything like that. I don't think either of us is ready for that. Besides, I know that's the last thing you'd want. But the two of us could set off together. Set up together. Stay together. Save each other — if that doesn't sound too melodramatic. I think it probably does. But I mean it. And if you think about it, you'll realize deep down that I'm right.

So let's just do it before we get too old and scared. Let's do this before we turn into <u>them</u>. I've got plenty of money saved in my own personal bank account, plus there's my regular monthly allowance from both Dad and my grandmother's trust fund. And we can both work. Just as long as we're together. All you have to do is say yes. I thought we could move right away from here. Maybe rent a place up north somewhere. Maybe in the country.

If you say yes.

Mother has finally agreed to my going to Chivers Boarding School and I'm leaving at two o'clock on Sunday afternoon. If I don't hear from you by then I'll know what your answer is. I'll wait for you right up until the moment I have to leave. But either way I'm going to get out of here.

Take me away from all this, Callum. Don't let me leave for Chivers. I want to be with you. Please don't let me down.

~~All my love~~
Yours for ever,
Sephy

I stuffed the letter back into its envelope as I heard footsteps approach the kitchen. I was in luck. It was Sarah.

228

'Sarah, I . . . could you do me a favour? A really big one.' I chewed on my lip nervously, trying to read her expression.

'Oh yes? What's that then?'

'Could you deliver this letter to Callum McGregor? He's staying with his aunt. I've written the address on the front.'

'I don't think so!' Sarah scoffed. 'I need this job.'

'Please, Sarah. I'm begging you. It's really important.'

'What is it?' Sarah asked.

'A letter.'

'I can see that. What does it say?'

I chewed on my lip some more. A horrified look appeared on Sarah's face.

'You . . . you're not pregnant, are you?'

I stared at her, then burst out laughing.

'I guess not,' Sarah said dryly.

'Please,' I pleaded, my smile fading. 'I wouldn't ask you if it wasn't really, *really* important.'

Sarah regarded me thoughtfully. 'OK,' she said at last. 'I'll deliver it on my way home tonight. But only on one condition.'

'What's that?'

'That you don't do anything . . . hasty.'

'It's a deal!' I wrapped my arms around her and hugged her tight. 'Thank you. Oh, thank you.'

'Hhmm!' Sarah didn't sound convinced that she was doing the right thing at all.

I licked the envelope and sealed it before pressing it into her hand before she could change her mind.

'Thanks, Sarah. I owe you one.' I grinned at her as I skipped off.

'You owe me several, Miss Sephy,' Sarah called after me.

'I know.' I twirled around before heading up the stairs.

Hasty! This wasn't hasty at all. I'd thought and considered and planned this for days, weeks, months, all my life. Everything Callum and I had ever done had been leading up to this moment.

Callum would read my letter and come for me and together we were going to *escape*.

Wasn't life glorious?!!

Callum

'Callum, there's someone downstairs to see you . . . What're you doing?'

I closed my eyes briefly, my back towards Mum. I'd hoped to escape any kind of explanation.

'I'm going away, Mum.'

'Where?'

'Away,' I replied. 'Somewhere where I can make a difference.'

Silence. When I could bear it no longer, I turned to see what Mum was doing. She stood in the doorway, watching me.

'I see,' she said at last.

And she did see. That was the trouble.

'When will you be back?'

'I don't know,' I answered truthfully.

Pause. 'Will you see your brother?'

'I don't know. Probably.'

'Tell him . . . Give him my love,' Mum said at last, adding, 'Do one thing for me, will you?'

'What's that?'

'Keep your head down. And tell your brother to do the same.' Mum turned to walk out of the door, her whole body slumped and drawn in on itself. She turned her head. 'What about Sarah downstairs?'

'Sarah?'

'Sarah Pike who works for Mrs Hadley. She's downstairs.'

'Tell her I'm busy at the moment. I don't want to see her.' I shook my head. The last thing I needed right now was a stale morality lecture from Mrs Hadley's dogsbody. 'I can't take all my stuff,' I decided. 'I'll be back tomorrow afternoon for the rest.'

Mum carried on downstairs. I flung a clean T-shirt into my rucksack and closed it, waiting for the sound of the front door to close downstairs. My leaving would please Aunt Charlotte, at any rate. I'd already received my orders. Go to the bus garage just outside town, sit on the bench outside the bus garage and wait. All very hush-hush, cloak-and-dagger. It was a big waste of time and effort if anyone were to ask me, which no one did. But if it kept my brother happy then fair enough.

I felt quite upbeat about what was going to happen actually. I was going to join the Liberation Militia. It wasn't what I'd planned for myself a couple of years ago, but at least I'd stopped drifting. At last, I belonged.

The moment I heard the front door shut, I headed downstairs.

'Sarah left this for you.' Mum pointed to a letter on the hall table.

'I'll pick it up tomorrow with the rest of my stuff,' I said, impatiently, without even looking at it. What Sarah couldn't say to my face she'd written down, eh? Well, it could wait. I was off to spend my Saturday evening outside a bus garage.

'I'm off now, Mum.'

Mum nodded. 'Take care of yourself.'

'You too.'

We stood in the hall like two lemons on display.

'See you, Mum.'

'Bye, son.'

I skirted round Mum trying to make sure I didn't knock her with my rucksack. And then I was out of the door. Mum closed it quietly behind me as I walked off towards the other end of town.

Sephy

He's coming. He's not going to come. He's coming. He's not going to come. He's . . .

'Persephone, move it!' Mother snapped. 'D'you want to go to Chivers or not?'

'I'm coming,' I called out. I took one more look around, searching the grounds, the path, towards the gate.

Nothing.

He wasn't going to come. The desire to cry came and died. Dry-eyed, I moved towards the car. Karl, the chauffeur, stood by the passenger door, holding it open for me.

'Sephy!'

I turned as Minnie came hurtling out of the door. She stopped right in front of me.

'Enjoy yourself at Chivers,' she said at last.

'I wish you could come with me,' I told her.

'Do you?'

I nodded.

'Well, Mother can't do without both of us and as I'm the oldest and my exams are only just around the corner, and going to a new school would be too disruptive, I might as well stay here . . .'

Mother's arguments, not Minnie's.

'I'm sorry, Minerva.'

Minnie shrugged. 'Yeah, so am I.'

'Couldn't you have another word with Mother? Maybe she'll . . . ?'

'It wouldn't do any good,' Minnie interrupted. 'She's determined that I should stay.'

'You worry too much about pleasing everyone,' I told her.

'Unlike you. You couldn't give two hoots for anyone else's opinion.' Minnie smiled.

If only that was true. I sometimes acted first and thought about it afterwards but I did care what other people thought. That was the trouble.

'Don't . . . don't get too . . . like Mother – OK?' I said.

'I'll do my best.' Minnie winked conspiratorially. 'And you lay off the booze. Agreed?'

'I'll try,' I told her.

'I thought you stopped for a while?'

'I did.'

'What made you stop?'

I shrugged. How to answer that? Feeling wanted. Being cuddled. Not feeling sorry for myself any more. Any number of answers. Lots of reasons.

'Well, what made you start again?'

I shrugged again. Being lonely. *Missing him.* The absence of hope until I'd written my letter.

'Sephy, you're not Mother. Stop trying to be,' Minnie said.

I started at Minnie's words, staring at her. Is that what I was doing?

'Sephy, please come on,' Mother called out from behind us.

'Bye then.' Minnie bent forward awkwardly and kissed me on the cheek. I couldn't remember the last time she'd done that. I couldn't remember the first time come to that! I headed for the car, still looking around.

He wasn't coming.

Wave goodbye to Dreamland, Sephy. I sat down next to Mother.

'At last!' she said, annoyed.

Oh Callum . . . Why didn't you come? Didn't you believe me? Or maybe you didn't believe in me? Or maybe you were the one who had to have sense enough for both of us. Or maybe you were just scared enough for both of us.

Karl walked around the car to the driver's seat – and we were off.

Callum, why didn't you come?

Callum

Faster. Move. I have to do it. I just have to. Wait. Please wait.

I race like the wind towards Sephy's house. Faster than I've ever run before. As fast as if my life depends on it.

Please God, if you're really up there . . .

I clamber up the rise to the rose garden, just in time to see a car turn out of the security gates. Sephy is in the back, next to her mum. But she's looking down, not at me, not anywhere near me.

Please God . . .

'WAIT! SEPHY, IT'S ME. WAIT!'

Run. Move. I sprint after the car. I stop breathing so drawing breath won't slow me down. Run. Race. Sprint.

'SEPHY . . .'

The car is several metres ahead of me now. The driver's eyes meet mine in the driver's mirror. Sephy's Mercedes accelerates smoothly but noticeably away from me.

'SEPHY . . .' I speed after the car. My lungs are about to implode and every muscle, every bone in my body is on fire. But I'll follow that car to hell and back, if I have to.

If I can.

Please, please God . . .

I trip over my feet and hit the ground face first. Dazed, I look up, but the car is almost out of sight. I grip Sephy's letter in my hand, lying on the ground, listening to the sound of all my hopes and dreams moving further and further away. Like listening to the sound of a door being slammed in my face.

GENTLEWOMAN

BY
LAURA DOCKRILL

1.

'Don't laugh.'

'OK.'

'You're already laughing.'

'That's just my normal face.'

'OK. Can't you just keep a straight face?'

'This is as straight as my face gets.'

'*Please*, Isaac.'

'I'm one of those people who just laughs at bad news. Don't take it personally.'

He's joking. I know he is. But I can't *help* taking everything personally. Like how I think people in clothes shops are saying an overly emphasized *hi* to me when I walk in. A *hi* that is much bigger and prouder than the one they give everybody else. It singles me out: a hi that stands for 'Are you *sure* you're meant to be in *this* shop?'

I suffer from paranoia. I never buy anything.

'This isn't *bad* news.'

'So why are you acting like this?'

'Like what?'

'Like all . . . I dunno . . . not like you used to.'

'Why? What am I acting like? How did I used to be? Because I don't feel like *me*. I don't feel like . . . look, this is why I wanted to talk to you, Isaac. About something.'

'Talk to me then. I'm listening.'

But he isn't listening. He hasn't listened to me for years. He's already ready to leave. Isaac's too simple, too black and white. If there's one thing I've learned through all this, it's people. Understanding them. I know them now. Their mannerisms and habits, their body language.

And I can't do it. I think he *knows* what I'm going to say anyway, or at least suspects, but I can't actually say it. Out loud. Because then it becomes real. A fact. An elephant in the room. And I don't know what he'll think of me after I say it, and once I have, I can't take it back.

I want to prolong this moment; having him in my grasp like this, vulnerable to my secret still. Being the one in charge.

I fold my hair behind my ears. It's really long now. I smile, try to make him feel comfortable. Act normal.

But I don't know what normal is.

Does anybody know what normal is?

I must have been silent for longer than I thought. Isaac rubs his face. We're fifteen now, and he's changed so much. Lost his chubby face. Developed a strong jawline. Stubble, no bum fluff. An Adam's apple. His eyebrows darker, bigger, more spread out. And he has these naturally long eyelashes, like a camel. I don't – I hardly have any eyelashes, but *it's a waste of time to compare*, as Mum says.

'Look, I've got football.'

He gets up to leave. I cross my legs.

'OK. I'll catch you later then.'

'Sure there's nothing you wanna say or whatever?'

'Oh, I can't even remember what it was now.'

'You can't remem— What's going on with you?'

I chew my lip. Chew my nails. I have to stop doing that. I'm meant to be growing them.

'Nothing. I'm sorry. It's been a weird week.'

'Sure?'

'Positive.'

''Cos you can talk to me. If you, you know, like, *need* to.'

'I know. Thanks. Honestly, I'm fine.'

'OK then. Anyways, I gotta bounce. Sure you don't wanna come, at least watch? See the boys?'

'No; thanks though.'

'K. Well, text me if you change your mind.'

Watching football only makes me feel weirder. It reminds me of more things that my brain or body don't like to do. Isaac knows I hate it.

Everything makes me feel weird. School. Eating. Washing. Talking. Even being around people.

The boys have all started to distance themselves from me anyway. Isaac's only stuck around for so long because our mums are friends. He feels obliged. He doesn't have a problem, like me. He's sorted. We have nothing in common except the past.

And I'm already trying to forget that.

We do an awkward handshake before he leaves. He calls me 'bruv'. I watch him wriggle his feet into his worn-down trainers without even untying the laces. He has dirt behind each nail, like he's been digging with his hands. Then I watch the way he opens my front door, says *Later* without even looking me in the face. He can't wait to get out.

'Bye, June!' he calls to my mum, who peeps her head, all flustered, round the kitchen door.

'Oh, going already, are you, Isaac? That was quick.'

'Yeah, I got football.'

'OK, well, come round again soon, for dinner next time. And tell your mum I'll give her a call.'

'Will do. Bye. Bye, Dan.'

'Bye.'

And I watch him, rushing down the garden path as though he's desperate not to be seen coming out of mine. Not looking back. Not even once.

'How did it go?' Mum asks. She wants to hold me, but I won't let her. She knows that.

'It didn't.'

'Oh, Danni.'

'I couldn't.'

'I thought we discussed this?'

'Yeah. Well . . .'

'It's almost ready.'

'I don't want to eat.'

'Danni.'

'What? I'm not hungry.'

'I've already told you: we're not going through with this unless you eat. Remember?'

Her love for me is like a rash. I hate it. It makes my skin crawl. But it's all over me. As close as it can possibly get. It's the only thing that I know is real about me.

'What is it?'

'Chicken. Without the sauce for you. Cooked in the spray oil that you like. And ri—'

'I'm not eating rice.'

'Danni, you're not doing this, not today.'

'I'll eat the chicken. But I'm not eating rice. Is it breast?'

'Yes.'

'I don't want it off the bone.'

'I know that. No flavour what-so-bloody-ever.'

'No salt.'

'I know. Dry as a bone.'

'OK, but no bones? It is breast, isn't it?'

'Yes, of course it's breast. Do you not listen?'

Awkward forever silence.

'I wish you had told him, Dan.'

I wish I had too. But I don't say that. It has to look like my decision. Her words just annoy me.

I boil the kettle. We wait in silence as it boils. The sound of it rushing to a climax is almost too much noise for me to bear.

Of course I wish I had told Isaac too.

Dad walks in. He has been walking Sherbet, our Jack Russell. Dad still kisses my mum when he sees her. He does this now when he enters the kitchen: a kiss on the side of the face, in between the eye and mouth somewhere. I don't see why they have to do that. They only saw each other a couple of hours ago.

I know Mum sent Dad out deliberately to give me space for my 'chat' with Isaac, because usually Sherbet just has to walk himself at this time, in the garden. Dad looks at me with loaded eyes, hoping that I've changed my mind. The way he looks at me every day; hoping he can change my mind.

'All right, Dan?' says Dad, all big and caveman.

'Nni,' Mum adds under her breath for him. 'NNI.' As if her saying it out loud cancels him not saying it.

'*Danni*. Sorry. Are you OK?' The question is a gun, aimed between my eyes.

He takes Sherbet's brace off and Sherby begins hurling himself around the kitchen, rebounding off the cupboard door, excitedly hoping for a meal. It's not his usual mealtime. The walk has thrown him. Poor Sherbet's had his itinerary messed with only for me *not* to do what I set out to do.

The kettle finishes shaking. I reach for my Nescafé sachets. I like the light low-fat ones and I like it that everything is included inside one sachet. I like the way it's neat and tidy and all done for you. The smell of powdered baby milk fills the room with the dense heavy reek of processed caffeine. On the back of the Nescafé box they recommend waiting thirty to forty seconds for your coffee to set before stirring it. To demonstrate this, I guess in case you either don't know what waiting looks like or you can't understand English, they have a picture of a blissfully happy woman with her chin perched proudly on her fist. She is *waiting*. I always think about trying that pose while I'm waiting for my coffee to set, but I never do. Instead I stir it. Incessantly. I'm always fidgeting, you see. I never know what to do with my hands. And then I begin blowing on it automatically, even though I know it's still too hot to sip. The ripples of the coffee froth move like passing clouds. I sip. It's too hot. I sip again. It's still too hot. I know it is.

Dad and I catch eyes. I do that short smile; that one you give when you see a neighbour in the street. Polite, distant acknowledgement.

My coffee gives me something to *do*. I am in control.

I wish we could move somewhere else. But Dad has his job here. And Mum says, *It's not about running away, it's about adjusting*.

I know she still wants me to wait a year. Another

year. But I think I've already waited fifteen years too long. She says the start of college might be a better time, but I don't think there's any good time for a thing like this.

They have a schedule, my parents. Of how it will all work. They have written the jobs in different coloured pens to show who each job is delegated to, so that the *stuff* doesn't lean on one parent too much.

Tablets.

Doctors.

Therapist.

Tablets.

Eyelash implants.

Laser surgery.

More implants.

Hair removal.

Tablets.

Therapist.

Doctors.

Shopping.

Beautician (at home).

Hair stylist (at home).

Laser surgery.

Tablets.

Therapist.

Mum's jobs are written in green and Dad's jobs are written in orange. Mum deliberately chose those colours, I think; colours without identity. Without sex. Without prejudice.

The schedule is mostly covered in green. And even though there is *some* orange pen on the schedule, I've seen him, Dad, drunk, hating me. Hating that he has to even *have* a colour. That there has to *be* a schedule. That I have to *be* Danni. And that there are no brothers and sisters.

Just me.

I was more than enough.

2.

Mrs Swan always said that *God makes no mistakes*.

She calmed us down at the end of the day by making us *sit nicely on the carpet*. We sat nicely by having our *bottoms on the mat* and our *mouths zipped up*.

On the rare occasion that this exercise didn't get results for Mrs Swan, she made us take out an imaginary pair of 'spectacles' from our pockets and unfold them and put them over our eyes.

For some reason, it worked. We'd concentrate in silence. We listened to a story afterwards, and then went home.

There was no opportunity at school to put my hand up in the air and say, 'Mrs Swan, I don't think I am a boy.'

Even if I had, I knew the other kids would laugh at me. Or think I was gross. Or weird. Or trying to be funny. And thinking back, Mrs Swan, as accommodating as she was, wouldn't have a lesson plan up her sleeve for *Identity Crisis*, and wouldn't know what to say to the tiny five-year-old on the carpet. Granted, in that big building, the teachers must have been expecting *one* of us to not feel the gender we were born into – but I'd never *really* thought that person was going to be me. Would you have?

You are on your own, kid.

Years passed and I thought perhaps I should talk to my best friend, Isaac, who I'd known since we were both babies, and our mums were mates too, so I knew I could trust him. But we were both kids and we didn't really *do* talking. So I pretended to laugh at the same jokes with the other boys my age, and I played football and computer games and learned to like girls in the same way that boys do, and hoped it was just a phase that would wear off like a sleeping pill or a bad cold. But Monday rolled into Tuesday and Tuesday into Wednesday and Wednesday into Thursday and weeks into months and months into years and I knew, I knew that my body had let me down and that Mrs Swan was incorrect. That she didn't know everything. And that actually, Mrs Swan, God did make a mistake.

God made me.

3.

I've been wearing this grey tracksuit. It feels like a comfort blanket; a cocoon to wrap myself in until I'm ready to show my new self to the world. Until then, this is all I'll wear. Something brandless, ageless, sexless, comfortable. Sometimes I imagine the same grey will feed up my throat and wrists and hands and feet and cover me completely. Cover everything. We could all just be grey. Uniformed. Then none of this would even matter.

I don't want the little hairs sprouting out of the follicles. The sprawling eyebrows. Sideburns. The snail trail. The armpit and leg hair. The BO. The blackheads. The acne.

I want to be clean. Natural. Effortless. Beautiful. Pretty. A girl. A woman.

After eating in my bedroom with the door closed, I look at my school uniform again. The one I'm going to wear on my first day back. I'd wanted to move schools, but Mum said *Better the devil you know*, which is a weird way of saying that no school is perfect and at least I know what I'm dealing with at the school I'm at now.

The bra is white. Lacy. Pretty, I guess. Boys' underwear is never pretty. It's comedy, if anything. The chicken fillets aren't too big, because I'm skinny and I want to start small first. Mum says I should put on weight, really, that other girls of fifteen are more soft and *squidgy* and that everything would look more natural if I plumped up a bit, but I can't put on weight because I don't want to take up any more space than I already do. I want to go unnoticed, to slip through school like a ghost. A shadow. Just to fit in.

I'm going to wear the skirt. At my school it's OK for girls to wear trousers too, but if I'm going to start the new year as *Danni* I can't be in this in-between phase any more. They all know I'm different by now, anyway. I haven't used the *Boys* or the *Girls* toilet for months; I use the disabled toilet and I go there to change for PE, too. I have to stick to this rule even when I go back, because I haven't had my op yet.

I have a complex about not acting 'too female' in front of my friends or the wrong company and then I beat myself up about hiding my femininity and true self when I'm alone. Then, because of the self-guilt, I practise being me for when I *get* to be me; how I should speak, sit, hold cutlery, walk.

That kind of hyper hawking can send a person crazy.

I know Isaac knows. I'm sure of it, even though he hasn't ever said. And Luke. And James. And Lee. And Eddie. And Andre. And Callum. And all the other boys that put up with hanging out with me because of Isaac. I'm sure they all know, because when you've got a different person living on the inside to what's on the outside, it's not easy to go around unnoticed. I guess they think there's enough of them being all *masculine* and *macho* and *alpha male* and that it cancels me out. I'm a glitch. I know that.

Sometimes I think it would be easier for me if I didn't have Isaac, because I could just make this change without having to think about how it will affect him. His reputation. His relationship with me.

And then there's her . . .

4.

'I like you.'

'I like you too.'

'You don't act like it.'

'I'm sorry.'

'Why do you always say sorry so much?'

'Sorry. *Sorry*. I just said it again, didn't I?'

'Yeah. I can't help but feel like there's so much more to you than the others.'

'Yeah?'

'Yeah. I can't explain. You're just more *gentle*.'

'Sure it isn't just my hair that gives that impression?'

'Hahaha! I know, it is good hair.'

Sara kissed me on the mouth. She tasted of coconut lip balm. Her lips were soft. I was shy, my mouth loose. Tender. Like a two-day-old bruise.

'Did I do something wrong?'

'No! Not at all. Sor—'

'I thought you liked me?'

'I do! I do. Sara, I *really* do.'

'This has been going on for too long though now, Dan. I'm sick of this "Will they, won't they?" Everybody keeps asking me what's going on between us. It's getting embarrassing. I sit on your front wall every day before school and wait for you like a total mug.'

'I like it that you sit on my wall.'

'Yeah, I do too, but everyone must be laughing at me! So desperate! Like some stalker!'

'Why do we have to care what everybody else thinks about us?'

'We don't. We don't. But I care. I want you to be my boyfriend. I want you to be my boyfriend, Dan.'

I LIKE YOU SO MUCH. I NEVER WANT YOU TO NOT SIT ON MY FRONT WALL. **YOU SAY YOU LIKE ME** BUT IT IS **NOT ME THAT YOU LIKE**. YOU DO **NOT** KNOW ME BECAUSE I AM **NOT** ME. NOT IN FRONT OF YOU. AND I AM TOO AFRAID TO SHOW YOU WHO I AM BECAUSE I AM TERRIFIED THAT YOU WILL NEVER SHOW YOURSELF TO ME AGAIN ONCE I DO. AND I DON'T WANT TO LOSE YOU. AND **RIGHT NOW I AM CHOOSING YOU OVER ME BY NOT BEING ME.**

I wanted to say this, but I didn't. I just got up. Sara's eyes searched me for an answer. For a decision. She's popular. She has friends she could talk to about what a dick I am, and they will nod their heads and agree. I don't have that privilege. I *could* tell Isaac how she kissed me and I went like a cold wet fish and he and the boys would laugh about what a pussy I've been.

HA. HA. HA.

I walked away, feeling sick and gross, licking my lips from her coconut balm. Then I changed my mind and used my sleeve to wipe her kisses off. The way she'd do when she found me out.

I was always less worried about what the girls at school would think. The girls were easier. They were more understanding with me, said I was a *gentleman* because I was sensitive, took my time. I wasn't a gentleman. Not at all. I was a gentle*woman*, if anything. The boys were worse; they'd all just decided I was frigid or gay. Gay was easier for them. Gay was a pigeonhole. But I hated being called gay, because . . . well, because I kind of was, really. If you thought about it. They were right, they just didn't know it.

I wanted to kiss girls. I fancied girls. I wanted to sleep with Sara. Truth be told, I wanted Sara to be my girlfriend.

But if Sara was my girlfriend, it would mean Sara being a lesbian. I guess. And she didn't even know it.

And the only way I was going to get close to Sara was to stay as Dan. Dan the gentleman. Dan who she fancied. Not Danni, who I really was inside.

It was all so much to digest. Not only was I a girl: I was a girl that was attracted to girls. Could I have drawn a shorter straw?

I didn't feel gay. But then, what does gay feel like?

A girl who was born a boy and was in love with a girl who loved the boy she *wasn't* – not the girl she was.

I just wanted to be accepted. But it seemed too much to ask.

5.

Dear . . . . . . ,

The reason for this letter may be a little unexpected and out of the blue. We wanted to write to you all personally, and we felt a letter was the truest way to give you this news.

As you know, we are very proud of Dan and love him very much. Although Dan has had a wonderful childhood and is growing up to be the adult we always hoped (and more!), something has not sat right with Dan since a young age. I think we always knew that Dan was different and unique, special for all the right reasons, and it has been a great weight off our shoulders to understand what that issue was.

From now onwards, Dan would like to be known as Danni and would like to be referred to as 'she'. This change is making Danni much more confident and happy already and that, in turn, is making us a happier family too. You will notice some changes in Danni in the coming weeks, and some of you that we have the pleasure of seeing more regularly will have noticed some changes already. We trust you will be sensitive and supportive about these changes and treat Danni no differently to anybody else.

We feel very fortunate to have the pleasure of watching a healthy young person find their brave way in the world, and in no way do we feel we have lost Dan. It's always been Danni. It's just Danni.

Please don't be a stranger; Danni would love to hear from all of you.

Lots of love and hope to see you soon,

June and David x

I watch Mum stack the letters up. I don't see it as anybody else's business, to be honest, but Mum says that people are very simple, simpler than you think, and that if they believe they are invited to be a part of something, then they will back it. Support it. It's about involving them.

Sara hasn't come to sit on my wall once since I walked away from her that day after the kiss. So there's nothing to lose now. Still, I feel sick. The white envelopes look like bank letters. Buying envelopes was a 'colour orange' job, so I think that was Dad's doing. Making this reality as disconnected as humanly possible.

Together with Sherby, we post the letters. I start to panic. Once I saw somebody pour a can of Sprite into the postbox. What if somebody does that this week and all my letters get drenched and ruined? Or would that be better?

I start to care. *Really* care, about everybody and what they're going to think of me.

It isn't my fault that there was a mix-up. Maybe I was wired wrong, or incomplete? Or maybe I was *meant* to have this challenge? This obstacle?

The letters leave our hands like confetti. There's no going back.

I see Sara and her friends catching the bus into central. Sara's long hair hangs down around her chest and shoulders. She has a freckle under her brown eyes. She wears bright colours. She is always laughing. She wears coconut lip balm and her teeth are wonky. When she finds something funny she grips her hand around your wrist like she needs something to hold onto, just in case she floats away. Her nose scrunches up.

She sees me from across the road and waves politely.

Her friends sort of wave too. I am a dick, remember.

And I'm glad I'm wearing a grey tracksuit today, with no personality. I want to clutch the air and keep this moment. It's the last time she'll look at me like that.

Mum says we should go and get some pizza and expresses her desperation for a glass of Sauvignon while I decide it's time to write a letter myself.

Dear Sara,
I'm sorry this has taken so long to explain. It's just, I'm sure you've probably noticed some changes in me over the last couple of years and thought, What the hell is going on with D—

I scrunch that one into a ball and start again.

Dear Sara,
You know how much you mean to me. I'm sorry I was so rude when you—

ARRRHHGHHHHH. NO. NO.

Dear Sara,
I'm so glad I'm writing to an open-minded person, like yourself—

OH, WHAT A WANKER. SHUT UP!

Dear Sara,
I know I've been weird recently. I'm weird because I am not who you think I am—

OH, NO. I'M JUST A SERIAL KILLER? NO. NO.

Dear Sara,
I am not the 15-year-old boy, Dan, that you think I am.

> My name is Danni and I am 15 and I am a girl.
> I have love- NO- liked you for the past-

I rip it up. I know she will never sit on my front wall again, like she used to before school. I know I will never know her again.

6.

I know the letters have been received because we get one back and we're even sent some flowers, as though I've died. The letter asks:

Is this the right choice as a mother?

Are you sure Dan isn't too young?

Has he had enough time to think about it?

And it's from a woman that Mum really likes at her work. Mum's hurt.

'What a load of bullshit!' Mum rips the letter up right in front of me. 'She lives in the dinosaur years!' She throws the letter in the bin but then clenches her forehead, which sometimes wears lines that tell another story. Of fear, maybe. Or doubt. But she's my mum.

Dad rolls his eyes. He's thinking, *That woman is right*, but holds his tongue, the way he hasn't held me for years.

I still haven't heard from Isaac. They would have got a letter. I try to call and text, but no response. Mum calls his mum too, to ask about him, even though I ask her not to.

Isaac's mum says, 'You know what the summer

holidays are like, June, they're out more than in, you barely see them!'

And Mum looks at me on the same spot on the couch wearing that same grey tracksuit, that sexless hybrid middle ground, like a deep fog that's never going to lift, and fake laughs. 'Yeah, tell me about it. Just get him to give Danni a call when he can.'

The night before my first day back at school I am a mess. Six weeks is long enough to change, but it's also long enough to go insane. Forty-two days of difference and denial, of going through the motions when you're not even sure what the motions really are, and nobody has replied to your messages and nobody has called you back. And then I get a message, from Isaac.

> Hi Danni, obviously things are really
> different, happy to still be your mate,
> like online and that and if you're
> ever in trouble, then just call. Isaac.

I calmly read the message. I feel sick. I brush my hair. Then I wash it again, because I've brushed it and played with it so much that it's gone greasy.

I make the shower really hot. Female shower products are much more fruity than male shower products, all berries blasting and mangoes crushing and lavender in the wind, but they don't make me feel as clean so I always opt for scentless body wash.

The hot water pounds on my back. I think of Sara. Then I wash the thoughts away like grains of sand after a day at the beach.

I dry myself with a clean towel. I catch my reflection in the mirror. My hair is long. I am pale. I am scrawny. I am tired-looking. My ribs show. I don't look like a boy. I don't look like a girl. I look unfinished. An unfinished alien. One that Sara will never be attracted to. One that Isaac will never get along with. One that my parents will never be proud of.

They peel me off the floor, my parents. In front of the mirror. Collapsed. I must look like a broken tree. I am shivering.

'It's OK. I've got you. I've got you,' says my mum and her touch stings my skin but I know it's what has to happen and even though I hate it I can't tell her to stop, and Dad begins to cry even louder than me because he hasn't seen me naked in so many years and that's what makes me stop crying and before I know it, he pulls me in, like a tiny baby. And we cry together.

'I am sorry,' he says. 'You are my baby. You will always be my baby. I love you. I haven't been a very good dad to you, Danni. I am sorry.'

7.
I wear the bra and the fillets. They feel weird and the bra feels tight, but it's OK. I have practised.

The skirt is actually more comfortable than the trousers, but I don't really like the tights. They're itchy and blue, like the tights the other girls wear.

I wear my hair down. My eyes are open. The lash implants have made a big difference. My brows are smooth, aligned. I apply just a little bronzer and blush to my face, and some lip salve; a plain-flavoured one for now.

I am beautiful, I think. *Natural. Myself.* I can see it now. Even though I've rehearsed before, now it's for real. I can't believe it's me. I feel lighter. Breezier.

Like myself.

School has been prepped about my change. Apparently they've been *really good,* according to Mum. So they should. My behaviour has always been impeccable.

'Ready, Danni?' Dad asks as we leave the house.

'Ready,' I say, and he squeezes my hand and opens the front door.

Sara is sitting on the wall outside mine. Just like she used to. She hasn't changed. My heart is smashing against my chest. My heart, which has always been the same.

'I'll walk with her,' Sara says, and Dad looks at me to see if that's something I want to do.

She loops her arm in mine and, linking, we walk to school. A change in the weather brings falling leaves that dance behind us in relief.

FROM
HEROIC

BY
PHIL EARLE

Sonny

So you probably want to know who the girl in the crowd was. And that's fine by me. I could talk about Cameron Thompson all day long. Although, inevitably, thoughts of her bring me back to Jammy, and another of his commandments.

Thou shalt not cop off with thy mate's sister.

Keeping to this was proving more difficult than the stealing one.

I mean firstly, they wouldn't have got away with this in Jerusalem or wherever Moses was when his hormones kicked in, and secondly, it was clearly aimed at Cam, as there's only Wiggy who also has a sister.

No disrespect to Tina or anything, but she's . . . ample. So big there's a health warning tattooed under her bra strap about the danger of suffocation.

Don't get me wrong, she's a nice girl, big heart,

big everything really, but she's not interested in me, and frankly, phew, ditto and amen to that.

Cam on the other hand is . . . well, it's impossible to explain. She's just Cam.

A stupid, gorgeous, tough, quirky mess of contradictions.

People who don't live on the estate would tell you she's typical of a girl from the Ghost, that she's brassy and confrontational. But if you actually watch her, I mean *really* watch her, you'll see that she's never the first to speak. All right, she'll fight her corner if pushed, in fact she's tastier with her fists than any of the lads from the west side of town. But you'll never see her strike first, only strike back.

That's *one* of the things that makes her rock my entire world, but by no means all of it.

I mean, the girl is fit. Tall without being lanky or scrawny, everything in the right place, without her ever feeling the need to flaunt it like others I could mention.

She's everything I'm not, basically, and for that reason I always reckoned she was leagues above me. She's Man Utd to my Grimsby Town. If any of us were ever going to stand a chance with her, it was Jammy.

Which is why the whole thing messes with my head on such an epic scale.

No one knows about it of course. Not Wiggy, Hitch or Den, and especially not Jammy or Tommo. Though if it did get out, the news wouldn't take long to reach them. Ghost estate gossip could easily reach Afghanistan, believe me.

I tried to work out who would be most hacked off if they heard, Tommo or Jamm. Tommo's her brother, after all, so you might say him, but the rules belong to Jammy, so he'd probably try and come down hard to mark his territory.

I thought about it for a few minutes then gave up. It wasn't like I signed a contract or anything, and I didn't chase it either. These things just happen sometimes. And when they do? Well, you just have to roll with it, don't you?

You see, Cam and Tommo's situation is complicated.

Actually, that's not true. It's not complicated at all, they just have a disgrace for a dad. The kind of disgrace who likes to hide behind his drink; the kind who can't hold his beer by the end of the night, because by then his hands have clenched into fists. Fists he can't straighten out until they've had a go on someone who he's supposed to love.

It's when I see his ratty face that I'm glad I don't have an old man of my own. He'd only disappoint me too.

We've known about what Larry does for years, how he rules the house and how the drink rules him, but it's not like we can do anything about it. Police aren't interested unless someone in the family makes a statement, and the chances of that, knowing the beating that would follow? Well. It's never going to happen.

I often wondered if that was the reason for Tommo joining up. He'd never gone on about the army before. Maybe he'd just had one too many pastings from Larry. I don't mean he signed up out of fear. Tommo wasn't scared of his dad. He'd often take one for the team. Two black eyes and a split lip meant his ma and Cam were left alone. No, he might've followed Jamm because he was about to snap and put the idiot in the hospital. And if he did that? Well, Larry would have no problem dialling 999.

The issue I had with him going to Afghanistan was Cam. I mean, if she was my sister, there's no way I'd leave and put her next in the firing line.

But Tommo had his reasons, and he's sound. One of us. An Original.

On the day he left with the rest of them, I saw his face. What it meant. I could see some of the other soldiers, all screwed up out of fear for themselves, wondering whether they'd ever come back. I'm sure Tomm was feeling that too. But the way he held on to Cam, the way their bodies shook without a word? It said everything I needed to know, and what I needed to do.

I know what you're thinking when you hear all this. That I engineered it, me and her. But that's not how it happened. First week I dropped her a few texts:

```
how u doing?
```

Nothing heavier. Responses were brief.

```
Fine.
```

```
All gud.
```

Then everything changed with a knock at the door about two and a half weeks in. Listen to me being vague. I know exactly when it was. Eighteen days after they left. It was a Wednesday. Three in the afternoon.

I'd not been in long, still burning up after a run in the heat. It wasn't a clear-your-head-and-keep-fit kind of run, more the if-you-stop-you'll-have-your-head-caved-in variety, but either way, I was sweating. Shirt off and Coke in hand, I'd collapsed in front of the box and was surfing for something to watch. The knock was irritating, but not for long. Not when I saw who it was through the frosted glass.

'Can I come in?' Her words were out before the door was fully open, before I had time to stick my pecs out and pull my stomach in.

'Course,' I said, resisting the urge to sniff my pits.

'Sorry to barge in,' she went on, turning to face me.

Her cheeks and eyes were red, the top of her chest above her vest was blotchy. Instantly I thought of Larry, of rearranging his face.

'What's up?' I offered her the chair but she wouldn't sit. 'Is it your dad? What's he done?'

Reaching for my phone I scrolled for Den's number. He was the biggest of all of us, the one you wanted at your shoulder when it all went down.

'It's not Dad. I haven't seen him for days. He does this, goes under for a week or so then pitches up like nothing's happened. Longer he's face down in a pint, the better.'

'Then what's up? What's going on?'

Her face dissolved. Not in a pathetic way. She could never be that.

'It's the telly. The news. I've barely switched it off since Tommo went. It's on twenty-four hours. Always about bombs and shootings. I want to turn it off and leave the house, Sonny, but I can't. I keep thinking if I leave it on I'll catch a glimpse of him, and be happy. But he never shows up, and now there's reports of another explosion. One of those improvised ones. The worst yet. Then they said where it was and I couldn't remember if it was the same place that Tommo and Jamm went . . .'

No more words came. She just swayed and looked at me, so scared she couldn't even manage to wipe the smudged tears that fell to the carpet.

I didn't know what to do. Hold her, calm her, stick the news on myself? I daren't do any of them for very different reasons, but had to pick one, so I stabbed at the remote until I reached News24.

As the camera settled on a raging cloud of smoke, I felt nerves prickle across my chest.

It summed up why I'd been resisting the news ever since they left. It was bad enough the scenarios playing out in my head without being confronted with it on the TV too.

I thought about others on the estate going through the same thing. Young mums little older than us, their kids screaming as Daddy left for Helmand. They told me about stuff they did to keep the little ones calm. Jars full of sweets: a Smartie for every day Daddy was away. And when the jar was empty? Then Daddy would be home.

It seemed so simple. Made me wish I was ten years younger and a hundred times more innocent.

It was clearly getting to Cam. She wasn't blinking as she stared at the screen. She didn't even react when the newsreader told us that the family of the blown-up soldier had been informed. All she did was pull the phone from her pocket and jab at the keypad before pushing it to her ear.

'Mum?' Her voice was calmer than when she'd been talking to me. 'Anyone been in touch?'

I presumed the answer was no as she exhaled loudly and slumped on to the settee, hanging up in the process. Immediately I checked my own mobile. Couldn't face the prospect of a missed call from Mum.

'I never understood why they always said that stuff about families being informed,' she gasped. 'I do now.

It's so idiots like me can stop bricking themselves 24/7.' She looked angry at herself, which I wasn't going to have.

'Give yourself a break. It's not easy, I know that.'

'I can't help it, though, Sonny. I can't walk past a newsagent without looking at every page in every rag, just in case I've missed something. If there's a telly in a shop, I'll watch it till the news rolls round to the start again.'

'I understand. I do. But you've got to try not to worry. It's not like we can do anything about it, except trust they'll look after each other.'

I thought for a second that her face had softened from panic to mild dread. It didn't last long.

'Do you ever find yourself Googling Jamm's name? In case it's leaked on to the web before it reaches the news on TV? I try to stop myself but it's . . .'

'*Hey!*' I interrupted, then let my voice soften. 'It's OK. I get it.' I really did, but had no idea how to make it any easier for her. So I did what I always do and winged it.

'Look at us. All of us, and the scrapes we've got through to be here. All right, it's not easy, but we're still in one piece despite it all. That's why I reckon they'll be all right. There're as many knives here as there are guns over there, and there's none sticking out of us yet, are there? They'll be all right if we are.'

I made a joke of it, patting for an imaginary blade across my shoulders and hers. My fingers turned pure electric as my skin touched hers, especially when she didn't flinch. I left them there, squeezing gently as Jamm disappeared from my head for the first time in weeks.

'And we are all right, aren't we?' she asked, eyes all the more magnetic for the make-up smudged around them.

I felt brave. Don't know why or how, but for once, around her, I felt invincible.

'You tell me? I reckon so.'

And that was it. The gap between us disappeared. Not because I lunged or took advantage. It just happened. And happened. And happened. The footage on the news disappeared. Jamm and Tommo were looking the other way, for now at least.

Breaking a rule had never felt so good.

MISS LUCY HAD A STEAMBOAT

BY
DAVID LEVITHAN

The minute I saw Ashley, I thought, *Oh shit. Trouble.*

You have to understand: I grew up in a house where my mother told me on an almost daily basis that until I got married, my pussy was for peeing. In her world, all lesbians talked like Hillary Clinton and looked like Bill, and that included Rosie O'Donnell especially. My mother didn't know any lesbians personally, and she didn't want to know any, either. She was so oblivious that she stayed up nights worrying that I was going to get myself pregnant. There was no way to tell her the only way *that* was going to happen was if God himself knocked me up.

Luckily, I'd learned that the best defence against such holeheaded thinking was to find everything funny. Like the fact that all the sports teams in our school – even the girls' teams – were called Minutemen. All you had to do was pronounce the first part of that word 'my-newt' and it was funny, like suddenly our football team had *Tiny Dicks* written on their jerseys. Or the fact that in the past calendar year, my mother had hit so many mailboxes, deer, and side mirrors that her licence had been suspended. I chose to think she did it on purpose, just so I'd have to drive her around and hear her advice on boys, school, and how bad my hair looked. Hysterical. And, best of all for a quick laugh, there was Lily White – that was her name, swear to God – who certainly enjoyed kissing me in secret. But then when I brought up the idea of, hey, maybe doing it outside of her house, she shut down the whole thing and said to me, 'None of this happened.'

Well, I knew a punch line when I saw one. So the next day at lunch, when no one was looking, I spilled her Diet Coke all over her fancy shirt and said, 'None of this happened.' And the next day, my bumper just happened to ram into the side of her daddygirl Cadillac. I left her a note: *None of this happened*. And it didn't happen the next day, either.

I, for one, was amused.

It was hard for me not to feel a little stupid about Lily White. Not because it ended or that it had gone on for three months, but because I'd started it in the first place. Lily was the popularity equivalent of a B-minus student – never the brightest bulb in the room, but still lit. She never laughed at a joke until she saw other people laughing at it, too. Even when we were kissing, she never seemed to admit that we were kissing – it was like I was saying something she couldn't hear, and she was just nodding along to be polite. The first time we got together, it had less to do with romance and more to do with Miller Lite. It took just two cans for her to turn playful. We kissed; it was nice. And for three months we pretty much stuck to that. The kissing was hot, but Lily was pretty insistent about not letting the fire spread. Every time I tried to take her clothes off, she suddenly had somewhere else to be. Every time I felt her up, she acted like my hands were cold. And every time I tried to go near her pussy, it jumped away.

I could lie and say I swore I was through with girls, but really I figured I needed to find someone better than Lily White. When Ashley Cooper came to town, I was primed.

She made one hell of an entrance.

She was ten minutes late to homeroom, because in her old school homeroom was at 8 and in our school it was at 7:50. Nobody'd told us there was going to be a new girl; they never do.

What I'm saying is: I wasn't expecting her. Then suddenly there was this girl in front of our class, trying to explain to Mr Partridge who she was, only Mr Partridge hadn't heard a complete sentence since he was eighty, which was a long time ago. He was telling her she was late, and that he was going to mark her down for being late. She made the mistake of asking him if he even knew who she was, and he shot her a look like she'd just told him that World War II was over. Then he shook his head and said, 'Sit down, Antonia.'

Man, she looked awesome. Short red hair, full full lips, shirt so tight you could check for tattoos underneath. Most of us put up with Mr. Partridge when we had him for history because at the end of each marking period we could steal his marking book, change the grades, and know we'd be getting As. But Ashley wasn't the type to let it go. 'Who's Antonia?' she asked. 'I'm not Antonia.'

'Hell you're not,' Mr Partridge chided. 'Sit down!'

I thought she'd storm back out; she had that pose. But instead she turned to the class – we were all treating this like gossip unfolding before our eyes – and said, 'Who *the fuck* is Antonia?'

I was so snagged. There was no way I could say something to her. But there was no way I could ignore her, either.

'Antonia's my sister,' I said.

Ashley walked over to me.

'Do I look like her?' she asked.

'No,' I told her – it was really the truth. 'But I don't look like her, either, and that's what he calls me all the time.'

'So he thinks I'm you?' She didn't sound offended by this, which was a start.

'He's looking forward to the day that a man walks on the moon,' I replied. 'Don't take it personally.'

'I try not to take anything personally, Antonia's sister.'

I had looked at her eyes for a split second, but now I was looking at her arm. The light from the window was hitting it and I couldn't stop staring. I'll admit it – I have a thing for a little hair on a girl's arm. Not head hair or anything like that – just that soft, translucent hair that looks like a spider wove it. She had that, and some freckles, too.

'You're new here,' I said. I mean, duh.

'It shows?' she said in a dumb-little-girl voice. She tilted her head to the rest of the class. 'Do they always stare like that?'

'I'm not sure they've ever seen a nose ring before. They probably think you're from MTV.'

I don't think Ashley was expecting me to joke. Her laugh caught even her by surprise. She kinda laughed like a barking seal. It wasn't very cute, but it was definitely sexy that she didn't care.

'I'm starting to see why Mr Ancient up there thought I was you.'

If she'd asked me to jump her right then and there, I swear I would've. It's like my mind and my body had the same voice, and they were both yelling, *Hell, yeah*. The only difference being that my mind, which knew a little better, added, *Oh shit. Trouble*.

'So do I get your real name?' she asked as the bell rang and we had to head to class.

'Lucy,' I told her.

'I'll be seeing you around, Miss Lucy,' she said.

That sealed it. I was completely in danger of falling in love.

Nobody'd ever called me Miss Lucy like that before.

Only a certain kind of girl could make *Miss Lucy* sound tough.

There's some history here.

With all due respect to my mother (although I'm not sure how much respect she's truly due), Lucy has never been the right name for me. The role models were all wrong. Like Lucy from the *Peanuts* comics. Okay, so she was probably a lesbian. I mean, her brother's gay (thumbsucker!) and Schroeder, the boy she pretends to have a crush on, is so gay it hurts my teeth. Plus she's friends with Peppermint Patty and Marcie, whose relationship has lasted longer than my grandparents'. But even if she was a lesbian, I wasn't going to be like Lucy. I didn't want to be. You get a sense from watching her that she's going to end up being somebody's evil boss.

And then, of course, there was Lucy Ricardo from *I Love Lucy.* I wanted to love Lucy, really I did. I kept waiting for the episode where Lucy and Ethel finally ran off together and made out. But eventually I realized that wasn't going to happen. Lucy was scatterbrained like me, all right, and I could definitely relate to the way everything she touched turned into a complete mess. But I knew I'd last a whole five minutes with a guy like Ricky. Maybe not even that. I understood that deep down he was supposed to love her and all, but most of the time I found him to be a whining prick. I'd been there – thank you, Lucy – and I had no intention to go back again.

That left me with the only famous Lucy remaining: the one who had a steamboat. She came into my life in the same way she comes into most girls' lives – at recess. I was in second grade, and the second-grade girls were sharing the pavement with the fourth-grade girls – the fourth-grade girls being, in my second-grade eyes, girls of infinite wisdom and certitude. I never would have gotten close enough to hear a single word the fourth-grade girls said, but Mrs Shedlow, the recess supervisor, was a firm believer in democracy, so she'd lined us up second-fourth, second-fourth for the jump-roping. She took one end of the rope and Rachel Cullins's older sister, Eve took the other. My friend Grace was the first girl to jump, and the rhyme she got was a familiar one:

> *Strawberry shortcake*
> *Cream on the top*
> *Tell me the name*
> *of your sweet heart.*
> *Is it A . . . B . . . C . . . ?*

Grace's foot hit the rope on B, shackling her in

eternal devotion to Barry Lefner for at least the next ten minutes. A fourth-grade girl got to R. But most of the second-grade girls couldn't make it past Evan Eager. I don't know if it was the fact that we were exhausting the alphabetically early boys, or whether it was because Eve knew my name since I was friends with Rachel, but whatever the case, when the rope started turning for me, the strawberry shortcake was sent back to the kitchen, and Miss Lucy sailed right in.

> *Miss Lucy had a steamboat*
> *The steamboat had a bell*
> *Miss Lucy went to heaven*
> *And the steamboat went to*

At this point I tripped up in a downward direction, skinning my knee and coming way too close to smudging my favourite shirt. When the next girl went, the shortcake had returned. I walked over to Rachel and asked her who Miss Lucy was.

Now, of all the Cullins sisters, Rachel was always the one to blush fastest. And I'm sure just the mention of Miss Lucy was enough to make her feel like the worst kind of sinner. There was no way she could share the rhyme with me. No decent girl would. My older sister, Antonia, certainly wouldn't. She was already in junior high, planning her hypothetical wedding day.

Luckily, a girl named Heron overheard my

question. Heron was fairly new to our school, and generally untested. When Mrs Park had introduced her to the class, she'd said Heron's name was 'Hero . . . with an n.' That set Heron back a couple of months. She wore clothes – even then – that seemed like hand-me-downs from when her mother had been in second grade. I didn't know what to make of her.

'C'mere,' she said to me now.

Curious, I obliged. She told me to sit down with my legs making a wide V. (Don't worry: I was wearing pants.) Then she sat across from me and touched her feet to mine. She started to make a patty-cake patty-cake motion, and I knew that I was supposed to clap my hands to hers according to a certain order. So far, so good.

'It's like this,' she said. And then she presented me with my last possible role model.

Miss Lucy had a steamboat
The steamboat had a bell
Miss Lucy went to heaven
And the steamboat went to
Hello, operator
Please give me number nine
And if you disconnect me,
I'll chop off your
Behind the 'frigerator
There was a piece of glass
Miss Lucy sat upon it

And it went right up her
Ask me no more questions
And I'll tell you no more lies
The boys are in the bathroom
Zipping up their
Flies are in the belfry
And bees are in the park
And boys and girls are kissing
In the D-A-R-K
D-A-R-K
D-A-R-K
DARK DARK DARK

It's not a rhyme, because it doesn't really rhyme. It's not a song, because there's no real music. It's not a limerick because it's not Irish. At some point, I guess I just started thinking of it as a biography.

By the time I got to senior year of high school, I figured I'd run Miss Lucy's story in my head at least a thousand times. In the beginning it was a source of endless amusement. Then it was one of my earliest pieces of nostalgia – when I was a sixth grader, I used it to remember the fond innocence of second grade. Then it became a place my mind went from time to time. Science class boring? Well, Miss Lucy had a steamboat. Dying to get off the phone with the friend who won't shut up? Miss Lucy had a steamboat. Stuck in the car while Mom runs in for the dry cleaning? Miss Lucy had a steamboat.

I had no idea what it meant. That was the beauty of it.

I could relate to Miss Lucy because her life made absolutely no sense.

I'd say I was itching to see Ashley again after our first brief conversation, but an itch is something you can scratch, while absence is something you can't really do shit about. She wasn't in any of my classes; since I was in all of the average classes, this meant she was either really smart or really dumb. There was a slim chance she'd just decided this place wasn't for her and had left after homeroom. But that wasn't the option I was hoping for when lunch began.

'You misplace your attention span?' my best friend, Teddy, asked when he caught me looking around.

'There's this new girl,' I said.

Teddy snorted. 'Now, that didn't take long, did it?'

Teddy was once the new kid, too. He was born in California, but he spent most of elementary school in Korea. Then his parents moved back to California when he was in sixth grade. In tenth grade, they moved again, this time to our town. That's when I met him – the first day of tenth grade. I hated him almost instantly.

His first words to me were 'If you're not a [not nice word for lesbian], you sure as hell dress like one.'

I must've immediately looked miffed, because he

quickly added, 'Hey, to me [not nice word for lesbian] is an affectionate term. After all, I'm a big ol' [rather sexually explicit word for a gay man].'

I wasn't ready for terms, affectionate or otherwise from him. I was still coming to terms with myself, dealing with the anxiety and disappointment and exhilaration of being into girls. I tried avoiding him for months. It didn't work.

'You got it bad, and that ain't good,' he said to me now.

'She called me Miss Lucy,' I told him.

This made Heron, also at our table, perk up. She'd been reading. She was always reading. She was the only person I knew who'd gotten carpal tunnel syndrome from holding books for too long.

'Miss Lucy is our thing,' she said. She wasn't saying it out of jealousy or possessiveness. It was like she wanted to remind herself.

'Where is she?' I asked Teddy. 'Use your gaydar.'

'You *know* gaydar isn't like air-traffic control,' he tsked. 'The person actually has to be in the room.'

'Well, she's not here,' I said. 'So I'm going to find her.'

'That's ballsy,' Teddy said.

I looked to Heron for some help.

'Why not?' she said. That was her version of advice.

As I left the cafeteria, it became a test: if I found her, surely that was a sign that things were meant to be. Granted, the sign wouldn't really spell out what those things were — it would be like a street sign that said stuff ahead. But that was good enough for me.

I found her in the parking lot, leaning on a blue car, eating French fries.

'I had to reward myself for surviving this morning,' she explained, offering me some.

'That bad?' I asked, taking a few.

'Yeah, but not without its prospects.'

I was so used to being the brazen one that I just about flipped to have someone be brazen in my direction.

'Prospects, eh?' I said, fishing for confirmation.

'Yes, Miss Lucy,' she replied, stretching away from the car, toward me. 'And I believe the afternoon's already getting better.'

You should never kiss someone in the first ten minutes. I know that now, but back then it just seemed like nine minutes too long to wait.

'So, are you girlfriends or what?' Teddy asked me, three weeks after Ashley and I started our thing.

The only place I called her *girlfriend* was in my head. Sometimes I'd say it about a million dozen times in a row, staring at her in class. I wasn't secret about it or anything. Hunger is something you can't hide.

'I dunno,' I told him. 'I think I'm her girlfriend, and I guess she's mine. We don't talk about it.'

'If you're not girlfriends, then what are you?' he pestered.

I didn't tell him the answer, because I was too proud of it and also a little embarrassed by my pride.

Even if I wasn't her girlfriend, I was definitely her Miss Lucy.

'Come over here, Miss Lucy, and give me a hand,' she'd say, and I'd be over in a flash, whether it was to sort out her locker, fill in her homework, or unhook her bra.

'I like you, Miss Lucy,' she'd tell me, and I'd have to do everything I could not to lob a *love* back at her.

But she could tell. Oh, she could tell.

Lily White could also tell. She could try to hide herself in the cheer squad at lunch or look away when she got near my locker, but damned if the news didn't spread to her ears anyway. I made sure to smile extra wide whenever I saw her. One time, Ashley gave me a big ol' love bite, right under the collar. That day, when I was passing Lily White in the hall, I couldn't help myself. Right when she was looking at me, I pulled the collar down a little to show her.

'That's gross,' she said.

'Didn't happen,' I told her.

Nobody'd ever bothered to tell me that if you get too caught up in running away from the wolf, you end up in the arms of the bear.

As for Lily White, a few days later she started dating Pete, who was much much nicer than me. But I doubted he was as good a kisser.

'You're a great kisser,' Ashley would say.

'Miss Lucy, I'd be lost in this town without you,' she'd tell me.

'You're so pretty,' she'd swear.

The things she'd do to me, I'd never even had the imagination to imagine.

'When's she going to hang out with us?' Teddy would ask. 'Why do the two of you always have to be alone?'

I didn't know how to explain it to him. 'It's not that she doesn't like you—' I started.

'How could she? She's never really *met* us.'

'She just wants to spend her time with me. Is that so wrong?'

'Yes,' Teddy said. 'Like this, it is.'

Heron didn't say a word.

'I'm through with you,' I said. 'Can't you think about me for once?'

'You're doing enough of that for all of us,' Teddy shot back.

'Forget it. Forget all of it,' I said, grabbing my backpack and storming out to the parking lot. I thought I'd find her there, but her car was gone.

'Where are you?' I asked, then felt stupid for doing it.

I didn't go back to the cafeteria. I found my own space, sitting on the floor around the corner from the gym.

I told myself the emptiness I felt was the space hollowed out from missing her. A negative space that was positive. The loss that meant I had something to lose.

I desperately wanted to have something to lose.

Mostly we stayed in places that were public or possibly public – we'd move items from aisle to aisle in Target, trying to come up with the sickest combinations possible, like putting condoms next to the Barbie dolls or hemorrhoid cream with the toothpaste. We'd sneak into crap movies and try to find the characters' crap lines for them. Then we'd make out in her car and hope nobody came by. We steamed up the windows so much that I could trace hearts in them afterward. Her initials looked good with mine.

My mother couldn't stand it. She needed me to drive her around and listen to her carry on about the sorry state of the world (which stretched about as far as the mall). All I'd told her was that I had a new friend. She said she wanted to meet this new friend. I told her the new friend wasn't a boy, and she got less excited. She had no real advice to give about friendship because she'd never managed to keep a friend in her life. Not that she saw it that way. She felt she had plenty of friends. She just didn't spend any time with them.

I had no intention of introducing her to Ashley, or even of having Ashley in the house. But finally the time came when I wanted us to use a bed. Call me old-fashioned, but I was getting tired of having to do the pleasure thing with a seat belt pressing against my back. Ashley flat-out refused to bring me to her house, so I told her, fine, we'd go to mine. My mother's one great indulgence was getting her hair done, so one afternoon after I dropped her off at the beauty parlor, I sped through a few lights and picked Ashley up to take her home.

'This is such a Miss Lucy bedroom,' she said when she saw it.

'What does that mean?' I asked her. For some reason, I didn't think Miss Lucy would have black-painted walls.

'You try so hard not to be frilly,' she replied, like she was the queen of frill.

I must've looked a little put out, because she said, 'Now, don't be hurt. You can't be hurt, 'cuz I wasn't meaning to hurt you.'

She came over and started to cuddle me into her, and it was like my mind stopped having any other thoughts about her besides *now now now*.

I was thirty minutes late picking my mother up.

She took one look at me and said, 'What happened to you?'

Ashley, I wanted to tell her. *Ashley's happening to me.*

But instead I told her I'd gotten a flat.

This was a stupid lie.

'Where's the old tire?' she said when we got home.

'The triple-A guy took it,' I told her.

'You're a very bad liar,' she said.

'Your hair looks like a camel peed in it,' I said back, then stormed to my room and called Ashley to tell her all about it.

'*A camel peed in it?*' Ashley said, laughing.

Suddenly it didn't seem as serious.

'Well, that's what it looked like,' I said.

Already the edge was gone. My life could be curvy again, and all it took was a laugh on her end of the phone.

More weeks passed.

I wanted something from her.

I wanted the l-word.

I wanted her to call me her girlfriend.

I wanted to make her cry.

I wanted to know I had the same effect on her that she had on me.

I got careless.

I tried holding her hand in school.

'Slow down, Miss Lucy,' she said. 'Slow down.'

I said I wanted to see her house.

Her room.

Her bed.

She told me they weren't worth seeing.

I asked her if there'd been other girls before me.

She laughed and said yes.

I asked: 'Am I the second? The seventh? The thirtieth?'

But she didn't tell me any more than that.

I had told her about Lily White, and now whenever I didn't want to do something she wanted me to do, she'd tease me about getting back together with Lily White, about how we'd be perfect together.

'Lucy likes to lick Lily,' she'd tease.

'Don't be mean to me,' I'd say.

'I'm not,' she said. 'It's a joke.'

Later, we'd be with each other and it would seem right – the perfect rhythm, the desire clouding us. Afterward, she'd hold me close – the perfect daze – and she'd say, 'Miss Lucy, you and I are a pair, aren't we?'

But then she'd tell me not to be so attached.

The more this happened, the deeper I fell in love with her.

The more she made me want it, the more I wanted it.

'Open your eyes,' Teddy told me, one of the few times I talked to him.

But that wasn't the problem.

My eyes were wide open.

Seeing her.

All our conversations in our relationship started to be about our relationship.

I was always the one who brought it up.

'What am I to you?' I would ask.

'Oh Lord,' she'd groan. 'Not again.'

'Are we girlfriends? *Lovers?* Nothing at all? What?'

'I'm Ashley and you're Miss Lucy. Isn't that enough?'

'No, it's not enough!' I'd protest, not even sure what I was defending.

'I don't need this, Miss Lucy. Really.'

Miss Lucy had a steamboat
The steamboat had a bell
Miss Lucy went to heaven
and the steamboat went to

'What are you mumbling?'

'Nothing.'

'C'mon.'

'I love you.'

'No.'

'I do.'

Hello, operator
Please give me number nine
And if you disconnect me
I'll chop off your

The kissing was supposed to be the escape. The kissing was supposed to be the moment when nothing in the world mattered but us. The kissing was supposed to take me away from all the problems. All the thoughts. All the doubts.

But now when I kissed her, I was always measuring how much of her was there. And I was wondering how much of me was left.

Behind the 'frigerator
There was a piece of glass
Miss Lucy sat upon it
And it went right up her

It was, I thought, a simple equation:
You find the right person.
You do the right things.
And from that, everything goes right.
Like you have a contract with the universe, and these are the terms.
I had no doubt Ashley was the right person.
I had to hope I was doing the right things.
But everything wasn't going right.
Some things were.
But not everything.

Ask me no more questions
And I'll tell you no more lies
The boys are in the bathroom
Zipping up their

Miss Lucy disappears from her own story.

> *Flies are in the belfry*
> *Bees are in the park*
> *And the boys and girls are kissing*
> *In the D-A-R-K*

I felt I was disappearing from my own story.

> *D-A-R-K*

I had no control over my own story.

> *D-A-R-K*

It was hers.

> *DARK DARK DARK*

I had to take my SATs a third time.
Ashley knew this. I'd told her.
Before I went in, I texted her:

WHAT DO YOU WANT TO DO TONIGHT?

It was a Saturday, and I thought we'd made plans.
After a few months of going out, this was pretty routine.

Of course, I forgot to turn off my phone. So ten
minutes into the SATs, my bag starts to chirp, and it

will not shut up. Now, I knew I wasn't supposed to take out my phone during the SATs, and I swear to this day that my intention was just to silence it until I was done penciling in those stupid bubbles. But as I went to hit the off button, I happened to look at the message on the screen:

WE HAVE TO TALK.

The test proctor was immediately yelling at me, asking what the hell did I think I was doing, as if I'd been about to call some math expert for help. I threw the phone back in my bag, but I couldn't get rid of the message as easily. It was like every problem on the SATs became my problem.

5. WHAT DO YOU WANT TO DO TONIGHT?: WE HAVE TO TALK:: ASHLEY, I CARE ABOUT YOU:
   a) LUCY, I CARE ABOUT YOU, TOO
   b) LUCY, WE'RE SO COMPLETELY OVER, IT'S NOT FUNNY
   c) LUCY, YOU'RE THE LOVE OF MY LIFE
   d) STEAMBOAT, I CARE ABOUT YOU, TOO

6. Which of the following phrases does not belong with the others?

    a) WE HAVE TO SEE MORE OF EACH OTHER

    b) WE HAVE TO TALK

    c) WE HAVE TO REMEMBER TO PICK UP A MOVIE

    d) WE HAVE TO BE TOGETHER ALWAYS

12. If the diameter of a cone is doubled, its volume:

    a) WILL QUADRUPLE

    b) WILL NOT BE ENOUGH TO SAVE YOUR RELATIONSHIP WITH ASHLEY

    c) WILL HALVE

    d) WILL STAY THE SAME

Of course, all the right answers were (b).

I might as well have used that number-two pencil to fill in the hollow dots that my eyes, my ears, my mouth, and my heart had become. Not only had I not seen it coming, but I had seen its opposite coming instead.

Doofus, I said to myself. *Idiot*.

I started crying in the middle of my third try at the SATs and I couldn't stop. I had to leave, and there was no way to explain to the proctor how a single sentence had stumped me more than any test question ever would.

All I needed was the confirmation. And all I needed for the confirmation was a simple two-letter word spoken in her voice. I called her as soon as I got to the parking lot. I knew she'd see my number on her phone, so when she answered, she'd be answering me. So the way she said that first word – *hi* – made the landslide complete. Her *hi* wasn't high at all – no, this *hi* was *lowwwwwwww*. The kind of *hi* that says *I've already scattered the ashes of our relationship somewhere over the land of yesterday*. All in two letters.

I began to cry again, and she told me she'd known I was going to be this way. I cried some more. She mentioned something about me still being her best friend in town. Not her best friend, mind you – her best friend *in town*. I wiped some snot with my sleeve. She asked me wasn't I supposed to be in the SATs right now? I just lost it and took that phone and threw it right at my car. Which is how I managed to lose a girl-friend, break a phone, and crack a windshield all at the same time.

And then I drove over to her house.

I didn't make it past the front door.

'What are you doing here?' she asked, stepping onto the porch and pulling the door shut behind her. 'And what the hell happened to your car?'

'What do you think I'm doing here?' I said, the tears already coming.

'It doesn't have to be like this,' she said, completely bored with the whole thing.

'Really? What can it be like? Tell me. I'd really like to know.'

'You see, this is why it was never going to work.'

'Because I'm upset that you're dumping me? That's why it was never going to work?'

'You were always too into it.'

'But you said we were a pair! You were into it, too.'

'Yeah, but not like you. And I wasn't always telling the truth.'

It had never occurred to me that a person could know all the right things to say and deploy them to get what she wanted, without having to mean any of it.

Dear Lord, I staggered then. Staggered back. Staggered away from her. Staggered to my car and cried for a good five minutes before I could get my key in the ignition. When I got home, I staggered past my mother, who called out, asking what was wrong. My breathing was staggered. My memory was staggered. And there was no way to get it right again.

I was waiting for her to call and say she'd made a mistake.

That was my own mistake.

I didn't want to go to school, but when my mother threatened to stay home with me if I didn't go, I knew I didn't have a choice.

'Is it some boy?' she asked, unable to keep the hope out of her voice.

'No, I'm just garden-variety suicidal,' I told her.

'Fine,' she replied, annoyed. 'Be that way.'

I tried to shut myself down completely, put up my best screen-saver personality to coast through the day. I didn't want to see her. I was desperate to see her. I wanted to hold it together. I wanted to melt down right at her feet and scream, *Look what you've done to me*.

I was going to skip lunch entirely, but Teddy found me and steered me toward his table.

'Spill,' he said.

'I can't,' I told him.

'Why not?'

'Because if I start, I might not stop.'

That's what it felt like — that if I let a little of the hurt out, it would keep pouring out until I was a deflated balloon of a person, with a big monster of hurt in front of me.

'You know what?' I said. 'I'm not Miss Lucy at all. I'm the goddamn steamboat.'

'Come again?' Teddy said with his usual shoulder-tilt pout.

'Let's just say this is *not* heaven,' I said with a sigh.

Heron, of course, knew exactly what I was talking about.

'It's just that Mercury's in retrograde,' she said.

'*This has nothing to do with a fucking planet*,' I groaned.

'Down, girl,' Teddy sassed. 'Down.'

I put my head in my hands and took a deep breath, hearing the air suck against my palms.

I felt Teddy pat my back, then start to rub it. Mmmmmm.

'A little better now?' he asked.

I nodded a little and he moved to my neck.

'Let it go,' he said. 'Let it go.'

I tried to. I wanted to block it out.

Miss Lucy had a steamboat. Miss Lucy had a steamboat.

'What are you saying?' Teddy whispered in my ear.

I lifted my head and told him. Then Heron and I explained what it meant.

'So you've sat on the glass,' Teddy said.

'Repeatedly.'

'And, let me get this straight, the boys are in the bathroom—'

'The boys don't really matter right now.'

'There will be other girls,' Heron comforted.

'I don't want other girls!' I cried.

What I meant then: *I only want Ashley.*

I couldn't stop thinking about her. My body missed her. My mind reeled at her absence. I was a fucking wreck. It wasn't pretty, and as much as I wanted to believe she was doing it to me, I had to begin to admit that I was doing it to myself, too.

Why is self-preservation so much more of a bitch

when it's your mental health that's involved? I mean, if there really *was* a piece of glass on my chair, I'd damn well make sure that I didn't sit on it twice. If a steam-boat *was* sinking, I'd know enough to head to the lifeboat. But a broken heart? At first I gave in to the temptation to think, nah, there was nothing I could do about it. I'd have to keep sitting on glass until someone was nice enough to take the glass away from my seat.

Then I thought, *To hell with that*. I actually had to think of it in terms of sitting on glass for it to work.

'What's up with the whole couple thing anyway?' I asked Teddy and Heron at lunch a week or so after Ashley had dumped me.

'What do you mean?' Teddy asked back.

'I mean, why is everyone so brainwashed into believing that they have to be in a relationship with one other person? Look at us, Teddy. If anyone were to tell us that the whole girl-boy thing was natural and anything else was unnatural, we'd know they were completely wrong. But have them tell us that every person needs to be with another person in order to be happy, and we nod along like it's the most obvious thing in the world. But there's no *reason* for it, is there? It's not a proven *truth*. It's just some thing that our culture has come to spin itself around, mostly so we'll procreate, and we're the dupes who fall for it over and over and over again.'

'I thought you were over the breakup,' Teddy said hesitantly.

'*I am*,' I insisted. 'Can't you see that this is more than that?'

Teddy clearly couldn't see, because he was looking at me like I was fifty-eight varieties of crazy all at once.

Heron, however, surprised me.

'You're totally right,' she said. 'And I'm tired of it, too.'

When I realized I was into girls, it was scary to let go of all the things I was supposed to be and all the things I was supposed to want. It's like you're a character in this book that everyone around you is writing, and suddenly you have to say, *I'm sorry, but this role isn't right for me.* And you have to start writing your own life and doing your own thing. That was hard enough. But that was nothing – nothing, I tell you – compared to the idea that I could let go of the desire to have a girl-friend. Maybe not forever. Maybe forever. Certainly for now. Talk about something that had been *ingrained*. I wasn't letting go of love or sex or the idea of companionship. I was just rejecting the package in which it was being sold to me. I was going to say it was okay to be alone, when it felt like everyone in the world was saying that it wasn't okay to be alone, that I had to always want someone else, that the desire had to fuel me.

I didn't want to feel like I needed it anymore. Because I didn't. Really, I didn't.

Ashley started fooling around with Lily White. She didn't tell me this, but I could figure it out easily enough. Lily White was more scared of me than ever. And she'd started to smell a little like Ashley's shampoo.

Betrayal. Lust. Secrecy. Devotion. I think we do these things to feel more alive. When the truth is that alive is alive – you can feel it in anything, if you give it a chance.

I thought more about Miss Lucy.

I'd never pictured her with anybody else, just her steamboat and her bell. Trying to keep things together, even when the world was constantly throwing glass under her ass.

'Do you think there was a real Miss Lucy?' I asked Heron.

'I don't know,' she said.

'I want to find out,' I told her.

The trouble I felt coming when I met Ashley was nothing compared to the trouble I felt when I first realized I didn't need her or anyone like her. People fall hard for the notion of falling, and saying you want no part of it will only get you sent to the loony bin. C'mon, you've seen the movie: As soon as the headstrong girl announces she's not going to fall in love, you know she'll be falling in love before the final credits.

That's the way the story goes. Only it's not going to be my story. I don't care for the way it's supposed to go. Some people find happily ever after in being part of a couple, and for them, I say, *good for you*. But that's no reason we should all have to do it. That's no reason that every goddamn song and story has to say we should.

I tried to explain myself to people.

'You don't know what you're missing,' Teddy, who usually had about four crushes going on at the same time, told me. 'It's the best excuse in the world for getting absolutely nothing done.'

When I called my sister at college and told her about my revelation, she acted like I'd announced I was shipping myself off to a nunnery. (Which would only be another form of crushing, if you ask me.)

'Did someone hurt you that badly?' she asked.

And I told her, no, it wasn't that.

'You *want* to be single?'

I said yes. And then I told her that I thought *single* was a stupid term. It made it sound like you were un-attached to anyone, unconnected to anything. I preferred the term *singular*. As in *individual*.

'Does this have anything to do with . . .'

My sister couldn't bring herself to say it, but I was still impressed. Besides a few gender-neutral terms (like *someone*, see above), she'd never really acknow-ledged that I was a [whatever term you want for lesbian].

308

'No, it doesn't,' I told her. 'I'd feel this way even if I were into guys.'

'Well,' she said, 'just don't tell Mom. You'll never hear the end of it.'

I didn't tell Mom. I did, however, finally speak to Ashley again. I couldn't avoid her forever. As soon as Ashley sensed me not wanting her anymore, she stepped right into my line of vision.

'I miss you,' she said.

'That's special,' I told her.

She laughed, and this time the laugh meant nothing to me.

'There's something I have to tell you,' she said.

'Don't,' I said.

'You know about me and Lily?'

'Yeah, I know.'

'I'm sorry. It just happened.'

'Let it, then. Why not let it?'

It felt so good not to care. Not to need.

'Miss Lucy,' she said. Quietly. Sweetly. Trying to pull me back in.

'Miss Lucy's gone to heaven,' I told her.

You never think of heaven in terms of who likes who, or who's with who, or whether this crush works, or whether the sex is good. In heaven you don't worry about what you're going to wear, or what you have to say, or whether someone loves you back, or whether

309

someone will be with you when you die. In heaven, you just live. Because it's heaven.

'Let's go on a trip,' I told Teddy and Heron. 'Let's drive until we find Miss Lucy.'

The three of us. The four of us. The hundred of us. The thousands of us.

You see, *us* doesn't need a particular number to make it fit.

I'm tired of convincing myself otherwise. I can put that energy to better use.

Let the boys and girls go on kissing in the dark.

I want more.

FROM
I AM THE MESSENGER

BY
MARKUS ZUSAK

Clown Street. Chips. The Doorman. And Me

It's the hottest day of the year, and I've got a day shift in the city. The cab has air-conditioning, but it breaks down, much to the disgust of everyone I pick up. I warn them every time they get in, but only one gets back out. It's a man who still has his last lungful of a Winfield in his mouth.

'Bloody hopeless,' he tells me.

'I know.' I only shrug and agree.

The stone that Lua Tatupu gave me is in my left pocket. It makes me happy in the festering city traffic, even when the lights are green and all the cars remain still.

Not long after I return the cab to base, Audrey pulls into the lot. She winds her window down to talk to me.

'Sweating like crazy in here,' she says.

I imagine the sweat on her and how I'd like to taste it. With blank expression, I slide down into the visual details.

'Ed?'

Her hair's greasy but great. Lovely blonde, like hay. I see the three or four spots of sun thrown across her face. Again she speaks. 'Ed?'

'Sorry,' I say, 'I was thinking of something.' I look back to where the boyfriend stands, expecting her. 'He's waiting for you.' When I return to Audrey's face, I miss it and catch a glimpse of her fingers on the wheel. They're relaxed and coated with light. And they're lovely. *Does he notice those small things?* I wonder, but I don't speak it to Audrey. I only say, 'Have a good night,' and step back from the car.

'You, too, Ed.' She drives on.

Even later, as the sun goes down and I walk into town and onto Clown Street, I see all of Audrey. I see her arms and bony legs. I see her smiling as she talks and eats with the boyfriend. I imagine him feeding her food from his fingers in her kitchen, and she eats it, allowing enough of her lips to smudge him with her beauty.

The Doorman's with me.

My faithful companion.

Along the way I buy us some hot chips with lots of salt and vinegar. It's old-style, all wrapped in the racing section of today's newspaper. The hot tip is a two-year-old mare called Bacon Rashers. I wonder how she went. The Doorman, on the other hand, cares little. He can smell the chips.

When we make it to 23 Clown Street, we discover that it's a restaurant. It's tiny, and it's called Melusso's. Italian. It's in a little shopping village and follows the small-restaurant ritual of being dimly lit. It smells good.

There's a park bench across the road and we sit there, eating the chips. My hand reaches down inside the package, through the sweaty, greasy paper. I love every minute of it. Each time I throw the Doorman a chip, he lets it hit the ground, leans over it and licks it up. He turns nothing down, this dog. I don't think he cares too much about his cholesterol.

Nothing tonight.

Or the next.

In fact, time is wasting away.

It's a tradition now. Clown Street. Chips. The Doorman and me.

The owner is old and dignified, and I'm quite sure it isn't him I'm here to see. I can tell. Something's coming.

On Friday night, after standing outside the restaurant and going home after closing, I find Audrey sitting on my porch, waiting. She's wearing board shorts and a light shirt without a bra. She isn't big up there, Audrey, but she's nice. I stop for a moment, hesitate, and continue. The Doorman loves her and throws himself into a trot.

'Hey, Doorman,' she says. She crouches down warmly to greet him. They're good friends, those two. 'Hi, Ed.'

'Hi, Audrey.'

I open the door and she follows me in.

We sit.

In the kitchen.

'So where were you this time?' she asks. It's almost laughable because usually that question is asked with contempt to unreliable-bastard husbands.

'Clown Street,' I answer.

'*Clown* Street?'

I nod. 'Some restaurant there.'

'There's actually a street called Clown Street?'

'I know.'

'Anything happen there yet?'

'No.'

'I see.'

As she looks away I make my mind up. I say, 'So why are you here, Audrey?'

She looks down.

Away.

When she finally answers, she says, 'I guess I missed you, Ed.' Her eyes are pale green and wet. I want to tell her it's barely been a week since we last got together, but I think I know what she means. 'I feel like you're slipping away somehow. You've become different since all this started.'

'Different?'

I ask it, but I know it. I am.

I stand up and look into her.

'Yes.' She confirms it. 'You used to just be.' She explains this like she doesn't really want to hear it. It's more a case that she *has* to say it. 'Now you're *somebody*, Ed. I don't know everything about what you've done and what you've been through, but I don't know – you seem further away now.'

It's ironic, don't you think? All I've ever wanted was to get closer to her. I've tried desperately.

She concludes. 'You're better.'

It's with those words that I see things from Audrey's perspective. She liked me being *just Ed*. It was safer that way. Stable. Now I've changed things. I've left my own fingerprints on the world, no matter how small, and it's upset the equilibrium of us – Audrey and me. Maybe she's afraid that if I can't have her, I won't want her.

Like this.

Like we used to be.

She doesn't want to love me, but she doesn't want to lose me either.

She wants us to stay OK. Like before.

But it's not as certain anymore.

We will, I try to promise.

I hope I'm right.

Still in the kitchen, my fingers feel the stone from Lua in my pocket again. I think about what Audrey's been telling me. Maybe I truly am shedding the old Ed Kennedy for this new person who's full of purpose rather than incompetence. Maybe one morning I'll wake up and step outside of myself to look back at the old me lying dead among the sheets.

It's a good thing, I know.

But how can a good thing suddenly feel so sad?

I've wanted this from the beginning.

I head back to the fridge and get more to drink. I've come to the conclusion that we have to get drunk. Audrey agrees.

'So what were you doing,' I ask later on the couch, 'while I was at Clown Street?'

I see her thoughts swivel.

She's drunk enough to tell me, at least in a coy kind of way.

'You know,' she embarrasses.

'No.' I mock her a little. 'I don't.'

'I was with Simon at my place and we . . . for a few hours.'

'A few *hours*.' I'm hurt but keep it out of my voice. 'How'd you manage the strength to get over here?'

'I don't know,' she admits. 'He went home and I felt empty.'

So you came here, I think, but I'm not bitter. Not at this moment. I rationalize that none of the physical things matter so much. Audrey needs me now, and for old times' sake, that's good enough.

She wakes me a bit later. We're still on the couch. A small crowd of bottles is assembled on the table. They sit there like onlookers. Like observers at an accident.

Audrey looks me hard in the face, wavers, then hands me a question.

'Do you hate me, Ed?'

Still stupid with bubbles and vodka in my stomach, I answer. Very seriously.

'Yes,' I whisper. 'I do.'

We both smack the sudden silence with laughter. When it returns, we hit it again. The laughter spins in front of us and we keep hitting it.

When it calms completely, Audrey whispers, 'I don't blame you.'

The next time I'm woken, it's by a cracking at the door.

I stammer there, open it, and there in front of me is the guy who jumped my cab. That feels like an eternity ago.

He looks annoyed.

As usual.

He holds his hand up for me to be quiet and says, 'Just' — he waits, for effect — 'shut up and listen.' He actually sounds a touch more than annoyed as he continues. 'Look, Ed.' The yellow-rimmed eyes scratch me. 'It's three in the morning. It's still humid as hell, and here we are.'

'Yes,' I agree. A cloud of drunkenness hangs over me. I almost expect rain. 'Here we are.'

'Now don't you mock me, boy.'

I reel back. 'I'm sorry. What is it?'

He pauses, and the air sounds violent between us. He speaks.

'Tomorrow. Eight p.m. sharp. Melusso's.' He walks away before remembering something. 'And do me a favour, will you?'

'Of course.'

'Cut down on the chips, for Christ's sake. You're making me sick.' Now he points at me, threatening. 'And hurry up with all this shit. You might think I don't have better things to do, but as it happens, I do, all right?'

'All right. It's only fair.' In my stupor, I try for something extra. I call out, 'Who's sending you?'

The young man with the gold-rimmed eyes, black suit of clothes and brutal disposition returns up the porch steps. He says, 'How the hell would I know, Kennedy?' He even laughs and shakes his head. 'You might not be the only one getting aces in the mail. Did you ever think of that?'

He lingers a little longer, turns and trudges off, dissolving into the darkness. Blending in.

Audrey's behind me at the door now, and I've got something to think about.

I write down what he told me about Melusso's.

Eight p.m. tomorrow night. I have to be there.

After sticking the note to the fridge, I go to bed, and Audrey comes with me. She sleeps with her leg across me, and I love the feel of her breath on my throat.

After perhaps ten minutes, she says, 'Tell me, Ed. Tell me about where you've been.'

I've told her once before about the Ace of Diamonds messages, but not in any detail. I'm so tired now, but I do tell her.

About Milla. Beautiful Milla. As I speak, I see her pleading face as she begged me that she did right by her Jimmy.

About Sophie. The barefoot girl with—

Audrey's asleep.

She's asleep, but I go on speaking. I tell her about Edgar Street and all the others. The stones. The beatings. Father O'Reilly. Angie Carusso. The Rose boys. The Tatupu family.

Just for now, I find I'm happy, and I want to stay awake, but soon the night falls down, beating me hard into sleep.

The Woman

The yawn of a girl can be so beautiful it makes you cringe.

Especially when she's standing in your kitchen in her underpants and a shirt, yawning.

Audrey's doing this right now as I do the dishes. I rinse a plate and there she is, rubbing her eyes, yawning, then smiling.

'Sleep OK?' I ask.

She nods and says, 'You're comfortable, Ed.'

I realize I could take that comment badly, but it's a compliment.

'Have a seat,' I say, and without thinking, I look at her shirt buttons and her hips. I follow her legs down to her knees, shins and ankles. All in a brief second. Audrey's feet look soft and delicate. Almost like they could melt into the kitchen floor.

I make her some cereal and she crunches it. I didn't have to ask if she wanted some. Some things I know.

This is confirmed later, once Audrey's had a shower and dressed fully.

At the front door, she says, 'Thanks, Ed.' She pauses before speaking again. 'You know, out of everyone, you know me the best, and you treat me the best. I feel most comfortable with you.' She even leans close and kisses me on the cheek. 'Thanks for putting up with me.'

As she walks away, I still feel her lips on my skin. The taste of them.

I watch her all the way up the street, till she turns the corner. Just before she does, she knows I'm standing there, and she turns one last moment and waves. In answer, I hold up my hand, and she's gone.

Slowly.

At times painfully.

Audrey is killing me.

FROM
GRASSHOPPER JUNGLE

BY
ANDREW SMITH

Stupid People Should Never Read Books

It took me a very long time to work up the nerve to kiss Shann Collins, who was the first and only girl I had ever kissed.

There was a possibility that I'd never have kissed her, too, because she was the one who actually initiated the kiss.

It happened nearly one full year after the *Curtis Crane Lutheran Academy End-of-Year Mixed-Gender Mixer*.

Like Robby explained to her: I was shy.

I was on the conveyor belt toward the paper shredder of history with countless scores of other sexually confused boys.

After the *Curtis Crane Lutheran Academy End-of-Year Mixed-Gender Mixer*, I tried to get Shann to pay more serious attention to me.

I tried any reasonable method I could think of. I joined the archery club when I found out she was a member, and I offered multiple times to do homework with her. Sadly, nothing seemed to result in serious progress.

At last, all I could do was let Shann Collins know that I would be there for her if she ever needed a friend or a favor. I do not believe I had any ulterior motives in telling her such a thing. Well, to be honest, I probably did.

I'd leave notes for Shann tucked inside her school-books; I would compliment her on her outfit. She laughed at such things. Shann knew it was a ridiculous thing to write, since all the girls at Curtis Crane Lutheran Academy dressed exactly the same way. Still, history will show that patient boys with a sense of humor, who can also dance, tend to have more opportunities to participate in the evolution of the species than boys who give up and mope quietly on the sidelines.

But I began to worry. Rumors were spreading around Curtis Crane Lutheran Academy about me and Robby, even though I never heard anything directly.

Then, in the second semester of eighth grade, I was called into the headmaster's office for something I wrote in a book report. Even though the book I read was in Curtis Crane's library, as well as the Ealing Public Library, apparently nobody other than kids had bothered to read the book until I wrote my report on it.

The book was called *The Chocolate War*, and the copy I read belonged to my brother, Eric. Mrs Edith Mitchell, who was the eighth-grade English teacher, assumed the book was about a candy kingdom or something. She probably thought there were magical talking peacocks in the book that shot gumballs and Sugar Babies out of their asses.

But there were teenage boys in the book – Catholic boys – who masturbated.

Boys who attend Curtis Crane Lutheran Academy are not allowed to masturbate.

My father nearly lost his job because I wrote a report on a book that had Catholic boys and masturbation in it.

Pastor Roland Duff, the headmaster at Curtis Crane Lutheran Academy, was very distraught.

He had the school's only copy of *The Chocolate War* resting on his desk when I came to his office.

There, he counselled me about masturbation and Catholicism.

'My fear is that when boys read books such as this,' he said, 'they will assume there is nothing at all wrong with masturbation, and may, out of curiosity, attempt to masturbate. In fact, Austin, it is true that masturbation has serious harmful effects. It makes boys spiritually and physically weak.'

The headmaster patted his forehead, which was

damp, with a handkerchief that had the Curtis Crane Lutheran Academy logo – a black cross surrounded by a bloodred heart – embroidered on its corner. I wondered if they had prepared him in his religious training for giving teenage boys talks about masturbating.

He went on, 'In history, entire armies have been defeated because their soldiers masturbated too frequently. It happened to the Italians in Ethiopia.'

When he said the words *too frequently*, I wondered if there was some number higher than once or twice per day that would get me off the hook to hell and military failure.

In any event, I hoped he was right. I hoped the bad guys in Afghanistan – where my brother, Eric, whose book got me into trouble, was fighting – were also excessive masturbators like the Italians.

Pastor Roland Duff continued, 'Masturbation can also turn boys into *homosexuals*.'

When he said *homosexuals*, he waved his hands emphatically like he was shaping a big blob of dough into a *homosexual* so I could see what he was talking about.

That frightened me, and made me feel ashamed and confused.

Then he called my mother into the office and he talked to her about masturbation, too.

Up until that day, I was certain my mother didn't know there was such a thing as masturbation.

As I stood there, shifting my weight awkwardly from one foot to the other, Pastor Roland Duff told my mother about the *Warning Signs of Masturbation*, so she could keep a better watch over me.

Then he sent me home with my mother and suspended me from classes for one day.

When I came back to school, Mrs Edith Mitchell made all the girls leave the classroom while Pastor Roland Duff explained the guidelines for books we were not allowed to read at Curtis Crane Lutheran Academy. We were no longer permitted to read any books that had masturbation, Catholics, or penises in them. Pastor Roland Duff gave the entire class of boys the same speech he'd given me about masturbation, weakness and homosexuality.

Once again, he blamed masturbation for Italy losing wars.

That kind of shit never made it into history books, either.

Sometimes, during his speech, he would remark, 'As I was explaining to Austin Szerba . . .'

And he would wave his hands as though he was shaping a doughy Austin Szerba in the air, so all the other boys could see what a boy who wrote a book report about masturbation and Catholics looked like.

Then he led the boys in prayer and excused us so Mrs Edith Mitchell could have a similar talk with the girls.

Robby and I whispered outside that after all that masturbation talk, a cigarette would be nice.

It was the worst day of my life since Eric left home.

Everyone knew that I was the one to blame for all the trouble about masturbating. At Curtis Crane Lutheran Academy you couldn't hear the name Austin Szerba and not think about masturbating.

I didn't speak in class again for the rest of the year.

Robby thought it was funny and told me I was brave.

Best friends do that kind of stuff.

When the boys were taken out of the room, I wondered if Mrs Edith Mitchell was telling the girls about Austin Szerba, and how teenage boys masturbate, or if maybe she had found a book with girls who masturbated in it. Thinking about a book like that made me very horny.

The library was quieter and emptier than usual for a long time after that day.

But when the boys came back into the classroom, Shann deftly slipped a note onto my lap beneath our desk. I thought she was going to tease me about masturbating, but the note said this:

Okay, I'll admit it, Austin Szerba, you have finally won me over. I read The Chocolate War, *too. I love that book. This school is full of shit. Let's go get a Coke after class and hang out. By the way, I like what you're wearing today.*

I was dressed exactly like every other boy at Curtis Crane Lutheran Academy.

Later that day, Shann Collins and I kissed for the first time.

It happened right after I said to her, 'Stupid people should never read books.'

The Death-Ray Gun

At one hour before midnight, Shann and I waited inside an old Ford Explorer parked behind the Del Vista Arms. Robby Brees, dressed in a pair of my clean white socks, best Adidas skate shoes, and Titus Andronicus T-shirt, dashed into his apartment to get us more cigarettes and wave, in passing, at his mother.

Events that night were going to set in motion a disaster that would probably wipe out human life on the planet. That night, I was going to say something to Shann I had never said to anyone. I was going to do something I'd never done, and see things I could not understand and never believed existed.

This is history, and it is also the truth.

I sat in the front seat.

Robby refused to chauffeur us around like he was some kind of limo driver, he said, so either Shann or I always had to sit up front with him. The rule increased the degree of difficulty in actually fulfilling my fantasy regarding Shann Collins and Robby's backseat.

But now, Robby was gone.

'What are you doing?' Shann said as I shimmied

my way between the front seats, over the centre console where there was still an assortment of cassette tapes that had belonged to Robby's dad.

I thought what I was doing was obvious enough, so I said, 'I'm looking for my death-ray gun.'

'Well, if your ray gun doesn't look like a pair of Robby's underwear or socks, it isn't back here.'

Robby needed to stop accumulating so much laundry this way, but it did keep the floor of his room tidy.

My foot got stuck between the passenger seat and console. My shoe came off. I left it there.

'I'm coming back there with you till Robby comes out.'

'Robby came out in the seventh grade,' Shann said.

A lot of things happened in seventh grade.

'There.' I said. 'I've never been back here alone with you, Shann. It's rather sexy.'

I thought using the word *rather* would make me seem mature and like I was not from Ealing.

'I've never heard you say anything like that before, Austin,' she said.

'*Rather?*'

'No. *Sexy*,' Shann explained. And she was right about that. I never had spoken about sex with Shann. I was too afraid to.

'Well, it is sexy,' I said. I kicked off my other shoe and scooted myself against her.

I put my arms around Shann. I leaned into her and brought my feet up onto the bench seat. I put my lips on her neck and licked her. She gasped.

'Shann, I want to tell you that I'm in love with you. I love you, Shann.'

I had never said that before, either.

'Oh, Austin. I love you.'

It was the first time Shann said it, too.

Then the dome light in the Explorer blinked on. Robby opened the driver's door.

'You are *not* having sex in my car – on top of my clothes!' Robby said.

I don't remember exactly how it happened, but the basketball shorts I'd been wearing that day were halfway down to my knees.

'Um. No. Robby. No.'

Shann coughed nervously and straightened up, while I pulled my shorts back over my hips.

'One of you,' Robby said sternly, 'up front now. Let's go get our shit.'

I squeezed my way back into the front seat.

Robby gave me an intense, scolding stare.

He shook his head and laughed at me. Robby wasn't angry. Robby was as shocked as I was. He and I both knew what probably would have happened if he had waited about one more minute before coming back to the car.

I extracted my shoe from the centre console. Somehow my socks had come off, too. I tried to find them. Clothing has a way of abandoning ship sometimes.

Then Robby dropped a pack of cigarettes in my lap and pushed in the dashboard lighter.

He started the car.

'Light one for me, Porcupine,' he said.

Robby Could Have Been A Preacher

We cased the Ealing Mall.

We sat across the street at Stan's Pizza, where we ate and watched through the window.

Stan's closed at midnight. Stan was visibly angry that we came in and ordered. There was nobody in the place, and Stan wanted to go home.

I ordered a large Stanpreme in an attempt to cheer Stan up.

'We'll have a large Stanpreme, please. For here,' I said.

In the same way that Johnny McKeon was proud for coming up with the names Tipsy Cricket Liquors and From Attic to Seller Consignment Store entirely on his own, and just as Dr Grady McKeon was considered a genius for inventing the brand Pulse-O-Matic®, Stan must have been very pleased with himself for creating the concept of the *Stanpreme*.

People from Ealing were very creative.

We didn't know for certain that Stan's real name was Stan. We never asked him.

Stan was Mexican, so probably not.

We sat, ate, and watched.

Stan watched us.

Everything was dark at the Ealing Mall across the street, except the sign over the Ealing Coin Wash Launderette. The launderette never closed. There was no need to. Between the hours of 2:00 and 6:00am., it was more of a public bathroom, a hash den, or a place to have sex than a launderette, though.

Thinking about having sex on the floor of the Ealing Coin Wash Launderette suddenly made me horny.

Nobody was out there.

This was Ealing at nighttime.

Nobody ever had any reason to be out, unless they were standing on the curb watching their houses burn down.

I wondered if Ollie Jungfrau had gone home. Ollie worked at Johnny McKeon's liquor store. Tipsy Cricket closed at midnight, too, but it was already completely dark by the time Stan scooted the tin pizza disk containing his eponymous creation down on our table by the window.

That was the first time in history anyone from Ealing, Iowa, used the word *eponymous*. You could get beaten up in Ealing for using words like that.

Just like Robby and I got beaten up for sitting there smoking cigarettes and being queers. But I don't know if I'm really queer. Just some people think so.

We ate.

Robby asked Stan for three ice waters, please.

Stan was not a happy man.

We couldn't finish the Stanpreme. It was too big. Stan brought us a box for the three slices we had left on his tin disk.

'Do you think we should make a plan or something?' I asked.

Robby said, 'This is Ealing. There's some kind of prohibition against making plans.'

If we didn't hate being Lutherans so much, Robby could easily have been a preacher.

Never Name A Pizza Joint Stan's

Robby parked the Explorer at the end of Grasshopper Jungle.

He positioned the vehicle facing Kimber Drive, so we could make a quick getaway if we had to.

Like real dynamos.

The pretense of doing something daring and wrong made the rescue of our shoes and skateboards a more thrilling mission to us. Nobody, ultimately, would give a shit about two teenage boys who'd been embarrassed and beaten up by some assholes from Hoover, who climbed up on an insignificant strip mall to get their shoes back.

Shann waited in the backseat.

When we were about ten feet from the car, Robby got an idea.

'Wait,' he said. 'We should leave our shoes in the Explorer.'

It made sense, like most of the shit Robby told me. Once we got up on the roof, it would be easier if we didn't have to carry so much stuff back down. We could wear our roof shoes to make our descent.

It was really good that Grant Wallace and those dipshits didn't throw our pants up there, too, I thought.

We went back to the car.

Shann was already asleep on top of Robby's underwear and shit.

We took off our shoes and left them on the front seat.

Robby grabbed his pack of cigarettes and a book of matches and said, 'Now we can do this.'

A narrow steel ladder hung about six feet down from the roof's edge. It was impossible to reach the bottom of it, so Robby and I rolled the heavy green dumpster across the alley and lined it up below the ladder.

Then, we climbed on top of the dumpster in our socks.

I didn't believe the garbage collectors ever emptied the thing anymore. The dumpster was sticky, and leaked a trail of dribbling fluid that smelled like piss and vomit when we rolled it away from the cinder-block wall beside the pubic-lice-infested couch.

From the top of the dumpster, we could barely

reach the lowest rung on the ladder. I gave Robby a boost. His socks, which were actually my socks, felt wet and gooey in the stirrup of my palms.

I felt especially virile doing a pull-up to get myself onto the ladder after him.

Soon, we were up on the roof, where we could stand and look down at the dismal, cancerous sprawl of Ealing.

We lit cigarettes.

Robby said, 'You should never name a pizza joint *Stan's*.'

We stood, looking directly across Kimber Drive at the yellowed plastic lens that fronted the long fluorescent tubes illuminating the lettered sign for Stan's Pizza.

Someone had painted an *A* between the *S* and *T*, so the sign read: *Satan's Pizza*.

People were always doing that to Stan.

They did it so many times that Stan simply gave up on cleaning the paint, and allowed the sign to say what the good people of Ealing wanted it to say:

Satan's Pizza.

People from Ealing had a good sense of humour, too.

'I have seen Pastor Roland Duff eating there,' I said.

'Did he order a *Satanpreme*?'

It was difficult to find our shoes and skateboards up on the roof at night. As I had originally theorized, there was plenty of cool shit up there, so Robby and I kept getting distracted. It didn't matter much, since Shann had fallen asleep, anyway.

We found a plastic flamingo with a long metal spike descending from its ass, so you could stick it in your lawn and fool passersby into thinking that flamingos were indigenous to Iowa.

Robby discovered two bottles of screw-top wine, full and sealed, and he placed them on the roof beside the top of the ladder.

We theorized that maybe back in the days when Ollie was thinner, he may have climbed up here to get drunk and talk to the flamingo. Ollie Jungfrau weighed more than four hundred pounds now.

Satan's delivered to Tipsy Cricket Liquors.

'Have you ever been drunk, Porcupine?' Robby said.

'No.'

'One of these days, let's get drunk together.'

'Okay,' I said.

Like considering most things that were against some well-intended list of rules, thinking about getting drunk for the first time with Robby made me feel horny.

We found two aluminium canisters that had reels of 16 mm film in them. Nobody watched 16 mm movies anymore. There was an old projector at Curtis Crane Lutheran Academy, but we decided not to take the films, just in case they were pornos or something.

We did want to take the flamingo, though.

Robby placed the plastic pink flamingo next to the bottles of wine.

'One of us can climb down first, then the other can toss down the bird and the wine,' Robby said.

Robby also found a Halloween mask. It was covered in fur and looked like the face of a grimacing lemur. It was the face a lemur in an electric chair would make. That had to come home with us, too, we decided.

'If you ever want to get shot in Ealing, walk through someone's backyard at night with a lemur mask on,' Robby said.

If You Ever Want To Get Shot In Ealing

We finally found our shoes and put them on.

I was embarrassed to admit it, but it was kind of emotional for us being reunited with our stuff after that very long day.

I could see Robby felt the same.

We put our skateboards down with the rest of the things we'd gathered, and then we sat beside the rooftop air ventilation unit to relax and have another cigarette.

'It feels good to have my shoes back,' Robby said.

'If we didn't find them, I was going to let you have those Adidas of mine.'

'Thanks.'

We both exhaled smoke at the same time.

'Austin?'

'Do you realize that today we got beaten up for being queers?'

'I know.'

'But you're not a queer,' Robby offered.

'I don't think so.'

'Well, I apologize.'

'You didn't do anything, Rob.'

Sometimes, I called him Rob.

'I've never done anything,' he said. 'I've never even been kissed or anything, but I still get beaten up.'

'Shann kisses you all the time.'

'That isn't what I mean.'

'I know.'

'Well, if I'm going to get beat up for being queer, at least I'd like to know one time what it feels like to be kissed.'

'Um. I guess you deserve that. You know. Everyone deserves to not feel alone.'

'Can I kiss you, Austin?'

The air suddenly became unbreathably thin.

I thought about it. I shook my head.

'That would be too weird.'

'Sorry.'

'Don't be.'

We sat there, smoking.

Everything was shitty and confusing.

Robby felt terrible.

I said, 'I guess I would kiss you, Robby.'

343

'Don't feel like you *have* to.'

'I don't feel that way.'

So Robby Brees, my best friend, and the guy who taught me how to dance so I could set into motion Shann Collins's falling in love with me, scooted around with his shoulder turned toward mine.

He was nervous.

I was terrified.

I watched him swallow a couple times.

Then Robby placed his cigarette carefully down on the gravel beside his foot. He put his hand behind my neck and kissed me.

He kissed me the way I kiss Shann, but it felt different, intense, scary.

Robby's tongue tasted like cigarettes when he slid it inside my mouth. I liked the taste, but it made me more confused. Our teeth bumped together. It made a sound like chimes in my head. I never bumped teeth with Shann when I kissed her.

When we finished kissing, Robby pulled his face away and I watched him lick his lips and swallow.

Robby's eyes were wet, like he was going to cry or something.

He looked away and wiped his eyes.

Robby said, 'I'm sorry.'

'No. It's okay. I said you could. I said let's do it.'

'Is it okay?'

'I said so, Robby. It was weird. Really. Are you okay?'

'I think that was the best moment of time in my entire life, Austin.' Robby wiped his eyes and said, 'Thank you. I've wanted to ask you to do that forever.'

'You could have just asked me.'

'I didn't want you to hate me.'

'How could I hate you?'

'For wanting to do that to you.'

'Oh. Well. I am sorry if it was clumsy. I didn't know if I was supposed to act like the man or the woman.'

Robby picked up his cigarette.

'You weren't supposed to *act* at all.'

'Good. Because I'm pretty sure I was just being . . . um . . . Porcupine.'

Robby puffed.

'You know what, Robby?'

'What?'

'If you ever want to get shot in Ealing, do *that* in someone's yard at night.'

FROM
ECHO BOY

BY
MATT HAIG

I ran to Iago's room.

But he wasn't there.

Downstairs, I heard the smashing of glass. I ran to my room and went into my pod, and in the mind-reader I commanded *Menu*. There was an option called 'House View'. I chose that, and then viewed the front garden. The part I couldn't see from my window. East of the gravel driveway. About ten protestors, all wearing masks, were climbing over a side wall. Where the police were meant to be guarding the house.

They carried small rocks and large sticks, and a few – more than a few, actually – had old guns. The kind that required bullets but could still kill. I needed a gun. There were guns in the house. Positrons. I needed a positron.

I switched to inside the house; saw that some of the protestors were in the lobby.

Three were engaged in a fist fight with an Echo. A tall dreadlocked Echo who was all muscle. I searched in other rooms, sometimes virtual running between them, sometimes by just mind-leaping.

The kitchen, the downstairs office, three of the living rooms, the therapy room – where Uncle Alex was, being protected by five Echos, including the blond boy – the indoor swimming pool, the gymnasium full of metal robots in boxing gloves, the dining room. I eventually found Iago in a small room hardly bigger than a cupboard. He was there with two Echos, taking a positron from the wall.

The weapons room.

He may have been holding an advanced antimatter weapon and he may have had a look of gleeful murder in his eyes, but he was still a ten-year-old boy and he was my cousin; I had stayed in an immersion pod while members of my family were being killed once before, and I wasn't about to let it happen again.

So I got out of the pod and my bedroom and ran downstairs.

I ran to the small room where the weapons were kept, but of course he had gone.

'Iago!' I shouted.

No response. Or none that I could hear above the sound of shouting and fighting and the occasional shot of an old gun. New guns were being fired too. I saw an Echo shoot a protestor into non-existence, his body disappearing before my eyes, but of course it was antimatter technology so it was unheard.

I ran to the therapy room to tell Uncle Alex that I couldn't find Iago.

'Oh, Audrey, you are safe. Come in here, come in here, and close the door behind you. Before any of those bastards see you.'

But I hesitated.

And the reason I hesitated was because Daniel was staring at me in such a way that hesitation was the only response. His words echoed in my head. *You are in danger here.*

I know it sounds irrational, but I was more scared of being shut up in a room with five Echos than I was of being out there with all those humans who had murder on their minds. Another of the Echos, the red-haired female, Madara, told me to come inside quickly. But she – unlike the blond Echo – was holding a gun. I remembered Uncle Alex telling me that she was designed for the army. To be a killer. I closed the door, and stayed on the other side of it.

It was a big mistake.

For the second after I had closed it, I felt something cold and hard press against my temple.

A gun.

An old twenty-first-century pistol, probably full of bullets.

Out of the corner of my eye I saw a man with a mask. The mask was the kind you would wear to a fancy dress party. He had come as a tiger. He was tall and smelled of tobacco gum.

'Where is your dad?' he asked me. His voice was harsh and rough and full of hate.

'My dad is dead.'

'Don't lie to me. Your dad. Alex Castle. The self-appointed God himself . . . Where is he? Tell me, or I will kill you. I swear to you I will squeeze this trigger and you will be out of here.' He did a quick mime to indicate my brains being blasted out of my skull.

'He's not my dad. My dad was killed three days ago. By an Echo.'

There was a pause. His voice changed. 'Your dad was Leo Castle?'

'Yes.'

He put the gun down slowly.

He seemed to be in shock.

'Leo Castle! He was a hero to me. To most of us! I watched all the pieces he did for *Tech Watch*. I'm sorry, I'm sorry. I wasn't really going to kill you. I just need to find your uncle. He must be stopped. The Resurrection Zone is evil. Everything he has done is evil. Neanderthals should not be kept in captivity. He cares more about Echos than real living things!'

'My dad didn't agree with violence,' I said, feeling a kind of defiance inside me. 'And he loved his brother. He would have been appalled by what you lot are doing.'

For a few moments I was just staring at the tiger

mask. Maybe my words were getting through. Maybe he wasn't going to do anything but leave, and tell the others who were rampaging around the house to leave as well. I would never know, for at that very moment he vanished into thin air and I saw Iago standing behind him holding his antimatter positron. A gun that was far too big for him (though seemingly as light as a feather, as it was far more aerogel than metal).

Unbelievably, he was smiling.

He had just killed a fellow human being and he was smiling. It was the first time I had ever seen him smile from genuine happiness.

'You owe me one, cuz,' he said, his voice jauntier than I'd known it.

He wasn't hanging around. He was heading past me, jogging through the unicorn holo-sculpture on his way to the lobby.

'Iago, come back! It's not safe!' I started running after him, but almost instantly someone burst out of an intersecting hallway and flung me to the floor. Another protester in a mask. This one wasn't a tiger, but the mask of a Neanderthal, with human eyes gleaming through. He was heavy and I was terrified. I screamed.

This one didn't have a gun. He had a stone. A stone large enough to be called a rock. He held it up high. He was about to smash it down on my head. Death was two seconds away now, and so my body was exploding with terrified life. But at that moment I saw someone else.

Daniel.

He was out of the therapy room and throwing himself towards us.

Daniel pushed the man with the Neanderthal mask to the floor. The man smashed the rock hard against Daniel's face and cut him, but Daniel already had his hand around the man's throat. He picked him up off the floor, holding him under his chin, his feet centimetres off the ground.

'Please,' the man wheezed, 'you'll kill me.'

'No,' Daniel said. 'Only if you hurt her again.' And then he threw the man far across the hallway, right through the holographic unicorn.

He turned to me and grabbed my arm, hard.

It was exactly where Alissa had grabbed me, and I automatically tried to resist. It was no use. He was even stronger than Alissa had been. He pulled me forward and started to run, and inevitably – being a human – I struggled to keep up. I could see the lobby, where the battle was still raging. A clock on the wall was hit; the face fractured, then instantly repaired itself. I could also see some of the protestors lying dead on the floor. The Echos – and Iago – clearly had the upper hand now.

'Slow down! You're hurting me!'

A thin stream of blood trickled down Daniel's cheek like a tear.

He went into the living room where I had been

taken on my first night. A female protester in a dolphin mask was in there, slicing through the Picasso painting with a knife. She roared and charged towards us with the knife, but Daniel held out his hand. The blade cut him, but he pulled the knife out of her hand easily, while still holding me with his other hand.

He looked out of the window to see Iago now out on the driveway with some Echos; many of the remaining protestors were fleeing.

The woman who'd had the knife ran out of the room. But we heard her scream a second later, a scream that ended too abruptly. And then we saw why. Madara was there with a gun, a gun she'd obviously just used, and she was running towards us.

Daniel saw her and led me towards a doorway at the far end of the room. 'Door open,' he commanded. The doorway led to some stairs. At the top of the stairs we ran along a landing I hadn't seen before.

I was scared, I must admit.

Beyond scared.

After all, here was an Echo, evidently malfunctioning and holding a knife. My parents had died this way. Maybe I would too.

Had he saved my life? Or did he want to kill me himself?

We reached a room with windows for walls. A room that showed the rear of the garden. I had been shown the garden before, the day I went to see Mrs Matsumoto, but then my senses had been dulled by the neuropads. Now, my mind hyper-sharp with adrenaline, I realized that it was an amazing garden, maybe the most amazing I had ever seen, the grass all shades and colours, the trees genetically perfect like something out of the wildest daydream. I saw the wall the protestors had climbed over. Madara was getting closer.

'Open,' Daniel called, and the window opened. And then, with troubling ease, he picked me up in his arms and jumped out onto turquoise grass. He landed awkwardly, but kept hold of me.

What was he?

Saviour, or monster?

I didn't even touch the ground.

He ran, and kept running. Behind us, I could see Madara at the window aiming the gun at Daniel. But she didn't fire it.

'I've disobeyed Master's order. Madara will have been sent to pursue me, but not to terminate me.'

Disobeyed Master's order.

'Order?'

'To stay with him. To protect his life at all costs.'

We passed through a row of silver birches. I struggled, trying to free myself from his arms. Above, in the distance, I could see a police car come to a stop on the magrail, and a robotic officer (a traditional metallic Zeta-One) leaned out of the window and switched his voice setting to loudhailer mode as he stared down at the driveway on the other side of the house.

'*Trespassers, you have ten seconds to leave the property. Failure to comply will mean death.*'

The Zeta-One wasn't talking to us, but Daniel was still running.

'Let me go! Where are you taking me? Let me go!'

'Don't worry. I'm not going to hurt you.'

Something about his voice made me almost believe him.

As he ran, he looked anxiously around at the grass, as if hidden danger lurked there.

'I heard your scream,' he said. 'I came to save you.'

'I want to go back. Take me back to the house.'

'No.' He cut left, behind some high, dense goji bushes, then stopped running. 'It's not safe. There are still protestors on the grounds and in the house.'

'The police are there now. Ten seconds has passed.' I thought about screaming. If I screamed the word 'police', then the police would surely come. But if Daniel wanted to kill me, he would have time to do so between my scream and the rescue attempt. He had superhuman strength and was holding a knife.

Daniel looked down at his bleeding hand. He winced, as though in pain, though I knew he couldn't feel pain.

'Listen, we probably don't have long. Madara will be telling Master that we escaped out of the window. I just need to tell you something. I tried to tell you before. I tried to come up to your room.'

I looked into his green eyes as if they were

357

possible to read, which of course they weren't. But I was here with him, at his mercy, so I could do nothing except go along with whatever weird Echo game he was playing.

'What did you try and tell me?'

'That I knew her.'

'Who?'

Blood dripped from his hand onto my cloth shoe, disappearing the moment it landed. Then he told me.

'*I knew Alissa.*'

Fear crept over my skin like an ice-cold blanket. 'What do you mean?'

'We had the same designer.'

I struggled to absorb this.

So was this what it was all about? Revenge? Was he going to kill me because I had terminated Alissa?

I knew this was a paranoid thought. I mean, Echos didn't feel loyalty to other Echos. They didn't *feel* anything at all. And besides, I thought of something else. Something that proved this Echo didn't know what he was talking about. 'No. That's impossible. Alissa was a Sempura product. You're a Castle product.'

'You are not safe here,' he told me. 'I tried to tell you. I was going to tell you that day in my room.'

I looked at his face. His eyes were wrong. Yeah. I had vaguely noticed it before, but now there was no mistaking it. There was too much there. He seemed more human than Echo. 'You're malfunctioning,' I told

him. 'And I think you've probably been malfunctioning since I got here.'

He held up his right hand, his cut hand. 'It is not
meant to be possible for me to feel pain, and I feel pain.
I feel all kinds of things. And I feel a duty to tell you
what I have wanted to tell you for a long time, and
would have just run up those stairs and done it if it
hadn't put you in danger.'

'What? Tell me.'

He took a breath. Came close. Whispered. 'You
have to get out of here. You have to escape. After I have
done this, there is no hope for me. Master will punish
me for my actions. I do not care. This was partly my
fault. Your parents' death. It was partly down to me.
I had her in my arms. I held Alissa the way I just
held you. I could have stopped it at the start, but I
didn't.'

Again, he looked anxiously at the grass around us,
waiting for something. Then he looked at the high
perimeter wall.

I didn't trust him.

There was no way in the world I could trust him.

Or at least, that's what I tried to tell myself.

Whatever silly weakness I had deep down inside
me, a weakness that came of being alone and wanting
someone to be there for me – well, I knew I shouldn't
let it get the better of me.

That dream I'd had . . . that had just been a dream.
He was an Echo, and a malfunctioning one. OK, so he

had read *Jane Eyre* and he could feel pain, but what did that prove?

But then he said it.

He said something that sent a jolt through me and made me question everything else. He said: 'Our designer's name was Rosella.'

Instantly Alissa's voice echoed in my mind. *Rosella*.

I looked into Daniel's green eyes and felt another shock. A deeper one than any spoken words could have caused. Because as I looked into his eyes, I realized that I felt for him. There was something gleaming there. Something like fear, or courage, or determination, or honour, or a combination of all four. Yes, for that moment at least, it felt like I was looking at someone who could be cared for. Worried about. Loved.

That is when the ground began to open up. Whole squares of blue and orange grass, tilting up and back like trapdoors all around us.

'Here come the hounds,' Daniel said.

'Hounds?' But even before Daniel explained, I remembered what Uncle Alex had told me.

'Echo dogs.'

Of course.

And then they started to prowl out onto the grass. They looked very much like Dobermans, although their chests were plates of naked titanium and their eyes were bright red.

'Step away from me,' Daniel told me, shouting

almost angrily. 'Step well away from me and they won't hurt you. They only want me. Trust me.'

I stepped away from him, like he said.

'So you wanted to kill me?' I asked him, still uncertain what to think. 'Was that your plan? Because of Alissa? She murdered my parents!'

'No. No, she didn't kill them. Not really.'

The dogs circled Daniel. There were five of them. They were all giving the same synthetic growl. Madara must have told Uncle Alex about us by now. And so he'd set the dogs on us.

'What are you talking about? I saw the footage. She was the only one there. She killed them.'

'You don't understand,' he said quickly. 'She did it, yes. But I told you – it wasn't a malfunction. She wasn't a normal Echo. Your parents thought she was, but she wasn't. She was a prototype, being made for Sempura . . . Rosella designed prototypes. One-offs. Tests.'

Something about this rang false. 'Designers only work for one company. Everyone knows that.'

'You don't understand. Rosella, she is the very best in the world. And she is a good human. Or she tried to be. The trouble was—'

One of the Echo dogs suddenly swept in, and bit Daniel's left leg. I caught sight of the gleaming titanium teeth, complete with two needlesharp fangs, longer than the rest. It was these that penetrated Daniel's flesh. Then another bit his right leg. A third jumped with a strength far beyond that of any purely biological dog, and pinned him to the ground.

Daniel looked at me with weary eyes. Those dogs had injected something into him via their fangs. 'You must escape. Find Rosella,' he said, before that third hound's fangs pierced his neck.

He managed a final word – '*Remember* . . .' – and then collapsed on the grass. A sleep beyond sleep. And as those Echo hounds ran towards the house, no doubt being remote-commanded to help the Echos and the police eliminate the last of the protestors, I went over to Daniel and crouched down to inspect him. The most visible wound was the knife cut on the palm of his hand, which was still leaking fresh blood onto the lawn. And he had a mark on his cheek from where the rock had caught him. Where the dogs had bitten him there were only the tiniest dark dots, as if from injections or vampire bites.

I no longer feared him. It was quite impossible to fear someone who was lying unconscious on the grass in front of you. In fact, I wanted him to wake up or come round. He had more information to give. But it wasn't just that. He had saved my life. And I knew I'd been wrong about him.

'Wake up! Wake up! Can you hear me? Daniel? Daniel! Wake up!'

There wasn't the slightest response, even when I slapped his face. I checked his pulse. I had never felt the pulse of an Echo before, but I knew that their hearts beat slightly faster than a human's, to ensure blood pumped more quickly around their bodies, leading to more efficient muscles and organs. And although Daniel's pulse wasn't beating quite that fast – he was unconscious, after all – it was still beating as fast as mine would in a state of absolute panic. To be honest, I wasn't far from that state.

A thousand questions sped around my mind.

Why had he saved me?

Why had he left my uncle's side when he knew he would be punished for disobeying an order?

Could any Echo ever feel guilt?

And had that really been Uncle Alex's order? Wasn't it more likely that Uncle would have told him to come and help me? After all, there were other Echos to look after Uncle Alex. But why had another Echo chased us?

And what was this stuff about Alissa? He had heard me say Alissa's name on that first night. He could have been lying. But then, he had mentioned Rosella. Why would he have said that name?

But was he lying? It came back to that.

Was he lying?

Was he lying?

He was an Echo. An Echo that Iago had already told me was weird. And even the least weird Echo in the world couldn't be trusted. But if he was lying, then why would he be risking everything to tell me that he knew Alissa? Why would he have brought me out here, into the garden, knowing that the Echo hounds were out here? And why had he told me to find Rosella?

I knew I didn't have long.

As soon as the protestors had been dealt with – maybe even before – someone would be out searching for me. Searching for Daniel. I looked at him lying there on the ground. At the arms that had carried me, at the hand that been cut trying to defend me, at the bruised and grazed cheek that had taken the force of a rock, at the strong pale neck that had been pierced by the fangs of an Echo hound. All those wounds. All for me. I looked at his closed eyelids, shielding those green eyes. I looked at his face, trying to see if there was some clue on it. If there was something that could tell me if he was lying or not.

Of course, it was impossible to tell. All I knew is that I was staring at a perfect face, and the trouble with perfection is that it doesn't give you any answers. Indeed, all it did was confuse me further. He was an Echo. I couldn't feel anything for an Echo except fear, and yet there I was, feeling all kinds of things.

But then I remembered. Echos have origin marks, singed onto the skin. It was roughly the same size as the mark on the back of an Echo's left hand. The E.

I had never seen Alissa's origin mark up close. Had never had any inclination to do so. But my parents would have done, I supposed, when they first purchased her. Yeah. Probably. Maybe.

There was the sound of footsteps, heading closer. I looked through the bushes and saw Uncle Alex, flanked by Madara and the other Echo who had been guarding him – the tall, muscular dreadlocked one – walking across the lawn towards me. Within twenty seconds they would be here.

Wasting no time, I tugged at Daniel's clothes until I saw his naked shoulder, and that origin mark. A band of text, neat bold capitals forming words almost too small to read:

DESIGNED BY
ROSELLA MÁRQUEZ (B–4–GH–44597026–D)
FOR CASTLE INDUSTRIES

'Activate info-lenses,' I said. And within a second the familiar green dot was hovering in front of me, to signify that the lenses were on. 'Camera,' I commanded. 'Take image.' I blinked. Rosella Márquez's ID number was now recorded. Just in time, as it turned out.

'Oh, Audrey, thank God.' Uncle Alex was standing there, looking worried. 'He didn't have time to hurt you.'

'I don't think he was going—'

He wasn't listening. 'Chester,' he said to the large Echo with the dreadlocks as he pointed at Daniel. 'Take that into the house.'

That. Why did it hurt me to hear him talking about Daniel like that? *Echos don't warrant sympathy. They're just machines.*

But still, when Chester scooped him off the ground and carried him into the house, I felt worried.

'What are you going to do to him? Is he going to die?'

My question seemed to puzzle Uncle Alex. Maybe not the words, but the way I said them.

'Audrey,' he said gently, 'this is my fault. An Echo never wins at chess if they are told not to win at chess.' Yes. Uncle's voice was gentle. But there was something new about the way he was looking at me. His eyes were harsh. 'We are going to make sure he never puts your life in danger again.'

'He didn't put me in danger. He . . . he saved my life.'

Uncle Alex came close to me. 'What did he say to you?'

'Nothing,' I said.

Madara must have done an instant voice-reading because she said: 'It is a lie, Master.'

Uncle Alex looked at Madara with an affection he couldn't hide from me. She was his favourite Echo, I could see that. But even so, he managed to say to her: 'Hush, Madara. She is young and she is human. She is allowed to lie. Indeed, it is expected.'

'He said some stuff, but it didn't make sense,' I explained. 'That is what I meant.'

Uncle Alex gave a small nod. '*Some stuff*.'

The Echo hounds skulked back across the grass and returned to their underground homes, the grass-covered doors closing and restoring the lawn to normal. I looked over towards the house.

'You are in shock. We all are, obviously, after what has just happened. Those protestors tried to kill me. They are animals. Monsters. Too scared to come out from behind their masks. They tried to kill Iago too. He is fine, though. In fact, he dealt with a lot of them himself. He is a sharp shooter. Whoever said that war games were bad for kids, eh? They might have just saved his life!' Uncle laughed a little. The laugh quickly died. 'Candressa wasn't so lucky, though.'

'What happened?'

'One of them shot her. In her arm. It won't be fatal. She's in surgery.'

'In hospital?'

'No. There's a medical room in the basement. Two Echos are fixing her right now.'

'I'm sorry to hear that.'

'There's been a lot of damage. I've lost a lot of money just in terms of the art they've destroyed. Picassos! They've destroyed Picassos! Clocks and furniture can repair themselves, but a painting can't. And all because of those terrorists. Terrorists fuelled by all that ridiculous anti-progress propaganda.'

'You mean, like Dad used to write?'

He sighed and looked at me for a while, maybe wondering if he should be polite. But eventually he came out and said it: 'Yes, exactly like that. Listen, I know you think I must have hated your dad. But I didn't. He was a stubborn man. I offered him money once. A lot of money. He turned it down. He didn't

367

start off radical; he became it. The more successful I became, the more principles he developed. It was classic sibling rivalry. Nothing more, nothing less. Now come on, I can't stand around out here all day. I've got to talk to the police. And assess the damage.'

And as I walked back with him, I wondered if Uncle Alex was the reason Daniel had told me to escape.

We were back inside the house. I was in my bedroom. Uncle Alex had told me to stay there until all the mess could be cleared away. I think he also wanted me in my room so I wouldn't ask any questions. Or see whatever they were going to do to Daniel.

I sat there staring out of the window. At the criss-crossing rails carrying traffic. At the distant floating bone that was the New Parliament building, directly above the old one, which had flooded and evacuated many years ago, though Big Ben had been left relatively intact. The bone contained what Dad always used to call 'a joke of a government', as most of the politicians who worked there were also getting money from one of the main technology giants, and significantly more money from Castle than from Sempura. Knowing this, and seeing that giant sphere going round and round with the blue castle on it, it was very easy for me to feel like Uncle owned the whole city. That he was a kind of king. And a king with far more power and wealth than King Henry IX.

King of the Castle.

The trouble was, if he was like a king, he was an unpopular one. One that many clearly wanted dead. So it wasn't safe here. Today had proved that. But it wasn't just the protestors – or 'terrorists', as Uncle Alex had been quick to call them – that bothered me. No. And it wasn't just the Echos, either. It was Uncle Alex himself. He had been kind to me, as Candressa had pointed out. And it was true. And I desperately tried to convince myself that my growing doubts were unfounded. Daniel had malfunctioned. How could I have taken his word for anything?

'Is Daniel going to be OK?' I asked when Uncle Alex came in with a cup of red tea for me.

'Audrey, I don't understand it. I thought you hated Echos.'

'I do . . . I do . . . I just want to know what will happen to him. I'd like to be able to speak to him again.'

Uncle Alex sat on a chair and leaned back, taking a deep breath. I'd felt like this before. When I'd had the interview for Oxford. It was the feeling of being assessed. 'Well, that's not going to happen, I'm afraid.'

'Why? What are you going to do to him?'

'Don't worry about that, Audrey. We're not going to terminate him. We're going to make a few little changes and then send him somewhere else.'

A few little changes.

'You see,' Uncle Alex said, 'there are things you don't know about Daniel.'

'*Things?*'

'He's not like the other prototypes. A lot more money was spent on him. Made by the best designer. By a genius, in fact. But there is very often a problem with genius. Sometimes the genius pushes things a little too far. It can create something that we're not quite ready for. It can create something that acts in unpredictable ways. And that might be what has happened here.'

'Like Alissa?'

'What?'

'Alissa acted in unpredictable ways.'

'Alissa wasn't a Castle product. If she was a Castle product, she would never have been on the market. None of the Echos I have here have been released yet.'

'But you said they were all safe. You said there was nothing to worry about.'

'They are all safe. Most of them. In fact, without them we'd be dead right now. Killed in cold blood by those terrorist monsters.'

He looked angry, but he was hiding something. I was becoming a bit scared. He reverted to his original topic. 'No Castle prototype has ever caused problems before. It's just Daniel. The most advanced. And therefore the most problematic.'

'So what are you going to do to him?'

'I don't know if you know about Echos. Their

brains look like ours but they are not like ours. They run on code. There is a chip inside them. This chip sends different instructions and triggers to different parts of the brain. The rear part of the brain deals with free thought. In his particular case – for some reason we can't identify – it seems to trigger imagination.'

I was confused. 'Imagination? Is that bad?'

'Imagination is dangerous, Audrey. Imagination makes them have a degree of unknowability. It makes them more advanced, but it increases the risk. But luckily, in an Echo, it is located right here.' He patted the back of his head. 'And it is very simple to remove, while still ensuring he maintains a degree of functionality.'

Degree of functionality.

'He's not a machine!'

'Oh, but that is exactly what he is. He is an Echo. He wasn't born, he was made. There are no blurred lines. And this machine has malfunctioned, so he is getting downgraded. And then I'll be putting him out there on the open market. There is a big market, you see, for rejects. Some go to the moon. Some end up in London, doing dirty or dangerous work. They are cheap. That place over there is full of them.'

'Where?'

He pointed out of the window, at the rotating sphere in the distance.

'The Resurrection Zone?' I remembered Dad's stories about that place. About violent encounters between the animals and the Echos that looked after them. Dad compared it to the Coliseum in ancient Rome, where Christians were fed to the lions for entertainment. But instead of Christians it was Echos, and instead of lions it was tigers. And though Dad wasn't a fan of Echos, I agreed that it was cruel – to the animals, if no one else. And yet, weirdly, I wasn't thinking about the animals. I was thinking about Daniel.

'Most Echos don't last more than a month there,' I said.

'Some do, some don't. That's hardly our problem.'

'But you own it. Castle owns it.'

He looked at me, and there was a sense that we both knew we were playing some kind of game. We were saying some things and not saying others. 'The Resurrection Zone is a fun place. It angers those terrorists, but everything angers them. I'll take you one day. I think you'll see that your dad was wrong about it. It makes a lot of people happy. It does a lot of good work.'

It was then that we heard a noise. A faint but alarming sound. A scream.

'Was that him? Was that Daniel?'

'It might have been.'

I realized they must have been operating on him right then. 'He sounded like he was in pain. Don't you do it painlessly?'

'Echos don't feel pain.'

'But he's advanced. *He* can. He can imagine and he can feel pain.'

Uncle Alex looked at the painting. Those huddled, cold, traumatized nudes listening to music. 'Interesting. I am sure artists like Matisse would have agreed. The price of imagination is pain. That may be true.' He laughed. 'Well, better he feels it than he inflicts it.'

And then he stood up to leave. The screams kept on. They triggered questions inside me. Questions I was no longer too scared to ask.

'Who was Rosella?'

Uncle Alex sighed. His nose whistled slightly as he did so.

'Whatever he said to you, you shouldn't trust it. He was playing with your mind.'

'How do you know he said anything about Rosella?' I said, my heart speeding as a revelation pumped adrenaline into me. 'Alissa did. I told you that at the media conference. But you are right – so did Daniel. Was she the genius? Did she make Alissa?'

Uncle Alex stopped just before he reached the door. 'You can tell you are your dad's daughter. Questions, questions, questions.'

'My dad was a good person.'

He nodded. And he looked at me with eyes that showed no sign of warmth. 'Yes, but look what happens to good people.'

'I need to know.'

He smiled. Looking back, I realize it was the first time I had seen open cruelty on his face.

'Well, then, come with me. You can ask Daniel everything you want to know.'

At the time I wasn't really sure why Uncle Alex wanted this to happen.

I mean, why he wanted me to see Daniel after the operation.

Why he took me down two flights of stairs to a part of the house I had never been in – to the surgery room, and that horizontal pod where Daniel was lying awake but lifeless beneath the aerogel casing.

Now, though, I realize it was about power. Everything in Uncle Alex's life was about power. The aggressive business strategies, the big house in Hampstead, the Matisse and Picasso paintings, the holosculptures. It was all to show how powerful and important he was. I wish Dad had told me more about what Uncle Alex had been like as a child. Maybe that would have explained a few things. Maybe one day I would discover the truth.

But anyway, this was about power. About showing the power he had over his products, of which Daniel was one; and also about showing the power he had over me. Because, really, this was the moment when everything changed between me and my uncle. It was the point at which the pretence was over. When I could no longer try and convince myself that he had my best interests at heart. Maybe it was the shock of the activists breaking into the house, but whatever it was, the mask had slipped.

We walked into the bare, perfectly clean white room.

'Open pod,' said Uncle. And the pod opened and Daniel was lying there looking up at us. Though his eyes were different now. They seemed blank and empty, the way Echo eyes were supposed to look.

'Right,' said Uncle, smoothing back his own hair. 'I'll leave you to ask your questions. Now, I am going to see how the house repairs are going.'

So he left us there. Alone.

But obviously we weren't really alone.

You couldn't really be alone anywhere in this house. You were always being watched, recorded, monitored. Uncle Alex could have been in his pod or in the security room, watching us in real time.

I tried not to think about this.

I tried to concentrate on Daniel.

It was weird. This whole thing was weird. Was he asleep with his eyes open? As I got closer I saw the blood. I was reminded that Echo blood and human blood is almost identical, except that Echos have fewer white blood cells, so theirs is darker. It was already drying, beneath the back of his head on the harsh-looking surgi-pillow and matted into his light hair.

'Hello,' I said.

Nothing. Not so much as a blink.

'Daniel, it's me, Audrey. You saved my life. I want to say thank you.'

There might have been something then. The smallest twitch between his eyebrows. A sign that he might be hearing my words.

And here's the thing . . .

He was not terrifying.

I had always been troubled by the way Echos looked; their perfect faces and bodies. It was a perfection that I had found ugly. Beauty was about imperfection because that was what made people special. Or maybe that's what I told myself because I had large shoulders and walked like a boy. Whatever. But if everyone was made to look perfect, then no one would be special because being special meant being different, by offering something that wasn't on offer elsewhere, and Echos were all the same. The models changed, but they were equals in perfection.

Echo skin wasn't quite like human skin. There were no pores or marks or blemishes. Everything was made to be symmetrical and visually appealing. Some people liked that sort of thing, obviously. (Which, I suppose, was the thinking behind Universal Affection and Echo Echo and 3.14 and Love Circuits, and all those other manufactured Echo 'boy' bands, which I had always seen as the absolute opposite of something real and messy and human like the Neo Maxis.)

But beauty was something else. Something hidden slightly away, something that existed inside every living thing, which could only be seen by certain people. And once they saw it, they couldn't unsee it, because like all those old dead poets said, beauty was truth and eternity and it connected you to the infinite.

Beauty did not belong to machines. It did not belong to Echos. And yet it was there, as difficult to spot as the little crease that had momentarily appeared on Daniel's forehead.

'This shouldn't have happened to you,' I told him. 'I am sorry. What happened? Why did you stay awake? Why didn't they switch you off? It's torture. That's what happened. You felt pain. You aren't meant to feel pain, but anyone who heard your screams knew you were in pain. I'm sorry.'

His eyes closed for the slowest of blinks, and when they opened again they were looking at me. But this was not the Echo boy who had saved my life. That boy seemed lost. Totally. He didn't seem to be there.

'Please. Say something. Anything. Just speak. I know you can hear me.'

I couldn't help but feel he was my responsibility. When somebody saves your life, you owe them a whole world. I touched his skin.

'You told me you had met Alissa. You told me you were designed by someone called Rosella Márquez.'

Another blink.

'You had more to tell me. About Alissa. About Uncle Alex.'

His eyes stared into mine, but it was hard to say what he was really seeing. I suddenly felt self-conscious, aware that I was just a mass of human imperfections.

His mouth moved.

He was about to speak.

'Who are you?' he said, in a voice that sounded empty and flat and neutral.

It was a weird feeling. Relief to hear him speak, but disappointment at the words.

'I'm Audrey. Audrey Castle. I am Mr Castle's niece. My parents were killed by an Echo called Alissa. She was a Sempura Echo, not a Castle one.' Then I whispered, 'I'm starting to think that I am only alive right now because I'm useful. I can help him score points against Sempura.' It was only as I said this that I realized, with a sudden jolt of fear, that it was true.

He frowned again. It was like someone trying to learn a language. He turned his head a little towards me. This movement appeared to cause him great pain. He winced. Instinctively I placed my hand gently on his face.

'Don't worry,' I said. 'I'm sorry. I'm troubling you. I don't want to trouble you. You saved my life.'

I remembered a poem. It was one of Mum's favourites. As I looked down at him, I tried to imagine what he was feeling, and the first line of that poem came out of my mouth: '*I am: yet what I am none cares or knows.*'

His eyes weren't so blank now. There was a sadness inside them. I didn't know if it was better that he was sad than nothing at all. I remembered that day in his room. I remembered him holding me. I remembered

378

his warm breath. I remembered feeling things I wasn't meant to feel.

And then I kissed him.

I leaned down and kissed him softly on the lips.

The kiss wasn't a silly romantic h-movie kiss. It was just the kind of kiss you give someone you care about. And I knew that I had once been wrong about him, and I knew that he was confused and in pain. I knew that he had risked a lot for me. He'd been trying to protect me all along. And I knew that, right at this moment, he was the only real ally I had in the world, so I wanted to bring him back and show that someone cared about him.

I had changed. I was feeling emotion towards something that was technically a machine. If a machine could develop enough to become almost human, maybe a human could develop enough to understand that. Maybe that is what growing up was all about. It was about changing your mind. Opening it right up. Admitting to yourself that you were wrong about stuff.

'You aren't like the others,' I said. 'You are different. You care. You feel pain. But one day you will feel other things. Nicer things, I promise you.'

He whispered something.

'*Audrey.*'

He knew my name. My heart felt like it would burst now that I knew I was helping to bring him back.

He looked like he might speak again. And he did.

'He changed Alissa.' That is what it sounded like, but I couldn't be sure.

'What? *What?*'

But then I stopped talking because the door opened and my uncle re-entered the room and said, 'All right, lovebirds,' he said. 'Time to say your good-byes. Because I don't think you'll be seeing each other again, do you?'

FROM
FORBIDDEN

BY
TABITHA SUZUMA

Lochan

He arrives at ten past seven. Maya has been on edge ever since she got in. For the last hour she has been upstairs, vying with Mum for the bathroom. I even heard the two of them laughing together. Kit jumps up, banging his knee on the table leg in his haste to be the first to greet him. I let him go and quickly close the kitchen door behind him. I don't want to see the guy.

Fortunately Maya doesn't invite him in. I hear her feet pounding down the stairs, voices raised in greeting, followed by: 'I'll be with you in a minute.'

Kit returns, looking impressed and exclaiming loudly, 'Whoa, that guy's loaded. Have you seen his designer gear?'

Maya rushes in. 'Thank you for doing this.' She comes straight over to me and squeezes my hand in that annoying way she has. 'I'll take them out all day tomorrow, I promise.'

I pull away. 'Don't be silly. Just have a good time.'

She's wearing something I've never seen before. In fact she looks totally different: burgundy lipstick, her long russet hair pinned up, a few stray wisps delicately framing her face. Small silver pendants hang from her ears. Her dress is short, black and figure-hugging, sexy in a sophisticated kind of way. She smells of something peachy.

'Kiss!' Willa cries, flinging up her arms.

I watch her hug Willa, kiss the top of Tiffin's head, give Kit a punch on the shoulder and smile again at me. 'Wish me luck!'

I manage to return the smile and give a small nod.

'Good luck!' Tiffin and Willa shout at the tops of their voices. Maya cringes and laughs as she hurries out into the corridor.

There are slamming doors and then the sound of an engine starting. I turn to Kit. 'He came by car?'

'Yeah, I told you, he's loaded! It wasn't exactly a Lamborghini, but Jeez, he's got his own wheels at seventeen?'

'Eighteen,' I correct him. 'I hope he doesn't intend to drink.'

'You should have seen him,' Kit says. 'That guy's got class.'

'Maya looked like a princess!' Willa exclaims, her blue eyes wide. 'She looked like a grown-up too.'

'OK, who wants more potatoes?' I ask.

'Maybe she'll marry him and then she'll be rich,' Tiffin chips in. 'If Maya's rich and I'm her brother, does that mean I get to be rich as well?'

'No, it means she dumps you as a brother 'cos you're an embarrassment – you don't even know your times tables,' Kit replies.

Tiffin's mouth falls open and his eyes fill.

I turn to Kit. 'You're not even funny, d'you realize that?'

'Never claimed I was a comedian, just a realist,' Kit retorts.

Tiffin sniffs and wipes the back of his hand across his eyes. 'Don't care what you say, Maya would never do that, and anyway, I'm her brother until I die.'

'At which point you'll go to hell and never see anyone again,' Kit shoots back.

'If there's a hell, Kit, believe me, you'll be in it.' I can feel myself losing my cool. 'Now would you just shut up and finish your meal without tormenting anyone else?'

Kit tosses his knife and fork onto his half-finished plate with a clatter. 'To hell with this. I'm going out.'

'Ten o'clock and no later!' I shout after him.

'In your dreams, mate,' he calls back from halfway up the stairs.

Our mother is next to come in, reeking of perfume and struggling to light a cigarette without smudging her freshly painted nails. The complete antithesis to Maya, she is all glitter and crimson lips, her ill-fitting red dress leaving little to the imagination. Soon she disappears again, already unsteady on her high heels, screeching up at Kit for having nicked her last packet of fags.

I spend the rest of the evening watching TV with Tiffin and Willa, simply too exhausted and fed up to attempt anything more productive. When they start to bicker, I get them ready for bed. Willa cries because I get shampoo in her eyes, and Tiffin forgets to hang the shower curtain inside the bath and floods the floor.

Teeth-brushing seems to take hours: the kiddie toothpaste tube is almost empty so I use mine instead, which makes Tiffin's eyes water and Willa gag into the basin. Then Willa takes fifteen minutes to choose a story, Tiffin sneaks downstairs to play on his Gameboy and, when I object, gets unreasonably upset and claims Maya always lets him play while she reads to Willa. Once they are in bed, Willa is immediately hungry, Tiffin is thirsty by association, and by the time the clamouring finally stops it is half past nine and I am shattered.

But once they are asleep, the house feels eerily empty. I know I should go to bed myself and try to get an early night but I feel increasingly agitated and on edge. I tell myself I have to stay up to check that Kit comes home at some point, but deep down I know that it's only an excuse. I'm watching some stupid action movie but I've no idea what it's about or who is supposed to be chasing who. I can't even focus on the special effects – all I can think of is DiMarco. It's past ten now: they must have finished dinner, they must have left the restaurant. His father is often away on business – or so Nico claims, and I have no reason to disbelieve him. Which means he has his mansion to himself . . . Has he taken her back there? Or are they in some dodgy car park, his hands and lips all over her? I begin to feel sick. Maybe it's because I haven't eaten all evening. I want to wait up and see for myself what kind of state she's in when she gets home. *If* she decides to come home. It suddenly strikes me that most sixteen-year-olds would have some kind of curfew. But I'm only thirteen months her senior, so am hardly in a position to impose one. I keep telling myself that Maya has always been so sensible, so responsible, so mature, but now I remember the flushed look on her face when she came into the kitchen to say goodbye, the sparkle in her smile, the fizz of excitement in her eyes. She is still only a teenager, I realize; she is not yet an adult, however much she may be forced to behave like one. She has a mother who thinks nothing of having sex on the floor of the front room while her children lie sleeping overhead, who brags to them about her teenage conquests, who goes out on the piss every week and staggers in at six in the morning with smudged make-up and torn clothes. What kind of role model has Maya ever had? For the first time in her life she is free. Am

I so sure she won't be tempted to make the most of it?

It's stupid to think like that. Maya is old enough to make her own choices. Plenty of girls her age sleep with their boyfriends. If she doesn't this time, she will the next, or the time after, or the time after that. One way or another it's going to happen. One way or another I'm going to have to deal with it. Except I can't. I can't deal with it at all. The very idea makes me want to pound my head against the wall and smash things. The idea of DiMarco, or anyone, holding her, touching her, kissing her . . .

A deafening bang, a blinding crack, pain shooting up my arm before I realize I've punched the wall with all my might: pieces of paint and plaster are flaking away from the imprint of my knuckles above the couch. Bent over double, I clutch my right hand with my left, clenching my teeth to stop myself from making a sound. For a moment everything darkens and I think I'm going to pass out, but then the pain hits me repeatedly in shocking, terrifying waves. I actually don't know what hurts more, my hand or my head. The thing I have feared and railed against these past few weeks – the total loss of control over my mind – has set in, and I have no way to fight it any more. I close my eyes and feel the coil of madness climb up my spine and creep into my brain. I watch it explode like the sun. So this is it, this is what it feels like after a long hard struggle – to lose the battle and finally go crazy.

Maya

He's lovely. I don't know why I ever thought he was some arrogant tosser. Just goes to show how flawed one's perception of others can be. He's considerate, he's courteous, he's polite; he actually seems genuinely interested in me. He tells me I look beautiful and then gives me a bashful smile. Once we are seated in the restaurant, he translates every single item on the menu for me and doesn't laugh or even look surprised when I tell him I've never tried artichokes before. He asks me lots of questions, but when I explain that my family situation is complicated, he appears to take the hint and backs off. He agrees that Belmont is a shithole and admits he can't wait to get out. He asks about Lochan and says he wishes he could get to know him better. He confides that his father is more interested in his business than in his only son and buys him ridiculous presents like a car to assuage his guilt for being abroad half the year. Yes, he is rich and he is spoiled, yet he is as neglected as we are. A completely different set of circumstances; the same sad outcome.

We talk for a long time. As he drives me home, I find myself wondering if he is going to kiss me. At one point, as we both reach out to turn down the radio, our hands touch and his lingers on mine for a moment. It feels strange, his fingers unfamiliar.

'Shall I walk you to your door or would that be . . . awkward?' He looks at me hesitantly and smiles when I do. I envision small faces peering from upstairs windows and agree that it's probably best if I get out alone. Fortunately, in the darkness, he has overshot the front door by two houses so no one from home can see us.

'Thank you for dinner. I had a really good time,' I say, surprised to find myself meaning it.

He smiles. 'Me too. D'you think maybe we could do it again sometime?'

'Yeah, why not?'

His smile broadens. He leans towards me. 'Goodnight then.'

'Goodnight.' I hesitate, my fingers on the door handle.

'Goodnight,' he says again with a smile, but this time he cups my chin in his hand. His face approaches mine and suddenly the realization hits me. I like Nico. I actually think he's a pretty decent person. He's good-looking and I'm attracted to him. But I don't want to kiss him. Not now. Not ever . . . I turn my head away just as his face meets mine and his kiss lands on my cheek instead.

As I draw back, he looks surprised. 'OK, well, till next time.'

I take a deep breath, groping for my bag at my feet, grateful for the darkness that hides the blush spreading across my face. 'I really like you as a friend, Nico,' I say in a rush. 'But, I'm sorry, I don't think I can go out with you again.'

'Oh.' He sounds surprised and a little hurt now. 'Well, look, just think about it, OK?'

'OK. See you Monday.' I get out of the car and slam the door behind me. I wave, and he is still wearing that look of perplexed amusement as he drives off, as if he thinks I am playing games.

I lean against a thick tree-trunk, staring up through the drizzle at a moonless sky. I have never felt so embarrassed in all my life. Why did I spend the whole evening leading him on? Acting fascinated by his stories, confiding in him? Why did I agree to see him again ten seconds before telling him we could only be friends? Why did I turn down a guy who, as well as being hot, actually turned out to be nice? *Because you're crazy, Maya. Because you are crazy and stupid and you want to spend the rest of your life as a social outcast. Because you so wanted this to work, you so desperately wanted this to work, you actually kidded yourself into believing things were going really well. Until you realized that the idea of kissing Nico, or any guy you could think of, was not what you wanted at all.*

What does this mean, then – I'm afraid? Scared of physical intimacy? No. I crave it, I dream about it. But for me there's no one. No one. Any guy, even imaginary, would just feel like second best. Second best to what? I don't even have an image of the perfect boyfriend. I just know he must exist. Because I have all these feelings – of love, longing, wanting to be touched, dreaming of being kissed – yet no one to focus them on. It makes me want to scream in frustration. It makes me feel like a freak. But worse than that, I feel so desperately disappointed. Because all evening I believed Nico was the one. And then, when he tried to kiss me in the car, I realized with total, earth-shattering certainty that it would never feel right.

I trail back up to the house. This stupid dress is so short and skimpy, I'm beginning to freeze. I feel so empty, so let down. Yet I have only let *myself* down. Why couldn't I have acted normal for a change? Why couldn't I have forced myself to kiss him? Maybe it wouldn't have been so terrible. Maybe I could have borne it . . . The lights in the front room are still on. I check my watch: quarter to eleven. Oh please, not another argument between Kit and Lochan. I unlock the door and it sticks. I kick it with the stupid high heels I doubt I'll ever wear again. The house, like a giant tomb, makes no sound. I slide off my shoes and pad in stockinged feet down the hallway to switch off the light in the front room. All I want to do is go to bed and forget about this whole lousy, self-deluded evening.

A figure seated on the edge of the couch makes me jump. Lochan is hunched over, his head in his hands.

'I'm back.'

Not even a flicker of acknowledgement.

'Is Kit still out?' I ask with trepidation, fearing another scene.

'He came in about twenty minutes ago.' Lochan doesn't even look up. Charming.

'I had a great evening, by the way.' My tone is caustic. But if he's feeling sorry for himself just because he had to put the children to bed on his own for once, I refuse to give him the satisfaction of knowing that my evening was crap too.

'You only went out for dinner?' Abruptly he lifts his head and favours me with a penetrating gaze. Self-conscious under his sudden scrutiny, I become aware that my hair is coming down, stray strands hanging over my face, damp from standing out in the drizzle.

'Yes,' I answer slowly. 'Why?'

'You went out at seven. It's nearly eleven.'

I can't believe this is Lochan talking. 'You're telling me I have to be home by a certain time?' My voice rises in outrage.

'Of course not,' he snaps irritably. 'I'm just surprised. Four hours is a hell of a long time to spend over dinner.'

I close the front-room door behind me as I feel my blood pressure begin to rise. 'It wasn't four hours. By the time we'd driven halfway across town, found a place to park, waited for a table . . . We just talked – a lot. Turns out he's a pretty interesting guy. He doesn't exactly have it easy, either.'

As soon as the words are out of my mouth, Lochan leaps up, strides over to the window, then swings back wildly. 'I don't give a damn about how poor little rich boy didn't get the exact car he wanted for his eighteenth – I've heard all about that at Belmont. What

393

I'm having trouble understanding is why the hell you pretend to have just been out for dinner when you've been gone four hours!'

This can't be happening. Lochan has gone mad. He's never spoken to me like this in his life. I've never seen him so furious with me before.

'Are you saying I have to account for my every move?' I challenge him, my eyes widening in disbelief. 'You're actually asking me for a blow-by-blow account of what happened throughout the whole evening?' My voice continues to rise.

'No! I just don't want to be lied to!' Lochan starts to shout.

'What I do or don't do on a date is none of your damn business!' I yell in return.

'But why does it have to be secret? Can't you just be honest?'

'I *am* being honest! We went out for dinner, we talked, he drove me home. End of story!'

'Do you really think I'm that gullible?'

This is the last straw. A row with Lochan after a week of being ignored: the perfect end to an evening of bitter disappointment that, had I allowed it, could have been so great. All I wanted to do when I came in was crawl into bed and try to put this wasted opportunity out of my mind. And instead I find myself subjected to this.

I start backing away towards the door, raising my hands in surrender. 'Lochan, I don't know what the hell your problem is but you're being an absolute bastard. What's happening to you? I come in expecting you to ask me if I had a nice time, and instead you give me the third degree and then accuse me of lying! Even if something *had* happened on this date, what on earth makes you think I'd want to tell you?' I turn for the door.

'So you *did* sleep with him,' he says flatly. 'Like mother, like daughter.'

His words slice the air between us. My hand freezes around the cold metal knob. Slowly, painfully, I turn. 'What?' The word escapes from me in a small puff of air, barely more than a whisper.

Time seems to be suspended. He is standing there in his green T-shirt and faded jeans, squeezing the knuckles of one hand with the palm of the other, his back to the giant slice of night. And I find myself facing a stranger. His face has a curious raw look, as if he's been crying, but the fire in his eyes scorches my face. How foolish I was to kid myself I knew him so well. He is my brother and yet, for the very first time, appears before me as a stranger.

'I can't believe you said that.' My voice, a quiver of disbelief, emanates from a being I barely recognize; one that is crushed, hurt beyond repair. 'I always thought of you as the one person' – a steadying breath – 'the one person who would never, ever hurt me.'

He looks stricken, his face mirroring the pain and disbelief I feel inside. 'Maya, I'm not feeling well – that was unforgiveable. I don't know what I'm saying any more.' His voice is shaking, as appalled as my own. Pressing his hands to his face, he swings away from me, pacing the room, gasping for breath, his eyes filled with a wild, almost manic look.

'I just need to know – please understand – I have to know, otherwise I'm going to lose my mind!' He shuts his eyes tight and inhales raggedly.

'Nothing happened!' I shout, my anger abruptly replaced by fear. 'Nothing happened. Why won't you believe me?' I grab him by the shoulders. 'Nothing happened, Lochie! Nothing happened – nothing, nothing, nothing!' I am practically screaming but I don't care. I don't understand what is happening to him. What is happening to me.

'But he kissed you.' His voice is hollow, devoid of all emotion. Pulling away from me, he crouches down on his heels. 'He kissed you, Maya, he kissed you.' His eyes are half closed, his face expressionless now, as if he is so depleted he no longer has the strength to react.

'He didn't kiss me!' I yell, grabbing his arms and trying to shake him back to life. 'He tried to, OK, but I didn't let him! D'you know why? D'you want to know why? D'you really, really want to know why?' Still gripping him with both hands, I lean forward, gasping, as tears, hot and heavy, fall down my cheeks. 'This is why . . .' Crying, I kiss Lochan's cheek. 'This is why . . .' With a muffled sob, I kiss the corner of

Lochan's lips. 'This is why . . .!' Closing my eyes, I kiss Lochan's mouth.

I'm falling, but I know I'm OK, because it's with him, it's with Lochie. My hands are on his burning cheeks, my hands are in his damp hair, my hands are against his warm neck. He is kissing me back now, with strange little sounds that suggest he might be crying too, kissing me so hard that he is shuddering, gripping the tops of my arms tight and pulling me towards him. I taste his lips, his tongue, the sharp edges of his front teeth, the soft warmth inside his mouth. I slide up astride his lap, wanting to get even closer, wanting to disappear into him, blend my body with his. We come up briefly for air and I catch sight of his face. His eyes brim with unfallen tears. He emits a ragged sound; we kiss some more, soft and tender, then fierce and hard again, his hands grasping at the straps of my dress, twisting them, clenching the material in his fists as if fighting back pain. And I know how he feels – it's so good it hurts. I think I'm going to die from happiness. I think I'm going to die from pain. Time has stopped; time is racing. Lochie's lips are rough yet smooth, hard yet gentle. His fingers are strong: I feel them in my hair and on my neck and down my arms and against my back. And I never want him to let me go.

A sound explodes like a thunderclap above us; our bodies jolt in unison and suddenly we are not kissing any more, although I cling to the collar of his T-shirt, his arms strong and tight around me. There is the sound of the toilet flushing, then the familiar creak of Kit's ladder. Neither of us seems able to move, even though the ensuing silence makes it clear Kit has gone back to bed. My head against Lochan's chest, I hear the magnified sounds of his heart – very loud, very fast, very strong. I can hear his breathing too: sharp jagged spikes piercing the frozen air.

He is the first to break the silence. 'Maya, what the hell are we doing?' Although his voice is barely more than a whisper, he sounds close to tears. 'I don't understand: why – why the hell is this happening to us?'

I close my eyes and press against him, stroking his bare arm with my fingertips. 'All I know right now is that I love you,' I say in quiet desperation, the words spilling out of their own accord. 'I love you far more than just as a brother. I . . . I love you in – in every kind of way.'

'I feel like that too . . .' His voice is shocked and raw. 'It's – it's a feeling so big I sometimes think it's going to swallow me. It's so strong I feel it could kill me. It keeps growing and I can't – I don't know what to do to stop it. But – but we're not supposed to do this – to love each other like *this*!' His voice cracks.

'I know that, OK? I'm not stupid!' I'm angry suddenly because I don't want to hear it. I close my eyes because I just can't think about that now. I can't let myself think about what it means. I won't think about what it's called. I refuse to let labels from the outside world spoil the happiest day of my life. The day

I kissed the boy I had always held in my dreams but never allowed myself to see. The day I finally ceased lying to myself, ceased pretending it was just one kind of love I felt for him when in reality it was every kind of love possible. The day we finally broke free of our restraints and gave way to the feelings we had so long denied just because we happened to be brother and sister.

'We've – oh God – we've done a terrible thing.' Lochan's voice is shaking, hoarse and breathless with horror. 'I – I've done a terrible thing to you!'

I wipe my cheeks and turn my head to look up at him. 'We haven't done anything wrong! How can love like this be called terrible when we're not hurting anyone?'

He gazes down at me, his eyes glistening in the weak light. 'I don't know,' he whispers. 'How can something so wrong feel so right?'

Lochan

I tell Maya that she needs to sleep but I know I can't – I'm too afraid to go upstairs and sit on my bed and go crazy in that tiny room, alone with my terrifying thoughts. She says she wants to stay with me: she's frightened that if she goes away, I'll disappear. She doesn't need to explain – I feel it too: the fear that if we part now, this incredible night will just vanish, evaporate like a dream, and we will wake in the morning back in our separate bodies, back in our ordinary lives.

Yet here on the couch, my arms around her as she sits curled up against me, head resting against my chest, I still feel frightened – more frightened than I've ever been before. What just happened was unbelievable yet somehow completely natural, as if deep down I always knew this moment would come, even though I never once allowed myself to consciously think about it, to imagine it in any way. Now that it has arrived, I can only think of Maya, sitting right here against me, her breath warm against my bare arm.

It's as if there is a great wall preventing me from crossing to the other side, from casting my mind out into the external world, the world beyond the two of us. Nature's security valve is at work, preventing me from even contemplating the implications of what just happened, keeping me, for the moment at least, safe from the horror of what I have done. It's as if my mind knows it cannot go there yet, knows that right now I'm not strong enough to deal with the outcome of these overwhelming feelings, these momentous actions. But the fear remains – the fear that in the cold light of day we will be forced to come to terms with what was, quite simply, an awful mistake; the fear that we will have no choice but to bury this night as if it never took place, a shameful secret to be filed away for the rest of our lives until, brittle with age, it crumbles to dust – a faint, distant memory, like the powder of a moth's wings on a windowpane, the spectre of something that perhaps never occurred, existing solely in our imagination.

I cannot bear the thought of this being just one moment in time, over almost before it started, already retreating into the past. I must hold onto it with all my might. I cannot allow Maya to slip away because, for the first time in my life, my love for her feels whole, and everything that has led up to this point suddenly makes sense, as if all this was meant to be. But as I gaze down at her sleepy face, the freckled cheekbones, the white skin, the dark curl of her eyelashes, I feel an over-whelming ache, like acute homesickness – a longing for something I can never have. Sensing my eyes on her, she looks up and smiles, but it is a sad smile, as if she too knows how precarious our new love is, how dangerously threatened by the outside world. The ache inside me deepens, and all I can think of is what it felt like to kiss her, how brief that moment was and how desperately I want to live it once more.

She keeps on looking at me with that little wistful smile, as if waiting, as if she knows. And the blood is hot in my face, my heart racing, my breath quickening, and she notices that too. Raising her head from my chest, she asks, 'Do you want to kiss me again?'

I nod, mute, heart pounding anew.

She looks at me expectantly, hopefully. 'Go on, then.'

I close my eyes, my breathing laboured, my chest filling with a mounting sense of despair. 'I don't – I don't think I can.'

'Why not?'

'Because I'm worried . . . Maya, what if we can't stop?'

'We don't have to . . .'

I breathe deeply and turn away, the air around me thrumming with heat. 'Don't even think like that!'

Her expression sobers and she brushes her fingers up and down the inside of my arm, her eyes heavy with sadness. Yet her touch fills me with longing. I never thought that the mere touch of a hand could stir so much.

'All right, Lochie, we'll stop.'

'*You* have to stop. Promise me.'

'I promise.' She touches my cheek, turning me back towards her. I take her face in my hands and start to kiss her, gently at first; and as I do so, all the pain and worry and loneliness and fear start to evaporate until all I can think of is the taste of her lips, the warmth of her tongue, the smell of her skin, her touch, her caresses. And then I'm struggling to keep calm and her hands are pressing against the sides of my face, her breath hot and rapid against my cheek, her mouth warm and wet. My hands want to touch her all over, but I can't, I can't, and we're kissing so hard it hurts – it hurts that I can't do more, it hurts that however hard I kiss her I can't . . . I can't—

'Lochie . . .'

I don't care about the promise. I don't remember why I even suggested it. I don't care about anything – anything except for—

'Easy, Lochie—'

I press my lips back down over her mouth, holding her tight to stop her from moving away.

'Lochie, stop.' This time she pulls away and pushes me back, holding me at arm's length, her fingers gripping my shoulders. Her lips are red – she looks flushed and wild and exquisite.

I'm breathing too fast. Much too fast.

'You made me promise.' She looks upset.

'I know, all right!' Jumping up, I start pacing the room. I wish there was an icy pool of water for me to dive into.

'Are you OK?'

No, I'm not. I've never felt like this before and it scares me. My body seems to have taken over. I'm so aroused I can hardly think. I've got to calm down. I've got to stay in control. I can't let this happen. I run my hands through my hair repeatedly and the air escapes from my lungs in a rush.

'I'm sorry. I should have said it sooner.'

'No!' I spin round. 'It's not your fault, for God's sake!'

'All right, all right! Why are you angry?'

'I'm not! I'm just—' I stop and lean my forehead against the wall, fighting the urge to head-butt it. 'Oh, Jesus, what are we going to do?'

'Nobody would have to find out,' she says softly, chewing the tip of her thumb.

'No!' I shout.

Storming into the kitchen, I rummage furiously through the freezer for ice cubes for a cold drink. Hot acid shoots through my veins and my heart is hammering so hard I can hear it. It's not just the physical frustration, it's the impossibility of our situation, the horror of what we've got ourselves into, the despair of knowing that I will never be able to love Maya the way I want to.

'Lochie, for goodness' sake, calm down.' Her hand touches my arm as I wrestle with the freezer drawer.

I knock it away. 'Don't!'

She takes a step back.

'D'you know what we're doing here? Have you any idea at all? D'you know what they call this?' I slam the freezer shut and move round to the other side of the table.

'What's got into you?' she breathes. 'Why are you suddenly turning on me?'

I stop abruptly and stare at her. 'We can't do this,' I blurt out, aghast with the sudden realization. 'We can't. If we start, how will we ever stop? How on earth will we be able to keep this a secret from everyone for the rest of our lives? We'll have no life – we'll be trapped, living in hiding, always having to pretend—'

She stares back at me, her blue eyes wide with shock. 'The kids . . .' she says softly, a new realization suddenly dawning. 'The kids – if even one person found out, they'd be taken away!'

'Yes.'

'So we can't do this? We really can't?' It's phrased as a question, but I can see by the stricken look on her face that she already knows the answer.

Shaking my head slowly, I swallow hard and turn to look out of the kitchen window to hide the tears in my eyes. The sky is on fire and the night has ended.

ENDLESS LOVE:
THE VALENTINE OF
DANIEL AND LUCINDA

BY
LAUREN KATE

1.
Love Long Ago

Luce found herself at the far end of a narrow alley under a slit of sun-bleached sky.

'Bill?' she whispered.

No reply.

She'd come out of the Announcer groggy and disoriented. Where was she now? There was a bustling brightness at the other end of the alley, some sort of busy market where Luce caught flashes of fruit and fowl changing hands.

A biting winter wind had frozen the puddles in the alley into slush, but Luce was sweating in the black ball gown she wore ... where had she first put on this tattered gown? The king's ball at Versailles. She'd found this dress in some princess's armoire. And then she'd kept it on when she stepped through to the performance of *Henry VIII* in London.

She sniffed at her shoulder: It still smelled like smoke from the fire that had burned down the Globe.

From above her came a set of loud bangs: shutters being thrown wide. Two women poked their heads out of adjacent second-story casement windows. Startled, Luce pressed herself against a shadowed wall to listen, watching as the women fussed about with a shared clothesline.

'Will you let Laura watch the festivities?' said one, a matronly woman in a simple gray cowl, as she pinned an enormous pair of damp trousers to the line.

'I see no harm in *watching*,' said the other, a younger woman. She shook out a dry linen shirt and folded it with swift efficiency. 'So long as she doesn't partake of those bawdy displays. Cupid's Urn! Hah! Laura's only seen twelve years; she's far too young to fetch a broken heart!'

'Ah, Sally' – the other woman sighed through a thin smile – 'you're too strict. Saint Valentine's is a day for all hearts, young *and* old. It might do you and the mister a bit of good to be swept up in its romance yourselves, eh?'

A lone peddler, a short man dressed in a blue tunic and blue tights, turned down the alley, pushing a wooden cart. The women eyed him with suspicion and lowered their voices.

'Pears,' he sang up to the open casements, from which the women's heads and hands had disappeared.

'Rotund fruit of love! A pear for your Valentine will make this next year a sweet one.'

Luce edged along the wall toward the alley's exit. Where was Bill? She hadn't realized just how much she'd come to rely on the little gargoyle. She needed different clothes. An idea of where and when she was. And a briefing on what she was doing here.

Medieval city of some sort. A Valentine's Day festival. Who knew it was such an old tradition?

'Bill!' she whispered. But there was still no answer.

She reached the corner and edged her head around.

The sight of a soaring castle made her halt. It was massive and majestic. Ivory towers rose into the blue sky. Golden banners, each emblazoned with a lion, billowed gently from high poles. She half expected to hear a blare of trumpets. It was like stumbling accidentally upon a fairy tale.

Instinctively, Luce wished Daniel were there. This was the kind of beauty that didn't seem real until you shared it with someone you loved.

But there was no sign of Daniel. Just a girl.

A girl Luce recognized instantly.

One of her past selves.

Luce watched as the girl strolled across the cobblestoned bridge that led to the tall doors of the castle. She moved past them, to the entrance of a fantastic rose garden, where the blossomless bushes were sculpted into tall, wall-like hedges. Her hair was loose and long and messy, trailing halfway down the back of her white linen gown. The old Luce – Lucinda – gazed longingly at the garden gate.

Then Lucinda stood on tiptoe, reached a pale hand over the gate, and from the middle of a bare-branched bush, bent the stem of a single unlikely red rose toward her nose.

Was it possible to smell a rose sadly? Luce couldn't say; all she knew was that something about this girl – herself – felt *sad*. But why? Did it have something to do with Daniel?

Luce was about to step fully from the shadowed alley when she heard a voice and saw a figure approach her past self.

'There you are.'

Lucinda released the rose, which snapped back into the garden, losing its blossom on the thorns as it crossed. The red teardrop-shaped petals showered down on her shoulders as she turned to face the voice.

Luce watched Lucinda's posture change, a smile stretching across her face at the sight of Daniel. And Luce felt that same smile on her *own* face. Their bodies might be different, their daily lives looked nothing alike, but when it came to Daniel, their shared soul aligned completely.

He wore a full suit of armor, though his helmet was off and his golden hair was lank with sweat and dirt. He'd clearly come from the road; the speckled white mare beside him looked weary. Luce had to fight every urge in her body not to run into his arms. He was breathtaking: a knight in shining armor to out-shine any fairytale knight.

But this Daniel wasn't her Daniel. This Daniel belonged to another girl.

'You came back!' Lucinda broke into a run, her tresses streaming in the wind.

Her past self's arms stretched out, inches from Daniel—

But the image of her valiant knight wavered in the wind.

And then it was gone. Disgust crept into Luce's stomach as she watched Daniel's horse and armor vanish into thin air and Lucinda – who could not stop herself in time – crash headfirst into a belching stone gargoyle.

'Fumble!' Bill cackled, spinning in a loop-the-loop.

Lucinda screamed, tripped over her gown, and landed in the mud on her hand and knees. Bill's craggy laughter echoed off the façade of the castle. He flitted higher in the air and then eyed Luce glaring at him from across the street.

'There you are!' he said, cartwheeling toward her.

'I told you never to do that again!'

'My acrobatics?' Bill hopped onto her shoulder. 'But if I do not practice, I win no medals,' he said in a Russian accent.

She swatted him off. 'I meant changing into Daniel.'

'I didn't do it to you, I did it to her. Maybe your past self thinks it's funny.'

'She doesn't.'

'That's not my fault. Besides, I'm not a mind reader. You expect me to realize you're speaking on behalf of all Lucindas ever, every time you talk. You never said anything about not razzing your past lives. It's all in good fun. For me, anyway.'

'It's *cruel*.'

'If you insist on splitting hairs, fine, she's all yours. I suppose you don't need me pointing out that what *you* do with 'em ain't exactly humane!'

'You're the one who taught me how to go three-D.'

'My point exactly,' he said with an eerie cackle that sent goose bumps running up Luce's arms.

Bill's eyes fell on a diminutive stone gargoyle capping one of the columns of the garden gates. He banked in the air, circled back to the column, and slung his arm around the gargoyle's shoulder as if he'd finally found a true companion. 'Mortals! Can't live with 'em, can't consign them to the fiery depths of Hell. Am I right or am I right?' He looked back at Luce. 'Not a big talker.'

Luce could no longer stand it. She ran forward, hurrying to help Lucinda up from the ground. Her past self's dress was torn at the knees and her face was sickly pale.

'Are you all right?' Luce asked. She expected the

girl to be thankful, but instead, she recoiled.

'Who— What are you?' Lucinda gaped at Luce. 'And what kind of devil is that thing?' She flung her hand in Bill's direction.

Luce sighed. 'He's just— Don't worry about him.'

Bill probably did look like a devil to this medieval incarnation. Luce most likely didn't look much better – some mental girl running up to her dressed in a futuristic ball gown that reeked of smoke?

'I'm sorry,' Luce said, glancing over the girl's shoulder at Bill, who seemed amused.

'Thinking about going three-D?' Bill asked.

Luce cracked her knuckles. Fine. She knew she had to cleave to this past body if she was going to move forward on her quest, but there was something in her past self's face – bewilderment and a hint of in-explicable betrayal – that made her hesitate. 'This, uh, this will just take a moment.'

Her past self's eyes widened, but as she was about to pull away, Luce seized her past self's hand and squeezed.

The solid stones beneath her feet shifted and the world before Luce swirled like a kaleidoscope. Her stomach lurched up toward her throat, and as the world flattened back out, she was left with the distinctive nausea of cleaving. She blinked and, for that one un-settling instant, saw the disembodied view of both girls. There was medieval Lucinda – innocent, captive, and terrified; and there, beside her, was Luce – guilty, exhausted, obsessed.

There was no time to regret it. On the other side of the blink—

A single body, one conflicted soul.

And Bill's fat-lipped smirk taking it all in.

Luce clutched her heart through the rough linen dress Lucinda had been wearing. It hurt. Her whole body had become a heartache.

She was channeling Lucinda now, feeling what Lucinda had been feeling before Luce inhabited her body. It was a move that had become second nature to her – from Russia to Tahiti to Tibet – but no matter how many times she did it, Luce didn't think she'd ever get used to suddenly *feeling* so keenly the landscape of her past emotions.

Right now it was the kind of raw pain Luce hadn't experienced since her early days at Sword & Cross, when she loved Daniel so much she thought it might split her in two.

'You're looking a little green around the gills.' Bill floated before her face, sounding more satisfied than concerned.

'It's my past. She's—'

'Panicked? Sick at heart with love for that worthless oaf of a knight? Yeah, the Daniel of this era jerked you around like a slot-machine pull on Seniors' Day at the casino.' He crossed his arms broodingly over his chest and did something Luce had never seen before:

He made his eyes flash violet. 'Maybe I'll be at the Valentine's Faire,' he said in a husky, affected tone, a grossly oversimplified impersonation of Daniel. 'Or maybe I have better things to do, like slash losers with my humungous sword—'

'Don't do that, Bill.' Luce shook her head, annoyed. 'Besides, if Daniel doesn't show at this Valentine's thing, he's got a good reason – I'm sure of it.'

'Yeah.' The croak returned to Bill's voice. 'You always are.'

'He's trying to protect me,' she argued, but her voice was weak.

'Or himself . . .'

Luce rolled her eyes. 'Okay, Bill, what is it I'm supposed to learn in this lifetime? That you think Daniel's a jerk? Got it. Can we move on?'

'Not exactly.'

Bill flew to the ground and sat beside her. 'Actually, we're taking a holiday from your education in this life,' he said. 'Based on your snippiness and the bags under my eyes' – he stretched out and displayed a wrinkly fold of saggy skin, which made a sound like a shaken bag of marbles – 'I'd say we both need a day off.

'So here's the deal: It's Valentine's Day – or an early form of it, anyway. Daniel is a knight, which means he's got his pick of the parties. He can grace the endless church-sanctioned nobleman's feast in the castle of his lord.' Bill jerked his head toward the towering white turrets behind them. 'Sure, there'll be a nice roast stag,

417

maybe even a sprinkle of salt, but you've got to hang with the *clergy*, and whose idea of a party is that?'

Luce glanced back at the fairy-tale castle. That was where Daniel lived? Was he inside those walls now?

'Or,' Bill continued, 'he can slum it at the *real* party out on the green tonight for that less-respectable sort of folk, where the ale flows like wine and the wine flows like ale. There'll be dancing, dining, and most importantly, wenching.'

'Wenching?'

Bill waved one tiny hand in the air. 'Nothing you have to worry about, darlin'. Daniel only has eyes for one wench in all of creation. I mean you.'

'Wench,' Luce said, looking down at her rough-spun cotton garments.

'There's a certain lost wench' – Bill elbowed Luce – 'who will be there at the Faire, scanning the crowd through the eyeholes of her painted mask for her hunky dreamboat.' He patted her cheek. 'Doesn't that sound like a great time, little sister?'

'I'm not here to have fun, Bill.'

'Try it out for one night – who knows, you might enjoy it. Most people do.'

Luce swallowed. 'But what will happen when he finds me? What am I supposed to learn before I burn up, before—'

'Whoa there!' Bill cried. 'Slow down, hothead. I told you – tonight's just about fun. A little bit of romance. A night off' – he winked – 'for both of us.'

418

'What about the curse? How can I drop everything and celebrate Valentine's Day?'

Bill didn't respond immediately. Instead, he paused thoughtfully, then said, 'What if I told you that this – tonight – is the only Valentine's Day you kids ever got to spend together?'

The words struck Luce immediately. 'Ever? We . . . never got to celebrate Valentine's Day?'

Bill shook his head. 'After today? No.'

Luce thought back to her days at Dover, how she and Callie would watch some of the other girls get chocolate hearts and roses on Valentine's Day. They'd made a tradition of lamenting how very, very single they were over strawberry milk shakes at the local diner. They'd spent hours conjecturing on the slim odds of ever having a date on Valentine's Day.

She laughed. She hadn't been far off: Luce had never had a Valentine's Day with Daniel.

Now Bill was telling her that she only ever had tonight.

Luce's quest through the Announcers, all her efforts to break the curse and discover what lay behind all of her reincarnations, finding an end to this endless cycle – yes, those were important. Of course they were.

But would the world end if she enjoyed this *one* time with Daniel?

She cocked her head at Bill. 'Why are you doing this for me?' she asked.

Bill shrugged. 'I have a heart, a soft spot for—'

'What? *Valentine's Day?* Why don't I buy that?'

'Even I once loved and lost.' And for the briefest of moments, it seemed the gargoyle looked wistful and sad. He stared right at her and sniffled.

Luce gave a laugh. 'Okay,' she said. 'I'll stay. Just for tonight.'

'Good.' Bill popped up and pointed a crooked claw down the alley. 'Now go, make merry.' He squinted. 'Actually, change your dress. *Then* make merry.'

2.
A Soul At Odds

Hours later, Luce leaned her elbows on the sill of the small stone casement window.

The village looked different from this second-story perch – a maze of interconnected stone buildings, thatched roofs angled here and there in something like a medieval apartment complex.

By late that afternoon, many of the windows, including the one Luce leaned out of, were draped with deep-green vines of ivy or dense boughs of holly that had been woven into wreaths. They were signs of the Faire taking place outside the city that evening.

Valentine's Day, Luce thought. She could feel Lucinda dreading it.

After Bill had disappeared outside the castle, for his mysterious 'night off', things had happened very quickly: she'd wandered alone through the city until a girl a few years older than her appeared from nowhere to whisk Luce up a flight of dank stairs into this small two-roomed house.

'Draw away from the window, sister,' a high voice called across the room. 'You're letting in Saint Valentine's draft!'

The girl was Helen, Lucinda's older sister, and the smoky, confining two-roomed house was where she and her family lived. The chamber's gray walls were bare, and the only furniture consisted of a wooden bench, a trestle table, and the stack of family sleeping pallets. The floor was strewn with rough straw and sprinkled with lavender – a meager attempt to clear the air of the foul smell from the tallow candles they had to use for light.

'In a moment,' Luce called back. The tiny window was the only place she didn't feel claustrophobic.

Down the alley to the right was the marketplace she'd glimpsed before, and if she leaned out far enough, she could see a sliver of the white stone castle.

It haunted Lucinda, that tiniest tease of a view – Luce sensed this through the soul they shared – because on the evening of the day Lucinda first met Daniel in the rose garden, she'd come home and coincidentally seen him peering pensively out of the tallest tower casement. Since then, she watched for him every chance she got, but he never appeared again.

Another voice whispered: 'What does she stare at

for so long? What could possibly be so interesting?'

'The good Lord only knows,' Helen replied, sighing. 'My sister is laden with dreams.'

Luce turned around slowly. Her body had never felt so strange. The part that belonged to medieval Lucinda was wilted and lethargic, flattened by the love she was certain she had lost. The part that belonged to Lucinda Price was holding fast to the idea that there might still be a chance.

It was a struggle to perform the simplest of tasks – like conversing with the three girls standing before her, alarmed expressions twisting their pretty faces.

The tallest one, in the middle, was Helen, Lucinda's only sister and the oldest of five children in their family. She was newly a wife, and as if to prove it, her thick blonde hair was divided into two braids and pinned in a matronly chignon.

At Helen's side was Laura, their young neighbor, who Luce realized was the girl she'd overheard the two women gossiping about over the clothesline. Though Laura was only twelve, she was alluringly beautiful – blonde with large blue eyes and a loud, saucy laugh that could be heard across the city.

Luce bit back a laugh, trying to reconcile Laura's mother's protectiveness with what Lucinda knew of the girl's own experience – pressing palms with the page boys in the cool recesses of the lord's wood. What Luce gleaned from Lucinda's memories of Laura reminded her of Arriane. Laura, like the angel, was easy to love.

Then there was Eleanor, Lucinda's oldest, closest friend. They'd grown up wearing one another's clothes, like sisters. They bickered like sisters, too. Eleanor had a blunt edge, often slicing dreamy Lucinda's reveries in two with a cutting remark. But she had a skill for bringing Lucinda back to reality, and she loved Lucinda deeply. It wasn't, Luce realized, so different from her present-day relationship with Shelby.

'Well?' Eleanor asked.

'Well, what?' Lucinda said, startled. 'Don't all stare at me at once!'

'We've only asked you three times which mask you're going to wear tonight.' Eleanor waved three brightly colored masks in Lucinda's face. 'Pray, end the suspense!'

They were simple leather domino masks, made to cover just the eyes and nose and tie around the back of the head with thin silk ribbon. All three were covered in the same coarse fabric, but each had been painted with a different design: one red with small black pansies, one green with delicate white blossoms, and one ivory with pale pink roses near the eyes.

'She stares as if she has not seen these same masks every one of her past five years of masquerading!' Eleanor murmured to Helen.

'She has the gift of seeing old things anew,' Helen said.

Luce shivered, though the room was warmer than it had been for most of the winter months. In exchange for the eggs the citizens had offered as gifts to the lord, he'd repaid each household with a small bundle of cedar firewood. So the hearth was bright and cheery, giving a healthy flush to the girls' cheeks.

Daniel had been the knight tasked with collecting the eggs and distributing the firewood. He'd stridden through the door with purpose, then staggered back when he saw Lucinda inside. It was the last time medieval Lucinda had seen him, and after months of stolen moments together in the forest, Luce's past self was certain she would never see Daniel again.

But why? Luce wondered now.

Luce felt Lucinda's shame at her family's meagre accommodations – but that didn't seem right. Daniel wouldn't care that Lucinda was a peasant's daughter. He knew that she was always and ever much more than that. There had to be something else. Something Lucinda was too sad to see clearly. But Luce could help her – find Daniel, win him back, at least for as long as she still had to live.

'I like the ivory one for you, Lucinda,' Laura prompted, trying to be helpful.

But Luce could not make herself care about the masks. 'Oh, any of them will be fine. Perhaps the ivory to match my gown.' She tugged dully at the draped fabric of her worn wool dress.

The girls erupted into laughter.

'You're not going to wear *that* common market gown?' Laura gasped. 'But we're all getting done up in our finest!' She collapsed dramatically across the wooden bench near the hearth. 'Oh, I would never want to fall in love wearing my dreary Tuesday kirtle!'

A memory pushed to the front of Luce's mind: Lucinda had disguised herself as a lady in her one fine gown and sneaked into the castle rose garden. That was where she first met Daniel in this life. That was why their romance felt like a betrayal from the beginning. Daniel had thought Lucinda something other than a peasant's daughter.

That was why the thought of donning that fine red gown again and pretending to make merry at a festival was a staggering prospect to Lucinda.

But Luce knew Daniel better than Lucinda did. If he had an opportunity to spend Valentine's Day with her, he would seize it.

Of course, she could explain none of this inner turmoil to the girls. All she could do was turn away and subtly wipe her tears with the back of her wrist.

'She looks as if love has already found and dealt roughly with her,' Helen murmured under her breath.

'I say, if love is rough with you, be rough with love!' Eleanor said in her bossy way. 'Stamp out sadness with dancing slippers!'

'Oh, Eleanor,' Luce heard herself say. 'You wouldn't understand.'

'And you *do* understand?' Eleanor laughed. 'You, the girl who wouldn't even put her name in Cupid's Urn?'

'Oh, Lucinda!' Laura cupped her hands over her mouth. 'Why not? I'd give anything if Mother would let me put my name in Cupid's Urn!'

'Which is why *I* had to toss her name into the urn for her!' Eleanor cried, seizing the train of Luce's gown and pulling her around the room in a circle.

After a chase that toppled the bench and the tallow candle on the casement ledge, Luce grabbed Eleanor's hand. 'You didn't!'

'Oh, a little fun will do you good! I want you dancing tonight, high and lively with the rest of the maskers. Come now, help me choose a visor. Which color makes my nose look smaller, rose or green? Perhaps I shall trick a man into loving me yet!'

Luce's cheeks were burning. Cupid's Urn! How did that have anything to do with a Valentine's Day with Daniel?

Before she could speak, out came Lucinda's party dress — a floor-length gown of red wool adorned with a narrow collar made of otter fur. It was cut lower across the chest than anything Luce would wear back home in Georgia; if Bill were here to see her, he would probably grunt a 'Hubba hubba' in her ear.

Luce sat still while Helen's fingers wove a stem of holly berries into her loose black hair. She was thinking of Daniel, the way his eyes had lit up in the rose garden when he first approached Lucinda . . .

A rapping startled them all; in the doorway, a

woman's face appeared. Luce recognized her instantly as Lucinda's mother.

Without thinking, she ran into the safe warmth of her mother's arms.

They closed around her shoulders, tight and affectionate. It was the first of the lives Luce had visited where she felt a strong connection with her mother. It made her feel blissful and homesick all at once.

Back home in Thunderbolt, Georgia, Luce tried to act mature and self-sufficient as often as she could. Lucinda was just the same, Luce realized. But at times like this — when heartbreak made the whole world cheerless — nothing would do but the comfort of a mother's embrace.

'My daughters, so fine and grown up, you make me feel older than I am!' Their mother laughed as she ran her fingers through Luce's hair. She had kind hazel eyes and a soft, expressive brow.

'Oh, Mother,' Luce said with her cheek against her mother's shoulder. She was thinking of Doreen Price and trying not to cry.

'Mother, tell us again how you met Father at the Valentine's Faire,' Helen said.

'Not that old tale again!' Their mother groaned, but the girls could see the story forming in her eyes already.

'Yes! Yes!' the girls all chanted.

'Why, I was younger than Lucinda when I was a

mother made,' her willowy voice began. 'My own mother bade me wear the mask she'd worn years before. She gave me this advice on my way out the door: "Smile, child, men like a happy maid. Seek happy nights to happy days . . ."'

As her mother dove into her tale of love, Luce found her eyes creeping back toward the casement, imagining the turrets of the castle, the vision of Daniel looking out. Looking for her?

After her story was done, her mother drew something from the pocket strung around her waist and handed it to Luce with a mischievous wink.

'For you,' she whispered.

It was a small cloth package tied with twine. Luce went to the window and carefully unwrapped it. Her fingers trembled as she loosened the twine.

Inside was a lacy heart-shaped doily about the size of her fist. Someone had inscribed these words with what looked to Luce like a blue Bic pen:

Roses are red,
Violets are blue,
Sugar is sweet,
And so are you.
I will look for you tonight—
Love, Daniel

Luce almost sputtered with laughter. This was something the Daniel she knew would *never* write. Clearly, someone else had been behind it. Bill?

But to the part of Luce that was Lucinda, the

words were a chaos of scribbles. She couldn't read, Luce realized. And yet, once the meaning of the poem was processed by Luce, she could feel an understanding break open in Lucinda. Her past self found this the freshest, most captivating poetry ever known.

She would go to the festival and she would find Daniel. She would show Lucinda how powerful their love could be.

Tonight there would be dancing. Tonight there would be magic in the air. And – even if it was the only time it ever happened in the long history of Daniel and Lucinda – tonight there would be the particular joy of spending Valentine's Day with the one she loved.

3.
Delight in Disorder

'Eleanor!' Luce shouted over a dense crowd of dancers as her friend bounced past in the spirited line of a jig. But Eleanor didn't hear her.

It was hard to say whether Luce's voice was drowned out by the delighted hoots of a crowd at a puppet show in one of the movable stages set up on the western edge of the dancing area or the raucous, hungry crowd lining up at the long food tables on the eastern side of the green. Or maybe it was just the sea of dancers in the middle, who bounded, twirled, and spun with reckless, romantic abandon.

It seemed as though the dancers at the Valentine's Faire were not just dancing—but also hollering, laughing, belting out verses to the troubadour's music, and hollering to friends across the muddy dance area. They were doing it all at once. And all at the top of their lungs.

Eleanor was out of earshot, spinning as she stamped out dance steps all the way across the oak-ringed green. Luce had no choice but to turn back to her clumsy partner and curtsy.

He was a spindly older man with sallow cheeks and ill-fitting lips whose slouched shoulders made him look like he wanted to hide behind his too-small lynx-face mask.

And yet Lucinda didn't care. She couldn't remember ever having had this much fun dancing. They'd been dancing since the sun kissed the horizon; now the stars shone like armor in the sky. There were always so many stars in past skies. The night was chilly, but Luce's face was flushed and her forehead was damp with perspiration. As the song neared its end, she thanked her partner and sidled between a line of dancers, eager to get away.

Because despite the joys of dancing under the stars, Luce hadn't forgotten about the real reason she was here.

She looked out across the green and worried that even if Daniel was somewhere out there, she might never find him. Four troubadours dressed in motley gathered on a wobbly dais at the northern edge of the green, plucking on lutes and lyres to play a song as sweet as a Beatles ballad. At a high school dance, these slow songs were the ones that made the single girls, including Luce, a little anxious—but here, the moves were built into the songs and no one was ever at a loss for a partner. You just grabbed the nearest warm body, for better or for worse, and you danced. A skipping jig for this one, a circling dance in groups of eight for another. Luce felt Lucinda knowing some of the moves innately; the rest of them were easy to pick up.

If only Daniel were here . . .

Luce withdrew to the edge of the green, taking a break. She studied the women's dresses. By modern standards, they weren't fancy, but the women wore them with such pride that the dresses seemed as elegant as any of the fine gowns she'd seen at Versailles. Many were made of wool; a few had linen or cotton accents sewn into a collar or a hem. Most people in the city only owned one pair of shoes, so worn leather boots abounded, but Luce quickly realized how much easier it was to dance in them than in high-heeled shoes that pinched her feet.

The men managed to look dapper in their best breeches. Most wore a long wool tunic on top for warmth. Hoods were tossed back over their shoulders – the weather that night was above freezing, almost mild. Most of their leather masks were painted to mimic the faces of forest animals, complementing the floral designs of the ladies' masks. A few men wore gloves, which looked expensive. But most of the hands

Luce touched that night were cold and chapped and red.

Cats stared from dirt roads around the green. Dogs searched for their owners among the mess of bodies. The air smelled like pine and sweat and beeswax candles and the sweet musk of fresh-baked gingerbread.

As the next song wound down, Luce spotted Eleanor, who seemed happy to be plucked from the arm of a boy whose red mask was painted like a fox's face.

'Where's Laura?'

Eleanor pointed toward a stand of trees, where their young friend leaned close to a boy they didn't recognize, whispering something. He was showing her a book, gesturing in the air. It looked like he took a great deal of care with his hair. He wore a mask made to resemble a rabbit's face.

The girls shared a giggle as they made their way through the crowd. There was Helen, sitting with her husband on a wool blanket spread out on the grass. They were sharing a wooden cup of steaming cider and laughing easily about something, which made Luce miss Daniel all over again.

There were lovers everywhere. Even Lucinda's parents had turned out for the Faire. Her father's wiry white beard scraped her mother's cheek as they sashayed around the green.

Luce sighed, then fingered the lace doily in her pocket.

Roses are red, violets are blue, if Daniel didn't write these words, then who?

The last time she'd received a note allegedly from Daniel, it had been a trap set by the Outcasts—

And Cam had saved her.

Heat rose on the back of her neck. Was this a trap? Bill had said it was just a Valentine's party. He'd put so much energy into helping her on her quest already, he wouldn't have left her alone like this if there had been any real danger. Right?

Luce shook the thought away. Bill had said Daniel would be here, and Luce believed him. But the wait was killing her.

She followed Eleanor toward a long table, where plates and bowls of casual, pot-luck-style food had been set out. There were sliced duck served over cabbage, whole hares that had been roasted on spits, cauldrons of baby cauliflowers with a bright orange sauce, high-piled platters of apples, pears, and dried currants harvested from the surrounding forests, and a whole long wooden table filled with misshapen, half-burned pies of meat and fruit.

She watched a man loosen a flat knife from a strap slung around his waist and cut himself a hefty slice of pie. On her way out the door that evening, Luce's mother had handed her a shallow wooden spoon, which she had threaded through a wool tie around her waist. These people were prepared for eating, fixing, and fighting, the way Luce was prepared for love.

Eleanor reappeared at Luce's side and held a bowl of porridge under her nose.

'Gooseberry jam on top,' Eleanor said. 'Your favorite.'

When Luce dipped her spoon into the thick concoction, a savory aroma wafted up and made her mouth water. It was hot and hearty and delicious – exactly what she needed to revive her for another dance. Before she realized it, she had eaten it all.

Eleanor glanced down at the empty bowl, surprised. 'Danced up an appetite, did you?'

Luce nodded, feeling warm and satisfied. Then she noticed two brown-robed clergymen sitting apart from the crowd on a wooden bench beneath an elm tree. Neither was taking part in the festivities – in fact, they looked more like chaperones than revelers – but the younger one moved his feet in time with the rhythm, while the other, who had a shriveled-looking face, glared darkly at the crowds.

'The Lord sees and hears this lewd debauchery perpetrated so near His house,' the shriveled-faced man scoffed.

'And closer than that, even.' The other clergyman laughed. 'Do you recall, Master Docket, just how much of the church's gold went toward His Lordship's Valentine's banquet? Was it twenty gold pieces for that stag? These people's festivities cost nothing more than the energy to dance. And they dance like angels.'

If only Luce could see her angel dancing toward her right now . . .

'Angels who'll sleep through tomorrow's working hours, mark my words, Master Herrick.'

'Can you not see the joy on these young faces?' The younger vicar's eyes swept across the green, found Luce's at the edge of the lawn, and brightened.

She found herself smiling back behind her mask – but her joy that evening would be vastly increased if she could be there in Daniel's arms. Otherwise, what was the point of taking this romantic night off?

It seemed that Luce and the shriveled-faced vicar were the only two people here *not* relishing the masquerade. And generally Luce loved a good party, but right now all she wanted to do was pluck the masks off the face of every boy who passed. What if she'd already missed him in the crowd? How would she know if the Daniel of this era would even be looking for her?

She stared so baldly at a tall blond boy whose mask made him look like an eagle that he bounded past the toymaker's stall and the puppet show to stand before her.

'Shall I introduce myself, or would you rather just keep staring?' His teasing voice sounded neither familiar nor unfamiliar.

For a moment, Luce held her breath.

She imagined the ecstasy of his hands around her waist . . . the way he always dipped her backward to preface a kiss . . . She wanted to touch the place where his wings bloomed from his shoulders, the secret scar no one knew about but her . . .

When she reached up to lift his mask, the boy grinned at her boldness – but his smile faded as quickly as Luce's did when she saw his face.

He was perfectly good-looking; there was just one problem: He wasn't Daniel. And so every aspect of this boy – from his square nose, to his strong jaw, to his pure-gray eyes – paled in comparison to the boy she had in mind. She let out a long, sad sigh.

The boy couldn't hide his embarrassment. He fumbled for words, then slipped his mask back over his face, making Luce feel terrible.

'I'm sorry,' she said, quickly backing away. 'I mistook you for someone else.'

Luckily, she backed into Laura, whose face, unlike Lucinda's, was cheery with the magic of the night.

'Oh, I hope they'll draw from Cupid's Urn soon!' Laura whispered, bouncing on her heels and drawing Luce mercifully away from the eagle boy.

'Did you sneak your name in there after all?' Luce asked, finding a smile.

Laura shook her head. 'Mother would slaughter me!'

'Won't be much longer.' Eleanor appeared at their side. She looked nervous. She was confident about everything except boys. 'They draw at the toll of the next church bells, to give the new sweethearts a chance to dance. Perhaps a kiss if they're lucky.'

The next church bells. To Luce, it seemed like the eight o'clock bells had only just rung, but she was certain time must be flying faster than she realized. Was it already almost nine? Her time to be with Daniel was running out – fast – and standing around obsessively scanning the gallery of masks wasn't doing any good. No eyes glowed violet behind their visor.

She had to act. Something told her she'd have better luck on the dance floor.

'Shall we dance again?' she asked the girls, pulling them back into the crowd.

The revelers had stamped the grass into mud. The musical arrangement had grown more intricate, a quick waltz, and the dances had changed, too.

Luce followed the light, fast steps, picking up the more complicated arm movements as she went along. Palm to palm with the gentleman in front of you, a simple curtsy, and then several skips in a wide circle around your partner to face the other side; then a swap with the girl to your left. Then palm to palm with the next young man, and the whole thing was repeated.

Halfway through the song, Luce was out of breath and giggling when she stopped in front of her new partner. Her feet suddenly felt welded to the mud.

He was tall and slender, wearing a mask with leopard's spots. The design was exotic to Lucinda –

there were no leopards in the woods around her city. It was certainly the most elegant mask she'd seen at the party. The man extended his gloved hands, and when Luce slipped hers cautiously inside, his grip was firm, almost possessive. Behind the holes around the leopard's eyes, there came a gentle glow as emerald-green irises locked with hers.

4.

Some Consequence Yet Hanging in the Stars

'Good evening, lady. How nimbly you dance. Like an angel.'

Luce's lips parted to respond, but her voice caught in her throat.

Why did Cam have to crash this party?

'Good evening, sir,' Luce responded with a quiver in her voice. From all the dancing, her face was flushed, and her braids had tumbled loose, and one of the sleeves of her dress had slipped off her shoulder. She could feel Cam's gaze on her bare skin. She reached to right her sleeve, but his gloved hand crossed hers to stop her.

'Such sweet disorder in your dress.' He drew a finger across her collarbone and she shivered. 'It inspires a man's imagination.'

The song changed keys, a cue for the dancers to change partners. Cam's fingers lifted off her skin, but Luce's heart still pounded as they danced away from each other.

She watched Cam from the corner of her eye. He was watching her. She knew somehow that this was not Cam from the present chasing her backward through time. This was the Cam who lived and breathed in this medieval air.

He was easily the most elegant dancer on the green. There was an ethereal quality to his steps that did not go unnoticed by the ladies. From the attention he was getting, Luce knew he was not from this city. He'd arrived specially to attend the Valentine's Faire. But why?

Then they were paired again. Was she still dancing? Her body felt stiff and rigid. Even the music seemed to stutter in an endless in-between beat, which made Luce worry that she and Cam would have to stay rooted to these spots, staring into one another's eyes forever.

'Are you all right, sir?' Luce hadn't expected to say that. But there was something strange in his expression.

It was a darkness even his mask could not conceal. This was not the dark of evil doings, not the terrifying way he'd appeared in the cemetery at Sword & Cross. No, this Cam's soul was crippled by sorrow.

What could make him look like that?

His eyes narrowed, as if he sensed her thoughts, and something in his face shifted.

'I have never been better.' Cam tilted his head. 'It's you I'm worried about, Lucinda.'

'Me?' Luce tried hard not to show how he affected

her. She wished for a different kind of mask altogether, an invisible one, which would prevent him from ever again thinking he knew how she felt.

He raised his mask to his forehead. 'You're engaged in an impossible endeavor. You'll end up brokenhearted and alone. Unless—'

'Unless what?'

He shook his head. 'There is so much darkness in you, Lucinda.' The leopard mask lowered again. 'Come back around, come back around . . .'

His voice trailed off as he began to dance away. For once, Luce wasn't through with him. 'Wait!'

But Cam had disappeared into the dance.

He was striding in slow circles with a new partner. Laura. Cam murmured something in the innocent girl's ear, and she tossed back her head and laughed. Luce fumed. She wanted to jerk simple, bright Laura away from Cam's darkness. She wanted to grab Cam and force him to explain. She wanted to have a conversation on her terms, not at momentary, melo-dramatic intervals between jig steps in the middle of a public festival in the Middle Ages.

There he was again, coming toward her in perfect control of the steps, as if influencing the tempo of the music. Luce couldn't have felt more out of control. Just when he was about to come before her again, a tall blond man dressed entirely in black deftly pushed him aside. He stood before her and made no pretense of dancing.

'Hello.'

She sucked in her breath. 'Hello.'

Tall, muscular, mysterious beyond all possibility. She would know him anywhere. She reached for him, desperate to feel some connection, to feel the sweetest flush at the touch of her true love's skin—

Daniel.

Just as the music was about to dictate that they change partners, it slowed – almost like magic – and morphed into something slow and beautiful.

Flames from the candles positioned all around the Faire flickered against the dark sky, and the entire world seemed to hold its breath. Luce stared into Daniel's eyes, and all the movement and colors around him faded away.

She had found him.

His arms came toward her, circling her waist as her body melted into his, buzzing with the thrill of his touch. Then she was deep in Daniel's arms and there was nothing so wonderful in all the world as dancing with her angel. Their feet kissed the ground with the lightness of their steps, and the flight was so obvious and innate in Daniel's body. She felt the buoyancy in her own heart, too, which she felt only when Daniel was near.

There was nothing so wonderful – except maybe his kiss.

Her lips parted in expectation, but Daniel just watched her, drinking her in with his eyes.

'I thought you'd never come,' she said.

Luce thought about escaping through the Announcers in her backyard, about chasing down her past lifetimes and watching them burn up, about the fights she and Daniel had had over keeping her safe and alive. Sometimes it was easy to forget how good they were together. How lovely he was, how kind, the way being with him made her feel like she was flying.

Just looking at him made the tiny hairs on her arms stand up, made her stomach flip-flop with nervous energy. And that was nothing compared to what kissing him did to her.

He raised his mask and held her so tightly against him she couldn't move. She didn't want to. She pored over every lovely feature of his face, her eyes lingering the longest on the soft curve of his lips. After all this buildup, she simply couldn't believe it. It was really him!

'I will always come back to you.' His eyes held her in a trance. 'Nothing can stop me.'

Luce rose on her toes, desperate to kiss him, but Daniel pressed a finger to her lips and smiled. 'Come with me,' he whispered, taking her hand.

Daniel led her past the edge of the green, past the ring of oak trees that encircled the revelers. The high grass tickled her ankles and the moon lit their way until they entered the chilly darkness of the forest. There Daniel picked up a small, glowing lantern, as if this was all part of his plan.

'Where are we going?' she asked, though it didn't really matter, as long as they were together.

Daniel just shook his head and smiled, holding out a hand to help her hop over a fallen branch blocking the path.

As they walked, the music faded until it was hard to discern, mingling with the low hooting of owls, the rustling of squirrels in tree branches, and the soft song of the nightingale. The lantern rocked on Daniel's arm and the light wobbled, reaching for the web of bare branches curling out toward them. Once, Luce would have been nervous about the shadows in the forest, but that seemed like millennia ago.

As they walked hand in hand, Luce's and Daniel's feet traced a narrow pebble path. The night grew colder and she leaned close to him for warmth, burrowing deep into the arms he wrapped around her.

When they arrived at a fork in the path, Daniel paused for a moment, almost as if he'd lost his way. Then he turned to face her. 'I should explain,' he said. 'I owe you a Valentine's gift.'

Luce laughed. 'You don't owe me anything. I just want to be with you.'

'Ah, but I received your gift—'

'*My* gift?' She looked up, surprised.

'And it touched me to my core.' He reached out and took her hand. 'I should apologize if I have ever made you wonder about my affections. Until just yesterday, I didn't think I would be able to meet you here tonight.'

A crow cawed, soaring overhead and landing on a wobbly branch above them.

'But then a messenger arrived and gave all the knights in my care strict instructions to attend the Faire. I fear I rode my horse to near exhaustion in my haste to find you here tonight. It's just that I have been so eager to repay you for your most thoughtful gift.'

'But Daniel, I didn't—'

'Thank you, Lucinda.' Then he produced a leather sheath that looked like it might hold a dagger. Luce tried not to look too baffled, but she had never seen it before in her life.

'Oh.' She laughed under her breath and fingered the doily in her pocket. 'Do you ever get the feeling someone's watching over us?'

He smiled and said, 'All the time.'

'Maybe they're our guardian angels,' Luce murmured jokingly.

'Maybe,' Daniel said. 'But happily, right now, I think it's just you and me.'

He guided her to the left-hand path; they took a few more steps, then turned right and passed a crooked oak tree. In the darkness Luce could sense a small, circular clearing, where a vast oak tree must have been chopped down. Its stump stood in the center of the clearing — and something had been placed on it, but Luce couldn't see what yet.

'Close your eyes,' he told her, and when she did, she sensed the lantern moving away. She heard him rustling around the clearing, and she came very close to peeking, but she managed to hold out, wanting to experience the surprise just the way Daniel had intended it.

After a moment, a familiar scent filled Luce's nose. She closed her eyes and inhaled deeply. Something soft, floral . . . and absolutely unmistakable.

Peonies.

Still standing with her eyes closed, Luce could see her dreary dorm room back at Sword & Cross, made beautiful by the vase of peonies in her window that Daniel had brought to her at the hospital. She could see the cliff's edge in Tibet, where she'd stepped through to witness Daniel doling out single flowers to her past self in a game that ended too soon. She could almost smell the gazebo in Helston, which teemed with the peonies' feathery white blooms.

'Now open your eyes.'

She could hear the smile in Daniel's voice, and when she opened her eyes and saw him standing before the tree stump decked with a vast bouquet of peonies in a tall, wide copper vase, she covered her mouth and gasped. But that wasn't all. Daniel had threaded peony blossoms through the slender branches. He'd made vases of the pocks in all the surrounding trees' stumps. He'd strewn the ground with the peonies' delicate, snowy petals. He had woven a wreath for her hair.

He'd lit dozens of candles in small hanging lanterns all around, so that the whole clearing glowed with a magical brilliance. When he stepped forward to place the wreath on Luce's head, she – and her medieval self – nearly melted.

Medieval Lucinda didn't recognize the vast array of flowers; she would have no idea how this was possible in February – and she still loved every inch of the surprise. But Lucinda Price knew that the pure-white peonies were more than just a Valentine's Day gift. They were the symbol of Daniel Grigori's eternal love.

The candlelight flickered on his face. He was smiling but looked nervous, as if he didn't know whether she liked his gift or not.

'Oh, Daniel.' She raced into his arms. 'They're beautiful.'

He swung her in a circle and steadied the wreath on her head.

'They're called peonies. Not traditional Valentine's flowers,' he said, tossing his head thoughtfully, 'but still, they are . . . something of a tradition.'

Luce loved that she understood exactly what he meant.

'Perhaps we could make them our Valentine's tradition,' she suggested.

Daniel plucked a large blossom from the bouquet and slipped it between her fingers, holding it close to her heart. How many times across history had he done the exact same thing? Luce could see a glimmer in his eyes that suggested it never got old.

'Yes, our very own Valentine's tradition,' he mused. 'Peonies and . . . well, there ought to be something else. Oughtn't there?'

'Peonies and' – Luce racked her brain. She didn't need anything else. Didn't need anything but Daniel . . . and, well . . . 'How about peonies and a kiss?'

'That's a very, very good idea.'

Then he kissed her, his lips diving toward hers with unsurpassed desire.

The kiss felt wild and new and exploratory, as if they'd never kissed before.

Daniel was lost in the kiss, fingers woven through her hair, his breath hot on her neck as his lips explored her earlobes and her collarbone, the low cut of her dress. Neither of them could get enough air, but they refused to stop kissing.

An itch of heat crept up Luce's neck, and her pulse began to race.

Was it happening?

She would die of love right here, in the middle of this glowing white forest. She didn't want to leave Daniel, didn't want to be cast into the sky, into another black hole with only Bill for a companion.

Damn this curse. Why was she bound to it? Why couldn't she break free?

Tears of frustration welled in her eyes. She pulled

447

away from Daniel's lips, pressing her forehead to his and breathing hard, waiting for fire to sear her soul and take this body's life.

Only – when she stopped kissing Daniel, the heat faded, like a pot being lifted off a fire. She flew to his lips again.

The heat bloomed through her like a rose in summer.

But something was different. This was not the all-consuming flame that extinguished her, that had exiled her from past bodies and sent whole theaters up in smoke. This was the warm, dazzling ecstasy of kissing someone you truly loved – someone you were meant to be with forever. And for now.

Daniel watched her nervously, sensing that something important had happened inside her. 'Is anything the matter?'

There was so much to say—

A thousand questions jockeyed for the tip of her tongue, but then a gruff voice jarred her imagination.

The only Valentine's Day you kids ever got to spend together.

How was that possible? So much love had passed between them, and yet they had never before spent or would never again spend the most famously romantic day of the year in each other's arms.

Yet here they were, stuck in a moment between past and future, bittersweet and precious, confusing and strange and incredibly alive. Luce didn't want to screw this up. Maybe Bill, and the kind young clergyman, and her dear friend Laura were each right in their way.

Maybe it was sweet enough just to be in love.

'Nothing's wrong. Just kiss me, and kiss me again and again.'

Daniel lifted her off the ground and held her cradled in his arms. His lips were like honey. She wrapped her arms around the back of his neck. His hands traced the small of her back. Luce could barely breathe. She was overcome with love.

In the distance, church bells rang. They would be drawing from Cupid's Urn now, boys' hands randomly selecting their sweethearts, girls' cheeks red with antici-pation, everyone hoping for a kiss. Luce closed her eyes and wished that every couple on the green – that every couple in the world – could share a kiss as sweet as this one.

'Happy Valentine's Day, Lucinda.'

'Happy Valentine's Day, Daniel. Here's to many, many more.'

He gave her a warm, hopeful look and nodded. 'I promise.'

Epilogue
The Guardians

Back on the green, four troubadours completed their last song and exited the stage to make room for the presentation of Cupid's Urn. As all the tittering single

449

young men and women pressed excitedly up to the platform, the troubadours sneaked off to the side.

One by one, they raised their masks.

Shelby tossed down her recorder. Miles strummed one more chord on his lyre for good measure, and Roland harmonized on his fretted lute. Arriane slipped her hautboy into its slender wooden case and went to help herself to a big mug of punch. But she winced as she tossed it back and pressed a hand to the bloody cloth dressing the new wound on her neck.

'You jammed pretty well out there, Miles,' Roland said. 'You must have played the lyre somewhere before?'

'First time,' Miles said nonchalantly, though it was clear he was pleased by the compliment. He glanced at Shelby and squeezed her hand. 'I probably just sounded good because of Shel's accompaniment.'

Shelby started to roll her eyes, but she only got halfway there before she gave up and leaned in to peck Miles softly on the lips. 'Yeah, probably.'

'Roland?' Arriane asked suddenly, spinning around to scan the green. 'What happened to Daniel and Lucinda? A moment ago they were right over there. Oh' – she clapped her forehead – 'can nothing go right for love?'

'We just saw them dancing,' Miles said. 'I'm sure they're okay. They're together.'

'I told Daniel expressly, "Spin Lucinda into the center of the green where we can see you." It's as if he still doesn't know how much work goes into this!'

'I guess he had other plans,' Roland said broodingly. 'Love sometimes does.'

'You guys, relax.' Shelby's voice steadied the others, as if her new love had bolstered her faith in the world. 'I saw Daniel lead her into the forest, thataway. Stop!' she cried, tugging on Arriane's black cloak. 'Don't follow them! Don't you think, after everything, they deserve some time alone?'

'Alone?' Arriane asked, letting out a heavy sigh.

'Alone.' Roland came to stand next to Arriane, draping an arm around her, careful to avoid her injured neck.

'Yes,' Miles said, his fingers threaded through Shelby's. 'They deserve some time alone.'

And in that moment under the stars, a simple understanding passed among the four. Sometimes love needed a lift from its guardian angels, to get its feet off the ground. But once it made its first early beats toward flight, it had to be trusted to take wing on its own and soar past the highest conceivable heights, into the heavens – and beyond.

FROM
MIDWINTERBLOOD

BY
MARCUS SEDGWICK

Eric sleeps late.

It's the curtains, the blinds, he tells himself.

'Nothing to wake me up,' he says.

He decides to set an alarm for the next morning, not remembering his device is dead, nor that his charger is missing.

He showers, for a long time, then goes downstairs to eat another huge and delicious breakfast. At the back of his mind is a vague thought, a mere feeling, like an itch that wants to be scratched. But it's so faint and he's soon able to ignore it. There are firm fresh raspberries in a bowl on the table. He takes a mouthful, then a few mouthfuls more, until the whole bowl is finished.

He sits back, and sighs happily.

Only then does he see a short handwritten note leaning against a vase of flowers in the centre of the table.

It's a lovely day for a swim. The south pier is the best.

He picks the note up, slowly.

'So it is!' he says.

After breakfast he rolls up a towel from the bathroom and sets off, to the south.

As far as he can remember, he hasn't been to the far south of the island yet, and it doesn't even occur to him why he can't remember if he has or not. Nor does he realise that he has lost track of time, though he only arrived a few days ago.

Homeway twists and turns past more colourful houses, until he reaches a junction, where a tiny wooden sign points the way to the pier. He follows this smaller path for a few minutes more, and then he sees the sea in front of him.

It's beautiful. It's so beautiful, it takes his breath away. It's not spectacular, it's not jaw dropping, it's simply a lovely sight, that makes the heart glad that such places exist. The greys and browns of the rocks, the trees and the wild grass, the sea, waiting for him, and only for him; the place is utterly deserted, he can see neither people nor houses.

He goes down to the pier and, taking his shoes off, sits with his feet in the water for a while, then undresses and slides into the water, swimming out far away from the jetty.

He turns and looks at the island, and feels that little itch at the back of his head again. He swims closer to the pier, ducking underwater for long spells.

Suddenly, as he surfaces, someone is there in the water with him, an arm's length away.

All he sees at first is a splash as they dive in, but moments later, a head and shoulders break the surface in a tumble.

It's Merle. Her wet hair is drawn back, and down her neck.

Neither of them say anything, and as Eric treads water, Merle edges closer.

There's that gently intense look on her face again, that's something he does remember, something that is pushing through the clouds in his mind.

She reaches out a hand, treading water, and their fingertips meet.

She whispers, just loud enough to be heard over the shushing of the waves.

'I followed you.'

Eric hesitates for a moment, wondering, but then he's laughing, and Merle is too.

'You.'

They swim together, far out to sea.

They duck under the surface, twisting and turning, hand in hand where they can, and gliding through the deep, Eric's lips brush her neck, just once. Finally they come up for air. And when they do, they do so laughing.

'This is ridiculous!' shouts Eric, and Merle shrugs, and smiles, as if to say, so what?

Eric tries again.

'Have we done this before?' he calls.

Merle is a few strokes away. He pulls his way over to her, and tries again.

'Have we done this before?'

Merle shrugs again.

'I feel like we've done this before,' he says, intently. 'But a long time ago. A very long time ago.'

She's gone, under the water again.

Eric thinks about his life, something he usually avoids, because it has not always been an easy one. He wonders if a few moments of utter and total joy can be worth a lifetime of struggle.

Maybe, he thinks. Maybe, if they're the right moments.

They swim some more, and finally, exhausted, climb onto the rocks to dry in the warm sun.

Eric turns and holds Merle's hands. He looks at his hands, a little older than hers. He looks at her younger ones. What if it were the other way round? What if his were the younger hands? Would it matter?

He asks himself why *this* hand, is *his* hand. Could it have been someone else's? And why is that *her* hand? Does it matter? And what if she were different? No, he thinks, as these strange and somehow foolish questions roll around in his head. No, it wouldn't matter. Even if she were different, she would still be *she*.

'This is ridiculous,' he says again, and she sits up, and gently takes his head between her hands.

'Why?' she says. 'Why is it? Why is it any more ridiculous than a thousand things? That the earth spins round the sun, that water can eat a mountain away, that a salmon can swim a thousand miles across the ocean to find the very stream it was born in. It's not ridiculous. It's just . . . how it is.'

Suddenly she fumbles in her clothes, spread on the rocks, and finds a watch.

'I have to go.'

'But, stay . . .'

'I'm sorry,' she says, shaking her head.

She will not be persuaded otherwise, and Eric watches her clothe her naked skin and then, like a dream that drifts out of reach on waking, she is gone.

He dozes on the rocks, the sense of Merle around and inside him, seeing her slender limbs, smelling the salt in her hair, imagining that the warmth of the sunshine is her hands on his skin. He realises that for the first time in a very long time, his heart is beating slow and calmly. Peacefully.

He wakes some time later, with that itch once more.

Something starts to rise to the top of his mind.

He walks home, trying to get a hold of it, whatever it is. He's sure that it's something he's supposed to be doing.

As he enters the house, he thinks he hears the back door, the kitchen door, shut.

He shrugs.

459

Maybe just the door slamming in the wind, though he doesn't get as far as noticing that there is no wind.

He hangs his towel over the balustrade to dry in the sun, and comes back into the kitchen, where he sees that someone has left him a jar of that tea, and he decides the best thing to do is have a drink, to think about whatever it is he's supposed to be thinking about.

He brews the tea, not really noticing that it has a slightly different taste, that it has become a little stronger.

And so he drinks, and the forgetting begins again.

The days pass.

The island is so beautiful, Eric thinks, every day as he wakes up, and every night as he goes to sleep. He's had Tor bring him some more of that tea in a tall glass jar, and he's quite proud of the little ritual he has created for himself every evening.

The days pass.

The sun burns strongly, the summer is young and fresh, the leaves and the grass bright, and vivid.

Eric passes his time walking round the island. He nods at people he's getting to know, and smiles. From time to time he stoops and sniffs at a flower in this garden or that.

Merle comes to see him sometimes, and he is just as happy to see anyone else as her. There was something about her, that's all. That's how the thought forms in his head. There was something about her. But it doesn't matter. Not really. She seems a little distracted, frustrated at times, and Eric starts to wonder what the cause might be, but he decides that that doesn't matter either. She ought to be like everyone else on the island. Sometimes she seems to look at him almost accusingly, but he can't fathom why, or what he might have done. He hasn't got the energy, his mind is too slow, and he soon gives up worrying about it.

The people are smiling and beautiful, and Eric feels happy and beautiful too.

His only other visitor during that time is not a person.

One morning he finds a rabbit sitting in the middle of the path to his door. He looks closely and realises it's not a rabbit but a hare, long and lean. It's sitting side on to him, but it is clearly watching him. Waiting.

He moves forward, expecting it to startle and bolt, but it does not. Puzzled, he makes a jump at it. It still stays exactly where it is. He is about to go right up to it, but something about its stare is unnerving, and in the end it is Eric who gives way to the hare, circling around it to go for a walk.

When he comes home that afternoon, the hare has gone.

The days pass.

One day melts into the next, the endless sun smoothing the journey round the calendar into one long chorus of joy. Of beauty, of joy, and of forgetting. Always forgetting.

The days pass.

It is the middle of what should be the night, when Eric suddenly wakes up, dreaming he is drowning.

He throws himself upright and out of bed, and cannot understand why there is actually liquid in his mouth. He falls onto the floor, choking, spluttering, retching some water that he has sucked into his windpipe.

The bedroom jar is ajar. Does he hear, or does he imagine footsteps on the wooden staircase? He stumbles downstairs and finds the front door wide open, but there is no one there. He scans up and down the lane, and across the meadows. But there is no one there.

Warily, and still spluttering, he shuts the door, and makes his way back to bed.

His blinds are drawn, and as he switches on the light in the bedroom, he sees a piece of paper on the floor, right in the middle of the rug by his bed.

It is a little damp from his choking, but the words on the paper are clear enough.

Wake up and remember. You were right. The answer lies beyond the hill.

He looks at it blankly, and shakes his head.

'Well, so it is,' he says.

He stares at the note for a long time, trying to think what to do, trying to think. He's so tired, though, so tired, and another wave of lethargy sweeps into him.

He gets back into bed, deciding the only thing is to forget all about it, and switching off the light, he shuts his eyes.

About five seconds later, the liquid that has made its way into his stomach gets to work, and then he's out of bed again.

He doesn't have time to get to the bathroom before he is violently and repeatedly sick on the floor.

His body heaves and shudders, aches and wails, and when it is over, he crawls back into bed, where he spends a grim night, half awake, half dreaming.

Is it this living nightmare, or is it whatever he was forced to drink in his sleep, that triggers a flood of memories from long ago, of other nightmares?

Nightmares that terrified not just him, but his devout and strict parents too. Blood-soaked dreams that came night after night as a teenager, dreams that upon waking seem more real than the drab surroundings of his mundane room, his grey house, his ever more distant mother and father. His life.

Blood-soaked nightmares. Of another time. Of another place. Another life.

It is the middle of the day when Eric finally feels he has enough energy to stagger from his bed, but when he does, something has cleared in his head. He has a long hot shower, trying to think, think more clearly.

Automatically, his hand reaches for the shower controls. He turns the power up, and reaches for the temperature control, and slowly, fighting the urge not to, he takes the temperature down, and down and down, until he is showering in what feels like ice water. It's agony, but he forces himself on, until his whole body is shaking with the cold, then heaving in great spasmodic shudders. He looks at his hands. They are virtually blue.

He falls backwards out of the shower, and shaking on the bathroom floor, everything comes back to him.

Images swim through his head – they are the broken pieces of fractured memories; the journey to Blessed, the flowers, his device. Merle.

He lies for an age on the floor, holding a picture of her face in his mind. Merle.

The answer lies beyond the hill.

He looks out of the window. It's very quiet, he guesses it's a Sunday, though he's not sure any more.

This is the perfect time. In five minutes he is whizzing fast on his bike, fully aware that he is having to pedal hard, as he makes his way up the steep, steep hill that he knows leads to the western half of the island.

As he cycles, he repeats her name in his head, using it as a mantra to keep his mind clear. Merle, Merle, Merle.

At the top, he takes time to look behind him, checking to see if he has been followed, and satisfied that he has not been, forces his way back through the undergrowth, looking for the eyes on the rocks.

He finds the first quickly, and crawls on hands and knees to the second and then the third.

By the time he gets to the fourth pair of eyes, he is able to stand, and at the sixth, he is in open country again.

The land slopes down in front of him, a mixed terrain of grasses, rocky patches, clumps of purple heather, and marsh. He follows the eyes, and very soon, he turns a corner, cresting a large outcrop, and there lies the narrow causeway that will take him to the western half of Blessed.

Again he glances behind, and seeing no one, hurries on, half running, half stumbling over the uneven ground.

THE LIAR'S GIRL

BY
CATHERINE JOHNSON

London, October 1829

You are there waiting at the door to let me in and I slip inside your parents' shop. No, that is too small a word. I know your mother calls it nothing less than 'the St James' Cloth Emporium'.

I would not set foot inside in daylight. One look from her would send me scurrying away again, back to the street. This is a fact. You know it's true. But in darkness all is possible. I say that aloud, to you, like a spell, and I feel the earth shift under my feet.

Everything is about to change. You do not know this yet. The candle you hold gutters in the draught, you lean down to kiss me and I have to think hard of something else.

Not the feeling of your lips on mine, tender and demanding, or the pressure of your fingers as they trace patterns on my neck. I could give in to those senses completely if I am not careful. But I am fifteen. And I have learned not to trust the fluttering in my insides – the swooping falling flying feeling – I must not, cannot fall.

I close my eyes and bring to mind a picture from my first few months in this city. A story I will never tell you, about a massive dray horse, beautiful, powerful, its smoke-grey coat beaded with sweat as it clattered over the cobbles down Whitecross Market. Out of control, its eyes rolling wild, knocking over stalls, the sound of its great iron hooves slipping – then its foreleg snapping, the bones splintering, and the scream. Did you know horses screamed? I did not. Then the louder noise when a man with a gun blew the beast's brains out right there on the corner of the Jewin, children watching, younger than me. I should have known, for your countrymen have less compassion than any street bitch would have for its pups.

So all those times when we were together, when we were kissing in the long grass at Copenhagen Fields, my eyes shut tight, or sometimes open in a reverie as we two lay together and watched the clouds scud past, when you would lean across and ask me earnestly, your honest eyes desperate to know what lay behind mine: 'What are you thinking of?'

Well, here, you have it: that dead horse, twitching in the gutter. A reminder that life is cruel, and all may turn on something seemingly of no importance. A word out of place, an accident of fate, and the ground will fall away and you may end up dancing at the end of a rope.

My first lesson: this world is a cruel place where the slip of a hand or the smile of a passer-by can result in oblivion for someone.

But I do not say this as I slip inside the St James' Cloth Emporium. I simply kiss you back, hurried, fast, my breath tasting of cinnamon and allspice. I am nothing if not exotic.

Under the shop counter in his truckle bed, Sam the apprentice stirs; his head pops up and you silence him with a look and a finger at your lips. You are kind, and you should know that makes this all both easier and harder.

On the outside, I am all a flutter. Across the street the bells at St George's chime for three o'clock. I whisper, 'We must hurry!' and I kiss you once more, upon your neck where you taste of salt and lavender.

You are more than passing fair. You know that, though, and it is another reason why your parents, with two shops, Mayfair and the City, would make a good match for you, marry you to a doctor's daughter. She is a girl who comes from money, safety and security. Her name is Jane; she has very light brown hair, the palest blue eyes and a fondness for kittens and the colour yellow. She sings. You recount her singing *The Girl Wrapt in a Wether's Skin* (I did not say that perhaps she was singing about me), and that is the only time I have heard you say anything cruel about anyone. But anyway, be assured she is not for you.

You have a bag stuffed with clothes and I guess — correctly, as it turns out — all the money from today's trade.

I ask for beer or water, something to slake my thirst. After all, I have run from the rookeries of St Giles, where the alleys are so narrow you may sit up in bed and shake hands with your neighbour on the other side of the street.

I wait while you fetch it, sit as quiet as can be and wish for a miracle. For you to change your mind and say you will not come. For your father to wake and find me here and shout loud enough to wake the dead. I wish, I wish it was him, not you.

I imagine that future for a moment, while you are out of the room. Imagine my mother waiting and waiting alone. I would vanish like a magic trick, somehow cease to exist, and with me all bitterness gone into the ether like a dream. The promise I made to him of your deliverance scrubbed out, rewritten.

Too late. You have returned, and I smile at you, the sweet half-smile of a maid.

I drink the water gratefully and make sure to offer you the rest. 'You'll need it,' I say.

You throw back your head and drain the cup. Our fingers brush, my heart is galloping. I lean close and say, a loud whisper to drown out all the shouting in my head, 'I love you.'

And at that moment, here in the dark of the shop,

Sam rustling in his bed, you must know that I never said a truer word.

You open the shop door, one hand on the bell to silence it. Outside, London is sleeping. Far away I can hear dogs barking, fighting maybe, and even further a woman sobbing and sobbing. I believe in the Scots vernacular (I am well versed in the varieties and oddities of language in these small islands) they call it *greeting*. Did you know that?

I forget myself. 'We have to hurry!' you say. And I think how I am doing you a kind of favour. I do believe you would wither, left in that shop, buried in bright muslin and pale linsey wolsey.

You look at me. 'We must reach Woolwich by six, you said . . .' And you smile.

You kiss my forehead. Sometimes it seems I am some kind of foolish child to you. So be it.

'Listen,' I say. 'Take my hand.' I'm glad you're with me, your fingers knitted fast in mine, your heart beating hard as mine under your skin. You grin, as if this is an adventure, an escape. Not life or death. Oh! You have been featherbedded in so many ways.

Your breath is making twin clouds of smoke in the cold air with mine. I tell you there is safety in numbers, even when that number is two.

My second lesson, and mark me well: the only safe number ever in this world is one.

I know all these streets; the filth and the dirt and the joy of them runs in my veins. I may not have drawn my first breath in this city, but it is my home now. I want to tell you to keep your eyes open, remember every stone and brick, for you will not see them again.

We must be quick! Out through the silent white-washed sugar-coated streets of St James towards the bridge at Westminster. Don't look back. Not once. We can make it out of the city by morning with this moon.

I have promised you my story, and tonight I will tell. You shall have the introduction as we run hell for leather down Pollen Street, across Piccadilly towards the river. And I am sad, for you will never see the new road, the Regent's Road, built. By the time we reach the prison hulks at Woolwich you will know enough to make a piece of it and some expectation of what is to come.

By then, you may want to let go of my hand, you may want to have nothing more to do with me.

Let me assure you I will understand. Even and beyond your heart breaking.

After tonight you can judge me, another blackbird from the stews, a born liar and deceiver. Neither black nor white, true nor false. You laugh when I say that. Is my face not solemn enough? Are my tears not still sticky on my cheeks?

You are sorry, then, and want to kiss away any offence you may have caused.

We cannot stop! At Swallow Street a drunken man

hugs the walls of the buildings singing a wailing version of 'The Nut-Brown Maid'. You laugh, and the drunken man looks our way and yells as if in pain or terror. Your hand flies to your belt.

'You brought a knife?' I say. I really hadn't thought it possible, and I fight the urge to ask if you know how to use it.

I pull you along; you are out of breath, more used to books and book-keeping. We are nearly at the river; if you take a deep breath you can taste it on your tongue, the tang of filth, the hundreds of years of life and death. The clock at St James' chimes for half past. We have to hurry, I want to fly across the bridge at Westminster, faster than minutes and seconds, faster than moments and ideas and kisses.

'We do not need a story about love, we're living it!' you say. Your eyes are shining.

'Love.' I am your echo. I think and have to look away or I know it will be simpler to be lost to kissing you and we shall not go another step. I take a breath and look at you for a long second. 'You must listen!' I say.

You look at me.

'This story is better than words, any words!'

I want you to know, I want to give you a chance to escape . . .

'Let me begin,' I say. 'Please.'

You say nothing, so I start.

'Imagine somewhere far away. A land where there

is never winter, and fruit drops from the tree into your hand all year round. One day some men came from the east and turned this Eden into Hell. They didn't see perfection, they saw only the possibility of gold, do you understand? Not real gold, only that it might be conjured from the soil, given enough blood. That was the moment this started. That's what is happening here, right now on these streets.'

'The West Indies?' you say. 'My father was there, for a year, I think, en route to America.'

You tell me I am exaggerating. That the only time your father spoke of it he said the air was so thick and moist he could hardly breathe. He said the whole island was heavy with the smell of rot and putrefaction, hardly any kind of paradise.

I have no facts to fight you with. I can't remember home at all, only what I have been told.

You tell me your father told you that in Jamaica white people died of sickness or debauchery or both. (Not unlike London, I want to add. But I stay silent.) That he came home in a hurry, his fortune made to open both his shops.

I have to quieten you. I want to shout – do you not see? Where did that money come from? You still do not realize I am telling the story of both our families. I am a Londoner by choice, where you have never known anything else, but one way or another our beginnings and our ends have their roots so very far away.

We creep past St James' Park, trying not to disturb the girls who still work undercover of the trees and bushes.

I whisper back that I am telling a story, my story. That you would do well to listen.

I begin again: 'Then one morning on the island another warm day dawns. The heavy sun shining on a sea so bright and blue you'd think you dreamed it. Down at the port, a red-faced man steps off a boat. He is unsteady on dry land, has come a long way. Where he lives the cold wind bites into your bones. He's come to be an overseer, to crack the whip and keep those wayward darkies on the straight and narrow. Green Mount Plantation. High up in the hills, round hills like a child's drawing, pudding bowls turned upside down and all alike, the road winds round and round. The heat is cooler but the sweat falls off him and the road never stops curling and the man vomits. Copiously. That means a lot. You would know that with your education. I know that because this is the way the story was told. Was passed down. That man, I say, was your father.'

'You're wrong.' Your voice is sharp. 'My father an overseer?'

'Buckra,' I say. But you have no idea what that means. When my mother says the word she spits into the fire and sparks fly.

You say nothing. There is the pressure of your fingers against mine. But you do not speak. Do you now recognize your father's story?

477

Inside I am begging for you to understand what's happening, but still you don't.

We reach the river. The water is black as molasses and just as slow, and the sound of the water slap-slapping heavy against the bridge like heavy shod heartbeats. There is a watchman crossing, and you pull me into the shadow, into the dark and we embrace. We are not a threat. Just another lost couple. We cross the bridge at a hurry, keen to show, should anyone be watching, that we do not intend to throw ourselves into the darkness below. But as we scurry across I feel such a pull I swear that if your hand was not firmly clasped in mine I would succumb.

We reach the other side. You point out where your father grew up in the back streets between the Magdalen and the Bethlem Hospitals, in one of those small streets where the houses lean in together like lovers listening for secrets.

You have lost interest, I think. In my story. Maybe you don't want to hear. Maybe, to you, it does not matter; to you all of it is so far in the past it cannot touch us.

The road opens out into a circus. We are south of the river now and the air smells of breweries and tanneries and hard work. A heavy laden dray plods into town from Kent or Sussex, laden high with hops.

In the centre of the road there is an obelisk. We are at St George's Circus, not quite halfway. I cross the street and run up the steps. You look at me, no trace of fear in your eyes. You seem at home in the city in the night. Perhaps we are more alike than I imagined. I kiss you. And this time I don't think of the horse, I think of the feeling. Of your mouth on mine, your hands, your tongue. And there is no room for any regret or fear or dread. And I pray. If not to God, who has never done anything for me since I drew breath, then to my mother's gods. The King of the Crossroads, the woman at the edge of the world. I pray to stay here, with you always. And I wish and wish that kissing was a way to stop the clock. To stop time and change the future. We could stay here for ever and ever, as the sun rises and the traffic flows. Clinging together.

But wishing and praying never changed one single thing. The course is set. The die is cast. My mother and her damned ship await.

Your father is already paying for what he did. He will wake up and your room will be empty. You will be gone. He deserves that. And you agree, you hate him almost as much as my mother does. Almost as much.

We hurry through Newington and through Bermondsey now. The streets are black with factories and brick works and distilleries. I walk along, two steps for every one of yours, hugged close to you as the city begins to wake. You have forgotten my story and are keen to tell me of the life you dream of, the one where you and I are free to live together, be together.

'Imagine that!' you say.

I wish I could.

All around from out of houses and tenements the city begins to stir. Early starters or those who never slept, the costers and the traders, readying stalls. No one looks at us. We are invisible. It is a spell of hers, the only one that works, I think.

I want to remind you of how we met.

That was no accident. She has watched you for a very long time. She has never forgotten what your father did to mine.

We were never slaves. There is no flogging in my story. I try and explain as we pass the docks at Rotherhithe and Deptford. How my father wed the Witch of Green Mount, and how your father killed and robbed him.

But I am holding you up now. Your strength is ebbing. You lean on me, and as we reach the turn of the river at Greenwich close to the Naval College, I am relieved to see my mother and her man, Jonathan, waiting with the cart.

She told me Woolwich; she is too clever for me. She must have dosed you to get no further than Greenwich, in case I changed my mind, in case you decided to run. I curse her under my breath.

One day, many days and months from now, when you wake up in a strange new land, you may ask yourself why I did it. Why I went along with her planning, plotting. You don't know that I took in tales of hatred and betrayal with my mother's milk. She hated your family so much she followed yours back across the Atlantic. This has been years in the making.

They scoop you up. I sit at the back with you, free to tell you anything now that your eyes roll back in your head and you cannot speak, only moan a little when the cart jolts and rocks. I put your head upon my lap so it is not such a hardship and count the nag's steps as she carries us away.

My mother has found room for you on a transport to the South, to Botany Bay. You will be swapped for a cutpurse who worked out of the tenement next to ours in Dyott Street, in the Seven Dials. Your parents will never see you again. You will be lost to them utterly and completely.

I was only the bait, the meat, the morsel that will convince you to walk into the web. And here we are, your head thrown back looking at the dull dawn sky as we trundle through the dockyard gates at Woolwich.

It feels as if we have reached the edge of the world, the city far behind us, across the river and beyond only marshes more marshes.

Mother whispers and tells me I have done a good job, the very best. She calls me Bridget.

You thought my name was Mary. That was a lie too.

The boat is sailing for Australia. You will be one more convict out of many.

My mother is old now, but Jonathan is still strong. He takes off your good clothes and passes your bag to Mother, he ties your hands quickly and roughly behind your back.

I beg him to leave you be, there is no fight in you but he ignores me and I am ashamed.

Your head lolls to one side. I only know you are not dead because I put my hand on your neck and feel the blood pumping there under the skin. A small relief. I feel sick as they take you away, half drag, half carry you up the plank. Exchange coins, a flash of bright silver.

I run after you, kiss you one last time, and the clouds part – the sun is there, struggling to shine.

Then it is gone and you with it.

That is the last I see of you.

What happens afterwards is this: Mother and her man take us to an inn. It is for sailors and I say nothing. My tongue is tied, and I will not drink a drop and lose the taste of you.

Mother toasts me.

Blood for blood.

I wipe a tear. Mother reminds me that we have no feelings – can never have. Not for the likes of you.

I look away.

I have spun such a web and I am stuck fast. I shut my eyes and see you once again half dragged up that gangplank to oblivion. It feels as if my whole insides, innards, heart, brain, muscles are collapsing. I struggle to hold myself together until I am outside the inn. Then I vomit – again you would say copiously – into a ditch.

And with the sky, at last my thoughts are clear. The sun has now peeped out and hangs like a perfect golden peach above the Thames. A thing of beauty.

I run back through the dock gates, faster and faster. For you.

But I am too late.

The *Amity* is half a chain out on the water. I could not swim out to you, could not reach you if I wanted. Even if I shout you will not hear me, walled in by wood and somewhere deep under the decks.

All I hear is the crying of those poor souls who never wanted to leave, or those who have been left behind. There is another woman on the quayside, tucked in her cloak, a tiny baby pale and wriggling like a rat. It mews and she shushes it with a song. The same one you sang to me once, as we walked out through Newington: 'The Nut-Brown Maid'. The song tells of a girl who lied, its words are true, and I was not.

My breath fails me. I am almost given up to self-pity. I will never see you, touch you, kiss you again. My eyes prickle with tears.

And even if I sail after you across the earth, to the far side of the world you will despise me. For I am guilty and complicit.

The liar's girl.

I turn away, walk back to the inn. Everything is ashes. At the door I look inside. The air is thick with smoke and the smell of ale. I see my mother, laughing with Jonathan, your bag, your clothes, those clothes that will still smell of you safe under her feet.

Mother does not look at me. I was useful; a cup, a hammer, a blade made flesh. She is talking to her Jonathan. He is a big man, arms like hams, lighter skinned than me; he looks straight at me like a dog eyes a bone. My mother smiles. I see the transaction has already been made.

There is a feeling in my throat, my head, my chest, a lack of breath, a knot of fear and something inside me tearing and I know that is my heart breaking.

I walk purposefully towards my mother and Jonathan. Offer to buy drinks and vittles for us all. But I take the money and run outside.

If your parents are lost to you then so are mine.

I reckon I will need every penny in order to buy your freedom so I offer the groom a good look at my breasts, and while he fumbles with his buckles and buttons I swing up onto the fastest-looking horse that is still saddled. A bay with a white blaze.

Then I turn her east and gallop for Sheerness. The *Amity* puts on its last human cargo there, on the Isle of Sheppey. There is a chance I can get you off, that I can talk whoever round – a slender chance, but I know I have to take it.

I hear shouting as the horse and I turn onto the road for Kent.

She is a good, kind horse. I pat her neck, lean forward and whisper magic words into her ear to urge her onward, and dutifully she flattens out into a gallop.

Since you are gone I tell the horse my final lesson, one I learned too late:

My love. All lies were true, all bets are off. I swear, I promise, I will follow you across the world and somehow make you love me all again. If not – I am certain of this – I shall die.

Record the nut-brown maid,
Which, when her love came her to prove,
To her to make his moan,
Would not depart; for in her heart
She loved but him alone.

THE UNICORN

BY
JAMES DAWSON

'. . . those who suffer from this disability carry a great weight of shame all their lives.'

Roy Jenkins, Home Secretary 1967

Now I am an old man. A very old man, one who both feels and looks his age: a hunched, shrunken gnome with white hair and skin like liver-spotted tissue paper. When I walk, I walk with a stick and I'm developing a mortal fear of icy pavements.

Oh, I see these colourful boys gallivanting outside the bars on Old Compton Street but they don't see me at all. With nothing solid left to offer, I move among them like a ghost. They wouldn't believe that I was quite the catch in my day, and even if they did, what good to them is a photograph? The Portsmouth girls used to compare me to Olivier, something about the dimple in my chin, although I never saw it myself.

There is one photograph, though, in which I almost take my own breath away. My first picture in uniform. In my head, this is how I look now, how I've always looked. Black and white, of course – it was 1950 – and so, so proud to be in that cap. Positively beaming. A black ribbon runs around the rim – HMS *Unicorn* – the vessel that was to be my home for two years.

We call it the Forgotten War. Over five thousand of our boys were killed, captured or maimed in Korea and, to my shame, I too only dimly recall the fighting. For me, when I think about that time, I think about a face; I think about a smile.

We met in the galley shortly after my transfer from the *Warrior* in the November of '51. The air was tacky with fried-egg-gammon grease and cigarette smoke. The change of vessel had unsettled all of us – newcomers upsetting the status quo. At sea, like a spot on your tongue, the smallest things seem enormous. Ships may look vast, but they're all just tin cans and we sardines.

Some fellas were rowdy, laughing and gambling, while others brooded over their jam roly poly. We were docked off Singapore, thousands of miles from the war, so we may as well have been on a cruise. A holiday during which we were to refit and repair the *Unicorn* before she returned to her duties.

The Aussies were the brashest, and one of them, a freckled hulk called Bronson, caught my eye as I went to retire. He was shirtless, wearing only his woollen britches. 'Oi, where you going, Fauntleroy?' My youth and Received Pronunciation had betrayed my schooling early into the voyage.

'I don't know. Back to the mess.' Truth was, I wanted to be on deck. I needed the sunset that night as much as I needed the air. However far from home I was, it brought me comfort to know I shared the same sun with Mummy and my brothers.

'Play with us a while!' Bronson demanded, slapping a paw on the table, jumping the cards. 'How much do you want to bet on an arm wrestle?'

I stifled a sigh. 'I wouldn't want to take that bet, Bronson.' I kept my voice unfailingly polite.

'What if I use my left arm to give you a shot?'

'I doubt it'd make a difference.'

'I doubt it'd make a difference,' he mocked my voice. 'Aw come on, you great Nancy. Don't tell me you didn't hold hands with boys at your boarding school.'

I did a great deal more than hold hands, but said nothing as I took my position opposite Bronson. I offered my right hand.

Bronson laughed, 'Here we go! Come on, fellas, how long do you think it'll take? Place your bets!'

'Are you sure you want to do this, Bronson?'

'Mate, I'm gonna snap your arm!'

'How much are you willing to bet?'

'Fifty dollars says I win.'

'Very well,' I said.

'Easiest cash I ever made.' Bronson offered his right hand and I took it, taking care to tuck my thumb under, rather than over, my fingers.

Poor Bronson. He wasn't to know my years at Highgate School had been entirely misspent and I was no stranger to an arm wrestle. Why else would I be here instead of at Oxford with my classmates? Off the pitch, my school career had been a resounding failure.

It's a common misconception that an arm wrestle is about brute strength. On the contrary, it's about skill. Our arms formed a peak in the centre of the table, Bronson's biceps twice the size of mine. I put my weight onto my forward foot and pressed my hip to the table's edge.

'Keep it clean, fellas,' said one of Bronson's Aussie friends. 'On three . . .'

I subtly flexed my wrist up, forcing Bronson's wrist to bend. He didn't seem to notice.

'One . . . two . . . GO!'

Predictably, Bronson tried to force my arm towards the table. Instead, I drew his towards me and left, into the corner of the table. This is known as the Top Roll, and he didn't see it coming. Straightening his arm gave him less leverage and me the drop. Throwing my body weight into it, I pinned his arm to the table.

I didn't gloat. No one likes a sore winner. The room erupted with laughter and applause. I'll say this for Bronson, he wasn't looking to start a fight. He knew he'd been beaten fairly although his freckled face turned beetroot. His comrades mocked him with hoots and backslaps, but, to his credit, he took it.

That was when I saw a hand appear to my right, palm up – waiting for payment.

Bronson reached into his pocket and withdrew crumpled notes.

I turned and looked into the bluest eyes I'd ever seen. I'd sailed the Atlantic, the Med, the Arabian Sea and the Bay of Bengal, but I'd never seen blue like that. The stranger, who *must* have joined the ship in Japan, smiled a cockeyed smile and handed me the money. 'I owe you a drink, mate! You just won me twenty-five bob.'

I shook hands with Bronson and left him at the mercy of his friends. 'Why did you bet on me?'

'Truth be told, mate, I felt sorry for yer.' His voice was undiluted Estuary but I liked it; it reminded me so strongly of London, of home. 'Why did you say he'd beat you?'

I shrugged. 'He's a proud man. He needed it more. Maybe I should have let him win.'

The newcomer looked confounded but held out his hand. 'I'm Frankie, mate. Frankie Cain.'

I shook his hand, his fingers Swarfega raw and calloused. 'I'm Reg. Reg Hastings.'

Checking no one was looking, Frankie pulled me into

the chapel. A fat, slumping candle flickered from a gold stand in the corner so he left off the main light. 'What are we doing in here?' I asked. I'd been raised a good Christian boy, but even I only visited the chapel when I remembered it was a Sunday.

'Holy Communion, my friend.' From under the altar, Frankie pulled out a small suitcase. He flipped it open and I saw it was filled with booze and cigarettes. Good booze too – single malt whisky. ''Ere.' He handed me the bottle. 'Bottom's up, or whatever it is gents like you say.'

I took a seat on the first pew. 'I'm from London, just the same as you are.' The whisky almost knocked my head off. It was strong stuff. Far more potent than the watered-down rum ration.

'Ha ha! I don't think your London's quite the same as my London, Reg.' He sat next to me and took a slug of the whisky. 'I like it in here. I dunno about you, but when I signed up I thought about life on the open sea, not twenty-four blokes sharing a bedroom. It's nice to have a bit of space to yourself.'

'I've lived in dormitories for as long as I can remember. Doesn't make a lot of difference. We're lucky they got rid of the hammocks.'

He took another swig. 'Maybe if we get drunk enough, Pennefather will put us in the cells! Private room!'

'I don't think I'd be able to sleep without the noise of other men snoring!'

He chuckled. 'You public school boys then . . . are the rumours true?'

I turned to him with a sly smile. This was dangerous and I didn't want to show my hand too soon. 'I vowed to take it to the grave . . .'

His lips curled at the edges, but he questioned me no further. He told me how he'd been docked at Iwakuni in Japan and had stayed on when we swapped crews. I asked his age and, although he looked older than me, he too was eighteen. 'I wasn't given much of a choice, to be honest. It was either the navy or the army or work for me granddad as a fishmonger and I never did like fish.'

'Me either,' I laughed. 'I'm much the same. My father died in action during the war. Service is rather the done thing in my family.'

Frankie smiled at me. 'Blood like yours, you'll be running the place in no time.'

'I hope not. Not really my scene.' By this stage I was more than a little merry.

'And what is?'

I shrugged. 'You know what I'd really like? A grocer's. A nice little grocer's somewhere in West London with fruit and veg in crates on the pavement. Hastings' Groceries.'

'Hastings & Sons?' He fixed me with his gaze and it felt like I was sinking in quicksand. Willingly. Now he *was* prying.

I shivered. 'I very much doubt it.' My throat was

tight, unbearably so. The chapel was a poky room, but the walls seemed to shrink in around us. Shoulder to shoulder on the pew, I could smell him, I could smell Frankie's scent – soap – Pears soap.

He laughed and the bubble popped. 'Well, as long as you don't sell fish!'

When the candle had burned down and the whisky was finished, Frankie had to escort me back to the bunks. I could scarcely put one foot in front of the other. I was off-duty, but if I was to be found like that I would have been in bother.

He hooked my arm around his neck and wrapped his own arm behind my waist. His arms were strong, muscular and so much hairier than mine. 'Come on, Reg, you can do it. Not far to go.'

'Sshhh!' I insisted, making far more noise than him. 'We'll be in the cells!'

He chuckled. 'Maybe we *should* go to the cells . . . what do you think?'

I stopped and steadied myself against the pipes. I couldn't tell if he was kidding or not. My heart was beating too fast – each beat echoed in my skull. His face was fuzzy, swimming in and out of focus. Almost of its own accord, my right hand reached for his left cheek. I missed, though, and he laughed. 'Come on, Reg, you need your bed.'

To be quite honest, I remember nothing more of that first night other than the splitting headache I awoke to.

When Mummy passed in '87, I found the letters I'd sent her during my time on the *Unicorn* and they were smothered with Frankie. I regaled her with stories of the time we had to shovel snow from the deck; of playing songs from the Sound Room; of him teaching me poker and me teaching him craps; of more secret moments in the chapel late at night.

There is so much love between the scrawled lines, it's a wonder Mummy didn't know. Maybe she did.

As far as I could tell, he felt the same as me. He'd always find a way to touch me. If someone *was* looking, he'd throw an arm over my shoulder and slouch into me, the way men do. If no one was looking, he'd hold my hand or massage my neck. Oh, we fooled around, of course we did – we'd been at sea for over a year. Alone in the chapel or in the Sound Reproduction Room . . . while we played songs over the radio, hands would inevitably wander.

We never kissed though. Not until the night in Sasebo.

Refit complete, the *Unicorn* returned to duties: ferrying crew from Japan and Singapore to the front line in North Korea. While we were in dock, we were able to set foot on land, and even if Sasebo wasn't quite as exciting or beautiful as Singapore, it was still sweet relief to be off the ship for a few hours.

It was an ugly town, made uglier by the naval presence – rusted grey docks welded onto a once serene bay surrounded by green-topped mountains. Of course, this was only a few years after the bomb was dropped on nearby Nagasaki, and I swear you could still feel a terrible silence in the air. No one spoke of it.

There was a naval club, and it was OK – although mixing that many crews, American, Australian and Royal Navy, always ended in fisticuffs. Instead, like many crewmen, Frankie and I headed into the village. The streets were ramshackle, washing lines hanging between the flat-top buildings in narrow alleys. Paper signs hung from shops and restaurants although we could read none of them.

Back then it was all so alien. You have to understand this was before Chinatown in Soho, although Frankie swore there were places in Limehouse where you could eat dog and find opium readily. I was wide-eyed, gawping at squid and octopi hanging in windows; buckets of fish heads on the street, dead eyes staring up at me. We meandered, getting ourselves lost just because we could.

We found a quiet restaurant, and Frankie managed to order for us using some sort of hand semaphore. He ate the raw fish, but I'm afraid I couldn't stomach it. I did have a stab at using chopsticks, though, with limited success. I was developing quite a taste for sake and by the time we left the restaurant, my feet felt decidedly airy. Arms around each other's shoulders – because it looked like nothing more than camaraderie – we began the trek back to the *Unicorn*. Suddenly Frankie stopped and I nearly fell. 'You know what we need to do?'

'What?' I couldn't stop smiling.

'We haven't got our tattoos yet.' I realized he'd brought us to a stop outside a tattoo parlour – the window full of swallows and pin-up girls and broken hearts.

'Oh no! Not on your life!'

'Reg, you're in the navy! You have to! It's tradition!'

He was right, of course: it was the done thing to commemorate your service at sea. I suppose I saw it as something temporary that I hadn't intended to do for long. 'I won't be in the navy for ever.'

He shook his head. 'You will, Reg! You won't always be at sea, but you'll always be a sailor.'

I could see that this was an argument I wasn't going to win. I also relished the idea of us going through this ordeal together. 'Very well. But just something small and out of sight.'

Frankie grinned and pushed his way into the parlour. The shop was sticky with condensation and smelled strongly of Dettol and sweat. Behind a dirty counter stood a Japanese girl who couldn't be much older than me, her belly heavily swollen, fit to pop.

'Two tattoos?' Frankie said.

'Who is it, Kizumi?' an American voice boomed, and a bald giant lumbered out from behind a bamboo curtain. I knew at once he must be ex-navy. Kizumi was lucky: most wouldn't have done the right thing by her.

'Hello,' Frankie slurred a little. 'We come to get our anchors.' Well, what else would we get?

'Both of you?'

'Yessir.'

'Come through.' My stomach clenched like a fist as we followed him into the back of the shop. 'You first, take your shirt off, son.'

The tattooist jabbed a sausage finger at me and I did as I was told. Feeling utterly naked, I saw Frankie's eyes look me over. I was embarrassed about my body, not realizing back then that it would never be so perfect as at that moment. I took to the seat and gripped the arm rest. Frankie sat alongside me and squeezed my hand. 'It'll be all right.' I believed him.

It hurt, but Bruce, the tattooist, was mercifully efficient. Within mere minutes, there was a perfect anchor on my left arm with HMS UNICORN underneath. 'Your turn,' he said to Frankie.

'Reg, I want you to do mine.'

'What?'

'That way I'll remember you for ever.'

'Isn't the tattoo enough?' I laughed.

'No. I want you to do it.'

'Frank, it'll look a right old mess if I do it.'

'I don't care.'

Bruno shrugged. 'It's your money, you can do what you want.'

I caved and took Bruno's seat. 'Are you sure?'

'I am.'

I took the gun, a chunky, clunky metal thing like a fountain pen strapped to a pistol, and dipped the nib in the same ink used on me. 'Frank, I'm not sure I can do this.'

'You can. It doesn't matter what it looks like, anyway, just that you did it.'

I started small – a practice mark. As I took the needle to his skin, Frankie tensed, the muscle in his bicep swelling under my touch. He inhaled sharply and I stopped. 'Keep going,' he said. 'Just do it.'

I continued, trying as hard as I could to draw in straight lines. The ink bubbled and spurted over his skin, beads of blood mixing in. He closed his eyes and I hated that I was hurting him. But I'd started so I had to finish. I couldn't leave him scarred but unfinished.

It took minutes, but felt like hours. His was little more than a stick drawing, lines crudely making a shape that looked more like a fish-hook than an anchor. Still, Frankie seemed pleased enough. 'Mate, I love it.'

I examined my own, my arm looking foreign, more manly somehow. 'Come on, it's getting late.'

We paid Bruce and started back for the *Unicorn*. Frankie acquired a bottle of rum en route which I wasn't convinced was a champion idea. Once more keeping each other upright, we wove through the narrow streets towards port.

'Hey, faggots.' I didn't realize at first that the Yank outside the naval club was talking to us. 'What did ya mama say when you told her you was queer?'

Frankie whirled to face him. There were three of them, all bigger than us. They were sucking on fat, oaky cigars and puffing smoke doughnuts into the night air. 'You talkin' to us, mate?'

'Frank, ignore them.'

The mouthy one stepped forward, his shoulders like mutton. 'You wanna listen to your girlfriend, sailor.'

Frankie lunged for him, giving the Yank the fight he so desperately wanted. It was brief. Painfully so. A couple of ugly pig grunts and a scraping of boots and Frankie was flat on his back. I pulled him up and away so fast it's a wonder I didn't rip his arm out of its socket. Luckily, the Yanks didn't chase us.

I could only hope it *looked* worse than it actually was. This time I dragged his floppy, half-conscious body up the gangway. 'Dear Lord, you're heavy.' He looked a state: red teeth, blood crusting on his chin and all down his shirt. 'Let's get you to Matron.' Matron was our name for Dr Lawson, the ship's medic. He was known for his 'busy' hands.

'No! No! I just wanna sleep.'

'Act right in the head. You might have a concussion.'

'What?'

I sighed. 'Come along, Frank. Come along.'

At this time of night, there were no feet clanking up and down ladders to cover the creaking of metal plates as they cooled. Down below was quiet and it almost felt like there was only Frankie and me on the whole ship. Not wanting to wake those who were sleeping, I did as best I could to carry him through the narrow passageways to the sick bay.

Lights were dimmed, but I could see the infirmary was empty. Where the bloody hell was Lawson? I elbowed my way in. The desk lamp was on and the room smelled of recent cigarette smoke, but the doctor and indeed the nurse were nowhere to be seen. It wasn't even that late, damn them.

I rested Frank on the nearest bunk. Ironically the beds in the sick bay were by far the nicest on the ship, I often wondered if being ill might be something of a treat. I pulled his boots off his feet and swung his legs up onto the crisp, mint-green sheets. 'Gerroff! Leave me alone!'

'We need to get you cleaned up or you'll be in the cells,' I said sternly, echoing my grandmother who'd cleaned us up when we'd fallen out of the orchard as boys. 'Now, button your lip and take off your shirt.'

A sly smile crossed his lips but he did as he was told while I filled a kidney-shaped metal tray with warm water. I found towels easily enough and carried them back to the bunk. I knelt before him to get a better look. His nose was bruised black and swollen twice the size it should be. 'I think he broke your nose.'

'I'll square with ya, Reg, that's what it feels like.'

'Pipe down.' I delicately bathed his face with a damp flannel, avoiding his nose. During rugby we'd be given ice packs, but there was no freezer here and I couldn't very well break into the galley. Instead I returned to the sink and gave him a cold flannel for the swelling.

'That oaf was right . . . you'd be a bloody brilliant wife, Reg!'

'Don't you start.' I carried on cleaning him up. Without all the blood, he didn't look too bad. I wiped his chest and collarbone with my now pinkish flannel. His body was taut and muscular, not an ounce of spare fat. My eyes lingered.

'What would I do without ya, eh?' And then his hand was on the side of my face, his thumb stroking my cheek. He put his flannel to one side.

His eyes were on mine and so sincere I had to look away. 'You're drunk, Frankie.'

'Drunk and brave, Reg. Drunk and brave.' He leaned down and kissed me. I shivered to my bones. He was not the first boy I had kissed, but it was the first time I'd felt a kiss in my toes.

I hooked my hand behind his head and pulled him closer, kissing him deeper. There was a familiar stirring inside. But I knew I had to stop it. If we were caught . . . well, it didn't bear thinking about. 'Frank, stop.'

'No . . .' he said petulantly.

'We have to.' I kissed him again, fleetingly, allowing myself a second taste – one to remember.

He shuffled over to make room for me on the bed. 'Lie with me.'

'I can't . . .'

'Aw, come on . . . just lie with me.'

I kicked off my boots and lay alongside him, scared rigid. Scared we'd be caught, scared of what might happen. I didn't trust myself and I certainly didn't trust him. I looked over and his eyes were already closed. He was passing out – I prayed from drink rather than concussion. 'Stay with me.'

'I will,' I said to his ear and wrapped my arms around him.

I don't know precisely what time it was when I woke, but sun poured in through the porthole and Dr Lawson was standing in the doorway. 'Just what do you think you're doing?'

No man has never moved so fast. I was off the bed in a flash, disturbing Frankie as I leaped up. My mouth blubbered like a goldfish as I composed my lie. 'I . . . we . . . Frank got into a fight. I brought him to find you, but you weren't here.'

John Lawson was a fox-like man with a full ginger beard and ruthlessly clever eyes. He knew. Oh, he knew all right. 'We have more than one bunk.'

'I . . . I had to watch him. To make sure he didn't swallow his tongue. And *you weren't here*.'

It's hard to say what the greater sin was: sleeping with another man or abandoning your post. And John Lawson knew that as well as I did.

His eyes blazed for a moment before he drew his lips thin. 'Does he require further attention?'

'I'm fine,' Frankie said, sitting up. He was now sporting two black eyes, each with a yellow rim.

'You don't look fine. You'll stay here and rest. Hastings, is it? I suggest you return to the mess at once.' He positioned himself between Frankie and me so I was left with little choice but to obey.

Frankie stayed in the sick bay for the rest of the day and I busied myself in the wireless office, throwing myself into my duties. As I did every evening, I sought him out in the galley for dinner. As I sidled onto the bench next to him, he stiffened.

'What's wrong?'

'Nothing,' he replied. 'Just don't sit so close. Give me room, mate.'

I'd seen this before. Alfie Reed, Upper Form Prefect. The coldness that followed his kisses.

'How's your nose?' I said, changing the subject.

'Hurts. And I can hardly see out of my eye.' And, just like that, everything returned to normal.

Or so I thought.

But a few days passed by, during which everyone heard about the three Yanks he'd singlehandedly fought off, and though I ate and drank and played cards with him, Frankie, it became clear, was actively avoiding being alone with me. One time, I passed him in the tight corridor leading down to the shell store and he squeezed himself into a corner, doing everything he could to avoid pressing his body against mine. 'Frank,' I said, reaching for his waist.

He recoiled. 'Don't!' he snapped. He leaned in. 'Just forget about it, Reg. Just forget it ever happened.'

I won't lie, that hurt. A physical pain, a lump in my chest like my heart had got itself knotted. But what else can you do? You can only have so many sleepless nights – and I did – before the tiredness catches up with you. I consoled myself in the knowledge that the next time we docked and he'd had his skin-full of sake, we would no doubt relive the exhilaration of that night in Sasebo.

Over the coming weeks, things returned to some form of normality and, like a timid puppy, I could feel the closeness creeping back.

In the April of '52 the *Unicorn* was 'adopted', if you like, by the Middlesex Regiment. Having a ship full of land troops changed everything. We were even more cramped than before and it rather felt like we were having our ship taken away from us. They were cuckoos in the nest. We were just to ferry them to Korea but their presence unsettled everyone.

There was a natural division between the army and the navy, except of course for Frankie. He welcomed them aboard, almost acting as tour guide – settling them in to their new home with poker nights and dominoes tournaments. He even taught them our songs! I couldn't help it. I felt like day-old bread.

I did not own Frankie Cain, for no one ever owns another, but on the night of the 3 May 1952 when I found him coming out of the punishment cells with a square-jawed lieutenant, he broke me.

It was late and I'd gone searching for him, almost knowing what I would find. Sometimes you just know.

There were two cells, both empty of detainees, so they had been unmanned.

Being proven right was a hollow victory. I stood, gormless, as they slunk out.

Frankie's eyes widened. 'Reg!' At least he had the grace to look appalled.

'Sorry,' I said. 'I shouldn't be here.' I turned and headed for deck, not once looking back. It was spring, but it was cool and a wind sliced across the open deck. I made for the back of the ship, where I knew it'd be quiet at this time of night. I gripped the rail and looked to the furthest point of the horizon where the black sea fell off the edge of the world.

'Reg.' He'd followed me. I didn't reply. 'Reg, that was nothin'.'

I could only bite my tongue for so long. 'It doesn't feel like nothing, Frank. It feels like a lot.'

He moved as close to me as he dared. I stood my ground. He lowered his voice and I could only just hear him over the engines and the waves. 'Reg, people were startin' to talk. That doctor. He knew.'

I shook my head. 'And sneaking out of the punishment cells is your idea of discretion?'

'He's no one! That was just . . . passin' time. That's completely different . . . you and me . . . you and me are somethin' else.' His fingers were touching mine on the safety rail. 'I'm sorry, Reg.'

'I'm sorry too. I am sorry I ever met you.'

Pain flickered through his eyes and for a second, I was glad. He deserved it. 'Aw, you don't mean that.'

'Yes, I do. Everything was easy before I met you and now you're all I think about. When I close my eyes, all I see is you.'

His hand was now on top of mine. I looked over my shoulder to make sure there was no one watching us. 'Me too. This wasn't meant to happen, you know. I wasn't supposed to feel this way, Reg. But I do.'

For a long time I stared out to the ocean without saying anything, content to feel his hand on mine. He was there. With me. 'So what are we to do?' I finally said.

'I dunno. But I am yours.'

I looked him dead in the eye. 'And only mine?'

'If you say so. You're the guv'nor.'

I nodded and gripped his hand. We stood where we were until the sea birthed the sun.

He was true to his word. Now when we met at ladders or in quiet storerooms, we would make the most of every spare second. The fear of getting caught, if I'm honest, only made it more arousing. Sometimes after lights out we'd meet in the chapel or the punishment cells if they were free.

I was happy, so happy my face ached. When I woke, I woke with the sun in my face even if it was cloudy.

It wasn't to last. Nothing ever does.

In the summer we were sent to assist HMS *Ocean*, a larger carrier to assist aircraft landings. Damaged planes were to come with us so as not to disrupt the operation.

You know how you just *know* when something's wrong? I think it's a tribal thing, a race memory – I sensed something was afoot at once. I was in the wireless office when I became aware of officers scrabbling around, practically throwing themselves down ladders or running out onto the gun platform. 'What's going on?'

'Smoke on deck!' someone shouted back. I ran onto the bridge to see what the fuss what and was greeted by a thick black mushroom of smoke. And I saw. A plane had come down badly.

Frankie was on deck, working on damaged planes. He was down there and we were on fire. The alarm screeched. I ran.

By the time I reached the deck, the fire was out but it was carnage. There was a body laid out, battered and bloody – the pilot. But others were injured too. I couldn't find him – I couldn't see him. Half the ship had come out to assist.

I pushed through the crowd. 'Where's Cain?' I grabbed a junior officer. 'Frankie Cain?'

The boy's face was covered in blood and I released his arm. 'Over there – he was over there – with them.'

I ran to where he pointed. Frankie was splayed on the deck, but he was alive. He writhed and howled with pain. There was so much blood. There was nothing I could do. I froze. A jagged chunk of fuselage jutted out of his middle. 'Oh, God. Frank!'

'Stand aside!' Hands picked me up and moved me out of the way. 'Get him to the infirmary!'

All I could do was watch as, screaming, he was stretchered inside by four men. 'He's not going to make it,' said a captain, far too casually. He would. He *would* make it.

I didn't care any more. I loitered around the sick bay and Lawson tolerated my presence. They got the shrapnel out and stitched him up but Lawson told me with medical school sympathy that Frankie was unlikely to survive the night. If his wounds didn't kill him, the morphine might. 'Can I stay with him?'

Lawson regarded me. 'You may. He shouldn't be alone. Should I call for the priest?'

'No. No, I don't think he'd want that. Doctor, you have to save him. You *have* to.' He regarded me sadly and shook his head.

I pulled up a chair and sat at Frank's bedside all through the night. I held his hand and didn't care who saw. In my mind's eye I imagined that I was lending him my heartbeat, aiding his to beat stronger. I didn't let go, and when I woke with my head on the edge of his bed, he was still alive. He'd made it through the longest night.

As he improved, I was forced to return to duties, threatened with disciplinary. Each day after work, I returned to the infirmary to sit with Frankie. As you might expect, soon you couldn't shut him up, but he was immobile. There was talk of him getting shore leave when we reached Japan in a week or so.

One night, as he prepared to retire for the evening, Lawson took me to one side. 'Hastings, this has to stop. You'll get us all court-martialled. People are talking.'

'People have a habit of doing so.'

'I'm serious, Hastings. Go back to the Mess. He's out of the woods.'

'No! I've had enough. I don't want to sneak around in shadowy corners any more like a rodent. I lo—'

'Oh, pull yourself together, man. We're not in a radio play.'

I could feel my insides steaming. 'Tell me, how do you do it, Doctor? How can you *pretend*?'

He narrowed his eyes. His voice was terse. 'I don't know what you're talking about.'

We reached Japan in August. Frankie was now up and about, but unable to fulfil his duties. He would leave the *Unicorn* until her return.

And I was leaving with him.

I told him in the infirmary. 'Frankie. I'm coming with you.'

He looked blankly at me for a moment as if I were joshing. 'You can't abandon your post.'

'I can and I shall.'

'Reg, no.' He winced and held his side. 'I mean, how?'

'I don't care. We'll go home. Back to London. I've had enough of this ship, this war' – I waved my hands around my head and at him – 'all of this.'

'Reg . . .'

'My family have a cottage in Worthing. We could go there. Together. I've always wanted a dog – a springer or a setter or some such. Just imagine – you and me walking on the shore, far away from prying eyes. We could do as we pleased. It would be so peaceful. I could even get that grocer's . . .'

Frankie sat on his bunk, head hung. 'Stop. Reg, Reg, Reg, Reg, Reg . . . you and me . . . we *are* this ship. We *are* this war. When I go home it's back to real life, ain't it? My Jean's waiting for me.'

Have you ever felt like the world has fallen away from under your feet like a trapdoor? I fell. I almost tumbled into the sink, scattering metal trays and tools. 'Your Jean? *Your Jean?* You . . . you kept her quiet!'

He looked up at me, and so help me God, there was pity in those blue eyes of his. 'I thought you knew, Reg. You must have . . . all those letters I get from home, who did you think they were from?'

I couldn't stop them. Bastard tears rolled down my cheeks. 'I loved you.'

'Reg, I . . .'

'I am a fool.' I backed towards the door. 'And you are a stranger.' And I left him.

I watched him leave the *Unicorn* from the bridge. He limped onto dry land, looking over his shoulder onto deck, perhaps searching for me, perhaps not. There wasn't to be a goodbye. He did not return to HMS *Unicorn* when we next docked.

I don't know what became of him and the war fizzled out a year later.

As we set sail for Blighty, I was no longer angry, only full of a longing I couldn't rid myself of. Frankie lingered in my veins.

By the time I arrived back in London, things were changing, improving – slowly – but improving. Politicians talking, talking, talking, the way they always do. Life went on. I was strong enough to never seek him out, but sufficiently weak to remember him – even now.

The memory of that man, Frankie Cain, outlived my ill-advised marriage. Poor, sweet Brenda. It even surpassed Hastings & Sons in Chiswick, which is now, naturally, a Tesco Metro.

I am an old man now, and I was lucky enough to fall in love again. I survived a plague that killed almost everyone I knew. But he's still there, like that feeble, pale anchor tattoo on my arm: always there, under my skin.

'I ask those [homosexuals] to show their thanks by comporting themselves quietly and with dignity . . . any form of ostentatious behaviour now or in the future or any form of public flaunting would be utterly distasteful . . .'

Lord Arran, 1967, after homosexuality was decriminalized

FROM

NORTHERN LIGHTS

BY

PHILIP PULLMAN

'How long do witches live, Serafina Pekkala?· Farder Coram says hundreds of years. But you don't look old at all.'

'I am three hundred years or more. Our oldest witch mother is nearly a thousand. One day, Yambe-Akka will come for her. One day she'll come for me. She is the goddess of the dead. She comes to you smiling and kindly, and you know it is time to die.'

'Are there men witches? Or only women?'

'There are men who serve us, like the Consul at Trollesund. And there are men we take for lovers or husbands. You are so young, Lyra, too young to under-stand this, but I shall tell you anyway and you'll understand it later: men pass in front of our eyes like butterflies, creatures of a brief season. We love them; they are brave, proud, beautiful, clever; and they die almost at once. They die so soon that our hearts are continually racked with pain. We bear their children, who are witches if they are female, human if not; and then in the blink of an eye they are gone, felled, slain, lost. Our sons, too. When a little boy is growing, he thinks he is immortal. His mother knows he isn't. Each time becomes more painful, until finally your heart is broken. Perhaps that is when Yambe-Akka comes for you. She is older than the tundra. Perhaps, for her, witches' lives are as brief as men's are to us.'

'Did you love Farder Coram?'

'Yes. Does he know that?'

'I don't know, but I know he loves you.'

'When he rescued me, he was young and strong and full of pride and beauty. I loved him at once. I would have changed my nature, I would have forsaken the star-tingle and the music of the Aurora; I would never have flown again – I would have given all that up in a moment, without a thought, to be a gyptian boat-wife and cook for him and share his bed and bear his children. But you cannot change what you are, only what you do. I am a witch. He is a human. I stayed with him for long enough to bear him a child . . .'

'He never said! Was it a girl? A witch?'

'No. A boy, and he died in the great epidemic of forty years ago, the sickness that came out of the East. Poor little child; he flickered into life and out of it like a mayfly. And it tore pieces out of my heart, as it always does. It broke Coram's. And then the call came for me to return to my own people, because Yambe-Akka had taken my mother, and I was clan-queen. So I left, as I had to.'

'Did you never see Farder Coram again?'

'Never. I heard of his deeds; I heard how he was wounded by the Skraelings, with a poisoned arrow, and I sent herbs and spells to help him recover, but I wasn't strong enough to see him. I heard how broken he was after that, and how his wisdom grew, how much he studied and read, and I was proud of him and his goodness. But I stayed away, for they were dangerous times for my clan, and witch-wars were threatening, and besides, I thought he would forget me and find a human wife . . .'

'He never would,' said Lyra stoutly. 'You oughter go and see him. He still loves you, I know he does.'

'But he would be ashamed of his own age, and I wouldn't want to make him feel that.'

'Perhaps he would. But you ought to send a message to him, at least. That's what I think.'

Serafina Pekkala said nothing for a long time. Pantalaimon became a tern and flew to her branch for a second, to acknowledge that perhaps they had been insolent.

Then Lyra said, 'Why do people have dæmons, Serafina Pekkala?'

'Everyone asks that, and no one knows the answer. As long as there have been human beings, they have had dæmons. It's what makes us different from animals.'

FROM
WE WERE LIARS

BY
E LOCKHART

Summer fifteen I arrived a week later than the others. Dad had left us, and Mummy and I had all that shopping to do, consulting the decorator and everything.

Johnny and Mirren met us at the dock, pink in the cheeks and full of summer plans. They were staging a family tennis tournament and had bookmarked ice-cream recipes. We would go sailing, build bonfires.

The littles swarmed and yelled like always. The aunts smiled chilly smiles. After the bustle of arrival, everyone went to Clairmont for cocktail hour.

I went to Red Gate, looking for Gat. Red Gate is a much smaller house than Clairmont, but it still has four bedrooms up top. It's where Johnny, Gat, and Will lived with Aunt Carrie – plus Ed, when he was there, which wasn't often.

I walked to the kitchen door and looked through the screen. Gat didn't see me at first. He was standing at the counter wearing a worn gray T-shirt and jeans. His shoulders were broader than I remembered.

He untied a dried flower from where it hung upside down on a ribbon in the window over the sink. The flower was a beach rose, pink and loosely constructed, the kind that grows along the Beechwood perimeter.

Gat, my Gat. He had picked me a rose from our favorite walking place. He had hung it to dry and waited for me to arrive on the island so he could give it to me.

I had kissed an unimportant boy or three by now.

I had lost my dad.

I had come here to this island from a house of tears and falsehood

and I saw Gat,

and I saw that rose in his hand,

and in that one moment, with the sunlight from the windows shining in on him,

the apples on the kitchen counter,

the smell of wood and ocean in the air,

I did call it love.

It *was* love, and it hit me so hard I leaned against the screen door that still stood between us, just to stay vertical. I wanted to touch him like he was a bunny, a kitten, something so special and soft your fingertips can't leave it alone. The universe was good because he was in it. I loved the hole in his jeans and the dirt on his bare feet and the scab on his elbow and the scar that laced through one eyebrow. Gat, my Gat.

As I stood there, staring, he put the rose in an envelope. He searched for a pen, banging drawers open and shut, found one in his own pocket, and wrote.

I didn't realize he was writing an address until he pulled a roll of stamps from a kitchen drawer.

Gat stamped the envelope. Wrote a return address. It wasn't for me.

I left the Red Gate door before he saw me and ran down to the perimeter. I watched the darkening sky, alone.

I tore all the roses off a single sad bush and threw them, one after the other, into the angry sea.

Johnny told me about the New York girlfriend that evening. Her name was Raquel. Johnny had even met her. He lives in New York, like Gat does, but downtown with Carrie and Ed, while Gat lives uptown with his mom. Johnny said Raquel was a modern dancer and wore black clothes.

Mirren's brother, Taft, told me Raquel had sent Gat a package of homemade brownies. Liberty and Bonnie told me Gat had pictures of her on his phone.

Gat didn't mention her at all, but he had trouble meeting my eyes.

That first night, I cried and bit my fingers and drank wine I snuck from the Clairmont pantry. I spun violently into the sky, raging and banging stars from their moorings, swirling and vomiting.

I hit my fist into the wall of the shower. I washed off the shame and anger in cold, cold water. Then I shivered in my bed like the abandoned dog that I was, my skin shaking over my bones.

The next morning, and every day thereafter, I acted normal. I tilted my square chin high.

We sailed and made bonfires. I won the tennis tournament.

We made vats of ice cream and lay in the sun.

One night, the four of us ate a picnic down on the tiny beach. Steamed clams, potatoes, and sweet corn. The staff made it. I didn't know their names.

Johnny and Mirren carried the food down in metal roasting pans. We ate around the flames of our bonfire, dripping butter onto the sand. Then Gat made triple-decker s'mores for all of us. I looked at his hands in the firelight, sliding marshmallows onto a long stick. Where once he'd had our names written, now he had taken to writing the titles of books he wanted to read.

That night, on the left: *Being and*. On the right: *Nothingness*.

I had writing on my hands, too. A quotation I liked. On the left: *Live in*. On the right: *today*.

'Want to know what I'm thinking about?' Gat asked.

'Yes,' I said.

'No,' said Johnny.

'I'm wondering how we can say your granddad owns this island. Not legally but actually.'

'Please don't get started on the evils of the Pilgrims,' moaned Johnny.

'No. I'm asking, how can we say land belongs to *anyone*?' Gat waved at the sand, the ocean, the sky.

Mirren shrugged. 'People buy and sell land all the time.'

'Can't we talk about sex or murder?' asked Johnny.

Gat ignored him. 'Maybe land shouldn't belong to people at all. Or maybe there should be limits on what they can own.' He leaned forward. 'When I went to India this winter, on that volunteer trip, we were building toilets. Building them because people there, in this one village, didn't *have* them.'

'We all know you went to India,' said Johnny. You told us like forty-seven times.'

Here is something I love about Gat: he is so enthusiastic, so relentlessly interested in the world, that he has trouble imagining the possibility that other people will be bored by what he's saying. Even when they tell him outright. But also, he doesn't like to let us off easy. He wants to make us think – even when we don't feel like thinking.

He poked a stick into the embers. 'I'm saying we should talk about it. Not everyone has private islands. Some people work on them. Some work in factories. Some don't have work. Some don't have food.'

'Stop talking, now,' said Mirren.

'Stop talking, forever,' said Johnny.

'We have a warped view of humanity on Beech-wood,' Gat said. 'I don't think you see that.'

'Shut up,' I said. 'I'll give you more chocolate if you shut up.'

And Gat did shut up, but his face contorted. He stood abruptly, picked up a rock from the sand, and threw it with all his force. He pulled off his sweatshirt and kicked off his shoes. Then he walked into the sea in his jeans.

Angry.

I watched the muscles of his shoulders in the moonlight, the spray kicking up as he splashed in. He dove and I thought: If I don't follow him now, that girl Raquel's got him. If I don't follow him now, he'll go away. From the Liars, from the island, from our family, from me.

I threw off my sweater and followed Gat into the sea in my dress. I crashed into the water, swimming out to where he lay on his back. His wet hair was slicked off his face, showing the thin scar through one eyebrow.

I reached for his arm. 'Gat.'

He startled. Stood in the waist-high sea.

'Sorry,' I whispered.

'I don't tell you to shut up, Cady,' he said. 'I don't ever say that to you.'

'I know.'

He was silent.

'Please don't shut up,' I said.

I felt his eyes go over my body in my wet dress. 'I talk too much,' he said. 'I politicize everything.'

'I like it when you talk,' I said, because it was true. When I stopped to listen, I did like it.

'It's that everything makes me . . .' He paused. 'Things are messed up in the world, that's all.'

'Yeah.'

'Maybe I should' – Gat took my hands, turned them over to look at the words written on the backs – 'I should *live for today* and not be agitating all the time.'

My hand was in his wet hand.

I shivered. His arms were bare and wet. We used to hold hands all the time, but he hadn't touched me all summer.

'It's good that you look at the world the way you do,' I told him.

Gat let go of me and leaned back into the water. 'Johnny wants me to shut up. I'm boring you and Mirren.'

I looked at his profile. He wasn't just Gat. He was contemplation and enthusiasm. Ambition and strong coffee. All that was there, in the lids of his brown eyes, his smooth skin, his lower lip pushed out. There was coiled energy inside.

'I'll tell you a secret,' I whispered.

'What?'

I reached out and touched his arm again. He didn't pull away. 'When we say *Shut up, Gat*, that isn't what we mean at all.'

'No?'

'What we mean is, we love you. You remind us that we're selfish bastards. You're not one of us, that way.'

He dropped his eyes. Smiled. 'Is that what *you* mean, Cady?'

'Yes,' I told him. I let my fingers trail down his floating, outstretched arm.

'I can't believe you are in that water!' Johnny was standing ankle-deep in the ocean, his jeans rolled up. 'It's the Arctic. My toes are freezing off.'

'It's nice once you get in,' Gat called back.

'Seriously?'

'Don't be weak!' yelled Gat. 'Be manly and get in the stupid water.'

Johnny laughed and charged in. Mirren followed.

And it was — exquisite.

The night looming above us. The hum of the ocean. The bark of gulls.

That night I had trouble sleeping.

After midnight, he called my name.

I looked out my window. Gat was lying on his back on the wooden walkway that leads to Windemere. The golden retrievers were lying near him, all five: Bosh, Grendel, Poppy, Prince Philip, and Fatima. Their tails thumped gently.

The moonlight made them all look blue.

'Come down,' he called.

I did.

Mummy's light was out. The rest of the island was dark. We were alone, except for all the dogs.

'Scoot,' I told him. The walkway wasn't wide. When I lay down next to him, our arms touched, mine bare and his in an olive-green hunting jacket.

We looked at the sky. So many stars, it seemed like a celebration, a grand, illicit party the galaxy was holding after the humans had been put to bed.

I was glad Gat didn't try to sound knowledgeable about constellations or say stupid stuff about wishing on stars. But I didn't know what to make of his silence, either.

'Can I hold your hand?' he asked.

I put mine in his.

'The universe is seeming really huge right now,' he told me. 'I need something to hold on to.'

'I'm here.'

His thumb rubbed the center of my palm. All my nerves concentrated there, alive to every movement of his skin on mine. 'I am not sure I'm a good person,' he said after a while.

'I'm not sure I am, either,' I said. 'I'm winging it.'

'Yeah.' Gat was silent for a moment. 'Do you believe in God?'

'Halfway.' I tried to think about it seriously. I knew Gat wouldn't settle for a flippant answer. 'When things are bad, I'll pray or imagine someone watching over me, listening. Like the first few days after my dad left, I thought about God. For protection. But the rest of the time, I'm trudging along in my everyday life. It's not even slightly spiritual.'

'I don't believe anymore,' Gat said. 'That trip to India, the poverty. No God I can imagine would let that happen. Then I came home and started noticing it on the streets of New York. People sick and starving in one of the richest nations in the world. I just – I can't think anyone's watching over those people. Which means no one is watching over me, either.'

'That doesn't make you a bad person.'

'My mother believes. She was raised Buddhist but goes to Methodist church now. She's not very happy with me.' Gat hardly ever talked about his mother.

'You can't believe just because she tells you to,' I said.

'No. The question is: how to be a good person if I don't believe anymore.'

We stared at the sky. The dogs went into Windemere via the dog flap.

'You're cold,' Gat said. 'Let me give you my jacket.'

I wasn't cold but I sat up. He sat up, too. Unbuttoned his olive hunting jacket and shrugged it off. Handed it to me.

It was warm from his body. Much too wide across the shoulders. His arms were bare now.

I wanted to kiss him there while I was wearing his hunting jacket. But I didn't.

Maybe he loved Raquel. Those photos on his phone. That dried beach rose in an envelope.

★ ★ ★

At breakfast the next morning, Mummy asked me to go through Dad's things in the Windemere attic and take what I wanted. She would get rid of the rest.

Windemere is gabled and angular. Two of the five bedrooms have slanted roofs, and it's the only house on the island with a full attic. There's a big porch and a modern kitchen, updated with marble countertops that look a little out of place. The rooms are airy and filled with dogs.

Gat and I climbed up to the attic with glass bottles of iced tea and sat on the floor. The room smelled like wood. A square of light glowed through from the window.

We had been in the attic before.

Also, we had never been in the attic before.

The books were Dad's vacation reading. All sports memoirs, cozy mysteries, and rock star tell-alls by old people I'd never heard of. Gat wasn't really looking. He was sorting the books by color. A red pile, a blue, brown, white, yellow.

'Don't you want anything to read?' I asked.

'Maybe.'

'How about *First Base and Way Beyond*?'

Gat laughed. Shook his head. Straightened his blue pile.

'*Rock On with My Bad Self*? *Hero of the Dance Floor*?'

He was laughing again. Then serious. 'Cadence?'

'What?'

'Shut up.'

I let myself look at him a long time. Every curve of his face was familiar, and also, I had never seen him before.

Gat smiled. Shining. Bashful. He got to his knees, kicking over his colourful book piles in the process. He reached out and stroked my hair. 'I love you, Cady. I mean it.'

I leaned in and kissed him.

He touched my face. Ran his hand down my neck and along my collarbone. The light from the attic window shone down on us. Our kiss was electric and soft,

and tentative and certain,

terrifying and exactly right.

I felt the love rush from me to Gat and from Gat to me.

We were warm and shivering,

and young and ancient,

and alive.

I was thinking, It's true. We already love each other. We already do.

Granddad walked in on us. Gat sprang up. Stepped awkwardly on the color-sorted books that had spilled across the floor.

'I am interrupting,' Granddad said.

'No, sir.'

'Yes, I most certainly am.'

'Sorry about the dust,' I said. Awkward.

'Penny thought there might be something I'd like to read.' Granddad pulled an old wicker chair to the center of the room and sat down, bending over the books.

Gat remained standing. He had to bend his head beneath the attic's slanted roof.

'Watch yourself, young man,' said Granddad, sharp and sudden.

'Pardon me?'

'Your head. You could get hurt.'

'You're right,' said Gat. 'You're right, I could get hurt.'

'So watch yourself,' Granddad repeated.

Gat turned and went down the stairs without another word.

Granddad and I sat in silence for a moment.

'He likes to read,' I said eventually. 'I thought he might want some of Dad's books.'

'You are very dear to me, Cady,' said Granddad, patting my shoulder. 'My first grandchild.'

'I love you, too, Granddad.'

'Remember how I took you to a baseball game? You were only four.'

'Sure.'

'You had never had Cracker Jack,' said Granddad.

'I know. You bought two boxes.'

'I had to put you on my lap so you could see. You remember that, Cady?'

I did.

'Tell me.'

I knew the kind of answer Granddad wanted me to give. It was a request he made quite often. He loved retelling key moments in Sinclair family history, enlarging their importance. He was always asking what something meant to you, and you were supposed to come back with details. Images. Maybe a lesson learned.

Usually, I adored telling these stories and hearing them told. The legendary Sinclairs, what fun we'd had, how beautiful we were. But that day, I didn't want to.

'It was your first baseball game,' Granddad prompted. 'Afterward I brought you a red plastic bat. You practiced your swing on the lawn of the Boston house.'

Did Grandad know what he'd interrupted? Would he care if he did know?

When would I see Gat again?

Would he break up with Raquel?

What would happen between us?

'You wanted to make Cracker Jack at home,' Granddad went on, though he knew I knew the story. 'And Penny helped you make it. But you cried when there weren't any red and white boxes to put it in. Do you remember that?'

'Yes, Granddad,' I said, giving in. 'You went all the way back to the ballpark that same day and bought two more boxes of Cracker Jack. You ate them on the drive

home, just so you could give me the boxes.
I remember.'

Satisfied, he stood up and we left the attic together.
Granddad was shaky going downstairs, so he put his
hand on my shoulder.

I found Gat on the perimeter path and ran to where
he stood, looking out at the water. The wind was
coming hard and my hair flew in my eyes. When I
kissed him, his lips were salty.

Granny Tipper died of heart failure eight months
before summer fifteen on Beechwood. She was a
stunning woman, even when she was old. White hair,
pink cheeks; tall and angular. She's the one who made
Mummy love dogs so much. She always had at least
two and sometimes four golden retrievers when her
girls were little, all the way until she died.

She was quick to judge and played favorites, but
she was also warm. If you got up early on Beechwood,
back when we were small, you could go to Clairmont
and wake Gran. She'd have muffin batter sitting in the
fridge, and would pour it into tins and let you eat as
many warm muffins as you wanted, before the rest of
the island woke up. She'd take us berry picking and
help us make pie or something she called a slump that
we'd eat that night.

One of her charity projects was a benefit party
each year for the Farm Institute on Martha's Vineyard.

We all used to go. It was outdoors, in beautiful white tents. The littles would run around wearing party clothes and no shoes. Johnny, Mirren, Gat and I snuck glasses of wine and felt giddy and silly. Gran danced with Johnny and then my dad, then with Granddad, holding the edge of her skirt with one hand. I used to have a photograph of Gran from one of those benefit parties. She wore an evening gown and held a piglet.

Summer fifteen on Beechwood, Granny Tipper was gone. Clairmont felt empty.

My house is a three-story gray Victorian. There is a turret up top and a wraparound porch. Inside, it is full of original *New Yorker* cartoons, family photos, embroidered pillows, small statues, ivory paperweights, taxidermied fish on plaques. Everywhere, everywhere, are beautiful objects collected by Tipper and Granddad. On the lawn is an enormous picnic table, big enough to seat sixteen, and a ways off from that, a tire swing hangs from a massive maple.

Gran used to bustle in the kitchen and plan out-ings. She made quilts in her craft room, and the hum of the sewing machine could be heard throughout the downstairs. She bossed the groundskeepers in her gardening gloves and blue jeans.

Now the house was quiet. No cookbooks left open on the counter, no classical music on the kitchen sound system. But it was still Gran's favorite soap in all the soap dishes. Those were her plants growing in the garden. Her wooden spoons, her cloth napkins.

One day, when no one else was around, I went into the craft room at the back of the ground floor. I touched Gran's collection of fabrics, the shiny bright buttons, the colored threads.

My head and shoulders melted first, followed by my hips and knees. Before long I was a puddle, soaking into the pretty cotton prints. I drenched the quilt she never finished, rusted the metal parts of her sewing machine. I was pure liquid loss, then, for an hour or two. My grandmother, my grandmother. Gone forever, though I could smell her Chanel perfume on the fabrics.

Mummy found me.

She made me act normal. Because I was. Because I could. She told me to breathe and sit up.

And I did what she asked. Again.

Mummy was worried about Granddad. He was shaky on his feet with Gran gone, holding on to the chairs and tables to keep his balance. He was the head of the family. She didn't want him destabilized. She wanted him to know his children and grandchildren were still around him, strong and merry as ever. It was important, she said; it was kind; it was best. Don't cause distress, she said. Don't remind people of a loss. 'Do you understand, Cady? Silence is a protective coating over pain.'

I understood, and I managed to erase Granny Tipper from conversation, the same way I had erased my father. Not happily, but thoroughly. At meals with the aunts, on the boat with Granddad, even alone with Mummy – I behaved as if those two critical people had never existed. The rest of the Sinclairs did the same. When we were all together, people kept their smiles wide. We had done the same when Bess left Uncle Brody, the same when Uncle Jonathan left Carrie, the same when Gran's dog Peppermill died of cancer.

Gat never got it, though. He'd mention my father quite a lot, actually. Dad had found Gat both a decent chess opponent and a willing audience for his boring stories about military history, so they'd spent some time together. 'Remember when your father caught that big crab in a bucket?' Gat would say. Or to Mummy: 'Last year Sam told me there's a fly-fishing kit in the boat-house; do you know where it is?'

Dinner conversation stopped sharply when he'd mention Gran. Once Gat said, 'I miss the way she'd stand at the foot of the table and serve out dessert, don't you? It was so Tipper.' Johnny had to start talking loudly about Wimbledon until the dismay faded from our faces.

Every time Gat said these things, so casual and truthful, so oblivious – my veins opened. My wrists split. I bled down my palms. I went light-headed. I'd stagger from the table or collapse in quiet shameful agony, hoping no one in the family would notice. Especially not Mummy.

Gat almost always saw, though. When blood dropped on my bare feet or poured over the book I was reading, he was kind. He wrapped my wrists in soft white gauze and asked me questions about what had happened. He asked about Dad and about Gran – as if talking about something could make it better. As if wounds needed attention.

He was a stranger in our family, even after all these years.

When I wasn't bleeding, and when Mirren and Johnny were snorkeling or wrangling the littles, or when everyone lay on couches watching movies on the Clairmont flat-screen, Gat and I hid away. We sat on the tire swing at midnight, our arms and legs wrapped around each other, lips warm against cool night skin. In the mornings we'd sneak laughing down to the Clairmont basement, which was lined with wine bottles and encyclopedias. There we kissed and marveled at one another's existence, feeling secret and lucky. Some days he wrote me notes and left them with small presents under my pillow.

> *Someone once wrote that a novel should deliver a series of small astonishments. I get the same thing spending an hour with you.*
> *Also, here is a green toothbrush tied in a ribbon.*
> *It expresses my feelings inadequately.*
>
> *Better than chocolate, being with you last night.*
> *Silly me, I thought that nothing was better than chocolate.*

> *In a profound, symbolic gesture, I am giving you this bar of Vosges I got when we all went to Edgartown. You can eat it, or just sit next to it and feel superior.*

I didn't write back, but I drew Gat silly crayon drawings of the two of us. Stick figures waving from in front of the Colosseum, the Eiffel Tower, on top of a mountain, on the back of a dragon. He stuck them up over his bed.

He touched me whenever he could. Beneath the table at dinner, in the kitchen the moment it was empty. Covertly, hilariously, behind Granddad's back while he drove the motorboat. I felt no barrier between us. As long as no one was looking, I ran my fingers along Gat's cheekbones, down his back. I reached for his hand, pressed my thumb against his wrist, and felt the blood going through his veins.

One night, late July of summer fifteen, I went swimming at the tiny beach. Alone.

Where were Gat, Johnny, and Mirren?

I don't really know.

We had been playing a lot of Scrabble at Red Gate. They were probably there. Or they could have been at Clairmont, listening to the aunts argue and eating beach plum jam on water crackers.

In any case, I went into the water wearing a camisole, bra, and underwear. Apparently I walked down to the beach wearing nothing more. We never found any of my clothes on the sand. No towel, either.

Why?

Again, I don't really know.

I must have swum out far. There are big rocks in off the shore, craggy and black; they always look villainous in the dark of the evening. I must have had my face in the water and then hit my head on one of these rocks.

Like I said, I don't know.

I remember only this: I plunged down into this ocean,

down to rocky rocky bottom, and

I could see the base of Beechwood Island and

my arms and legs felt numb but my fingers were cold. Slices of seaweed went past as I fell.

Mummy found me on the sand, curled into a ball and half underwater. I was shivering uncontrollably. Adults wrapped me in blankets. They tried to get me warm at Cuddletown. They fed me tea and gave me clothes, but when I didn't talk or stop shivering, they brought me to a hospital on Martha's Vineyard, where I stayed for several days as the doctors ran tests. Hypothermia, respiratory problems, and most likely some kind of head injury, though the brain scans turned up nothing.

Mummy stayed by my side, got a hotel room. I remember the sad, gray faces of Aunt Carrie, Aunt Bess, and Granddad. I remember my lungs felt full of something, long after the doctors judged them clear. I remember I felt like I'd never get warm again, even when they told me my body temperature was normal. My hands hurt. My feet hurt.

Mummy took me home to Vermont to recuperate. I lay in bed in the dark and felt desperately sorry for myself. Because I was sick, and even more because Gat never called.

He didn't write, either.

Weren't we in love?

Weren't we?

I wrote to Johnny, two or three stupid, lovesick emails asking him to find out about Gat.

Johnny had the good sense to ignore them. We are Sinclairs, after all, and Sinclairs do not behave like I was behaving.

I stopped writing and deleted all the emails from my sent mail folder. They were weak and stupid.

The bottom line is, Gat bailed when I got hurt.

The bottom line is, it was only a summer fling.

The bottom line is, he might have loved Raquel.

We lived too far apart, anyway.

Our families were too close, anyway.

I never got an explanation.

I just know he left me.

Melvin Burgess was born in London and brought up in Surrey and Sussex. He has had a variety of jobs before becoming a full-time writer. Before his first novel, he had short stories published and a play broadcast on Radio 4. He is now regarded as one of the best writers in contemporary children's literature, having won the Carnegie Medal and the Guardian Children's Fiction Prize for his acclaimed novel *Junk*.
www.melvinburgess.net
@MelvinBurgess

James Dawson grew up in a quiet suburb of Bradford, West Yorkshire, writing imaginary episodes of *Doctor Who* for his grandma. After surviving secondary school by the skin of his teeth, James escaped to Brighton and became a teacher. He specialized in literacy, PSHCE and behaviour. James now writes full-time and lives in London.
www.jamesdawsonbooks.com
@_jamesdawson

Susie Day grew up in Penarth, Wales, with a lisp and a really unfortunate choice of first name. She has had lots of jobs, including guiding tourists and professional nappy-changing – but she always wanted to be a writer. Her first book, *Whump! In Which Bill Falls 632 Miles Down a Manhole*, won the BBC Talent Children's fiction prize, and was published in 2004. Susie now lives in Oxford, England, and eats a lot of cake and drinks a lot of tea.

www.susieday.com
@mssusieday

Named one of the top ten literary talents by *The Times* and one of the top twenty hot faces to watch by *Elle* magazine, **Laura Dockrill** is a young, talented writer/illustrator who is a graduate of the BRIT School of Performing Arts. She has performed her work at the Edinburgh Fringe, Camp Bestival, Latitude, Bookslam and the Soho Theatre and on each of the BBC's respective radio channels, 1–6. She has been a roaming reporter for the Roald Dahl Funny Prize, run workshops at the Imagine Festival on the South Bank, and is on the advisory panel at the Ministry of Stories.

www.lauradockrill.co.uk
@LauraDockrill

Jenny Downham was an actress for many years before concentrating on her writing full-time. She lives in

London with her two sons. Her debut novel *Before I Die* was critically acclaimed and was shortlisted for the 2007 Guardian Children's Fiction Prize and the 2008 Lancashire Children's Book of the Year, nominated for the 2008 Carnegie Medal and the 2008 Booktrust Teenage Prize, and won the 2008 Branford Boase Award.

Phil Earle was born, raised and schooled in Hull. His first job was as a care worker in a children's home, an experience that influenced the ideas behind *Being Billy* and *Saving Daisy*. He then trained as a drama therapist and worked in a therapeutic community in south London, caring for traumatized and abused adolescents. After a couple of years in the care sector, Phil chose the more sedate lifestyle of a bookseller, and now works in children's publishing. Phil lives in south-east London with his wife and children, but Hull will always be home.

www.philearle.com

@philearle

Matt Haig's first novel for young readers, *Shadow Forest*, won the Blue Peter Book of the Year Award and the Gold Smarties Award. He is also the author of various adult novels, including the bestsellers *The Last Family in England*, *The Radleys* and *The Humans*. Reviewers have called his writing 'totally engrossing', 'touching, quirky and macabre' and 'so surprising and strange that it vaults into a realm all of its own'. His books have been translated into 25 languages.

www.matthaig.com

@matthaig1

Gayle Forman is an award-winning author and journalist whose articles have appeared in numerous publications, including *Seventeen*, *Cosmopolitan* and *Elle* in the US. She lives in Brooklyn with her family.

www.gayleforman.com

@gayleforman

Catherine Johnson was born in London. Her father is Jamaican and her mother Welsh. After studying film at St Martin's College, London, she started a family and began to write. Catherine has been Writer in Residence at Holloway Prison, Royal Literary Fund Writing Fellow at the London Institute, and has mentored writers in Africa for the British Council. She has written three books for Oxford University Press – *Hero* (2001), *Stella* (2002) and *Face Value* (2005). Catherine also co-wrote the screenplay for the critically acclaimed film *Bullet Boy*, which starred Ashley Walters from So Solid Crew. Catherine lives in London.

www.catherinejohnson.co.uk

@catwrote

Maureen Johnson is a *New York Times* bestselling author whose novels include *The Name of the Star*, *Suite*

Scarlett, Scarlett Fever, Girl at Sea, The Key to the Golden Firebird, and *13 Little Blue Envelopes.* She lives in New York City, but travels to the UK regularly to soak up the drizzle and watch English TV.
www.maureenjohnsonbooks.com
@maureenjohnson

Lauren Kate is the internationally bestselling author of *Teardrop* and the *Fallen* novels: *Fallen, Torment, Passion, Rapture* and *Fallen in Love,* as well as *The Betrayal of Natalie Hargrove.* Her books have been translated into more than thirty languages. She lives in Los Angeles.
www.laurenkatebooks.net
@laurenkatebooks

David Levithan won the Lambda Literary Award for his debut novel *Boy Meets Boy,* but is probably best known for his collaborations with John Green (*Will Grayson, Will Grayson*) and Rachel Cohn (*Nick and Norah's Infinite Playlist,* which was also made into a movie). As well as being a *New York Times* bestselling author, David is also a highly respected children's book editor, whose list includes many luminaries of children's literature, including Garth Nix, Libba Bray and Suzanne Collins. He lives and works in New York.
www.davidlevithan.com
@loversdiction

E. Lockhart is the author of nine novels, including *We Were Liars*, *The Boyfriend List*, *Fly on the Wall* and *The Disreputable History of Frankie Landau-Banks,* which was a Michael L. Printz Award Honor Book, a finalist for the National Book Award, and winner of a Cybils Award for Best Young Adult Novel.

www.emilylockhart.com

@elockhart

Non Pratt's real name is Leonie, but please don't call her that unless she's done something really bad. She grew up in Teeside and now lives in London. She wrote her first book aged fourteen. After graduating from Cambridge University, Non decided to work in children's publishing. Unfortunately, she went to her first job interview with her top on inside out. Fortunately, they hired her anyway. Since then she has worked as a non-fiction editor at Usborne and a fiction editor at Catnip. She now writes full-time, and *Trouble* was her debut novel.

www.nonpratt.com

@NonPratt

Lauren Myracle is a graduate of the Vermont College MFA programme in writing for children and young adults. She is the author of the *New York Times* best-selling *Internet Girls* series (*ttyl, ttfn*, and *l8r, g8r*) and *Rhymes with Witches*, among many other books for teenagers and young people. She grew up in Atlanta

and currently resides in Fort Collins, Colorado, with her husband and their three young children.
www.laurenmyracle.com
@LaurenMyracle

Patrick Ness is the author of the *Chaos Walking* Trilogy – *The Knife of Never Letting Go*, *The Ask and the Answer*, and *Monsters of Men* – for which he has won numerous awards, including the Guardian Children's Fiction Prize, the Booktrust Teenage Prize, the Costa Children's Book Award and the Carnegie Medal. He lives in London.
www.patrickness.com
@Patrick_Ness

Philip Pullman is one of the most highly acclaimed children's authors of the decade. He has been on the shortlist of just about every major children's book award in the last few years, and has won the Smarties Prize (Gold Award, 9-11 age category) for *The Firework-Maker's Daughter* and the prestigious Carnegie Medal for *Northern Lights*. He was the first children's author ever to win the Whitbread Prize for his novel *The Amber Spyglass*. He lives in Oxford.
www.philip-pullman.com
@PhilipPullman

Bali Rai has written nine young adult novels for Random House Children's Publishers, as well as the *Soccer Squad* series for younger readers. His first novel, *(un)arranged marriage*, created a huge amount of interest and won many awards, including the Angus Book Award and the Leicester Book of the Year. It was also shortlisted for the prestigious Branford Boase first novel award. *Rani and Sukh* and *The Whisper* were both shortlisted for the Booktrust Teenage Prize. He was born in Leicester, where he still lives, writing full-time and visiting schools to talk about his books.

www.balirai.co.uk

@balirai

Marcus Sedgwick used to work in children's publishing and before that he was a bookseller. He now happily writes full-time. His books have been shortlisted for many awards, including the Guardian Children's Fiction Prize, the Blue Peter Book Award, the Carnegie Medal and the Edgar Allan Poe Award. Marcus lives in Cambridge.

www.marcussedgwick.com

@marcussedgwick

Andrew Smith has always wanted to be a writer. After graduating college, he wrote for newspapers and radio stations, but found it wasn't the kind of writing he'd dreamed about doing. Born with an impulse to travel, Smith, the son of an immigrant, bounced around the world and from job to job, before settling down in Southern California. There, he got his first 'real job', as a teacher in an alternative educational programme for at-risk teens, married, and moved to a rural mountain location. Smith has now written several award-winning YA novels; *Grasshopper Jungle* is his seventh and the first to be published in the UK. He lives with his wife, two children, two horses, three dogs, three cats and one irritable lizard named Leo.

www.andrewsmithauthor.com
@marburyjack

Tabitha Suzuma was born in 1975 and lives in London. She has always loved writing and would regularly get into trouble at the French Lycée for writing stories instead of listening in class. She used to work as a primary school teacher and now divides her time between writing and tutoring. Her first novel, *A Note of Madness*, was published to great critical acclaim.

www.tabithasuzuma.com
@TabithaSuzuma

Markus Zusak was born in 1975 and is the author of five books, including *I Am the Messenger* and the international bestseller *The Book Thief*, which is translated into more than forty languages. He lives in Sydney with his wife and two children.

www.zusakbooks.tumblr.com
@Markus_Zusak

PERMISSIONS